The Secrets of Hattie Brown

The Secrets of Hattie Brown

Copyright © 2020 by Barbara Brown Gathers

Published by Barbara Brown Gathers in Partnership with
The Literary Revolutionary

www.tlrpublishing.co

Editing By: Anjé McLish
Cover Design By: Opeyemi Ikuborije Olorunfemi

Publisher's Note:
Without limiting the rights under copyright reserved above, no part of this publication may be reproduced, stored in or introduced into a retrieval system, or transmitted, in any form, or by any means (electronic, mechanical, photocopying, recording, or otherwise), without the prior written permission of both the copyright owner and the publisher of the book.

Manufactured in the United States of America

ISBN #: 978-1-950279-18-0
Library of Congress Control Number: 2020905292

The Secrets of Hattie Brown

By: Barbara Brown Gathers

Dedication

Growing up in this family, I was in awe of the fact that these people, my father, aunts and uncles, had lost everything, at a moment in their lives, mother, father, home. Still they managed to put the pieces back together and provide a life of comfort and security for my brother, my cousins and me.

This book is dedicated to all of them.
The Browns
Bessie
Ernest
Florida
Robert Jr.
Lander
Virginia
Virtee
Azel RD
Rivers

Prologue

I got secrets.

Most folks keep secrets because they don't want anyone to know. Mine are secrets because I died before I could tell. I woulda told, if I coulda. But life swooped outta me before I could shape my thoughts and tell my stories to my children. My stories are my secrets. But they never got told...cause I died. Four days sick with the pneumonia, and then I was gone at thirty-nine years old. Lotta people died like that in those days. Then, weeks after my death, the house burned down and any fibers that coulda been woven together to reveal my stories, got destroyed. My tragically motherless and homeless nine children then had to see their papa buried the following year. This is how my stories became secrets that just never got told.

Since then, I have watched my children and their children build upon the voided stories that became secrets, and explore, unbeknownst to them, what were my dreams. I longed to hold them close to my breasts. To hear them call me as they approach the house, "Mama! Come and meet my husband....my wife.... your new granddaughter.... your new grandson...." voices that existed in my visions of the future. I saw myself sitting on the porch, rocking in my chair, proud, anticipating their visits. But only in my dreams. Today, almost ninety years later, those grandchildren and great grandchildren are living life, much like the answers to my prayers.

But I'm gettin' ahead of myself.

The Secrets of Hattie Brown

Holloways Township, Person County, North Carolina was home, although I was born in Black Walnut, Virginia in 1890. White folks call me a moo-lah-toe. They made up that name for black folks who have a white daddy or granddaddy.... light skinned, straight hair. White folks always makin up names for us.

My mama was a force of nature. She was unable to read or write, but she was a midwife, delivering black, white, and Indian babies across three counties. Her services were in high demand. I'm so proud of my mama! Eliza Cowen, was Person County's best kept secret for farmer's wives! Once you meet my mama, you will understand me better. I am gonna let my narrator tell you the story. She knows it well.

Barbara Brown Gathers

"Where is de house where de mouse is de leader? In de Africa soil, I cain't tell you bout de son, before I tell you bout de father." Barracoon, Zora Neale Hurston

"If you wanna know the end, look at the beginning."
Iyanla Vanzant

Book One

Eliza Cowen

Barbara Brown Gathers

Eliza was her name
That name created fame
As a bringer of new life
To the world
She walked where the ground was smooth
She tread where the road was rough
Eliza was known for being wonderfully gentle
And rest assured she could be ferociously tough
A misty-eyed star gazing girl
Became stronger with each of life's blows
And before life ended its turn with her
She'd had pains like nobody knows
Eliza was a trooper
Eliza didn't go down with defeat
With each disappointment and setback
Still, she landed on her feet
Folks wondered how she did it
All those children
The man gone astray
All those children
And then he passed away
But Eliza wanted something as much as she wanted a man
She wanted for life to teach her how to stand
And teach her how to rebound
And teach her voice to resound
With the truth
So, she could live by it
And strive by it
So, she could shift lives with it
And die by it
Eliza! We have heard you
Eliza! You did well.
Your grandchildren and great grandchildren
Are now drinking from your well
You reached far beyond what most brown colored women
could attain

The Secrets of Hattie Brown

You left behind a legacy
Of knowing how to sustain while working through life's pains
God bless your spirit and the memory of your name
As long as we remember you, this legacy cannot wane

Chapter One

"Mama Etney, I think she ready." He was clearly nervous and anxious to turn this 'project' over to one who was trained to manage the birth, and the hysterical woman. "De water done broke."

"Well now Sam, you bout to be a daddy! I'll be ready in no time."

Eliza went along as her mother's assistant. She grabbed the tapestry bag which contained the necessary instruments, herbal tinctures, borax powders, ointments and clean cotton cloths. The Carley's cabin wasn't far. When Eliza saw Sam's wife Harriet, lying in bed, her eyes looked like two sunny side up eggs! The contractions had already begun.

"Eliza, put some more wood on that fire in the kitchen and start heating up some water."

She heard her mother begin preparing the soon-to-be new mother for what was ahead.

"Now listen, Sarah," she said, pointing her finger and lowering her voice, "you 'bout to bring a life into dis here world. It's one of the bravest things you have ever done, and it will change you from now on. Time for bein' scared has passed. Now is the time for being ready to push dis here baby out yo womb. Now I'm here wit ya. And you know I ain't gon let nuthin' happen to ya. So, you got to relax, trust me, and do what I say. You and me and God, gon' bring this baby into the world. You understand me?"

Sarah nodded. Still a little petrified but more confident. "My back is hurting so bad."

"Eliza, get them quilts over there and spread them out on the flo' "Eliza created a pallet on the floor next to the bed. "Okay Sarah, now take your time and move down here," she pointed to the pallet. "This gon help your back. "Dis yo first chile. So, we gon be here for a while. You know, the railroad tracks ain't been laid yet."

The next of many contractions had begun.

"Breathe Baby. Breathe. In through yo nose out through your mouth. Jus keep breathin'..." Edna held one hand and Eliza held the other. Eliza had done this many times with her mother. She had been assisting her for more than two years.

"Ahhhhhhhhhhhhh!" Sarah screamed. "Mama Etney, I gon die. I gon die tonight."

"You gon be fine honey." Edna was calm. Eliza admired her stoic posture and disposition.

The contraction ended and the room was quiet again. Edna gently examined Harriet. "Okay, you doin' great. The baby done dropped some. We movin' along. After a while you gon feel like pushin'. But don't push unless I tell you."

The contractions came and went out like the tide, faster and faster. Each one was harder than the one before. Sarah was screaming and sweating but holding her own. She would curse Sam, call Jesus, and pray to God, all during the same contraction. Edna put her hands on the bulging belly, and masterfully assessed the position of the child.

"Oh yes. It done dropped way down. You gon soon be outta yo misery. This is a big baby. You gon have to work! These things don't happen on they own. We almost done. Eliza you can bring that water now and get those cloths out my bag. Sarah, get up on your hands and knees, head down. Lemme help you." She assisted Sarah to move into position on the pallet. "Next time the pains come; I want you to push wit everything you got!"

Sarah was ready. When her pain came again, she gritted her teeth, pursed her lips tight, and pushed with all of her might. Edna was at her bottom, watching for the baby's head. Eliza was at her side, rubbing her back. With each pushing contraction, the baby makes a little bit more progress exiting the birth canal. When Edna saw the head crown--the little round circle covered with a fuzzy crop of hair about to pop out of Sarah's womb--she exclaimed, "This is it gal. Puuuuuuuuuusssssssssshhhhhhhhh!" Her deeply pitched vocal expression of the word push synchronized and harmonized with Harriet's high-pitched scream as she pushed one last time. Edna's practiced hands took hold of that baby and pulled as its mother pushed. The baby came out with a swoosh of blood and other liquids. Edna's white dress and apron were covered with splashes of red. She held the baby's head up to keep it from strangling. Together they had brought this new life--a little boy screamin' his head off--into the world! Now on to the next part.

"Eliza, look in the bag and bring me that string."

Eliza knew what was coming next. She loved watching this part, and she also got to help. When she brought the string to her mom, Edna was examining the navel cord. Eliza knew that this cord was attached to what her mom called "de afterbirth." Edna was holding the cord.

"Why are you holding it like that, mama?"

"Well first I have to check and make sure that the pulses are beating right before I cut the cord. This baby's pulses are just fine."

Eliza was watching every step with intent. Edna reached for the piece of string Eliza was holding and she tied the cord on the end nearest Harriet's belly. She knew that this would help Harriet when she delivered the afterbirth in about thirty minutes. She tied the other end of the string about three inches from the baby's abdomen and cut the cord. Then she turned that end of the cord, back into the belly band.

"Did I have a piece of cord on my belly when I was born, Mama? Cause I don't have none now."

Edna smiled. She seemed happy that Eliza was so interested in her life's work. "Of course, you had one. Everybody has to have one. It's how we all get here, attached to our mamas. After a while it will fall off. Dat's why you don't see yours."

While talking with her daughter, Edna was steadily working. Now that the baby was detached, it was time to clean the eyes. "Bring me those borax powders, and dat jar of water."

She mixed the solution until the powders had dissolved in the sterile water and very carefully began to clean the baby's eyes. Next, she washed out his mouth with the same solution.

"Eliza, is that tub of water ready?" Eliza had prepared a small tub full of warm water with a sprinkling of borax powders dissolved in it.

"Yes, mama."

Edna carried the baby across the room and gently laid him in the water to clean him. The water was also a sedative.

Getting born was hard work, and a little scary for babies. When he was clean and falling asleep, Edna put on a cloth diaper and wrapped him in one of the swaddling quilts Sarah had sewn for her baby. This was the part Eliza loved the most. She got to hold the baby while Edna worked on getting the afterbirth from the Mom. She sat by the hearth, perched on a stool. Her arms cradled to receive the new life from her mom.

"Now Sarah, this will be hard cause you had a big baby. I want you to take your two fists and blow into them hard as you can." Sarah obeyed. She kept blowing and pushing and before long, with the help of Edna, the afterbirth was out.

Eliza was rocking the baby and watching her mom work. She had seen this many times before. If you have ever seen a pig slaughtered, you would know that the afterbirth looks like a hog liver.

Edna said to Sarah, "I have to study it carefully before we call ourselves done. It should be smooth and round with no chips. Gotta make sure we got everything. I don't want you having no pains later on." Sarah nodded in appreciation.

The afterbirth was a perfect specimen, and the birthing of James Carley was now complete. Edna lifted the baby from Eliza's arms and placed him on his mama's chest so he could smell her and feel her close up. Eliza put some rolled up quilts and pillows behind Sarah's head and propped her up so she could nurse her baby for the first time. He started to pull in on that nipple like he had done it a hundred times before.

Edna and Eliza began cleaning up the cabin so they could invite Sam into the bedroom to meet his son. Later they could go home to get a few hours rest. It had been a long night and would soon be time to start breakfast (for Edna) and for Eliza to get up and feed the chickens.

"Yes, mama?" Jesus! It was daybreak. She had overslept. The aromas of coffee brewing and biscuits baking confirmed her realization that she should have been up already.

"Eliza get up .... Go out there and feed those chickens and bring me some eggs."

Eliza stumbled--still dazed with only two hours sleep--into the dew-kissed dawn farmyard and opened the pen to let the chickens out. The red cardinals nesting in the dogwood trees were singing and celebrating the dawning of a new day.

"Humph," she grumbled. "When I grow up I ain't gonna marry no farmer.... scratching and diggin in the dirt!" As the chickens waddled out through the opened gate, clucking their thank yous for freedom from being penned-up and pecking at the dried cracked corn she was throwing in handfuls, Eliza saw a familiar figure walking towards her.

"Mornin' lil sis," Her brother Nelson chirped cheerfully, smiling like the sun and knowing that she hated this early morning ritual of stumbling out of bed to feed the chickens. He was headed back from laboring in the fields since before dawn and milking the cows.

"Is breakfast ready? I ain't got much time to eat and get back to work.... lots of land to plow today and that mule is movin' mighty slow."

"I saw mama in the kitchen on my way out, and I heard the crackling bacon in the frying pan, so I guess it's ready. You know she never late." Eliza was feeling a little bit more awake now.

"Then let's go! I'm starving." He took her basket and went into the pen to gather the freshly laid eggs and they headed back towards the cabin that was home. Eliza loved her brother.

"Well thank you for helping me. You know I hate any kind of work in the yard."

Nelson handed her the basket filled with fresh eggs.

"I am always gonna help you and look after you, no matter what. I am your big brother. That's, of course, unless you get on my nerves!" He ran ahead to dodge her fist in motion towards his head. He was two years older than her, but his twelve years somehow dwarfed her ten. She felt like a baby compared to him and how hard he had to work to help support the family. He never complained; that's what made him seem even more grown up.

"Get on your nerves! Ha! Where's Papa?" She had not seen her dad return with Nelson.

"He'll be here soon. Barn door needed fixin'."

Through the cabin's front door, they entered the kitchen. There was mama in her glory. This was her domain.

It was the heartbeat of the home. The room was dominated by a magnificent floor-to-ceiling hearth. From just above mama's head, to the ceiling, the hearth was a solid brick wall which concealed the chimney. Below that was the brick-lined, wood-burning space, where all of the nourishment for the family was prepared. There was a metal pole suspended across the middle of the cavern, and four heavy weight chains that were spaced apart by at least twelve inches. The chains were wrapped around the pole several times. One end of the chain had a sort of "s" hook (to hang a pot handle) and the other was just a round circle to make it easy to hang on a wall when not in use. The length of the chain determined the pots proximity to the fire, which was adjusted by how many times it was wrapped around the pole. One of the pots was filled to the brim with steaming white grits that mama was slowly stirring as she added a big hunk of butter which Eliza had helped her to churn the day before.

The floor, walls, benches, and trestle table of the kitchen were made of wood. This wood was alive with the aroma of the forest, and the meals prepared in that space. This very same wood also knew the history and culture of the family. Everything that was important in the home took place within the view and hearing of this wood. Family meals prepared and eaten, sewing of quilts to keep them warm on winter nights, and whispered conversations between mother and father while the children slept.

The kitchen was the warmest place in the house. Entrance into this space meant the immediate vanquishment of any chill in your body The smell of the goodies ready for consumption, the sight of the woman who loves you more than any other, the temptation to join her in the singing of her favorite inspirational song, and the taste of that food in your mouth before you even park your bottom in your space on the bench.

Edna Brooks Betts looked up when they entered through the percussive-sounding door. Her beautiful chocolate brown face--sweat on the brow from the heat of the hearth--lit up when she saw her children.

"Mornin'!" She had a way of singing the salutation.

Mama worked from 'cain't see in the morning to cain't see at night', but this was her life. It had been the life of every family member Eliza knew and didn't know, for generations before her. So, complaining was simply not a thing to entertain. One just did what was required for the survival of the family. At least slavery had ended five years before. Edna had lived the life of an enslaved girl, and then woman, from birth to twenty-eight years old, by the time it was over. There's promise. Things will get better. She had to believe this. Eliza prayed for it. Mama rarely spoke about the slavery life.

"Mornin Mama," Nelson greeted her. He then plopped himself down at the end of the bench closest to the head of the table where Papa would sit. "I'm so hungry I could take a bite out of your arm!"

"Boy you ain't got no bottom to yo stomach. You always hungry!" Mama laughed. Eliza handed her the eggs. She washed them and immediately began cracking them into a bowl. This was the last part of breakfast prep. There were two younger ones in the family. Malinda (Lindy) who was four, and Nannie was two. Cute as two lil brown buttons. They were seated at the table opposite Nelson.

"Eliza you gotta get up earlier," her mother said. "I want you to start training Lindy to feed the chickens and bring in the eggs. You need to get up on time so you can get her up and out with you. I need your help in the kitchen, and it's time for you to sharpen up yo cookin skills"

"Yes mama. I promise I will do better." Eliza was an obedient child with a rebellious spirit. So of course, in her mind she was sucking her teeth and clucking like a chicken at the thought of getting up on time instead of lying there until mama screamed at her.

"Hey everybody," a thunderous booming baritone voice entered the room. Papa Isaac was a robust man with a jovial disposition. He was only twelve years older than Eliza, so not her biological daddy, but he was the only father she had known. Edna was eleven years his senior. The enslavement experience had created some family configurations that look abnormal under the lens of our modern standards. Slave masters controlled the potential for nuclear families to remain intact. If his business needed cash flow, he might sell the father or the mother or the children. Most often they were sold away from one another, like used furniture being sold off in separate pieces. This left many family units tattered and truncated. The trauma was devastating and often left individuals alone without loved ones. So, they latched on to others who would take them in and nurture them as a family member.

Isaac was a teenager when he bonded with Edna on the plantation where they were enslaved. His father had been sold long before. Then his mother and sister were sold away to a place unknown to Isaac. The master kept him because he was young and strong and capable of doing a heavy workload on the plantation. When slavery ended in 1865, he and Edna decided to be together as husband and wife. He had no family, and she had a son and daughter whose father had died. They would go and find the meaning of freedom together, as a family. Despite his youth, he provided a well-grounded, hard work and love-based leadership of the family seated at the table, waiting for his blessing of the food. People matured faster in those days.

"Mornin Papa," Eliza beamed a smile at him.

"Papaaaaa!" His two daughters jumped off of the bench and ran over to him as their screeching voices sang out the sound of his name. He gathered them both into his generous arms and kissed their cheeks. They giggled, hugged him and scurried back to their seats on the bench.

Once Papa was seated, Edna covered the table with bowls of food. Biscuits, butter, molasses, hot grits, fried eggs and a platter of crispy fried bacon. She poured a mug of steaming hot coffee for herself and for Isaac.

Bowed heads, clasped hands, Papa started, "Dear God. We thank you for another day. We thank you dear God for this roof over our heads, the food on the table and the shoes on our feet. May we always remember that you have brought dis family from a mighty long way. Bless the hands that have prepared this meal. Lord, help us to live so that we will see you, when all is said and done. In the name of your son, our lord and savior Jesus Christ. Amen."

After the grace was said, the only sound in the room was the clinking of spoons and forks and the swooshing of jaws chewing and savoring the food. Mealtime was a sacred family time.

Into the quiet, came a knocking on the door. "Come in," Papa said from his seat at the table's head. It was Mitchie Henderson, the neighbor from the farm next to theirs.

"Mornin Isaac, Miss Etney." He nodded his head as a greeting to the adults in the room.

Isaac greeted his neighbor, "Mornin Mitchie. Come on join us. There's plenty food."

Mitchie stood still in the place near the door, where he had entered the room. "Thank you. That's mighty kind. Sorry to interrupt your meal, but Randall asked me to come and git you, Miss Etney, cause Harriet is having pains. They think it's her time."

Edna had been trained as a midwife, by her former slave master, Dr. Henry Easley, when she was a young girl. He had noticed that whenever he had to attend one of the slave cabins to deliver a baby, she always showed up, standing in the doorway, watching. On one occasion, he called to Edna, "Girl. Bring me that bowl of water over there!" That got her into the room and up close. Then, "Look in my bag on the table and bring me the instrument that looks like a spoon." In the time it took for him to say the "n" on the word spoon, she was handing it to him.

After that she would just stand there, watching his every move. Eyes asking questions that she didn't dare verbalize. Not at first anyway. So, it was and so it became that whenever a woman was in labor, they would come for Dr. Easley, and on his way to the cabin, he would send someone to get Edna. She was thirteen when this started. By the time she was sixteen, they would go for Dr. Easley and he would say, "Go get Edna. Tell her I'll be down there after a while." He would show up an hour later (at first), then two hours after he became more confident in her skills. Finally, he would just come by few hours later and inspect her work, nodding and grunting as he scrolled the checklist in his mind, and then he would leave. Sometimes he would ask her certain questions to get her affirmative response. Once he was satisfied that the mother and new baby had been properly handled. He would leave. If he made no comment,

Edna knew she had done a good job. By the time she was eighteen, nobody even thought about going for Doc Easley. This is how Edna became gifted with the profession that would dominate her life and the life of her oldest daughter Eliza. This is also how Eliza became somebody who did not want to be a farmer. Her passion was in attending to the health of women.

All of the farmers and their wives there in Black Walnut depended upon her herbal remedies for guidance through their pregnancies as well as the safe delivery of their babies. The local doctor was too far away, too expensive. And anyway, they trusted Edna. Many of these families had been enslaved right there on the Easley plantation, or one of the neighboring farms where Edna also sometimes went to administer to new mothers. Randall and Harriet were at the farm next to Mitchie. She had known that Harriet was due to give birth soon, but she thought it would be at least another week, when she had examined her a few days before.

"Okay Mitchie. I'll be right with you. Eliza you stay here with the girls and clean up after breakfast."

When Harriet heard Her husband open the door and greet Mama Etney, she felt relieved.

Eliza loved spending time with her sisters, but she sure didn't like being left behind when mama had a baby to deliver. There was still so much to learn about the art of midwifery. She was determined to learn all that her mother could teach her, but Isaac and Nelson still had a full day of work to complete. It was the planting season, so Eliza had to stay with Lindy and Nannie.

When the kitchen was sparkly clean, and all dishes, bowls and pots had been put back into place, Eliza swept the floor with the long handle broom made of fine tree branches tied to a stick. Her little sisters were clapping and singing, entertaining themselves without disturbing Eliza with any "behaviors". She had promised them that if they were "good" while she did her work, she would tell them a story when she was done.

As soon as Lindy saw Eliza lay the broom in the corner, she started up." Liza, we was good. We ready for our story. Which one you gon' tell us?" Nannie looked on in anticipation of the response. Sometimes Eliza retold Bruh Rabbit or lion or turtle stories that her mother had already told them, and sometimes she made up tales. Today she had a new story for them.

Eliza had learned and then taught her sisters, that when the story is about to be told, the teller says, "Once upon a time...." and the listeners must say, all together, "Time". This is to indicate that they are ready to listen. Her mother had told her that this was a tradition from way back in the Africa time.

Eliza began, "Once upon a time...."

"Time!" Came the anxious and synchronized response.

"Back in the old old days.... back in which days?"

"The old old days" Nannie and Lindy said

"Bruh Lizard was an awful lot like Bruh Frog. He could sit upright like a dog. Things had been like this for a very long time. Then one day as they were walking down the road by their swamp, Bruh Lizard and Bruh Frog spotted something real nice. Lindy get up and show us how Bruh Lizard was walking."

Lindy stood up and put her two hands up in front of her body and sauntered forward while swaying her hips.

"There you go! Now Nannie, can you walk like a frog?"

Nannie jumped up and down with her two-year olds display of how a frog "walks."

"Good girl! So, they saw a pasture with a great big ole pond that was on the far side of a huge fence. Ooo that land looked lucious! So green and so fresh! Bruh Lizard knew he could catch insects and other good food. And Bruh Frog couldn't wait to jump into that pond. Bruh Lizard and Bruh Frog went right up to the fence. But it was a reeeally big fence. Say reeeeally big fence!"

"Reeeally big fence," the girls called as they spread their arms up towards the ceiling like Eliza had done.

"That's right. And the boards of that fence were mashed together so tight that it seemed like one solid piece of wood. The bottom of the fence went deep into the ground. Neither of them could hop over it and did you ever see a lizard, or a frog dig a hole?"

"No!" shouted Lindy. "Lizards and frogs can't dig no hole!"

"That's right. So, they couldn't go under. There was a sign that said, 'keep out', but they couldn't read. Even if they could read, they would not have cared about that sign. Cause they saw something they wanted."

"So, Bruh Lizard and Bruh Frog sat beside that tall fence with their bottoms on the ground and their front ends leaning against the fence, cause Bruh Lizard could still sit upright then jest like a dog.

'Bruh Frog, there's gotta be a way to get to the other side of that fence!' Said Bruh Lizard.

They got up and started to movin along the fence to look for some opening in the wall. Suddenly, Bruh Frog saw a narrow opening...like a lil crack. It was low to the ground. 'I'm going ta squeeze through that crack over there,' he croaked. 'I think my body can squeeze through it.' So, he pushed himself and squeezed himself and grunted and made loud noises to help him to achieve his goal.

Finally, Bruh Frog popped out on t'other side.

'Come on Lizard,' Bruh Frog called through the crack.

'I'm a-comin'!' Bruh Lizard called back. And he started tryin to do the same thing he had seen the frog do. He pushed and squeezed and squeezed and pushed. He grunted and groaned and groaned and grunted. Lemme hear you grunt like Bruh Lizard." The two girls both started making guttural sounds from the middle of their throats.

"Yes .... and help me to groan like Bruh Lizard." The three sisters started to groan like someone with an unscratchable itch.

"Oh yeah. He was givin it all he had. Well, with all of this carryin on, Bruh Lizard and Bruh Rabbit hadn't noticed that there was a loose rail sitting on top of the fence. All of the to do, made the rail fall. It hit poor Bruh Lizard and mashed him flat. The only thing he could do was crawl backwards and lay down to try and pull himself together. So, from that day to this, the Lizard has never been able to sit upright again. And he never did get through the fence to eat them insects."

Eliza's two little sisters squealed with delight at the conclusion of the story. Then she began singing:

Juba dis an' Juba dat, Juba kill a yaller cat;
Juba up an' Juba down, Juba running all around.

As soon as they heard the word juba, they joined in singing with her. Then Eliza sang, "can I see your juba?" To Lindy.

"Yes, you can, "Lindy replied swinging her hips and twirling around.

"Can I see your Juba?"

Lindy continued her movement. "Yes, you can."

Then it was Nannies turn. "Can I see you Juba?"

"Yes, you can," Nannie said spinning around and waving her hands in the air.

"Can I see you juba?"

Still spinning, Nannie said, "Yes you can."

Eliza was about to take her turn at showing her moves, her "juba", when she turned to see her mom coming through the door.

"Mama! How's Miss Harriet?"

"Aww she okay. It's her first baby. She don't understand how it goes and she scared her time will come and I won't be there. I examined her belly and looked her over really good. She ain't ready yet. Still gon' be bout another week before her baby is ready to come." Edna turned to hug her two little ones, "You girls go on in there and lay down for a nap. Me and Eliza will start getting ready to prepare dinner."

Lindy and Nannie respectfully, although clearly reluctant, disappeared from the kitchen. They had probably hoped that mama would come back later so that their play time with Eliza could be extended past nap time.

"Eliza, we gon' make a pot of chicken stew with dumplins. While I go change my clothes, you git that big stew pot and three onions off the shelf. Get my knife out. I'll be right back."

And so, this was life for Eliza Easley Betts growing up into young womanhood. One year flowed into the next. She complained less about work, enjoyed cooking, and was dedicated and attentive to learning the craft of midwifery from her mom. This kept her busy, feeling fulfilled and away from farm work. Ah, such a waste of her talents, she felt. Her social outlet was mainly attending church services and church social events.

At a certain age though, all young people respond to nature's call. The boys at the church had been eyeing Eliza for quite a while already. She was tall and stately. So, they probably thought she was older than her actual 16 years. One of these boys was Marshall Mason. He was always trying to get Eliza's attention by smiling when she walked by, or saying things like, "Nice frock you wearing today Miss Eliza". She would hardly turn her head in his direction.

He was like a peacock! Putting on airs like he was such a big deal. His daddy was a farm laborer just like most of the other people in the church. They was poor and mostly illiterate. Eliza wanted something more for herself. She wanted a man who had a trade, like a carpenter or a blacksmith. He should at least be able to sign his own name, instead of just putting the letter x when his signature was required.

Still she realized that she was getting older and there weren't many boys her age around. Girls were expected to get married and start families. Most of the boys were either much younger or already married. Even some of those married men would be peaking at her when their wives weren't looking. But she definitely didn't want no parts of them. She had heard about how some girls used to sneak off into the woods at night and be lettin those married men touch and feel on them in ways that Eliza thought were just not right. Those married men didn't get as much as a sniff from Eliza Betts. Would she ever find someone who she liked?

Every fall at the end of harvest time, there was a big social event at the church. Each family would cook something that was produced from their farm. Those who raised chickens, cows, or pigs would slaughter an animal. The night before the celebration, the men would gather behind the church and dig huge pits for the cooking of the meat in the yard. They would start the fires and place screening over the fire in the pit. One pit fire had a metal pole suspended over it. This was for the all-night roasting of the pig. Isaac, along with the other men of the church would camp by the fires overnight and take turns curating the roasting meats. This was also bonding time for them. They would share stories about that year's harvesting experience and other spicy topics the women were not privy to. By the time the women and children showed up the next morning and set up the tables in a big circle, the entire church grounds were radiating with the aromatic essences of barbeque pig, roasted beef, and grilled chickens. Oh, what a mighty feast it was every year. All ages of all families looked forward to this event. Even the trees that surrounded the church danced in the gentle breezes that caressed the people and food. The women showed off their cooking and baking skills. Hand sewn quilts were exhibited on clotheslines in a lovingly competitive spirit.

Malinda and Nannie were now teenagers and they loved this chance to get with the other young girls and play jump rope and clapping games. They both still loved a good game of Juba. It was in this festive atmosphere that Eliza spotted HIM. The love of her life. She was helping her mom set up the table with the cakes and pies. He walked by with Mr. Henry Jones, carrying a big pot, and his wife Ann. HE was carrying a crate full of ears of corn. Ann was carting her baby girl in one arm and had their little son by the hand. Eliza spotted him right away. He was tall, light skinned and gooooood lookin'. A perfect match for Eliza's solid lanky frame. She caught his eye as they passed by the table.

"Mornin' Mama Etney. Mornin Eliza," chirped Ann. Of course, Eliza and her mom had delivered Ann's baby girl. Eliza had played a very big part in the delivery of this little girl, since her mama, Etna, had also been very pregnant at the time of this birth. She had stayed for a few days to help Miss Ann with the new baby. While there, she had heard tell that Mr. Jones' nephew was coming to visit them to help with the harvesting.

"Mornin Ann. How's that baby doin'?" Ann brought the baby over and lifted her into Edna's waiting arms. Ann leaned over to admire Etna's new son, laying on the quilt in the grass next to their table. Mr. Jones and his nephew continued walking towards the area where they had the fire ready for the steaming of the corn. Eliza pretended to be interested in the baby girl, but she had one eye on that handsome tall drink.

Here come Nelson with his always empty stomach! "I'm hungry. They still setting up the other tables. Even the corn ain't ready. Can I get a piece of pie?" He asked his sister since Mama was busy holding the baby and talking to Miss Ann.

Eliza gave her brother, who was now a towering, good looking, twenty-one-year-old eligible bachelor, a snide smile. She could always use food to bribe him or get his help.

"It's gon take me a minute to get the plates and forks out. Plus, I gotta find the knife. Which pie did you want?" She was baiting him. Making him salivate. He looked over the table of delicious looking apple, blueberry, sweet potato and cherry pies, alternated with the pound cake, chocolate cake and white cake with pineapple filling and coconut icing....

"Um I don't know. You think I could get a slice of pie AND cake?" He smiled his most, 'come on you my sister, my best friend', smile. He had played right into Eliza's hands. She gave him back her 'you can get what you want if you do what I say' smile. They both knew the shorthand for one another's smiles. But this time, Nelson was clueless as to what she wanted. "Okay. What?" He looked at her amused and curious.

She spoke in a voice just above a whisper, with her head facing away from her mom and Miss Ann who were engrossed in a conversation about newborn baby care. "You see that tall light skinned boy over there with Mr. Jones?"

"Yeah," replied her brother. "That's his nephew. Came from Richmond County to help with the harvest since Mr. Jones doesn't have any big sons yet." Eliza stood, arms akimbo, staring at her brother, waiting. Slowly, he reads with sheer amusement the meaning of his sister's smile. "No! Don't tell me ole stuck up done seen somebody she like?"

"Shut up Nelson," she commanded, feigning annoyance. "All I know is if you want a piece of this pie now, before it's time for the desserts to be served, you need to go over there, make friends, he bein' new to town and all, and then bring him over to meet your mother and sister!" Nelson was tickled by his sister's scheme to meet a boy, and happy to conspire with her.

She watched him saunter over to the table where the newcomer was shucking ears of corn to add to the big pot of boiling water.

"Hey man. How you? You from Richmond, right?" Nelson started.

"Yes I am. Here visiting my uncle for a short time," Alex replied in a friendly tone.

"My name's Nelson. Nelson Betts," he introduced, extending his hand for a shake.

"Well, pleased to meet you Nelson. I'm Alex. Alex Cowen," he replied while shaking Nelson's hand.

"How bout I give you a hand." Nelson began helping with the corn shucking.

Eliza was impatiently viewing the two young men and wondering what was taking her brother so long to get the job done. But Nelson was talking and laughing and when they finished with the corn, the two went off to get some slices of sweet red watermelon and then to play stick ball with some of the other young men. "Hmph! No cake or pie for him!" She said aloud to herself.

Truthfully, Nelson hadn't forgotten but the day was young. He figured he had plenty of time. Plus, he kinda liked this guy and wanted to get to know him better, especially since his sister was interested in him. So far, he was impressed. Alex was pretty smart and seemed like a good-hearted person. He had spoken about the importance of helping family when they needed you. He had also told Nelson about his plans for the future, which included owning his land. Nelson figured when it was time to eat, which would be soon, he would introduce them at the dessert table. At just that moment, one of the deacons started hitting the huge bell in front of the church to announce mealtime. People started lining up with plates in hand. There were people at every table in the circle. The elderly folks were served first, and then the others. On the church lawn there were chairs under the trees, for the elderly and others had spread quilts on the grass. Everyone assembled for the saying of the grace, giving thanks for the harvest and the families assembled, as well as the good cooking of the food and then, it was on! Plates were piled sky high. Barbecue pork, roasted chicken, fried chicken, beef ribs and roasted beef, potato salad, boiled corn, candied sweet potatoes, collard greens, steamed cabbage, and corn bread with fresh churned butter! There was lemon aid and iced tea to wash it all down. And then there was the dessert table....

Eliza was ready with her most prize-winning white teeth showing grin when Nelson came over to her with Alex. Each of the young men had so much food that one wondered how they could carry it all.

"Eliza, I want you to meet a new friend of mine. This is Alex. He's visiting with Mr. Henry and Miss Ann." Then he turned to Alex, "Alex, dis my sister Eliza. She a great cook. You gotta taste that sweet potato pie. Dats her best!"

"Hello Eliza. Nice to meet ya." He smiled, and all she could do was smile. The words were stuck in her throat like old peanut butter. Jeezus, he was so handsome! And so tall. Instead of just standing there grinning, she figured since she couldn't speak, she should be about the business of getting them served so they could go, and she could pull herself back together. He pointed to the sweet potato pie. She cut him an extra-large slice, put it on a plate and handed it to him. Her brother got his cake and pie (after all he did what she asked) and the two balanced their food on hands and forearms as they went to sit on the grass and eat.

Eliza fixed herself a plate and went to join some of the girls her age. As she sat down, they were in a conversation about 'the new boy'.

".... And he so cute."

"I heard he ain't staying long."

"Girl you gotta be careful. You know them boys from Richmond is wild."

Eliza pretended to be preoccupied with her food.

"Eliza. What do you think? I saw you grinning at him."

Eliza shrugged. "He all right. My brother seems to like him."

Competition. Hmph. She wasn't worried about that. He was lookin at her jus like she was lookin at him. Bet Nelson didn't even see that.

The conversation changed to other girlish topics, like menstrual cramps and the latest fashions, but Eliza was still thinking about Alex. She couldn't wait to get another chance to talk to him. This time she wouldn't freeze.

Just about when folks were finishing up with eating and it was time for games and recreation, dark clouds started to roll across the sky. In a matter of about two minutes rain started falling in buckets everywhere. Men, women, children, everybody started grabbing food, blankets, pots bowls and running towards the church sanctuary. This brought the harvest celebration to an abrupt and somewhat rude ending. Leftover food was divided up so that everybody had something to take home and folks started leaving.

Mama came up to her daughter. "Eliza have you seen Nannie?"

"No mama. I thought she was with you and Lindy. I will go back outside and look for her."

She looked everywhere, in back, in front, on the both sides of the church building. "Nannie! Nannie!" The rain was still coming down. She was getting scared and quite drenched. It wasn't like Nannie to wander off by herself. Eliza decided to check the outhouse, which was a little bit far away from the church building. As she approached the small wooden building, she heard knocking from the inside. "Nannie! Nannie?"

A high pitched, somewhat frantic frightened voice yelled," I's here Eliza! The do' is stuck. I cain't get out!"

Eliza got a big rock and forced her way into the lightweight wood door. She grabbed her sister and hugged her. "What happened? How did you get locked in here? Why didn't you call somebody?"

"I went to the bathroom and then it started raining. I couldn't get out cause the door jus wouldn't open when I pulled on it and nobody heard me calling for help. The rain was so loud." Her voice sounded whiny, as if she had been crying.

"Aw. I'm sorry. Well I'm glad you okay. Come on, everybody is waiting for us." Luckily, the rain had stopped.

When Eliza returned to the sanctuary with Nannie, both girls drenched and cold, their mom was relieved and wrapped them each in a quilt. Now, the family could go home. As they headed towards Papa Isaac, waiting in the buggy, she looked around and everyone else had left. Nelson came over to her, "Alex was lookin for you to say bye. We couldn't find ya, and his folks was ready to go. I promised him I'd let you know."

Her heart sank. Would she ever see him again? Maybe at church Sunday.

The next Sunday, Eliza got all gussied up. She had two church dresses. The blue one with the white lace collar was her favorite. It was tightly fitted in the waist and then flared out as it cascaded down towards her hips. The hemline lightly brushed over her black Sunday dress up shoes, which she was very proud of. She had washed clothes for white people and saved her money to buy those shoes. As she brushed and combed her hair and pinned it up into a tight knot at the back of her head, she was almost dizzy with anticipation. Folks are supposed to go to church to worship God, but honestly, this preparation and excitement didn't have a thing to do with saying hallelujah, thank you Jesus. It was about hoping to get to see that fine specimen of colored manhood that she had not been able to, nor did she want to, stop thinking about.

As she was finishing up her hairdo, Nannie came up behind her, "Ooh lookie here! You lookin mighty nice today Sista." Eliza blushed but didn't say a word more than a very curt, "Thank you."

When they entered the church sanctuary, she immediately turned her head towards the section where Henry and Ann Jones always sat. They had not arrived yet. As the Betts family took their seats, Eliza positioned her body on an angle in the chair so that she could have a direct line of vision to where she knew the Jones would sit when they came. Finally, after about the third congregational song and the second prayer, Henry and Ann came in with their two children. No Alex....

"Nelson," he was sitting next to Eliza, "Where is he?" She whispered.

"I don't know. After church I'll see what I can find out."

The pastor's eloquent, rhythmically delivered sermon sounded like "blah blah blah blah blah" to Eliza on that Sunday. Normally she enjoyed hearing the word of God, but on this day, her mind was totally filled with all of the words she had practiced she would say when she saw him again. 'Nice to see you again.... how long are you staying? Are you enjoying your time with your uncle?.......'How is Richmond different from here?' Mostly, she just wanted to look into his beautiful eyes again. It seemed like the church service was endless. Finally, after the benediction, when folks were standing around talking, shaking hands, Nelson made his way over to Brother Jones.

"How you Bruh Jones?" he asked as he extended his hand for a shake.

"We are well. Thank God. And how are you Nelson?"

"I'm just fine, thank you. I was looking forward to seeing Alex."

"Ah yes. Alex was such a great help to me. He went back to Richmond yesterday."

Nelson gave the news to his sister.

"Yesterday?!" Eliza felt deflated.

"Yeah. He took the train back to Richmond yesterday. Seems he has a job to get back to. His uncle hopes he can come again, but no idea when," Nelson explained.

The many well-crafted dreams and plans that she had been conjuring up in her mind suddenly became liquid as they were flushed from possibility by a reality that she had not expected to have to accept. She might never see him again.

Chapter Two

Eliza and her mom were now partners in the business of delivering babies. While Edna was recovering from giving birth herself, Eliza had worked solo. The women of Black Walnut trusted Eliza the same way they trusted her mom when it was time for their babies to come. Sometimes, if the birth had been a difficult one, she would stay for a week or so to make sure that the new mother did not overexert herself. This also gave Eliza the chance to get to know the women and families in their community on a more intimate level, such as hearing their stories.

Rhody and Barnet Pool had four daughters. Her most recent pregnancy had gifted them, finally, with a son, Edom. The labor had been long and very difficult. Eliza had used every skill, every herbal concoction, and every prayer she had learned while in training with her mom to get that boy born. Finally, after almost two days of monitoring, coaching, and then Rhody pushing and Eliza pulling, the big-headed boy arrived, screaming, with a scalp full of bushy hair. Eliza knew that Barnet and Rhody would need for her to stay for a while. Normally the neighbors and or family members of the new parents would come and help out. This couple was new to town. They have recently moved from Newbern. Most of their family members were back there. One elderly auntie lived with them.

Staying with them after the birth of Edom gave Eliza the chance to get to know Aunt Mazie, who was about 75 years old and as alert as an owl. She liked Eliza. The young midwife appreciated the opportunity to ask questions of someone who had lived during a time that was very different for people of color. She brought Miss Mazie a cold glass of lemonade. She was sitting in her rocking chair out in front of the house. Eliza sat on the top step, just nearby Miss Mazie's worn out old slippers.

"Miss Mazie, my folks don't talk about slavery very much. I want to know more about what happened before I was born. What was slavery like? What kind of work did you do? Are there any stories you can tell me that will help me to understand what it is they don't want to discuss?"

"Whoa gal..." Miss Mazie admonished. "You sho wants to know a lot." Eliza was excited. She could feel that this was her chance to get something she had longed for. Her mom and dad had not been so willing to talk about this time in their past. Both Edna and Isaac had been reluctant whenever she'd ask about their experiences before her birth. Eliza was born in 1860, five years before enslavement ended. She had very little recall of where they were or what it was like. She only remembered that they had hurriedly packed the few personal items they owned and left from where they used to sleep every night. In fact, she only recalled her mom and her brother. It seemed like Isaac showed up sometime later, but he was the only dad she had known.

Mazie began, "I was sixty years old when the Yankees came and told us that we were free. My whole life had been lived as a slave on the Morgan plantation in Newbern. I was born a slave. The last time I saw my mammy, I was nine years old and she was sold to a massuh who took her to somewhere I don't know. I never saw her again. I stayed there with the massuh who had sold my mammy. When I was fourteen, he told me to go and sleep in the cabin with John. That was his way of "marrying" me to John, who I did not really know. He was quite a bit older than me. Slaves were matched according to what the massah thought would be a good combination for baby making. The children belonged to him. If a man was strong and a woman was smart, for example, he would put them together to make smart strong children who could bring better sales prices at the slave auction."

"That sounds like how my daddy breeds the cows on our farm," Eliza sighed

Miss Mazie was now in the flow of her story, so she continued without responding or reacting to Eliza's remark. "My life was spent working in the fields and caring for the children I bore. In the morning on my way to the fields, I would leave my baby with the cook in the big house. She would nurse my child whilst I worked in the fields. This was better than some. There were those who had to lay their babies under a tree and nurse them when they cried whilst picking cotton in between. One day there was a terrible rainstorm that came suddenly and before we could get to where the babies were lain, they all drowned. The overseer didn't care, and as soon as the rain stopped, he made those women go back to pickin cotton. Those were hard times girl."

"Oh my." Eliza was in awe. "What kind of person would be so cruel?"

"We asked that question many times over during my life as a slave. Never did get an answer that made sense. We just knew that prayer was the only thing to get us through what we didn't understand. I had three babies. Each of them was sold off when they got big enough to work in de fields and pick cotton. I never did know what happened to them. There was another woman named Rachel, who had a husband and seven children that got sold off and she had no idea where they went to either."

"Can you tell me your story?" Eliza was so anxious to get an understanding of what had happened to her people.

"Well I really don't like to talk about these things. I knows everything about slavery. I was born amongst the slaves. Jesus! We have suffered. I still can't talk about my children, or my husband who died. It hurts too much. Breaks my heart again every time I tell it. But I know you want to hear about slavery. So, I can tell you Rachel's story. How's that? "

"Miss Mazie, thank you for being willing to share with me. I'm sorry to bring up these painful memories. One day I hope to be able to tell my children and their children about where we came from and who we are," she spoke, feeling humbled.

"Well all right. I will tell you Rachel's story. I have many stories in dis here ole head, but Rachel's story is one that give some happiness in the end, so it's one of my favorites. Many of the stories end in death, whippings, or some kinda deep sadness, but this one has a lil light in it. Rachel was my friend on the plantation in Newbern. Around the time they sold my mammy, they bought Rachel. She was new on the plantation and alone. We became friends right off and we stayed like dat until she died. She told me the story of her life before she came to Newbern. From the time I met her, we shared our secrets and dreams with one another.

Rachel had fond memories of the mama who had been sold off from her. One thing she always talked about was how strong and direct her mama had been. She didn't allow nobody to take her for a push over and had been born in Maryland. Rachel said her mama would make the 'fur fly'. She always quoted what her mama would say if she wanted to set somebody straight: 'I warn't born in de mash to be fooled by trash! I'm one of de ole blue hens' chickens I is.' Blue hens' chicken is what folks born in Maryland called themselves. If Rachel got upset or angry with one of us, she would say this quote from her mom. She made it her own. It seemed to give her satisfaction when she was riled up. Made her feel like she had some power over her surroundings. She couldn't say it to Massuh or the overseer, but she wore us out with it. Hot like a pepper, that Rachel.

"So, round about the same time Massuh put me with John, he moved Rachel to Sam's cabin. Well Rachel was mighty glad cause she and Sam had already been a kissing behind the barn at night anyway. He loved him some Rachel and she wouldn't take nuthin for her Sam. They started having children right away. Before they were done, they had seven! Round the time the last one, a boy named Henry, was born, Massuh took sick. He got weaker and weaker and finally died. The mistress tried to keep things going. She tried hard for a few years. But finally, she came and said that she broke, and she got to sell all de niggahs on de place."

"So, we was all put in chains and taken off to Richmond where they made us stand up about twenty feet in the air, on a platform, like a porch. White men came by and touched us everywhere on our bodies; even looked in our mouths at our teeth. They made comments like, 'Dis one too skinny,' 'Dis one don't mount too much, 'Dis one too ole, and 'Dis one lame.'

"After they finished looking us over, the sale began. They sold Rachel's husband and took him away. Then one by one, they sold her children, each to a different white man. When the last one was left, she grabbed him and hugged him and begged, then threatened them, not to take him. 'I'll kill de man that touch him!' She screamed at them. Then her little sweet boy, whispered in her ear, 'Don't worry mama. I will run away and then I will work to earn money so's I can buy yo freedom.' Her terrified heart was so warmed by his grown uppity thinking. But they took him and sold him to someone she had never seen and away he went. She never saw her husband or six of her children again. Rachel and I were both good cooks. We got sold to the same massuh, who took us to his plantation. We were still in Newbern. The years came and went. Before we knew it, twenty-two years had gone by and the white folks had a war dat made us free, so they said."

"The Yankees had fought with the southerners and beat them. When the Yankee soldiers came to Newbern, the white folks ran for their lives, leaving everything behind except what they could grab as they fled. Me and Rachel and some other slaves was left in that big house all by ourselves. One day, we heard the hooves of the yankee horses approaching. It sounded like thunder and we was scared fo our lives. We only knew that white folks always bring bad news fo' us niggahs. They came into the house and we stood, straight as arrows, waiting for whatever was coming. The man who seemed to be in charge came over to Rachel and asked who the cook was. She told him it was me and herself. He could see we was very nervous. Then he said, 'Don't worry, you amongst friends now. Would you be willing to cook for me and the other officers while we stay here to plan our next maneuvers?'

"Of course, this was a relief, since cookin is what we know. We said, 'That's what we here for.' That man was the captain. He said, 'Well then you two are in charge of the kitchen. If anybody come meddling with you, make um walk chalk! Don't you be afraid. Then he and the other officers moved into the house. So, the house became their headquarters. They have different platoons in the area that would take turns guarding the house. One night, a big platoon of negro soldiers came. It was a Friday night and captain had allowed them to have a big party. The kitchen was a big and warm place. Always plenty food around. They went to congregatin in the kitchen and making noise and dancin around. Me and Rachel was not happy. We was jus a waiting for them to break something so we could run them out. There was one particular soldier who was jus a waltzing around and around with this young girl on his arm. Rachel and I was just a swelling and a swelling up! Secretly we was enjoying the show, but we didn't let them know that. When they got near Rachel, they kind of went to dancing around and around like to make her dizzy. Almost like they was making fun of her. Kept lookin at her red turban. 'Git along wid you! – rubbage!' Rachel said in a voice rough like tree bark.

The young man's face look like he heard something worth noticing, but just for about a second, and then he went to smiling again, same as he was before. Then the band members came around. They was also making fun at us. The more we showed our anger, the more they laughed and kept up making fun at us. When they laughed, and that made us worse, the rest of the niggers got to laughing! Rachel's eyes was just a blazing! I knew Rachel was going to rip into them any minute. Sho nuff, she stood up, put her fists into her hips, an' says, 'Look-a-heah!' she says, 'I want you niggers to understan' dat I wa'n't bawn in de mash to be fool' by trash! I'm one o' de ole Blue Hen's Chickens, I is!' Then I saw that young man freeze where he was a standing. He seemed to be in a daze, lookin up at de ceiling like if he forgot sumthin' and tryna remember it."

All of this time, Eliza had been on the edge of her seat, listening carefully and trying not to interrupt Miss Mazie with questions. She was so anxious to know how the story ended and inpatient to wait. But she didn't want Miss Mazie to get annoyed with her and stop her telling of the tale, so she kept her lips closed tightly. She almost lost control at this moment. She opened her eyes wide as the sun disc at dawn.

Miss Mazie continued. "Rachel picked up one of her black iron pans and went to swinging at them fellas. They took off runnin', still laughin as they went. As that particular young man was goin out, he told one of the other niggers, 'you go 'long and tell de cap'n I be on hand about eight o'clock in the mornin'; There's something on my mind, he says; I won't sleep no more this night. You go along and leave me by my own self."

"This was about one o'clock in de mornin. Me and Rachel went on to our beds to get some sleep. The next day, around seven we was gettin breakfast ready for the officers. Just as Rachel was gettin a hot pan of biscuits out of the oven, she sees a black face come round and look right into hers. He was lookin right into her eyes. I was standing there wondering what this here young man, the one from last night, was up to. But I am waiting ready to pounce if he was up to no good. Rachel stood still like she was frozen. She jus kept looking in his eyes, while he was staring into hers. Next thing I knows, the hot pan starts a trembling and she drops it on the floor. She grabs his left hand and shove back his sleeve. She was lookin' for something, I could see dat there was a scar. An then she pushed back his hair around his forehead. Another scar shaped like a crescent moon. An then I see Rachel's eyes fill up with tears, flowing like a river down her face. 'If you ain't Henry,' she said, 'then Henry is a dream I once had, and he never was born! Lord God oh heaven be praised! I got my own again!"

By this time Eliza's eyes were dewy. She felt happy and sad, all at once. "So, Miss Mazie. What happened then?"

"Well Mother and Son cried and hugged one another and shared their stories. Twenty-two years was a lot of history to tell. Henry had served time in the northern army after escaping slavery and moving to New York. He had a home up north and a wife and had hoped to find his mama to take her back with him. We stayed there, in Newbern, until it was time for the officers and their platoons to move on. Then Rachel's Henry came and got her and took her north to live out the rest of her life with him and his wife. She died last year', but not before she lived to see a new baby grandson come into de world, born free.

Eliza felt a surge in her level of respect for Miss Mazie, her parents, and all of the people who had survived this awful thing called slavery. She knew, like never, before that she was made of tough stuff. If her ancestors had survived to tell stories like the one, she had just heard, and many even worse, then there was nothing she could not achieve. She was indeed woven from unbreakable, unshredable threads.

She stayed there with the family for a few more days until mother and child were well on their way. When she said goodbye to the Pool family, she felt like she had delivered a baby for them, but also had been reborn herself. Eliza knew that she was now a woman and it was time for her to be about starting a family with a good man and have a few sweet babies.

Chapter Three

Eliza stayed busy all the time. She was now nineteen years old. Her parents had four younger children, Malinda, Nannie, Henry and the newest addition, Becky. This meant that Eliza had to help out around the house and farm. She also performed most of the midwife work now. Her days started before dawn and ended well after darkness had fallen. Still, she never forgot about Alex Cowen. She hoped that he was also thinking about her and that she would get to spend some time with him...just the two of them. Maybe they would even.... kiss... She never gave up the notion that he would return one day, and they would.... well what would they?

Her big brother, best friend, Nelson was now twenty-four and very popular with the girls at church. He knew he was handsome, and charming. Nelson was a flirt. Girls both loved and hated him for this way he had. He would say something, or smile his special all teeth showing crescent smile, when his eyes would twinkle. Then some girl would think, "Oh I'm the one. He favors me!" But before she could begin strategizing on how she could make him her man, she would see him giving that very same full mouth grin to some other girl who would be giggling like a ninny! Eliza told him he was gonna get himself in big trouble one day. That trouble never came cause Nelson, well Nelson got sick.

It was September. Time for harvesting. The days had begun to shorten and the green in the leaves of the trees had begun to surrender their pompacious allure to welcome the brown, orange, yellow and pink pallet of fall. The air was crisp with just a hint of summer warmth lingering. The coolness of winter's breeze whistled high up in the clouds, "I will soon be down to get ya!"

Eliza remembered this moment in time like a crystalline shard of ice, frozen in her heart, for the rest of her life. It was the season when her beloved brother took sick and died in a flash. Nobody saw it coming. Consumption was the evil horseman that rode into their lives and stole his light, and his breath.

With Eliza and Edna being women, who folks would call, sometimes before they'd call a doctor when they were sick, it wasn't the first time they had seen someone become very tired and have sweats at night. At first, they thought it was just a bad cold. The weather was changing. Nelson hadn't been dressing with clothes that were warm enough. Both mother and sister were looking after Nelson and urging him to rest and drink the bitter teas they were making for him. But when he started coughing really bad about the third day, and then spitting up thick white phlegm, they knew it was more serious than a cold. Isaac went to town to get the doctor, who was very busy. Almost every day, there was someone dying from Consumption or from Pneumonia. The doctor would go and tend to them, but it usually didn't change very much.

By the time he came to see Nelson, it was too late for him to offer even a glimmer of hope. He just shook his head, and said, "I'm sorry. The most you can do is make him comfortable."

Eliza did not move from his side. She sat by his bed feeling so hopeless. Still she would not leave him. The coughing was terrible. When the spasms would come, Eliza felt the rupture in her very own lungs. Nelson was so weak, and each coughing spasm seemed to subtract from the moments he had left to live. She didn't sleep. She didn't eat. Somehow, she hoped against hope that if she was vigilant, her lifeline could wrap around her brother and snatch him back from this illness. She would have given days, weeks, months or years from her own life if it were possible to add time to her brother's. As we know, it doesn't work that way. It wasn't long before Nelson Easley Betts departed this life. Eliza fell into an abyss of disbelief of anger of pain. Nelson was no more. That twinkle in his eyes was blackened forever and his enigmatic smile had no animation. Her most private hopes, dreams and aspirations, had been shared with the mind and heart of her beloved treasured brother. How would, could, she go on without him? Jesus!

Eliza sank into a state of isolation. Neighbors, family, friends, church members came and went, expressing their most heartfelt regrets. "So sorry for your loss", "Ah, he was so young", "The Lord knows best". Somewhere in the recesses of her being, Eliza knew that they meant well. However, at this moment, she just wished they would shut up. They could never understand what she had lost. She didn't want their "kind" words or their fried chicken. He had slipped away like the morning mist. Eliza had an empty space inside of her that was void, vacated. That space, had just lost it's only tenant, because nobody would ever replace her brother in her heart. There was nobody, just nobody like Nelson. She wanted Nelson to come back.

After the doctor returned to pronounce him dead, the elder women of the church came to the house and began the preparation of Nelson's body for burial. They washed him and rubbed oils of frankincense, myrrh and cedar all over his body. They cut his hair and dressed him in the suit he always wore to church. The whole time they were working on him, they were also administering to the family by expressing joy and hope for Nelson's time well spent on earth. Some of the other women from the church who were not directly involved with preparing the body, sang songs and clapped their hands. This was of great comfort to Edna and the rest of the Betts family. One song they sang was:

Someday, someday
I'll go where Jesus is
Someday, someday
I'll go where Jesus is
Someday, someday
I'll go where Jesus is,
I'll be caught up to meet Him
I'll be Caught up to meet Him
I'll be caught up to meet Him in the air.
I'll be caught up to meet Him
Caught up to meet Him
Singing joy and happiness,
Peace is mine!
Some day in glory,
I'll tell the story
I'll be caught up to meet Him in the air.

Isaac had made the wooden box that would be his coffin and they placed Nelson inside of it cradled in his favorite quilt that was sewn by Eliza and Edna. The coffin was placed near the kitchen door, under an open window, where Nelson would lay in state for three days. The air outside was cool and crisp with a gentle breeze. His death was an important event in the Black Walnut community. Nelson had been young, dashing, and loved by people of all ages. They came and went in continuous streams, from dusk to dawn, and never empty handed. They brought food and drinks and those who could, gave 'a lil piece of money' to help with expenses. The men dug the cavern where Nelson would be laid to rest in the church yard. The three days at the house were called "settin' up," that was "The Wake". Then at the church, there would be the funeral followed by the burial.

Amongst those who came to the house was Ann Jones. Edna greeted her warmly and thanked her for the double layered coconut cake she had brought. Malinda took the cake and put it on the kitchen table. The other children were outside in the yard. Sadness permeated even the normally jovial mood of the younger ones in the Betts family. Normally they ran up and down and sang songs like Juba Dis and Juba Dat or One For Your Money, which both involved clapping and singing out loud. Instead, on this day, they sat in circles, the girls fussing with one another hair, the boys rolling a ball on the ground between their feet. Their big brother had been their champion.

"Miss Etney, I am in shock. Nelson was a wonderful young man." Ann's sadness was genuine.

"Thank you, Ann. We are all just doing our best. He was my first born. He was my rock," her voice trembled. Her face was swollen and moist. Many teardrops had caressed those ample cheeks. "How's the baby? Where's your husband Henry?"

"Baby is doing very well thank you. Walking and running all over the place. Henry dropped me off on his way to the train station. His nephew Alex is coming in from Richmond this afternoon. They will come back here after Henry picks him up from the train station."

Eliza was laying down in her small bedroom which was just off from the kitchen where this conversation was taking place. Through the haze of her grief, she heard 'nephew

Alex' and something stirred inside of her despite her almost catatonic condition. There was a numbness inside that engulfed her. She felt remote and had no desire to come out. But the sound of that name, Alex, created a hairline of a crack in her entrapment.

It wasn't long before she heard Henry Jones' wagon approaching the front of the house. All at once she felt happy, sad, disheveled and listless. After all of this time she prayed for and wished to see Alex Cowen again. How many times had she done a little something extra to her hair, or wore a new dress with the hopes that he just might show up at church? And now, with no preparation and probably the worst day of her emotional life, he is here outside her door. Well she could finger brush her hair quickly, and pull together her clothes, but she couldn't do anything about her eyes looking like a river swollen in the flood season.

"Eliza", her mother spoke gently at the doorway, "you have a visitor." After greeting Edna and Ann and expressing their condolences, Henry went out to the barn where Isaac was working, and Alex had asked, "Miss Etney, is Eliza around?"

Every cell in her body was trembling. She wanted to smile but couldn't. She wanted to erupt with the telling of how much she had hoped to see him again. But because of the timing of his return, the thing that stood out most in her heart at that moment was the part that Nelson had played in introducing them. Alex appeared in the doorway of her sitting room, and the flood gates broke. She saw him with clarity for all of about four seconds, and then he was a blurred vision, like looking through a waterfall from the inside. One minute she was sitting on the side of her bench while he stood in the doorway, and the next, he was sitting at her side, cradling her, rocking her, and stroking her head.

He kept saying, "It's alright. It's alright. It's alright," almost like a lyrical chant. His voice was so soothing. Eliza went from bawling to sniveling to whimpering to quiet and in fact, at some point, she fell asleep. At some point, Alex must have gently slid from her side, covered her with a quilt and left the room.

She woke up the next day at dawn with a start. That was the first night's sleep she had managed to get since Nelson first got sick. She felt rested. Then she remembered, ran out into the kitchen where her mom was making biscuits, "Where is he? When did he leave? What did he say?" Bordering on hysteria and even wondering if she had dreamed Alex's reappearance.

"Good morning. You slept." Edna was sedate.

"Yes mama. I'm sorry. How are you this morning?" She went over and gave her mom a kiss on the cheek.

"I am okay. I have prayed and asked The Lord to hold my hand. So, I'm okay. God knows, I miss him so much," she spoke, kneading biscuit dough.

"Yes. I have also prayed. I know he is at peace." Eliza agreed.

"Today will be a long day. We have the funeral and burial and the repast at the church afterwards. I am sure you will see your young man there. For now, I need you to help me get the children ready while I prepare breakfast. I thanks de Lawd for you Eliza."

"I love you mama. Of course. I will get them up, bathed, and dressed."

Henry Jones and Mitchie Henderson came to the house to put the casket on a wagon and take Nelson to the church. Isaac assisted. He was clearly overwhelmed by grief. Somehow, Isaac felt that he had failed Nelson. He thought that perhaps if he had gone for the doctor that first day, when Nelson told him that he was feeling cold standing in the midday sun, maybe Nelson would still be alive. Nelson had been his "stepson", his little brother, and sometimes they were even just like friends. As he watched the casket slowly roll away, his heart felt like it was being crushed in a vice grip.

The funeral was both a wonderful celebration of the life of Nelson, and a sacred ceremony to commemorate his home going. The pastor spoke of him from personal knowledge and then quoted and expounded upon Bible texts that would comfort the family. He said that he could sympathize with them because he too had lost a young daughter to Consumption. There was talking and tears, hearty hallelujahs, and amorous amens. When it was time to view the body, Isaac, Edna, Eliza, Henry, Malinda, Nannie and Becky stood in front of the casket to say goodbye to their brother and son. The congregation hummed, "Precious Lord Take My Hand" which Eliza only noted later when she reflected on her brother's service. At that moment she only heard his voice, laughing, teasing her, and then coughing to his death.

Isaac, Mitchie, Henry, Marshall Mason (still trying to impress Eliza), and Alex were the pallbearers who carried Nelson's casket to the burial site. Everyone stood in a circle while the pastor prayed and said a few more words of encouragement. Eliza was a midwife. She had seen a lot of blood, tears, and even seen deep remorse when babies were stillborn. She had learned how to internalize her anguish in order to comfort those who needed it most. But there was nothing in her experience that had prepared her for the words "ashes to ashes, and dust to dust" to be spoken over the body of her deceased brother as soil was sprinkled upon his casket. Nothing.

The sisters of the church had prepared a sumptuous feast for the repast, after the burial. There was fried chicken, baked chicken, boiled ham, collard greens seasoned with fatback, potato salad, baked sweet potatoes, cornbread, biscuits and gravy. Outside in the front of the church, there was a fish fry in progress. Of course, the dessert table was covered with cakes, pies, and puddings of all sorts. This is how the people of Black Walnut came together to support one another when in need. The gathering after the burial was one that Nelson would have not wanted to miss. It was reflective yet respectfully festive.

Eliza was outside getting some fish for Isaac when Alex came up next to her. She had seen him earlier, but they had not spoken.

"How are you doing?" He asked.

"Oh! Alex. I'm doing okay. Listen. Thank you for yesterday. I didn't mean to fall apart like that. But I had not slept and ...."

"You don't have to explain. I was so glad that I could be there for ya. I really liked your brother. And I really like you."

All right now Eliza, here's your moment. Grab it girl. Don't freeze up, she thought

"Well I am glad to know that. My brother told me that he thought you were smart and kind and he liked you. I like you too Alex. I thought you might never come back," she said, her face wrinkled in sadness.

"How bout we go for a walk?" Alex asked

"Well lemme give this plate to papa. I'll be right back."

Isaac was sitting with some other men who were talking about helping him with harvesting since Nelson would not be there to do it. He hardly noticed Eliza putting the plate of hot fried fish in front of him. She quickly rejoined Alex, who was still outside waiting for her.

The sun was shining brightly in the cloudless blue sky. The branches of the trees on either side of the dirt road under their feet seemed to hold hands, creating an arch over their heads. They walked in silence at first. The silence seemed to scream with an urgency. From that urgency, came his first words.

"I can't explain what I'm bout to say, but I missed you."

Eliza stayed silent listening, marinating in the meaning of his words. He continued, "Since that day when Nelson introduced us, I knew there was something special about you. I felt it. Then I couldn't find you to say goodbye, and I haven't been able to forget about you since."

Eliza broke her silence. "I looked for you at church the following Sunday. When you weren't there, Nelson asked your uncle and learned that you had left town. I been looking for you from that day until yesterday Alex. Why didn't you come back sooner?"

There was a huge rock on the side of the road. They stopped and sat down on it.

"A lot has happened in my life since I saw you. My mama got sick and then died. She was the only family I had besides Uncle Henry and my mother's sister, Aunt Mary. After burying her, I had to decide how I was going to feed, house, and clothe myself. I moved to Woodsdale in Person County where I got a job working on a farm. It has taken me this long to put my life back together. My mama was a wonderful and strong woman. I miss her so much. But she taught me to work hard and keep my head up. So that's what I've been holding on to. It's been hard being alone in the world. I was coming back to see you and tell you how I feel, how I was missing you. But when my uncle picked me up from the train station, he told me that Nelson had died. Eliza, my whole reason for coming here, was to see you."

If eyes were mouths and could eat, Alex would have disappeared through the wide-open disks on Eliza's face. She looked at him with such adoration. "Alex. I'm so sorry about your mom. Burying her must have been the worst thing you have ever had to do. To know that you came here to see me, makes me happier than words could ever express. I have dreamt of you, wanted to see you and looked for you at church, ever since you left. I hope I never have to lose you again."

Alex looked remorseful. "I can't stay. It is harvest season. I stayed this long because of the funeral. But now I have to get back to work. My plan was to see you, tell you, and talk about when we could see one another again. I just couldn't wait any more. I am leaving in the morning. But I promise, this time it won't be long. And more important, you know that I want you to be my girl."

Those last seven words shot straight to Eliza's heart and sent a ray of light from heart to face. She lit up. She wanted to grab him and hug the juice outta him, but nice girls didn't do that. So, she hugged him with her eyes, with her smile, with her rounded shoulders arching forward, pointer finger resting on her middle teeth.

Alex reached over and pulled Eliza into a warm, enveloping embrace and whispered in her ear, "Be my girl?"

The stoic young woman, known as midwife Eliza Betts, normally stern and very serious, let out a giggle fit for a little girl who just received a piece of candy before dinner. She looked at this handsome strong man, with whom she was totally smitten, and whispered, "Yes. I am your girl."

And that was that. They walked back to the church, hand in hand, while they made plans for when he would come again.

After that Eliza's life was never the same. Alex came to Black Walnut every weekend. First, he spent time with her and the Betts family, and then he would go to see his uncle Henry and Aunt Ann. Sometimes on Saturdays, they went for long walks and had long talks with lots of hand holding and warm embraces. On Sundays they sat together at church and then he would come for dinner with her family. Eliza hated it when dinner was over because she knew that Alex would be leaving to head back to Woodsdale. Her parents liked him and approved of their budding relationship.

One Sunday night, as he was leaving, he said, "Next weekend when I come, I want to take you out somewhere. Jus' me and you.

Eliza smiled, showing all her teeth, "Where to Alex?"

"Don't worry. Just pretty up yourself," he replied smiling.

The week went by in a flash. Eliza hardly slept she was so excited. He took her to the local music club, which was the precursor to what would later be called a juke joint. She didn't know anything about this type of social environment, being just a simple hardworking church girl. But apparently, Alex had sewn some oats, some very wild ones. He had been "around". "Truth be told, it was your Brother Nelson who told me about this place that day we met," he said.

Hmmm. Eliza knew Nelson used to go out sometimes at night, but clearly, he didn't tell her EVERYthing.

The social club in Black Walnut was in a house owned by an African American family. Folks could stop by to hear local musicians play music, get some food to eat, drink some bootleg whiskey, and then if needed, even get a room upstairs for the night. It was often the only option for black folks who were traveling long distances, since they were not permitted to stay at the inns owned by whites.

The music was like nothing Eliza had ever heard. The lyrics to the songs were very suggestive and very frank. They spoke about things that concerned grown folks; love, heartbreak, money, racism, and poverty. They sat and listened for a while. Eliza was in awe. Then....

"Wanna dance?" Alex held his hand out

"Me? I don't know how to dance!" She was in a panic. She knew everything about birthin babies, makin' biscuits or feedin chickens, but dancin'? Eliza was afraid of embarrassing herself.

"Come on babeh. Just listen to the music and folla me." Alex was so convincing and so smooth. He always made her feel like she could do no wrong.

"Okay," she took his hand and followed him on to the crowded dance floor.

The singer's voice wrapped itself around the guitar's blues chords like a serpent squeezing its prey.

Come on lil mama
Rock me all night long
Come on little mama
Rock me all night long
Give me some of dat honey
Come on lil mama come on

The tempo was moderate, allowing the fluid movement of their bodies swaying in sync. Alex held her close. She felt like oil that had been poured over his body, as she easily followed his movements. The lyrics, coupled with his feet, his legs, the arching of his back, all so hypnotic. Eliza felt like she had somehow forfeited possession of her own physique.

Come on lil mama
Shake yo hips and twirl
Come on little mama
Come on rock my world
Let my train run through your tunnel
Ooh baby, I knoooooooows you my girl

Alex was so worldly, and Eliza was very inexperienced. She was astute, and a pretty good judge of character. But matters of the heart was a whole different category. She could not think logically. Her whole sense of self was being dominated by what she was feeling at this moment.

The guitarist stepped forward and played a solo. It looked and felt like the guitar and the player of it were one and the same being. He played that guitar like he came out of his mother's womb with his fingers plucking those strings. He was bending and stretching the notes of the melody like they were trying to visit someplace the song had not gone before but knew they couldn't stray too far from home. His hips made a circle as his fingers danced on the guitar strings.

Eliza had been so engrossed in her mastication of the Alex experience, that she hadn't really paid attention to the other couples on the dance floor. It looked like she wasn't the only one who was feeling the heat. Folks bodies were chest to chest and pelvis to pelvis, and their eyes were close enough for lashes to touch. Ooh, so this is how it was.

"We move good together babeh". The sound of his voice jolted her. For a moment, she had been lost in the small but expanding world inside of her mind. She looked up into those orbs that always made her feel like she was his drink of cool water after a hot day in the sun. "Yeah. You were right. Following you and listening to the music, made it easy to dance," she replied, trying to sound light-hearted and carefree. Not!

During the weeks following that night, they would often visit that place. Eliza became better at dancing and following Alex's lead. There was no longer hesitation when he was ready to hit the dance floor!

Alex was ready to move forward with Eliza. He knew that she was his clay; to shape and mold into his cup, bowl, and plate. But he also believed that she was not the kind of girl he should fool with if he wasn't serious. First of all, their families were friends. Second, she was a good, kind, hardworking and intelligent woman. Eliza was the kind of woman he wanted to have a family and to build a future with. She would be the perfect partner for a colored man who wanted more than just life as a farmer. Alex had plans. He wanted to go places.

The next time he came to Black Walnut, he asked Isaac if he might have a word with him, privately.

"What has you looking so serious young man?" Isaac has been watching the two lovebirds and pretty much knew why Alex wanted to talk with him. But he played the game.

Alex looked sheepish. "Yeah. I guess you can read it on my face. I been courting Eliza for quite a while now. I can see that you and Miss Etney has been raisin her to be a good woman; a woman who knows how to take care of a home, a man and a family. I wouldn't be coming to you if'n I didn't understand that"

Isaac stood silent, staring into the eyes of the younger man. His posture made Alex nervous, but he waited patiently. Alex continued nervously. "Well I think that Eliza is the perfect woman to be my wife and the mother of my chilren, and I come here to ask your permission to marry her!" He spit the last ten words out like they were little flames, burning his mouth.

Issac looked very stern and gave a pregnant pause before broadly smiling, "Welcome to the family son."

Eliza was inside of the house watching Alex and her dad converse out front. She thought that Isaac looked very stern.

The Secrets of Hattie Brown

HIs eyes looked piercing under arched eyebrows, one of which was raised. She wondered what they were talking about. Alex was facing Isaac, and she could only see his back. It was the first time in her life that she had tried to read someone's disposition by their body language from behind. All she knew was that Alex was as straight as a board and he was speaking, but barely moving his head. Shoulders were squared and his hands were stiffened at the side of his thighs, like a soldier at attention.

As Alex continued, she saw her father's demeanor soften. Then he spoke, and Alex's shoulders dropped, becoming round. His head tilted to the side as Isaac smiled at him. They shook hands. Gee! What in the world was this about?

The two men stood there for a while, talking and laughing like two old pals. When they turned to enter the house, she saw Alex's face. It looked so joyful. He was smiling broadly.

"My baby girl, gonna be somebody's wife!" Isaac was beaming

She looked from Isaac to Alex, and back again. Alex exclaimed, "I asked your daddy for your hand in marriage and he said yes!"

She hugged her father, "Thank you Daddy. Thank you!"

It would not be appropriate for a girl to outwardly show intimate affection for her beau right there in front of her father, so she took Alex's hand, and looked deeply into his amazing eyes. Her look said, 'I love you and I am so happy.!'

"I can't wait to tell mama when she returns from the market!" Eliza was already planning the wedding in her head.

The wedding day was a sunny Saturday. They were married at the church by the pastor and then there was food afterwards for their guests. The reception was also a farewell party of sorts for Eliza. She would be relocating with her husband to Woodsdale in Person County, North Carolina.

When her old friend/ 'wish you coulda been mine', flame, heard this, he exclaimed, "Well now! Maybe I'll be seeing you there! I got a job working on a farm in Woodsdale! I'm moving up there next month. Be staying at the Saunders farm."

Eliza congratulated him sincerely, "How great Marshall. Good luck to you."

As for Eliza, her heart was swollen with apprehension (leaving her family for the first time ever), anticipation (new life, new home that was her own), and determination (that she would be a wonderful wife for Alex). Most important, she was happy.

Alex told Eliza that he was happy, hopeful, and inspired. He now had someone to call his own. Life for him was now complete and he no longer felt like he was all alone in the world. He had someone to share his dreams. He was just a little nervous though, having been born with the soul of a winged creature. He said that his mom had been known to complain about him wandering off and being gone for days at a time. He hoped that he could put that part of himself in a container and store it on some high shelf in the closet of his mind, at least while he managed to get his married life established and maybe start a family. Eliza had correctly assumed that his weekly visits to Black Walnut on Friday nights, and back to Woodsdale on Sundays, while courting her, had been due to a sincere desire to see her. However, they were also his most current mode of satisfying his need to be on the go. If she had known this, it would have been a new lens through which to see the man she was about to marry. Nevertheless, the new marriage had been consecrated by church and family. The winds of the town of Black Walnut gently swirled around them as Alex's wagon (wedding gift from Henry and Ann) sauntered down the road headed north to Woodsdale. The only light brighter than the glow of their faces, was the sun up above.

Eliza recalled her last private conversation with her mom before she waved goodbye to her family. "You's married now. I'm gone miss you so much. I done taught you everything I thought a young woman should know. Eliza, you is truly a gift to Alex, and the children you may have. I will pray for you every day. Marriage is not easy. Loving your husband makes it possible, but still challenging. Women bear a special weight in the marriage. Sometimes your husband may want to bed you, and it's not what you feelin' at that moment. Maybe you's jus' tired. Still you have to lay yourself down, and open yourself to him, without complaining. Never complain. There are other ways that women folk learn how to make they feelings known. You must always submit to your husband and be a perfect mate to him. Marriage is a lifelong commitment."

Eliza suddenly felt concerned "But mama, what if I'm unhappy and disagree about something? I cain't say nothin?"

Edna shook her head. "This is what has had me afraid of you becoming a wife. We didn't raise you to be silent when you disagree. As a wife, most times that's exactly what you should and can do. When you feel you jus' can't stand no more, then pray without ceasing. The Lawd will help you."

Eliza felt doubtful and a bit disheartened. But at the same time, she was thinking that mama doesn't understand. She and Alex are different. He always wants to know when she is not pleased. He always puts her first.

As if Edna could read her thoughts, she continued, "Men are less likely to sacrifice their own wants to make others happy. When they courting you, it's one thing. Once you're married it becomes another. If you make it your business to give him your list of complaints every day when he comes home, then you're asking for trouble in the marriage. Practice remaining calm and proud like a peacock whenever you can. If you two have a disagreement, which you will, be the one to make peace. It will keep your house a home. All these things, Eliza you do for yourself, for your marriage, and later for your children as well. Your job is to be a help mate and servant to your husband.

"Mama, I promise to try my best. Me and Alex is gone be fine! Thank you for being a wonderful mama to all of us." She hugged her mom and together they walked out to meet the other family members and Alex. She knew that she would miss her mom and their time together. Still, Eliza looked forward to creating her own life by her own rules. She did appreciate her mom's advice. But she felt that her mom didn't understand what she and Alex had together. He was different from other men. Her mom just didn't understand.

Their first intimate coupling had been sweet and tender. Alex was gentle and made the pain of her virginal submission bearable. The first-time hurts. The only thing that made it in any way pleasurable was that Eliza could see and feel that he cared about her discomfort. He kept asking, "You okay?"

Their new marriage was resplendent with frequent love making, laughter and intimate talks about plans for their future together. As the weeks went by, Eliza was transformed into a woman, his wife. She became a vixen in the bedroom and a lady on the porch.

One morning before Alex left for work, she asked, "Will you be coming home the usual time this evening?"

He cocked his head, "Yeah, why?"

She was beaming, "Don't you worry. Just get here." Her barrel chested, lanky hunk of a man bent over and kissed her with a twinkling glint in his eyes. "Okay Mrs. Cowen. I'll do just that." And he bounded out of the front door.

She spent the day in preparation for a special evening with this man who she adored. Outside in the storage shed, she retrieved a plump ham that she had gotten as payment for delivering the baby of a local farmer and his wife. She would cook it up just how Alex liked it; glazed with stewed peaches. Mr. Samuels up the road had let her pick some peaches from his tree earlier in the week. She cooked them down with cinnamon and syrup. Alex was gonna love it!

Ham could be eaten and enjoyed at room temperature. This was perfect for the evening she had planned. Hours later, the glazed ham and two loaves of freshly baked bread graced the dinner table, wrapped in cotton dish towels. Now to finish getting ready. Alex would be coming soon.

When he opened the door to their cabin at dusk, it was like walking into a cloud. The room was hardly lit. The only source of light was the embers glowing in the hearth. Otherwise the house was dark and very quiet. He smelled a blend of some tantalizing flavors but dismissed what he thought he smelled. "Couldn't be ham and peaches. It ain't Christmas."

This was odd. Normally when he came home, she met him at the door to greet him, take his coat to hang it up, and then help him with removing his work boots.

"Eliza." He called out. Silence

"Eliza!" He called louder this time "Where you at?" He was beginning to worry. There had been talk of some robberies in town.

Then he heard her voice and joy bubbled up in him. "I'm here Alex. In the bedroom. Come."

"Now?" He was confused.

"Yes. Right now." She sounded breathless.

Alex tore his jacket off and almost broke both of his feet getting out of those brogans quickly. He raked his fingers through his hair, as if to 'fix' himself, and made a dash for their bedroom.

He stopped short when he entered the bedroom and realized that it was lit only by several white candles on the table next to the bed. He could see the outline of Eliza's body under the quilt as the candlelight danced on her glowing face.

"Evenin' Mr. Cowen." The cicadas provided the soundtrack as they sang in the trees outside of the screened open window. The room smelled like the magnolias in the jar on the table with the candles. Alex was intoxicated by all of this. All he could utter was, "Eliza." As if he was seeing her for the first time.

"Well you gon' just stand there?" Her eyes flickered with desire "Or are you coming in?" She lifted the quilt if it was a doorway and gently, like a ballerina, slid on naked leg into view, then put it back under the quilt. Heat curled down his spine and his body came to attention. As passion ignited him, the corners of his mouth turned up.

Alex shed his shirt and pants faster than you can say jack rabbit. As he slid under the quilt next to his wife, she threw her head back and let out a low chuckle.

He drew in a long breath, "Well love, this is certainly a homecoming worth waiting all day for."

Her cinnamon colored satiny skin smelled like she had rubbed those magnolia blossoms all over her body. Desire radiated between them.

When Eliza wrapped her arms around his neck and arched her body into his, he pulled her closer and kissed her already pursed and waiting lips. Every inch of him craved her, his whole body was throbbing, as desire percolated between them. When he entered her, they took flight to the place where lovers go to romp in Utopia. They took it long and slow until they both were satiated.

"You hungry?" She whispered, as they luxuriated in the afterglow of their lovemaking.

"I'm starving. I smelled something in the kitchen but didn't see any plates on the table." He said.

"Now you know I ain't gonna have my husband come home from work and don't feed him." She was teasing.

"Wha chu got?" He tickled her ribs as if to torture her into to telling him.

Laughing out loud, she grabbed his hand, "Come see." Together they went to the kitchen, both naked. On the table, she lit an oil lamp and removed the red and white checkered cotton dish towels, from two platters on the table.

When Alex saw that ham, then he squeezed a loaf of the bread...his heart leaped!

"Aw Eliza! Girl I loves me some you. This is beautiful! Let's eat!"

Mr. and Mrs. Cowen sat there, naked as two newborn babies, eating ham and bread, sopped in peaches and syrup, while sucking their fingertips and feeling quite giddy.

There love life was easy. But their financial life, was a different story. Money was scarce. Eliza was new in town and did not know anyone except her husband. He worked on a nearby farm like most of the men in their community. The church, of course, was the social and civil center of the families there. Alex introduced Eliza to the wives of some of the other farm workers and she became a member of the church. Once folks learned that she was a midwife, her reputation grew and she began to be a bit more prosperous. Remuneration was not always in the form of cash money. Sometimes a family could not pay her, but they would give her food from their gardens, and eggs from their chickens. Most often the roasted chicken on their dinner table would have been given to Eliza as payment for her midwife services. In order to supplement their income, Eliza also took in work as a laundress for the wealthy white folks. This was constant work, there were always clothes to be washed. Delivering babies was now and then, but even that work was picking up. Sometimes she would be recommended to a pregnant woman from a neighboring town. All she needed was one successful delivery, and then someone else from that town would want her to come and deliver their baby. She had a reputation for being knowledgeable, gentle but tough at the same time. Delivery of a new life was a very emotional as well as physical experience for expectant moms. Eliza was compassionate and would comfort them with kind words and back rubs. At the same time, she knew when to say things like, "All right now. Do you want to get this baby here or not? Stop that crying and work with me. Time for tears is now over and you need to bear down and do what I tell you." Through in her practices. Women felt safe with Eliza. They knew that she cared about their health during AND after the pregnancy. In this way, finances became a bit more reliable and manageable by the end of their first year of marriage.

Alex enjoyed the benefits of having a little extra money in his pocket. He could stop by the juke joint after work and have a few drinks. Sometimes he'd even treat his friends to a shot of whiskey. He knew that his dinner table had beef and pork on the menu more often than many families in their community. Meat was expensive, and Alex loved himself some bacon for breakfast. Most folks raised their own chickens for consumption. Chickens were cheaper to buy and raise than a cow or a pig. Still, he dreamed of being able to support his family without his wife's income. At this time, that was not the reality. Without Eliza's income, they would have meat only every other Sunday. He would not have extra spending money, and his work shoes would be his only shoes. Instead, both he and his wife had Sunday, church shoes. They were not rich, but compared to others in their social circle, they were living pretty good.

When they arrived at church one Sunday, neighbor John and wife Salley pulled up alongside their wagon. "Well looka y'all. Is that a new wagon?"

"Naw. Nothin a can of paint won't do." Alex replied. He downplayed the fact the the wagon was new... to them. He had bought it used, from a white man in town who was selling his used wagon to buy a new one. Only because of Eliza's income, had he been able to make that purchase. Life wasn't bad at all.

Later that week, when Alex put his hand on the doorknob to enter their cabin, the most sensuous and enticing aroma entered his nasal passages. He opened the door and saw his wife standing in front of the fire stirring a big pot. "Sumthin' smells really good."

She was beaming, face glowing. Eliza turned to greet her man and said, "Well go on and get washed up. Cause I'm puttin this food on the table in just a few minutes." She smiled at him. Alex was curious. He always looked forward to coming home to Eliza's good cooking. But somehow today, he felt there was a little something extra special in the pots.

Alex went to wash up and take off his work clothes. When he returned to the kitchen, there were hot biscuits with boiled ham, collard greens and roasted sweet potatoes steaming in bowls on the table. There was an apple pie with golden brown crust on the side table. So many wonderful aromas mingling in the air. It was downright intoxicating. He grabbed Eliza and picked her up off her feet, squeezing her tightly. Then he hummed one of those songs they had heard at the blues club and started dancing around with her in his arms, moving in small circles.

Eliza giggled. "Well now Mr. Cowen, what done got into you?"

"I'm in love!" Alex sang a musical response as he was still trying to do a few dance steps with her. Eliza melted. She loved this man so much. He made her feel so important, so necessary for his life. And now she had news to tell him.

"Come on. Sit down before the food gets cold." Gyrating her hips around his, she slid her feet towards the waiting dinner table, and they sat down. Alex said the grace, then Eliza piled his plate high. He dived in with his fork in one hand, while reaching for a biscuit with the other.

They ate in silence for a few moments. Then, when Eliza felt that the sharp edge of his hunger had been dulled, she said, "We been so busy, you at the farm, me with the babies birthin' and laundry work. Since last week, I started feeling sick in the morning, and tired in the afternoon. I thought I mus' be coming down with with the flu. Then I realized that the last time I saw my blood, was a good two months ago. So, Alex, I am pretty sure that we are about to be parents!"

Alex looked at her with disbelief, and then sheer joy in his eyes.

Pregnant!? For Alex that changed EVERYTHING! His days of feeling like his lifeline could end when he died were over. He didn't have siblings and his mom had died. With her death, he wondered what would happen to the legacy of his family. He had a little person to love and work harder for. This officially made he and Eliza a family! PP break

Barbara Brown Gathers

He couldn't wait to announce it at the next church gathering. Everyone gathered around to congratulate the young couple. The men gave the proud papa to be the back slap and the women hugged Eliza who was ecstatic. She was livin' her dream!

PP Break The following weekend, Alex took her to Black Walnut so that they could share their news with the Betts and Jones families. Her mom examined her just to confirm what she already knew. There was jubilation and excitement. Edna knew that she would be the first one to embrace her new grandchild, as she delivered it from her daughter's womb.

Mother and daughter made plans for monthly prenatal exams. Of course, Eliza would come and stay with her parents when the time for the birth was near. Alex sat outside late into the night, talking with Isaac. She guessed he was getting new father talk from her dad. Men needed for men to translate the meaning of this new status, in a way that women didn't know. Issac was glad to be father and father in law to this young man who his daughter loved so much. Through the open window, the wind carried in a little piece of their conversation. "Things gon change. She gon be busy with the baby sometime when you want her to be busy with you. You gon have to work harder and find ways to make mo money. A new baby is a joy for the both of you. But, becoming a father brings a whole nother bucket of worries about survival, and needs to be filled. My daughter is strong and tough, but right now she need to be treated a lil gentle...." She couldn't see them but imagined Alex shaking his head and listening intently to the advice of her father, another man who has already walked the path now ahead of the new father. She could not know that with each day, Alex was falling deeper into a doubtful abyss with no idea of how to raise out of it.

Eliza continued with her midwife and laundress duties until she was quite well on into her pregnancy. She had noticed a change in Alex though. He seemed more thoughtful, quieter, sometimes downright broodish. "Alex…" she called his name because he was staring at a crack in the wooden floor plank below his foot. He jumped as if a moment of silence had been broken by a loud thunderclap. "What's the matter?" She asked, very concerned.

"Nothin," he mumbled, not looking at her.

"What were you thinkin' about?" She pressed, looking straight at him.

"Nothin' I said, just nothin," he grumbled. 'Nothin' was not what he was thinking about, it was exactly what he was willing to tell her. This hurt. She felt like a fence was being constructed through the middle of their relationship and she was a spectator at the building site. Did this mean she was a participant in the process? How had this happened? Could she stop it? Tear it down? As long as there was 'nothin' she could not know the answers to these questions that were burning a hole in her heart.

"Are you okay?" She was still trying

"What do you mean by okay? I get up. I go to work even when I'm tired, and I come home afterwards." His annoyance flared

"Well I'm jus' askin' cause you don't talk to me as much and even when you home, it seems like you somewhere else."

"Eliza, a man don't always wanna talk his mind. I have a lot to think about. We need a bigger living space. You gon have to stop work in a few weeks. Babies have needs that cost money."

"I know. But some of the ladies at the church is gon' give me some of the baby clothes theys finished with, and when I stop workin' they done set up a schedule to cook and bring dinner for us 'til I'm back on my feet. That's how we do for every woman dat has a baby." An alarm rang in her mind. So, this is what he is worried about.

"That's good, but I ain't one to ask for no handouts. I believe in having my own, earned by the sweat on my brow. People be nice and then later talk about ya." She could see his pulse throbbing in the side of his neck.

Eliza became frustrated. "Alex, you gotta trust somebody. Everybody needs help from time to time."

Rage flashed through Alex, "I ain't everybody!"

He glared at her, got up from the table, and left the house. When Alex returned much later in the night, she could smell the local bootleg whiskey as he wordlessly laid his body down next to hers on their bed. Eliza made a mental note to herself. He was traveling down two roads with one leg.

This was not the last time he went out and came home late smelling like a whole vat of moonshine. Sometimes he went out drinking straight from work. When he came home, there would be:

Cold dinner still on the table.
Cold wife laying in the bed.
Cold sentiments swirling in his head.

He wanted this baby. He loved Eliza, but he was scared. Could he provide enough for a family? Could he settle down and stay put for the rest of his life with the same woman and maybe more babies? Stay on one job picking and planting tobacco until he jus' drop dead in the fields one day? That wasn't the life he had imagined for himself. That life was for them other guys, with no ambition. He was Alex Cowen. Destined for greatness! But what kind of greatness was there for a colored man who was anchored to a life of farm work?

As the time for the baby's birth came near, and Eliza's belly was swollen like a juicy grape about to drop off the vine, Alex felt a combination of pride, love, anxiety, and dismay, well blended like a bowl of cake batter that would never bake properly. Sometimes he was affectionate. He'd say things like, "How's my girl? Come here gimme some sugar." And then some days he came home, and it was like a stranger had walked in the door. "I'm not hungry. Just leave the food on the table." He would take his jug of moonshine from the cupboard and go sit on the porch drinking until way past midnight when he would crawl into the bed and turn his back to Eliza.

Eliza had decided to focus upon the life that was moving inside of her. She would talk to her baby, hug her belly, and eat the best foods she could get to nurture the little bundle. Every evening, after dinner, she prepared the herbal tea concoction her mom had mixed up for her. If Alex was home to have dinner they ate together, and this felt good. If he didn't come home in time for dinner, she ate alone, massaged her belly and sang to it while she drank her tea and prepared for a night's sleep. She loved her husband no matter what. Maybe when the baby came, he would be more like the man she had married.

One song she loved to sing to her baby had been taught to her by her mom. "My mama used to sing this with me and my brother," she said while patting her belly. "It's from Africa. She learned it from her mama. But we had to sing it in the night when the white folks wasn't around. We weren't allowed to sing anything that wasn't in English. You could be whipped for that. It meant something to my mama for us to know this song, so she took the risk. But she warned us never to tell anybody, and never sing it in the daytime. Slavery is over now, so we can sing it loud when we want. We loved singing it with mama, deep in the night with only the fire in the cabin to hear the hushed but robust sound of our voices."

Eliza sang it to her baby. It was a call and response song. She looked forward to the time when she would hear that sweet little voice, she and Alex's creation, sing the response.

Che che koolay
Che Che koolay
Che Che Kofi sa
Che Che Kofi sa
Kofi sa langa
Kofi sa langa
Kaka shi langa
Kaka shi langa
Kum aden de
Kum aden de
Hey!

And she would sing it over and over until she felt like laying down and falling asleep. Eliza was content. Couldn't let no man ruin this miracle for her. He will come around. And so, it went until her mom examined her and decided it was time for her to stay in Black Walnut.

"Alex, you gon have to leave her here with me because the ride back in the wagon would be too much up and down for Eliza and the baby. Plus, the child is due very soon."

"How long is it gone be Miss Etney?" he asked excitedly.

"Oh, I am thinking it will be about a week."

Alex returned to Woodsdale alone, while Eliza stayed in Black Walnut awaiting the arrival of their gift. He was relieved in a sort of way. At least now Eliza was with her family and she seemed so happy when she had greeted them. He felt guilty about how he had been behaving in recent months.

Eliza knew that she was going to miss Alex. But at this moment, it was all about her baby being born safe, sound, and into a happy environment. Being with her family was a guarantee that this wish would be fulfilled, one hundred percent.

Edna could see that her daughter was not as emotionally robust as she had been when she was a newlywed. Although Eliza was clearly healthy, and had been taking good care of herself nutritionally, there was a sadness in her aura. Edna was quite capable of reading folks' spirits. It wasn't something she spoke about, but she used this skill to assist in her healing practices. Illness was almost never seated in the body, but always originated in the recesses of the spirit.

During slavery, it was considered "hoodoo," therefore taboo, to talk about healing arts involving anything other than taking medicines or doing what the doctor said. However, everyone knew that there were those women (and men) who were born with a gift. They could go into the woods, pick certain leaves and barks, cook them up and heal you quicker and more thoroughly than the village doctor. Often when doctors didn't know what else to do, they would cut the patient and "bleed" the illness out of them. When that didn't work...oh well.

These gifted healers could sometimes simply "lay hands" on a sick person and improvement in the condition would be noted, and then with herbal treatments, followed by complete recovery. As quiet as it was kept, slave masters sometimes engaged these gifted healers' services because they could get the workers out of the sick bed and back into the fields quicker than the white local physician. These men and women, if sold, went for a much higher price. They did not work the fields or cook in the kitchen. Either they "shadowed" the local doctor, who may have owned them (like Edna and her mom) or the slave master would use them to administer to the sick on his plantation. On a large plantation, there was always someone sick and or pregnant. For him, this was a win-win because he had no overhead for doctor's fees, and recuperation was more efficient and faster. In this case, the healer would have his/her own quarters to set up like a hospital. They would forage in the woods for herbs and then make the medicines that they kept on supply for the most common illnesses.

Edna and her daughter sat at the kitchen table, snapping peas for the dinner that evening. "Eliza, I know that you are not all right. You wanna talk about it? Thank God the baby is fine, but there's something else...."

She wasn't the cocky, self-assured, girl who had half listened to her mom's marriage advice when she rode off into the sunset with her new husband.

"Mama, I'm okay. I am happy to be having this baby and looking forward to being a mom. My husband has changed.

He says he is happy about the baby, but......" she didn't know what should come after the but. Her throat tightened. How could she verbalize something that was not in words? How could she say that love shouldn't hurt, and if her life with Alex was hurting then...Everything was all jumbled up in her head. She just didn't know how to talk about it.

Edna listened carefully, but more than that she studied her daughter's countenance. She remembered how Eliza used to light up a room when she entered. Her energy was so bright. She was always smiling. Sometimes she would check on her daughter while she was asleep and Eliza even seemed to smile in her sleep. Now her light was dim. Her skin was ashen and sallow. When she smiled, the look in her eyes did not match the rest of her face. It was like she was wearing a happy mask over a very sad face. The eyes still tell the truth to anyone who is really looking, as a mother always does. This was not due to the pregnancy. In fact, pregnancy was known to increase a woman's glow. Considering her strong body and great nutrition, Eliza should be radiant. But she was not. This was very telling.

She didn't wait for Eliza to find words. "I am concerned about your heart. A broken heart can lead to sickness down the road. I know it seems like what I am saying has nothing to do with what you are feeling but trust me. I am your mama. I care about you to the bone, to the middle of yourself. I get that you are disappointed; he is not the person you thought he was. Baby, you can't know a person until you live with them, and even then, folks change as life changes. I want you to get it in your heart that you are worthy of being loved and you are loving. Do not give over your personhood to another being. How you define yourself, is up to you and you only. You are gonna have another life depending upon you to be healthy in body mind and spirit. I know you will do a great job as a mama. You can only control and be accountable for yourself and your behavior. Your husband is an adult and responsible for his deeds. I want you to be happy, but more than that, I want you to be sure that you are one hundred percent wonderful and worthy of the best of life. We ain't come out of slavery to do nothin' but strive for the best life we can possibly make for ourselves. Do you want me to have your daddy talk to him?"

"Oh no mama. He would be so angry with me if he knew I said anything at all! We will be all right. Once the baby gets here. We will be just fine." She appreciated her mother's love and advice more than ever, but she was ashamed. Still she felt, there must be something she did wrong. Maybe she asked him too many questions when he didn't look like he wanted to talk. Maybe she was too independent. After all, wives were supposed to be subservient and rely on their husbands for advice and guidance. Could it be that Eliza wasn't the right woman for Alex? No. She wouldn't even entertain that thought another minute. She was his wife. They were about to be parents together and that was a bond for life. Period! She was determined to do better and then he would be like the man she fell in love with again. Yes, that was it. She had to be a better wife.

Eliza finished snapping the peas while Edna mixed up some corn bread batter. It felt good for mother and daughter to be together again cooking and talking about the goings on in Black Walnut. Being with Mama was easy. No need to be careful about what you say or how you say it. Eliza could just speak her mind. Her mother never judged her or misunderstood her intentions. She felt a brand of freeness that she had forgotten even existed.

Meanwhile, Alex was back in Woodsdale without his wife for the first time since they had married. He missed her, but at the same time an itch was being scratched by her absence. Always that yearn to be a free agent; to come and go and go and come as he pleased without explanations. He was acutely aware of how much he had missed that life. The thought of "losing" it again, and this time to a wife AND baby. Was he sure he could do this?

One evening after work, Alex stopped by the Colored Cafe to have a drink and listen to some blues. Seated at the bar was Marshall Mason.

"Marshall! How you doin' man?" Alex asked excitedly. He was glad to see a friend.

"I'm good. Just trying to shake some of this tiredness off my bones with a lil drink before I go home, sleep, and start all over again tomorrow. Sit down here man! How's Eliza doin'? She ready to have that baby yet?" Marshall said lightheartedly.

"Yeah. Hey barkeep. Bring me a glass of something strong," Alex asked before getting back to Marshall. "Yeah." I left her in Black Walnut with her folks. She bout to pop any day." The bartender brought a glassful of bootleg whiskey and Alex took a greedy gulp. He felt the liquid burn the lining of his throat. His mood melted as the stresses of the day began to evaporate.

"You a lucky man Alex. She is a good woman. Always been smart since we were lil kids. She always knew what she wanted. I remember when she first met you that day at the church. She knew she wanted you and she waited until you two could be together."

Alex blushed. "Yeah. She a good woman. I loves me some Eliza."

The two men sat quietly for a moment, both staring into the liquid in their glass. Each disappeared from the room and went away into the land of their own personal dreams. The silence hung in the air, thick and heavy.

Marshall began speaking again. "Sometimes I dream about leaving and going somewhere to be somebody else besides a farm worker from North Carolina. But then I ask myself, where can a colored man go and what can he be besides a colored man? You ever think about those things Alex?"

Alex sighed. "Marshall, every day of my life. I don't know what a colored man can be, but there's got to be something more than this. There's just got to be. For me, this here is like a prison. Sometimes I can't breathe. I wanna take off running down the road and not stop." The alcohol was opening him up. He wanted to verbalize things he had not said to anyone. "I have heard of places up north where men like us work in factories and bring home a regular paycheck. They live in big brick buildings and the streets are all paved with concrete. No farmers, coveralls, and boots for them. Nah! They wear shoes and suits. Go out partyin on the weekends. I want me some of that life. Yes, I do!"

"Man! That sounds like the life! You think Eliza would go for something like that?"

All at once, Alex's face turned from animated with anticipation to darkened with despair. "Eliza? Eliza. No. She ain't going nowhere. Everything is here for her. Family, church, and midwifin'. She is quite pleased with herself and her life."

In spite of his alcohol altered perception, Marshall was becoming a bit concerned. He knew that when a man felt that level of discontent, he normally did something about it. "So, what are you gon' do Alex?"

Alex shook his head. "I don't know. I'm tryna work it out in my head."

"Alex, I think you already know. You just ain't ready to tell me what it is."

About that time, the singer was seated with his guitar and ready to begin performing. He sang a song that was popular around town.

> I'm a workin on the farm everyday
> I'm a workin on the farm everyday
> Workin my fingers to the bone
> Sometimes I can hardly make it home
> Workin on the farm everyday
>
> Planting tobacco
> Then threshing it out
> Workin on the farm everyday
> Nobody cares what I'm a thinking about
> Workin on the farm everyday
>
> Workin ......
> Workin....
> Just workin in the dirt everyday
> Workin....
> Workin......
> Just workin my life away
>
> When is it my turn
> Workin on the farm everyday
> When can my fire burn
> Workin on the farm everyday

I'm just workin on the farm everyday
Oooooh ooooooh ooooooh
Workin' workin' workin'
On the farm everyday

Blues chords gave the melody a familiar line and rhythm. More familiar was the sentiment in the lyrics. Every man in the place was a colored farm worker. They all felt the same frustrations, the same sort of invisibility of self. But Alex, he intended to do more than just feel it and lament. He had a plan.

At the home of Isaac and Edna, all was well. Dinner had been wonderful. Edna and Eliza were sewing a quilt for Malinda's bed when Eliza's water broke.

"Ma!" Her eyes wide. "It's time!" she yelled with a calm on the edge of hysteria. Although Eliza had taken many women on this journey, now it was her turn and she was more nervous than she had expected to be. Her water flooded the chair where she was sitting as a little puddle formed on the floor below.

"Really," Edna replied smiling. Her first grandchild. "Okay, let's get you to the bedroom."

She guided Eliza to the bedroom where she had slept all the years of her childhood. Malinda ran to tell Papa Isaac it was time. Mama would need Ann's help.

"Nannie, put three pots of water to boil in the hearth!" Edna shouted ready for this moment.

For the first few hours it was easy. Every twenty minutes Eliza would get up and walk and pant through the pain of the contractions. Then she would lay down and wait for the next round. Her mom had used large sheets of paper creating a pallet under her to protect the bed from stains.

" Mama!" Eliza screamed. "It hurts. I had no idea it hurts like this. Ahhhhhhhhhhh!"

Ann had come and was there to comfort the new mother. She rubbed Eliza's belly and said things like, "Don't worry you're doing fine. Ooh your baby is ready! Yeah, gon be here soon lil mama", while Edna continued monitoring her daughter and also offering encouragement and guidance through the process.

It was 3AM. Nannie and Malinda had fallen asleep in front of the fire in the kitchen waiting. Isaac had also gone to bed. The contractions progressed to every ten minutes and then later every five minutes. At this point, Edna instructed her daughter to lay down and put her knees up, with legs wide open. "Still", she said, "Don't push until I tell you. When the pains come, I want you to breath like this: Hah, hah, hah, hah..." Edna panted in a rhythmic pattern. Eliza obeyed her mother's instructions. It was so different when she was the one, legs wide open, knees pointed to the ceiling, on the bed about to give birth.

Edna examined her daughter and she could see the black curly crown of the baby's head as Eliza panted through the contraction. "Now Eliza, next time the pain comes, I want you to push with all your might, like you're blowin' into a bottle." Then she turned to her other daughter. "Ann, I have a white cloth over there. Give it to me."

Ann handed her the white cotton cloth she had sterilized earlier for this very moment. Edna laid it on the bed so she could catch the baby when it was time.

Eliza's shrill scream filled the room "It comin! It's comin!

"Push Eliza! Push!" Edna was yelling at her.

Eliza let out a primordial wail that came from the very depths of her being. She screamed, she grunted, and she pushed. Edna now had her hands on the shoulders of her grandchild, pulling and breathing in sync with her daughter's push. "Come on baby! Bring this chile into the world!" She pulled. Eliza pushed and... the baby was out. A little girl.

But the baby wasn't breathing.

Eliza raised up on the bed. "Let me hold my baby! Let me hold my baby!" She knew what was supposed to happen. The room should not be quiet. The baby should not be so still. All of this and the baby was dead?! Oh no! It just couldn't be. The baby had been kicking in her womb just before the water broke! Oh no. Please God.

Edna immediately cut the umbilical cord, and handed it to Ann. Then she held the baby up in the air by her feet, head down, and hit her on the butt. Twice. Still nothing. No sound. No sign of life. Twice again...stillness...silence...the air in the room had become thick and heavy. Oppressive. Nobody was breathing.

The masterful midwife gutsy grandma did not give up. She took a corner of the sterilized white cloth, put it over the baby's mouth, and gently squeezed the baby's jaws to open the mouth. She placed her lips on the cloth and pushed her breath into the mouth of the new life in quick puffs of air. "Help me Lawd" Puff puff puff. Puff puff puff. Suddenly the baby sneezed! And then she sneezed again! There was a moment of pregnant silence. Like the void between life and death...the state of nothingness...the women waited for the sound they longed to hear, the exhilarating scream of a newborn baby. And there it was! A strong set of lungs, that one! There was a collective, simultaneous, exhale by the three women in the room, grandma, mama, and auntie.

Edna used a little rubber syringe in the baby's nose, then mouth, to suck out any remaining fluids that were left from the birthing experience. She bathed the baby in the basin of warm water that Ann had prepared. Then, she wrapped the beautiful little girl in a clean white cloth and laid her in her mother's waiting arms. Eliza cuddled her daughter and held her close to her breast. The beginning of a new life for both mother and child.

As the sun rose, Edna removed the afterbirth. Eliza knew when and how to push it out. Everything was fine. Jubilation time! The little girl was here. She was safe, healthy, beautiful and the breath in her lungs had been gifted by her very own grandma. A blessed arrival! The sky was illuminated by the joy of this family. The first grand baby. It meant something to Edna to know that her grandchild was born free, like her own Malinda, Nannie and Henry. She was owned by God and herself alone. The two women held hands encircling Eliza and her daughter while they whispered a prayer, giving thanks for God's grace.

Edna had been born into slavery on a plantation in Black Walnut. Life was hard and tightly controlled. She was put to task, it seemed, since she was a toddler. She would carry water for the master's wife to wash her feet. The only time worked stopped was when they were allowed to sleep so that work could begin again as soon as they awaken before dawn.

Barbara Brown Gathers

Slavery had ended some twenty years before, but Edna still had not been able to completely understand the meaning of freedom. In an environment that is hostile towards people of color, at a time when money was scarce, most were illiterate and rented rather than owned property. What exactly did this thing called freedom mean?

She wasn't sure that she would ever see the day when freedom would be a concept that she lived and understood, but one thing was for sure. This little girl, her first grand baby, had the chance to be in that number of those colored people who would walk about as they pleased. Who would be educated and own themselves for real. She would pray for that every day for the rest of her life.

Edna prayed, "Almighty God, we thank you for your grace. We asked for your help to bring the breath of life to this child and you gave it. Lord God we thank you, we love you, and we know that without your blessing, we would be preparing to bury this baby and tell her daddy that his daughter was born dead. God, we dedicate right now, this life, and the life of her mother to you. Lord God you have granted life to this little girl because she has a purpose. Her life will be dedicated to service to you and the deliverance of your message to the world. Thank you, father. Thank you. Thank you. Thank you. In the name of your son and our savior Jesus Christ, Amen, Amen, aaaaaaaaamen!!

On the weekend, Alex came. When he saw his wife and new daughter, there was an explosion of delight inside his heart. Eliza put the little girl into his arms. He looked at her sparkling eyes and saw his mother. She even blinked at him in a way that seemed to be saying, "I know you. I know you!" The tears puddled inside the lower rim of his eyes like a waterfall about to cascade. Eliza, knowing that this was a happy cry, stood aside and marinated in this first encounter between father and daughter. Her heart was also throbbing with a degree of love she had not known existed before this moment.

She was so happy and proud it had washed away her worries about their relationship. She looked at Alex, and believed he was feeling the same way.

"Oh Lord Eliza, she is beautiful! You did good!" He was beaming.

"No. We did good Alex! She's ours! We have a daughter. Me and you." A single tear rolled down her cheek.

"Aw honey now why you crying'?" He looked at her with eyes like a deer.

"I'm just so happy. I'm just so happy," she said trying to hold back the flood of tears she felt coming.

"Oh baby. I am happy too." He reached over and put one arm around Eliza, while the other arm cradled their daughter. Their first family hug! He looked at the baby's sparkling eyes. They decided to name her Mary, after his mom.

Edna suggested that Eliza and Mary stay with her for two weeks so that Eliza could rest and mend her body postpartum. This was a happy time in the Betts household. Nannie and Malinda fawned over their little niece and could not do enough to help their sister. Even little Henry was torn between being excited about the baby and jealous that he was no longer the youngest one. Isaac, the proud Grandpa, was like a rooster. He would bring folks by the house so he could cock a doodle doo to show off his new granddaughter. Eliza could not help but to wish that Nelson was there. He would adore this, her little girl.

When Alex came to get his family and take them home to Woodsdale, they were ready to go. Eliza had enjoyed being with her parents and siblings but was longing to return to the home and bed she shared with her husband. She had been thinking a lot about how she was going to reclaim her marriage. She would not make the same mistakes she had before. Talking too much. Asking him too many questions. She would be a better wife. He would see. Now they had Mary. This would also make all the difference.

When they arrived at their cabin, Eliza was delighted to see that her sisters from the church had cleaned the house and made a little pallet for her baby next to the bed where she and Alex slept. They had cooked a welcome dinner to celebrate her home coming and left it on the table.

"Alex! I'm so happy. Home sweet home." Joy filled Eliza like sunshine.

She looked around at the familiar spaces and places that now defined her life as a wife and mother. Life had promise. Life was good.

Mary began to sing the whiny song that babies sing when they are hungry. Eliza's breasts were aching and heavy with milk, after the long ride from Black Walnut to Woodsdale. Mother and daughter both knew it was time for them to unify in the breastfeeding experience. So, Eliza went into their bedroom and breast fed their daughter while Alex unloaded the wagon and brought the new things into the house. The baby things that had been gifted by the family and friends in Black Walnut. When breast feeding was finished and cloth diaper was changed, Mary was fast asleep. Now mommy and daddy enjoyed dinner together.

Both parents adored little Mary. One thing is for sure, when you have a baby, life takes on a rhythm. Babies demand schedules. So, days bled into weeks and weeks bled into months and months bled into years. Eliza was doing laundry and catching babies. Alex was working for a local white farmer, and life seemed normal. He came home after work, most nights. They had dinner, most times in silence, unless Eliza shared a story about how the day had been, and all was…well all was, what it was…

Eliza had kept the promise to herself, that she would be a "better" wife. Sometimes he was not very communicative. She didn't try to make conversation on those days. When he came home late, and she didn't know where he had been, his dinner was in a covered plate on the table and Eliza feigned sleep when he came to bed.

She had so many more tasks to attend to with a new baby, still keeping up with midwife work and doing laundry for local white women, she truly had less time to worry about Alex and whether or not he was disgruntled on a given day. One problem was centered around the fact that she could be called anytime to attend to an expectant mother. How did she carry her child and at the same time do her work? Most of the time, Alex was not at home.

Mary was growing like a well-fed garden flower and looking healthy and happy. When she saw her daddy, she would squeal with delight and reach her little arms upward for him to come and pick her up. Her first word had been "DADA." Alex melted like a piece of ice thrown into a cup of hot water. Eliza saw the lower rim of his eyes flooded with moisture, when he heard his daughter call him for the first time.

Alex worshiped his baby girl. Whenever he came home, the first thing he did after removing his brogans and outer clothing, was to take her in his arms, tickle her, kiss her, and make sounds that Eliza didn't know he had in him. If he came home late and she was asleep, he would tenderly kiss her cheek as she slept in the cradle, and then he would just stand and stare at her. Eliza often wondered what he was thinking at these moments, but she dare not ask for fear of being chastised and told that it was 'nothin'.

One night she tried to disguise an inquiry by asking, "So how are things at work? It's near about harvest time." She made sure her voice was very light and almost like she really didn't care what he said in response.

Even a simple question such as this was met with a tinge of animosity, "Work is work. I go every day and listen to the white man yell at me when he thinks I need to work harder. Harvest or planting time, it don't matter. It's all the same."

Was he angry at her? Or was he angry at the white bosses? She could not know. Nowadays, when Alex came to her for intimacy, it was the same every time. Grope her, mount her, ejaculate, and go to sleep. She would lie there listening to his snores and wonder if this was all there was to life for her as a woman.

Mary enjoyed being with her mommy around the house. Eliza would allow Mary to 'help' her with whatever chore she was engaged in. If she was making biscuits, she would give Mary her own little piece of dough to roll up. Then she'd bake it so Mary could see her daddy eat her biscuit. If Eliza was doing laundry, she would give Mary a little bowl of water with a dish cloth in it and Mary could "scrub" like she saw her mom doing.

This is how life was for a good three years. Eliza mostly worked, went to church, and took care of her husband and daughter. Trips to Black walnut were few and far between. As time for the Christmas holidays was drawing near, she was missing her family and the warm festive atmosphere that this time of year always brought.

"Alex, I would like to go home for a few days. When do you think we could go?"

"Well we are pretty busy over at the farm. There's a good deal of cleaning up to do and preparation next planting time. I am not sure I could get away anytime soon. I have an idea though. I was talking to Marshall the other day, and he told me that he is going to Black Walnut to see his folks this weekend. Maybe you and Mary could go with him."

She had been hoping for a family outing. A family get away was more her vision. But the "good wife" should be agreeable (this 'good wife' thing was getting old and oppressive), so of course she replied, "That would be great. Will you ask Marshall?"

"Of course. I will go by his place right now." Alex seemed just a tad too anxious, too willing, too happy about this proposition.

A few days later, Marshall showed up in the early morning at their cabin. He was happy to escort Eliza and her daughter to Black Walnut. Alex took the three of them to the railroad station in his wagon. Marshall had suggested that they take the train. It would be much better for little Mary than all of the dust and bumpity bump of a wagon journey. It cost more money, but Marshall chipped in with Alex to help pay for the tickets. His father was expecting their arrival and would pick them up at the station when they arrived.

The train ride was pleasant and surprisingly relaxing. Eliza and Marshall reminisced, revisiting stories from their childhood, growing up in the same town, knowing the same people. They laughed a lot. There was something about Marshall Mason and the rhythmical clackitty clack of the train that put her at ease. She had not realized how tightly wound she had been for a very long time. Living with Alex and relying on him for conversation and comfort was like swimming in a bowl of okra stew. It was uncomfortable most of the time. She never knew exactly how to behave around him. Some days, even her "good morning" seemed like it was a fly buzzing around his ear. When they arrived at the station in Black Walnut, Deacon Mason was there to greet them and to take Eliza and Mary to Edna, Isaac and the rest of Betts clan.

The joyous reunion of Eliza and her family was a colorful thing to behold. Whooping and hollering. Hugging and kissing. Isaac took Mary from Eliza and held her up over his head while laughing and shaking her little body up and down. She was so tickled, and giggling with such abandon, that when she opened her mouth, screaming with delight, she dropped spit right on Isaac's face. Peals of laughter by everyone standing around. Isaac was ecstatic.

Her parents thanked Marshall and Deacon Mason for bringing their beloved daughters home. Marshall said he would be back to get them in three days, and then left Eliza to enjoy her folks.

Home was home. It felt so good to be in a familiar space, with familiar people who loved her unconditionally. She could just be Eliza with no holds barred. Her inhale was deep and her exhale was authentic. How had her life gone so far away from this natural way of being? What state of being made someone feel okay to just be? Certainly, it was missing from Eliza's home life. They had it once. What thief of dreams had taken it from Eliza and her beloved husband? The man who owned her heart.

Nannie, Malinda, and Henry had swept Mary away to go play in the yard. They started teaching her the songs and games that Edna and Eliza had taught to them. Eliza heard, "Juba this and juba that..." being sung outside. After a few rounds, she heard Mary's sweet little high-pitched voice singing, "Can I see you Juba?" She thought it was so cute.

It was December in Virginia. Normally the weather was cool but clear. Occasionally they would have storms, but not often. On the evening of the second day of their visit, the skies began to look cloudy and the air was very crisp. By nightfall it had started snowing. A beautiful white coat laid across the land as far as they could see. By morning, it was still snowing. The accumulation got deeper and deeper as the day progressed. The railroad would not budge when there was this type of weather. Eliza was glad to extend her stay, yet still she was concerned about her husband's expectations for their return. Word was that the storm was also raging in North Carolina where they lived, so she knew that he understood her tardy return. It was a good three days before the roads and train tracks were cleaned up enough for them to make their way back to Woodsdale.

Marshall and his dad came to pick them up and they headed to the railroad station. Marshall told Eliza all about his visit with family and friends. He had also enjoyed his stay. She was happy to hear his stories, but deep inside her gut, she felt that something was not right. There was a little whirlwind turning, like a spinning top. She had no idea where this was coming from. On the surface, everything seemed fine and normal. Just a simple train ride with her daughter and a childhood friend, headed home after a delay caused by a snowstorm. Mary was quiet during the trip. She slept a lot, woke up mostly to eat a snack, play a little, and then back to sleep.

With the delay in their return, there had been no means of alerting Alex of their time and day of arrival. When they got off of the train in Woodsdale, Marshall spotted a farmer who he knew. That gentleman had come to pick up his brother from the station. Marshall asked him if they could possibly get a ride to Eliza's house. He figured Alex could take him home from there. They all squeezed themselves into the small wagon sat tight, while the sort of rickety racketty wagon made its way down the road. Whew! What a relief when they arrived. Eliza and Marshall graciously thanked the man for his kindness as they got down from the wagon and Marshall unloaded their bags.

Eliza, holding hands with Mary, and walked a little too fast for the little short legs to the front door of their home. She was surprised that Alex had not heard the wagon approach and then came to greet them at the door. She called his name, "Alex! We're home!" just before she opened the door. No answer. Then she realized, silly woman, he had said he would be working long hours. He was still at work and would definitely be home soon. Then she opened the door and entered the house. It was pretty clean, considering the fact that Alex had been living there without her to clean up after him. It almost looked just like it had the day she left. Well she would tease him about it when he came home. 'So, you CAN clean up when I'm not here to do it!' she thought.

Marshall brought their bags into the house. "Where's Alex?" He quizzed.

"Well I am thinking he is still at work. He should be home soon. Have a seat. Lemme get Mary settled and I will make us some coffee while we wait for him. I'm sure he will come soon and then he will be able to drop you home."

Marshall sat down at the table to wait. There was a staleness about the air in the room, like the house had been closed up for several days. He was not so sure that Alex was at work. He was not so sure that Alex had been home recently. He was not so sure that Alex was coming back. Marshall Mason had a very bad feeling about all of this.

"Ain't much food here, but I think I can make us a few biscuits to go with the coffee." Eliza was trying to appear normal, bordering on cheerful, but Marshall knew her. He had known her, and secretly loved her, for a very long time. She was frightened. In fact, he sensed an undercurrent of controlled hysteria.

"Eliza. Just some coffee will be fine. Sit yourself down and rest. It's been a long day."

They waited and waited and waited. When they had arrived, it was a bright clear sunny day outside. As the wait time stretched and expanded like a rubber band creating more tension as it lengthened, the colors of Eliza's world changed from bright yellow, to orange to burnt amber. Finally, she was engulfed by shades of muted blue transitioning to grey. Darkness inevitably fell and the temperature dropped. Marshall made a fire in the hearth. His heart shattered into a million pieces as he watched Eliza quietly crumble.

"Eliza. Why don't you go and lay down? I will wait for Alex and he can wake you when he gets here. You have got to be tired." Even as the words escaped from between his lips, Marshall knew in his gut that there would be no Alex that night, or any night soon. Eliza knew it too, but she played along.

She went and laid down on the bed. She could not recall her head touching the pillow. Almost instantly, she fell asleep. It was like a greater force was protecting her from the impact of what was actually happening by just knocking her out. She dreamed of walking in a densely flowered garden with her beloved Alex. They held hands, talking and laughing. It was very much like it had been when they first started dating. In the dream, they stopped by a stream and gazed into the water. Alex seemed very interested in the fish swimming with the current going downstream. He was pointing at one of the fish coming towards them from the opposite bank of the stream. It was a bright blue fish the same color of the shirt Alex was wearing in the dream. Eliza was amused, but Alex was fixated on that fish. As it got closer to them, he became more and more entranced. As the blue fish was about to reach the side of the stream where they were standing, Eliza heard a baby's cry. She turned her head in the direction of the sound and there was nothing. When she turned back, Alex was gone, and the blue fish was now swimming away, downstream. She screamed his name, turned in all directions, but no Alex. The blue fish never looked back. She awoke at daybreak with a start. Mary was still asleep in her bed. In the kitchen, there was Marshall, sitting in the chair where she had left him, head down on the table, fast asleep.

He woke up to the sound of her footsteps. When Marshall looked into Eliza's eyes, he just didn't have words to express what he was thinking about her husband. And even if he did, it would hurt too much. She understood.

"He gon Marshall. I dreamed it. Alex done left me," she said it almost as a matter of fact, rather than a matter of her life being broken.

Marshall didn't bother to dissuade her from this conclusion. After all, it was his own as well. He stood up, walked over to where she was standing, and completely engulfed the tall statuesque Eliza in both his arms. They stood like that for what seemed like a lifetime encompassing all of the years they had known one another and beyond. Eliza was the one who broke the embrace and walked away.

"I will go by the church and see if anybody has seen him." He knew that Eliza had heard him, and understood his words, but she seemed to have left the room. She was staring out of the window, at some distance place in her memory. Marshall felt helpless.

For three days, Eliza kept a bright disposition while she managed her duties as a mom. She cared for Mary as usual. Played with her, sang to her and fed her. When Mary asked about daddy, Eliza said that daddy had gone away and would return soon. She just didn't know what else to say. Once she had bathed Mary and put her to bed, it was her time to let go and literally fall apart. She would cry into her pillow laying in a fetal position on her bed until she wailed herself to sleep. Two or three hours of sleep, and then she would wake up and stare at the ceiling until nearly dawn. She would think, "Why Alex? Why? And How? What about our vows? What about your promises to love me forever?" Three days, she allowed herself to wallow in self-pity, and to bury herself in the misery of the moment. Marshall had come by and said that he spoke with the sisters from the church and they said that they had come by the spruce up the house for Eliza's return, but they found it clean and empty. They thought that perhaps Alex had changed his mind and gone with us.

On the morning of the fourth day, she woke up and decided that it was time to reclaim her life, and to accept the responsibility for her daughter's life. Also, there were two pregnant ladies who were both due to deliver any day.

Alex's abandonment hurt like hell. She hurt in places she didn't know she had. Yes, her heart was hurting, her physical heart and her emotional heart. Eliza had pain in her back, and aching in her legs, even her throat was sore. Of two things she was certain. The aches and pains would pass, as all things do, and she would eventually become emotionally restored. She was a warrior, made of the stuff of survival. But not today. Today, she felt empty and alone.

Chapter Four

Marshall would stop by to see Eliza and Mary most days after work, just to check on them. She was an amazing woman. He personally knew how her husband's leaving had cut at the core of her womanhood, but she seemed to be resurrecting herself. She seemed to be recuperating from the hit. At first Marshall would stop by and Eliza looked bedraggled. She was clean as was Mary. But they both looked drawn and devoid of emotion. Even the tone of her voice had become more bass in its timbre.

As time went on when he would check on them, he noticed that she had put on a freshly ironed house dress and Mary's hair had been brushed and put in cornrows. She spoke in lighter tones and seemed happy to see him. Sometimes he would bring a bag of groceries just to help out. Sometimes he would give her a little piece of money. Eliza really appreciated Marshall's friendship, generosity, and attention. He was faithful. Months went by and still he was diligent about checking on the two. He would always come by, stay for a few minutes and then leave once he knew all was well with them. Time was healing Eliza's wounds and finally her smile looked like it came from within and not just lifting the corners of her lips for a desired effect. She knew that Alex was the love of her life, but she also knew that she could and would live without him. One evening when Marshall stopped by, he brought a piece of beef. The farmer he worked for had slaughtered a cow and given him a small share of the meat.

"Marshall! Thank you. This is a big piece of meat for me and a little girl. Why don't you stay for dinner? It won't take long for me to stew up this beef." Ha! He'd been waiting for this moment.

"Well don't mind if I do," he said with a very coy side grin.

After that it was dinner two or three nights a week, then four or five, and then he started picking them up for church and having Sunday dinner with them afterwards. The church community would normally frown upon a married woman with a child keeping company with a single man like that. But somehow, as it always does, word had gotten out that Alex had simply left his wife and daughter. Folks admired Marshall for stepping up to help the "sister."

Intimacy between Eliza and Marshall was simply a natural transition. They were spending so much time together, and he had been so kind. Plus, she trusted him, which was something she wasn't sure she could ever have for another man. Inside she wondered where this was leading. Until now, Marshall had been like a brother. She never thought of him as anything more. It was easy to spend time with him and he was always honest and out front about his feelings. This was a pleasure after being with someone who was so closed off emotionally. So, she felt safe with Marshall.

One evening after dinner, she put Mary to bed and returned to the kitchen where he was still sitting at the table. She reached across him to refill his glass of lemonade. Marshall touched her hand as she sat the pitcher down on the table. She looked at him for a nonverbal clue to explain his gesture.

"I have been in love with you since we were kids Eliza. Did you know that?"

"Well not really. I mean we always teased one another. But love? No."

"Love, yes. I kept it to myself cause it seemed like you wasn't interested in me like that and then when I saw you and Alex together, I knew there was no chance for me." Marshall was sincere. "Why do you think I have never married?"

Eliza was at a loss for words. She had never imagined that Marshall being single had anything to do with her. "Well I don't know Marshall. I guess I just thought you prefer the free and single life."

"Not at all. Everybody wants and needs a family. I wanted you and nobody else Eliza. Plain and simple. I hate what Alex has done to you and Mary, but if you will have me, I'm ready to share my heart with you. I know that you are still healing. But why not let me be part of helping you to feel better. You deserve to be cherished and wanted and shown that you matter in a very real way," he finished with his eyebrows raised.

Well! Eliza thought to herself. You ain't never lied about that. I need somebody to show me that they value me the way I know I should be valued. With Alex, I was scratchin' in the dirt beggin' for him to give me that assurance that he knows how wonderful and worthy I am.

"What is it you want Marshall? I'm still married. You know that," she queried.

"I have thought about this a lot," he began. "I know exactly what I want. I want to make love to you as often you will allow me to. Cause I have a whole bunch of catching up to do. So many fantasies to act out," he smiled devilishly.

"Then I just want you to let me be the man who you come to when you need comfort, when you need money, when you need to be sure that you are the only juicy peach I need to bite into when I want something sweet." He watched as she blushed before continuing. That's what I want Eliza. What do you want?"

"Well of course I need help financially. Otherwise I want you to be honest with me. No matter what it is, whether I am gonna like it or not, I want you to tell me. Then I want you to come for dinner every night because it is what makes you happy. And I don't ever want to see you mistreat Mary cause she ain't your blood. If these things can work for you, good. If they can't, then let's forget this right now." This was new for Eliza, stating her conditions. It felt good. It felt like she was taking care of herself for the first time.

Marshall was smiling, showing with every single one of his teeth. "Well it sounds like we got us a perfect grown folks understandin'"

Chapter Five

It had been over a year since Alex's disappearance. Eliza and Marshall became a twosome. Like a well-oiled machine, they worked their relationship and created a life they both desired. Marshall was delighted and finally had what he wanted. Eliza was glad to have a man who had no problem with showing her how he valued her role in his life.

One evening when Marshall came home, he had his right arm tucked behind his back. She looked up from the bowl of cornbread batter she was stirring. "Good evening. Whachu hidin'?" She looked at him smiling

"Nuthin," he said bending forward in her direction and giving her a 'come over here and find' outlook.

She stopped stirring and went to him. As she reached for his arm he spun around fast. She got a quick glance but then he was facing her again, arm behind his back laughing at her.

"Okay. I give up. Marshall whachu hidin'? Come on pleeeze," she said in a sing songy voice. That always worked with him.

From behind his back, he lifted a gallon sized brown clay jug. "Molasses for your corn bread sweet lady."

"Aw thank you Marshall Mason. You too much."

At least once a week he surprised her like this. If it wasn't molasses it was a new coffee mug made of clay, or a piece of fabric to make a new frock for herself and or Mary. Marshall was always thinking of ways to try and make up for the painful blow she had been dealt by her husband, Alex. She knew that was what he was trying to do, and she didn't mind at all.

Mary continued to grow and develop a sense of herself. At first, she used to ask for her 'Dada' every day. Little by little she stopped asking and it seemed like she had forgotten him. Marshall played with her when he came home in the evening before she went to bed. She looked forward to that time with him and it seemed to be enough to dispel the memory of the man who used to just look at her as love poured out of his eyes into her heart.

"I am Mary. Mary Cowen," she would say. "I like to sing and I like to cook. My mommy teaches me."

Eliza was proud of her. She was thankful that Marshall had been able to fill the gap left by Alex's abandonment. Mary was growing up smart and happy and knowing that she was loved. The sex was okay, not as good as with Alex. Alex knew how to make her scream when they made love. She would never tell Marshall this of course, but inside her heart, mind, and body she was still craving that hit from Alex. Shameful, but she was. After all, he WAS the love of her life. Good, bad, or indifferent. Eliza didn't kid herself about this fact. She had just resigned herself to live with the naked truth. He has gone. He was her first love, knew how to knock the little man out of the boat, but he was gone.

When Marshall had gone home to see his parents shortly after Alex had left, he went over to see Isaac and Edna to let them know what was going on. Eliza had asked him to do this. They were surprised to see him and welcomed him to come on in the house.

"How's everything Marshall?" Isaac asked.

"Not too bad. But I am here on behalf of Eliza. She asked me to come and let you know what is going on with her."

This was hard.

"What do you mean?" Isaac asked.

Marshall proceeded to tell them what had happened when they returned home and found Alex gone.

"Oh my God! How is my Chile doin' Marshall?" Edna exclaimed.

"Miss Etney she is doing okay. But I tell you I was frightened for a little while there. Eliza was hardly eating and hardly talking. She would take care of Mary, but otherwise she was walking around like she was dead."

Edna looked like she had just been slapped and didn't see it coming.

Isaac didn't say a word, he just looked like a man who wants to get his gun and do something to correct an injustice.

After some silence, he said, "That boy promised me that he was gonna take care of my daughter. He said he loved her. I believed him. I can't believe he has done this."

Marshall tried to be comforting. "I know Mr. Isaac. But try not to worry, I am looking after Eliza and Mary. They are doing much better day by day. She been through a lot but your daughter is strong. She so strong it scares me sometimes."

When Marshall told her parents that he was "looking after" Eliza and Mary, they were relieved. It was very difficult for a woman to survive alone, especially with a child in those days. Of course, any grown up knows what "looking after" means in its totality, but nobody talked about or asked for a full disclosure.

Consequently, it was no surprise, sometime later when Eliza announced that she was pregnant with Marshall's baby. He became somebody Eliza almost didn't recognize. Marshall had always been pleasant and calm spirited. He was now like a jumping jellybean. Always colorful, happy, and on his feet trying to do the bidding of his pregnant lover.

"Whatever you need baby. Just let me know, he would say."

"Marshall! Sit down! I'm fine." He just could not do enough to show her how happy he was.

What pregnant woman doesn't want the father of her baby to be enamored? She felt loved, appreciated and quite satisfied. But the real, quietly kept truth? Eliza did not love Marshall.

"Well what do you mean by 'love' Eliza?" Edna asked. With this pregnancy, she had taken to coming to see Eliza in Woodsdale. Very pregnant and having little Mary, it was a bit much for Eliza to travel.

"I can't tell you exactly in words, mama. I just know that it's not what I felt for Alex. Even after all of this time no word from him, and I still feel something deep inside with how he left me. I still desire him mama! I don't even want to. It is just sitting there, like an empty rain barrel praying for the skies to open up. Marshall is a very good man. He is the best. I just can't feel something that is not there!"

Edna, her head tilted towards her left shoulder, arms wrapped across her body, seemed to take a moment to drink in all that she was seeing and feeling. Eliza waited, knowing something was coming. She was not sure she would like it, but she knew it would be honest and based upon her mother's love for her. Mama could always see through her.

"Listen Eliza. Love is so many things. It definitely is what you hold inside for Alex. That may never go away. He is your first love and the father of your first child. Thank the Lord, love is not limited to that one and only definition. Try to change the way you look at what love is supposed to mean. Right now, as I speak and you listen, is your heart beating?"

"Yes."

"Did you ask for that? Or did you do anything to make that happen?"

"No"

"Exactly. God loves us so completely, that our hearts beat continuously, we breath and exhale, and we don't even think about it. If you had to make that happen, would you know where to start?"

"I wouldn't know."

"Can you possibly see that this is happening because you are receiving love, and it is unconditional"?

Eliza could see where this was going, she just didn't know if she was the one to follow through. "I guess..." she replied reluctantly.

"So, let's look at Marshall and the type of love he is offering to you and Mary and now this little baby. Do you have to ask him to treat you well? Does he require that you be anything in particular in order to be worthy of his affection?"

"No mama."

"Eliza, I ain't trying to tell you that what you feel for Alex is not real or even that it is not what most of us want. He is your husband which makes you a married woman. But where is he? Is he even alive? Or are you a Widow? I'm just saying that you have got to go with what is in front of you. What is behind you cannot put food on the table or even give you a hug at night...a hug or whatsoever else y'all wanna do," she winked at her daughter.

Eliza smiled. "Okay mama. I get it."

Chapter Six

Edna stayed with them to await the moment when she would deliver her next grandchild. She seemed happy to be with Eliza and so tickled to spend time with Mary, especially since it was almost Christmas. There were two other sisters at the church who were pregnant and hoping that Eliza would be their midwife. Edna was able to assist with both of those deliveries. It felt like old times, she and mama working together.

It happened late one night. They had eaten a delicious dinner prepared by Edna, cleaned the kitchen, and put Mary to bed. All was quiet. The next day was Christmas Eve.

Suddenly, "Mama! Mama!" A shrill scream pierced the silent darkness of the house.

"Miss Etney, Eliza says she is in labor, but something is wrong. She don't know what exactly, but something is wrong," Marshall said.

Eliza heard her mother give instructions. "Okay Marshall. I will see about Eliza. Can you go and get Sister Ella and Sister Myra? They know what to do."

The labor lasted well into the night. Eliza was in a tremendous amount of pain. She breathed through it. She walked between contractions. She screamed, she cried, she laid down, she sat up. As the length of time between the pains became shorter in duration and the urge to push began, Edna watched carefully for the right moment. She saw a little round head covered with blood laced black curly hair show itself in the opening of Eliza's vagina.

"We are there daughter, push!" Sister Myra was on her right side and Sister Ella was on her left. Each held one of Eliza's hands in a viselike grip. "Push Eliza!" She pushed and grunted and pushed and grunted. The baby slid forward and showed a little more of itself in the birth canal. And then it was over. The baby slid back up, but not all the way. Now to wait for the next one. With each pushing contraction, the baby comes out a little more, slides back up some, but not all the way.

It took several of these pushing episodes, each five minutes apart before finally, the baby slid out into his grandmother's capable hands. And the room went silent. Edna froze. Holding the baby in the same position she had "caught" it in, just staring at it. Ella and Myra staring. Eliza, exhausted, head resting on the pillow, eyes closed but ears waiting to hear exaltation and jubilations. Nothing. Absolute deadly silence. It was as if the four women had been engulfed in a cube of ice and could not speak or move. The ice cube was shattered by the scream of the baby. One big exhale filled the room, but still there were no words. Eliza sat up so she could see the baby. It was a brown little boy with curly black hair, but his legs were incomplete. He had only thighs but no calves or feet. Then his arms were too long! Eliza let out a wail that came from the depths of who and what she was. The volume of it wasn't the thing, but the eerie quality of the sound. Like a wild animal in excruciating pain, dying in anguish. The women, all mothers themselves, felt her pain and maintained a stoic silence as she vented, and then sobbed.

Edna was the first to break the trance. "Ella let's get this umbilical cord cut. Myra is the bath ready?" The women went into automatic 'this is what we do when a baby is born', mode. But nothing was normal, everything was abnormal, and it was Christmas Eve!

Chapter Seven

Eliza sat at her kitchen table and made a mental list of the items she needed to get at the General Store. There was very little flour left in the cupboard. She needed some corn meal; some sugar and she also needed some baking powder. Supplies for her business: washing powder, alcohol, and a box of Borax powders. This was a task she dreaded because going into town meant a few things:

First, driving the wagon with the two children in tow.

Second, the bags of flour and cornmeal were heavy. She could get help loading them into the wagon but when she got home, she had to do it herself. Eliza wasn't squeamish about hard work, but those fifty-pound bags were way out of the range of a woman's work. Still, she did what she had to do.

And third, folks would stare at little Willie. Children would point fingers and exclaim to their mama's "Mommy. Looka that boy. He look like a frog!" In fact, they had begun to call him "Frog Boy".

This was hard for Eliza. However, she was used to the mimicry and had set her mind to be immune to it. But, her little five-year-old had no such immunity. Each and every one of these pointed finger incidents, was a stab to his heart. Willie knew he was "different" but at home, and around neighbors and friends, he was just Willie; a lovable, smart, and energetic little boy. Thus, Willie hated it when they had to go to town as well. She also had to restrain Mary, who was protective of her little brother and would want to go and confront the offenders. Going to town was an ordeal to put it mildly, but one that had to be endured at least once a month.

There was no other option because Eliza was somebody who didn't leave her children with other people, especially since Willie was "challenged" and only she and Mary knew how to care for him best.

Willie was strong in body. His legs were abnormally short, and his arms were unusually long. This meant that he had to 'scoot' in order to move around. This made his arms very strong and muscular. Considering his disability, and the way people outside of the family and church treated him, he was a relatively cheerful boy. Always willing to help and if given a task to do he stayed on it until it was completed to perfection. Willie loved to play catch in the yard outside. Mary would throw the ball and he would scoot around the yard, retrieve it and throw it back to her.

One day Mary ran into the house, hysterical. "Mama! There's a snake outside. I'm scared he gonna bite Willie!"

Eliza ran outside carrying her big knife. She ran over to Willie and cut off the head of a poisonous snake that was headed straight for him. At first, he had not seen the snake and then when he did, he had frozen. Just sitting there on his haunches staring at it.

Eliza screamed at him and grabbed him into her arms. "Boy you gotta be careful! Oh Jesus! Thank you Jesus!"

While hugging Willie, she reached for Mary who was standing by and bundled both of her children up into her embrace.

These two children were her life. If something had happened to Willie she would just die!

Oh, Marshall. Well Marshall flew the coup. It wouldn't be fair to say he didn't try, cause he did. But both he and Eliza knew that he was faking affection for the little boy. He just couldn't embrace the fact that he had something to do with making a deformed child. Eliza had her own struggles with getting accustomed to the notion that her baby had been born "imperfect." She wondered if God was punishing her for some reason. Could it be that she was not supposed to be intimate with anyone since she was still someone's wife?

She had no tolerance for Marshall's shortcomings. Either way, he was her child and her first obligation was to him. She never really had romantic love for Marshall anyway, and he knew that. They agreed that it was best they separate. The arguments and discord that had become common in the house were not good for the parents or the children. He sometimes looked at Willie with disdain. Other times he didn't look at him at all. He ignored Willie. When Eliza asked him about this, he would say it wasn't true and that he was just tired when he came home. Or he claimed that Eliza was partial to Willie and didn't pay him any attention. She knew that this was an excuse. Just so he would have something to complain about. She knew that she had done her 'duty' by being nice to Marshall and showing appreciation for his kindness. They both knew that their friendship would not survive if they continued to live like this. So, Marshall moved out. He still gave Eliza money as often as he could, which was pretty often. Proof of his need, want, compulsion, to have a family is that it wasn't long before he married Ella Baird, a girl nine years his junior, who was a member of their church, and commenced to having a whole slew of children. In fact, Eliza the midwife, even delivered a number of Ella and Marshall's children.

She was on her own for the most part. From time to time deacons and their wives would come by and help her with certain tasks, if she asked them. But as independent as Eliza was, she didn't make a habit of doing that. And anyway, women were funny about their husbands doing work for you if you're single. Next thing you know, there'd be another scandal for the folk of Woodsdale to sink their teeth into. Lord knows Eliza didn't need any more scandals.

"Mary! Willie! Come on let's go."

Mary whined. "Aw mama! I hate going to town. Can't I stay here."

"You know the answer to that. Get your shoes and help your brother up on the wagon."

The store in town, R.P. Brooks General Store, was also the train station for Woodsdale. Whenever she went there, she couldn't help but to think about that holiday season when Alex had dropped them off with Marshall to take the train for a visit with her folks for a few days, unsuspecting that she would return home to an empty house. Yes, this tangible memory always gave her a little swirl, accompanied by the slight cramp in her stomach. Then, she would push it down and out of her consciousness and proceed with the task of getting her supplies.

The store was long and narrow. It had a front door and a back door. The back door led to the platform where one waited for the train. On both sides of the store there were shelves that reached the very high ceilings. There were counters on both sides and through the middle of the store. Every surface was covered with items that were needed to support the lifestyle of the farming community/church folks who shopped in this establishment.

Eliza had left Willie sitting in the back of the wagon, and Mary was there with him for safe keeping. She could shop more quickly and get back home if she didn't have to attend to them in the store. The flour and cornmeal were in the back.

Mr. Brooks greeted her. "Mornin' Eliza. How goes it?"

Eliza replied, "We are all fine and thanking God for another day, Mr. Brooks. How is your wife? And your daughter?"

Mr. Brooks replied politely. "Everybody is fine. Thank you for asking."

She proceeded to recite the list of supplies she had memorized, as she had never learned to read and write more than a few letters and bible phrases, while Mr. Brooks began to put the items on the counter.

While customers and the storekeeper were in the back, a tall man, very striking in appearance, had entered the front door. "Hey Sal!" Mr. Brooks greeted him.

"Mornin R.P." He said

He was taller than Eliza, which made him pretty tall. His skin was a light golden-brown tone and his jet-black hair was plaited into two shoulder length braids. There was a small round earring in each one of his ears. Light brown eyes with black specs of colored illuminated his face. Eliza was trying not to stare, but it was hard. He was odd in a very alluring kind of way. Actually, he was quite exotic looking. She found his attire unusual because clearly he was an Indian, but he was dressed like a preacher. His braids were crowned by a ten-gallon hat, not a feather or some beaded business. His tweed pants and vest were complimented by a pocket watch with a chain hanging from the vest pocket and a double-breasted jacket. His shirt was white with a sort of fancy looking collar. He was well dressed and clean, but clearly this outfit was his everyday wear. It wasn't crisp and new looking. Eliza thought he pretty much wore this every day, but he sho' did wear it well.

"Be right with you Sal."

"No hurry R.P. Take your time," he responded as walked to the back of the store where they were. Sal tipped his hat towards Eliza. "Mornin' mam."

She looked up into his eyes to return his greeting but was stunned by the power of his gaze. Enormous, dark brown piercing eyes. She had not seen any like them before.

Eliza smiled. "Mornin'...."

He chimed in, "Sal is my name, Sal Tobin."

"I am Eliza, Eliza Cowen. Pleased to meet you Mr. Sal."

Mr. Brooks had been tallying Eliza's order. "That will be twelve dollars and fifty cents Eliza. I will help you to load these things on your wagon."

Sal spoke up "Lemme help with that R.P. Can you get me a sack of beans, some cornmeal, and a box of bullets?"

Sal carried the heavy bags of flour and cornmeal to the wagon where he saw Mary and Willie waiting for their mom. "Do you have someone to help unload these heavy things?"

Eliza hated to have to admit that she had these two children and no man at home. But what the hell. "I unload them myself. A little at a time."

"How about I get my things and then follow you home to help. No woman should be lifting this kind of weight by herself," Sal offered.

Somehow, Eliza felt like this man was sincerely offering to help and meant her no harm. Like a neighbor, or brother from the church. Plus, Mr. Brooks had greeted him as if he was well known and trustworthy. So, she said, "Okay. That would be mighty nice of you."

And that was how Eliza Cowen met Sal Tobin. A man who changed her life.

When they arrived at her house, Mary was the first to get down from the wagon. She helped Willie to get down and he scooted off to play in the yard.

"You need any help Mama?" Mary asked.

"Here take these washing powders in the house and keep an eye on your brother."

As Eliza handed the box to Mary, Sal had pulled his wagon up behind hers and was getting down. He went straight to her wagon and picked up the fifty-pound bag of flour like it was a piece of paper and looked at Eliza for direction. She opened the front door and pointed him in the direction of the pantry.

Maybe he would have just brought in the second bag of cornmeal and then tipped his hat to leave. He would go on his merry way and Eliza would not see him ever again. But so much for maybe, an incident occurred. As Sal was ascending the four steps from the ground to Eliza's porch and front door, the third step broke under his foot. He lost his balance and fell right on to the porch. Sal, the bag of cornmeal, and Eliza's composure came crashing down.

"Oh no! I'm so sorry. That step has been loose for a long time. We always just avoid stepping on that part. Are you okay?" she asked exasperated and embarrassed.

"Please don't worry," he said as he picked himself up like nothing had happened. Sal grabbed the bag of cornmeal, which was still completely intact, and carried it into the house placing it next to the flour in the pantry.

A stunned Eliza was still standing on the porch, watching him through the open door.

He came directly back out of the house. "Well Miss Eliza, now I done broke your step. I feel obliged to fix it."

"Oh no. Please. You have been so kind. It was already broken."

He insisted. "It's no trouble. I am a carpenter. I can come by tomorrow with my tools and get it fixed in no time flat. See you then?"

Well the step needed fixing. If she didn't allow him to do it, then she would have to ask somebody's husband to do it for her.

"Okay. We sure do appreciate it Mr. Sal."

"Just Sal is fine...Eliza," he showed his teeth while stressing the E in her name. What a delightful smile.

He hopped onto his wagon seat and waved goodbye.

The next day, Sal showed up around mid-morning with his tools and a piece of wood to replace, not repair, the broken step. As he had promised, it didn't take long at all. When he was finished, he sat down on the new step to put his tools back in his toolbox. Eliza came out of the house and handed him a cold glass of iced tea. He was thirsty and grateful for the refreshment. "This is good. Something is different about the taste of it."

She sat down next to him on the step laughing. "Yes, that's my secret ingredient."

He looked at her, and something about those eyes made her feel naked." Well, I would love for it to be my secret too." He was teasing her.

"I add a pinch of baking soda," she said

"Aha! A neutralizer. That's why it tastes so smooth."

Eliza had not met a man who was so interested in her, and he was smart. "Neutralizer?" She didn't know what that meant

"Yes. By adding the baking soda, you take down the sharp edge in the taste of the tea. Make it more smooth tasting in the mouth. Then you wanna take your time with the drink and feel it go down your throat in slow motion." This man! Who was he? He had a way of saying things that made sense but didn't make sense.

"Hmmm. I never thought of it that way. Everybody just likes my iced tea. Sometimes, I also add a sprinkle of cinnamon."

"Now cinnamon is delicious. I bet that tea tastes wonderful too. You know cinnamon is also good for digestion and for your heart. My people use the cinnamon sticks to make a tea for medicine."

"Your people? Who are your people?"

"My people are called The Blackfoot, or Saponi."

"Where are you from?"

"I was born over by the Hyco River. I lived there with my family until about five years ago when I got married. My wife was not a native. We moved to Roxboro and I built a house for us to live in."

Eliza had not realized that she was hoping he was unattached. When he mentioned a wife, her heart skipped a beat. "How nice," she said. "To be able to build a house is a wonderful skill to have." She carefully avoided the "wife" word.

"It is. My father taught me everything he knows about carpentry. Now I am able to make a living by working for people, using my skill. It keeps me busy."

"Well I would love to thank you for this here new step." She thought she might as well bite the bullet... "Maybe you and your wife could come over for dinner this weekend."

"My wife died. We were very excited to start our family when we learned that she was having a child. Her pregnancy was difficult, but she carried the baby for the full nine months. When she went into labor, I sent for the midwife. All I know is that there was a complication and both my wife and son died that night. My life has been empty since then. I work hard, so I have money. But I am alone and sometimes feel like maybe I should go back to live with my people, by the river." He sounded so remorseful. Eliza noted the longing in his voice.

"Oh! I'm so sorry. What a terrible experience for you to have to go through. I am a midwife. I know what that is like."

"You? A midwife?!" he lit up. "Seems like you got a few secret ingredients Miss Eliza Cowen," he mused. "I will accept your dinner invitation."

Eliza really did appreciate the new step and his kindness. Life had been rough both financially and emotionally. It had been awhile since a man showed her some special consideration. She was a mother and a hard-working sole wage earner for her family. But she was still a young woman, wanting, needing, craving affection, adult conversations, a sense of belonging somewhere.

Her time was divided between caring for her children, administering to pregnant women, and white ladies whose laundry she picked up and delivered. None of these people were likely to treat Eliza like she was their one and only special person. She needed to talk about her feelings and hold somebody's hand. She wanted to feel treasured. So far in her life, womanhood had meant being a servant, one who tolerates her partner's short comings, and one who submits for the sake of keeping the peace, even when it conflicts with her own beliefs and desires. She just knew there had to be more to it than this. Could this man be that person for her?

Church was standard in the social/religious world of Woodsdale, North Carolina. Just about everybody in the community belonged to the same church, attended regularly and everybody knew everybody's business. Church was familiar and acceptable for most folks, but Eliza wasn't most folks. Then, especially after the Alex abandonment and the Marshall "affair" (non-married status), to the birth of Willie, a deformed child, folks looked at her funny. Some even thought she had some kind of hoodoo around her. She was definitely the go to midwife, herbalist/healer in the community and beyond the immediate neighborhood. Her reputation was stellar, but socially...not so much. Eliza was popular, and lonely. Most of the time she didn't think about it. She was too busy with work and mothering. Her religious life, her spiritual convictions remained strong, as had been established during childhood.

"It's only the love of Jesus that got us through slavery," her mom always said.

Eliza prayed without ceasing, and she was sure with no doubt that this had been what carried her through the painful emotional traumas that had threatened to smother her life on more than one occasion.

These encounters with Sal had forged a little crack in a door she had closed and never expected to reopen. Trust was the missing factor. To open that door inside of her heart again, meant to risk opening old wounds, and being vulnerable. Why would she want to do that? She no longer knew how to believe in anyone besides herself and perhaps her mom. Life's disappointments had committed homicide against her ability to trust. Resuscitation was impossible.

He showed up with a jar of apple cider for dinner, and a little tin of cocoa for the children. "I made the cider," he said as he proudly presented the gallon sized jar. "Picked the apples myself. Fell out of the tree and hit my head too." He was smiling and rubbing the back of his head. The look in his eyes said he was kidding.

"Well thank you. Have a seat here at the table. I grew the tree, chopped it down and then made this here chair." Now it was Eliza's turn to be humorous, eyes twinkling. She sat the jar of cider on the table and looked at Sal flirtatiously.

Sal liked her. His laughter was robust. "Well I did pick the apples and make the cider."

Eliza liked him too. "Dinner is almost ready. How was your day?"

Sal had a slow and easy walk; he glided more than stepped. He didn't drag his feet though. He held his head high like he owned everything and everybody he could see. Sal gave the impression of being calm and easy going like a lion taking a nap in the sun, still there was a feral cat just under the surface of his skin. As she got to know him, she could detect that he had a side to his personality that could be lethal if he was crossed. Yet, she felt completely safe, even protected, in his company. She loved listening to him talk. He knew so much about so many things in the natural world and beyond.

That dinner had been the first of many to come. It started out as a once a week occasion, which evolved into every weekend experience which they both anticipated. This had escalated over a period of weeks and months. Now, he came over almost every night. He always brought something to add to the dinner. Sal was a hunter and a fisherman. Often, he bought game or fish that he had caught. Eliza was not inclined to rush into anything serious with a man. She was guarded with her own feelings and then she was raising two children for whom she needed to set an example of piety.

Eliza told Sal that although she liked him a lot, they need to take things slow. He looked at her with those jewel like onyx eyes and said, "Well that's just how I like it." She could not help but to hear a double meaning there but left that alone.

He continued, "I want to get to know this mysterious, smart, and very strong-willed woman. I want to be an asset to you and these children who are everything to you. In order to do that, I need to know where your deficits are. I want to share my strengths with you, and my weaknesses too. This takes time. Talking, walking together, laughing, agreeing, disagreeing and sitting together in silence while sipping some of your special tea."

One evening after Eliza had put the children to bed, she joined Sal outside sitting on the steps in front of the house, enjoying the evening breeze. Sal pointed to the sky.

"Do you know the names of the stars?"

"No. I love looking at them on a clear night as they move across the sky. But, I don't know their names." Eliza was curious.

"My people have names for everything in nature and stories about most things. There's a beautiful story about the morning star."

Eliza sat silent, looking up at the sky and ready to hear the story.

"Once, many many years ago, in the earliest times, summer nights were very hot. A beautiful young maiden was sleeping outside in the tall prairie grass, where it was cool. She opened her eyes, looking at the sky, just as the morning star came into view. She stared at it for some time, musing about how beautiful it was. The longer she looked at it the more she admired it. Before long, she realized that she had fallen in love with it."

"The maiden went to find her sisters and told them that she had fallen in love with a star. Of course, they said, "You are crazy. A star isn't a man. How can you fall in love with a star? She went and told everyone in the village. They all said she was out of her mind and she became the subject of ridicule and much amusement in the community. This did not change her feelings for the morning star. She continued to sleep in the grasses and awaken in time to stare at her love in the sky."

"One day she went to the river to fetch water. She saw a most handsome man there. At first, she thought he was one of the young men of her tribe. This meant that she should behave very coyly, as was the tradition between young women and men other than their fathers or brothers."

"Then he came near to her and said, 'I am Morning Star. I know that you have been watching me and have fallen in love with me. I was also watching you in the Prairie grass. I know that it is only you who I want to be my wife.' He gave her a yellow feather, and said, 'I will call you Feather Woman. Come with me to my home in the sky.'

"Feather woman was awestruck. She was speechless. First that he was actually there in the flesh, and then he wanted her to be his wife and leave with him. 'I...I...I... well I need to say goodbye to my family'.

'There is no time for that.' He said, 'we have to go now.'

Sal turned to face Eliza. She was waiting to hear Feather Woman's decision. What was the outcome of this dilemma? Instead of delivering the story's end, he said, "What would you do if you were in her place Eliza?"

Now it was Eliza's turn to be speechless. "Um, well I don't know. Well she doesn't have children, so I guess she could just up and go...but then everybody will be wondering what happened to her..."

Sal let her words hang in the air like rising smoke, for a few seconds, then, "Well cause I kinda feel like Morning Star. And I feel like you been watching me and falling in love with me all of this time. I think you been like Feather Woman's sisters and the villagers, telling yourself you are crazy, not wanting to believe what you've been feeling. But believe it Eliza. It is real. What we have is just a real as apples on an apple tree. We are very good together. I am ready for you to be my woman in every way."

Just then they both heard a horse's hooves clip clopping in their direction from down the road.

"Evening," Marshall greeted got down from his mount.

"Evening Marshall," Sal greeted him. They had met before. Marshall came by periodically to give Eliza money or to check on her and the children. He came less now, since he had noticed that Sal was there every time he showed up.

"Marshall. How are you? Everything okay?"

"Everything is fine Eliza. I came because Ella's been having pains all day and her water just broke. We didn't want to alert you too soon in case it was a false notice like the other time. But once the water broke, she said I should come and get you. Her mama is there looking after her until you get there."

"You go ahead Eliza. I will stay here with the children," Sal assured her before she could even think about how to leave with Marshall while her children were asleep in the house. Normally, she would have to awaken them and take them with her.

"Thank you Sal," both Marshall and Eliza said at the same time. Eliza grabbed her bag and supplies and left with Marshall. When she returned the next morning, she found Sal in her kitchen frying some bacon and cracking some eggs into a bowl. Mary was putting plates on the table for the three of them.

"Mornin' mama. I will add another plate for you!" She seemed excited. "Mr. Sal said that I am his best helper."

"Thank you honey. I am so hungry." Eliza liked what she was feeling. Someone to have her back when she just couldn't be two places at once.

"How is Ella?" Sal asked

"She is just fine. Had a beautiful little boy. It's not her first child so the birth was pretty routine, just long. I'm tired now." She sat down at the table as Sal ladled hot grits onto her plate of eggs and bacon.

Mary called, "Willie! Come on."

Willie scooted himself from the back of the house into the kitchen and up on to his seat at the table. His arms were very strong, and he had become quite adept at lifting himself up and down as well as moving around the house and the yard. "Mornin mama!"

"Well good morning my little sunshine. You lookin mighty bright and shiny this morning." He was truly her heart.

"Mr. Sal said I am a good boy. He showed me how to get the water and bathe myself this morning mama." Ha. Mr. Sal this and Mr. Sal that. Mr. Sal was definitely a cog in the wheel of her life these days.

"Wow! Really Willie? I think Mr. Sal is right. You are a very good boy," she said to Willie, while looking at Sal with one eyebrow raised as if they were co-conspirators.

When they finished breakfast and the kitchen was all cleaned up, dishes put away, Mary was chirping like a little bird, "Mama. Mr. Sal said if it's okay with you, we can go into town with him. He has to go to Mr. Brooks store for some supplies."

"You want to go to town?" Eliza was surprised and suspicious. Normally going to town was not something Mary and Willie wanted to volunteer for.

"Yes!" Both children chimed in.

Willie said, "Mr. Sal said he gonna buy us some candy if we good." Oh, so candy was the bait. Eliza looked at Sal with her tongue in her cheek, suppressing a smile.

"Yes. I told them that. Good children deserve sweet things," he said, winking his eye at Mary.

Eliza knew that what this was really about was creating a space and time in her day for her to catch up on a little sleep. She appreciated this and him so much.

"Well as long as you each save me a piece of candy. Be sure to behave and listen to Mr. Sal," she said as she smiled and kissed them both. She was actually trusting Sal with her two most prized possessions. That was noteworthy. Before the two children and Sal could get into his wagon and head towards the main road, Eliza was asleep in her bed.

They returned much later in the afternoon full of stories and dust from the road. Eliza could see that Sal had enjoyed his time with the children and her children were exuberant. The sweetness he had given them reached far beyond that of candy for their mouths. He had made them feel special. They liked being seen in town with someone like Sal who people seemed to admire.

"Mama! Nobody was laughing at me. In fact, some of the boys looked jealous when they saw Mr. Sal letting me choose which candy I wanted from the store." Willie exclaimed, animated and proud.

Oh God. Eliza felt like crying. She didn't let them see tears, but inside they were flowing like a waterfall completely flooding her heart. This is all she ever wanted for her little Willie, a moment of feeling normal. He would forever remember that a time such as this had seen the light of day in his world. She owed it all to this mystical magical man who had sauntered, ever so gently, into her life.

"Well look at that Willie boy! And which candy did you choose?" Eliza was humoring him and prolonging the telling of the story of one of the greatest triumphs of his young life.

"Well, I said, now Mr. Sal, how many can I have? And I said it kinda loud so that those boys in the store could hear me."

"And then," Sal added, "I said, well Willie, a good boy like you can have at least ten pieces of candy, and even more if he wants it!"

Willie was more animated than Eliza had seen him in a very very long time. "So, I said, thank you, Mr. Sal. But I won't be greedy. Specially since I want to be sure to get some for my sister Mary too."

Now Mary added her part. "All this time, I was standing nearby watching those boys turn green. They was so jealous. Their mom was busy shopping and not really paying attention. But she sure wasn't buying them no candy. I said, kinda loud and sing songy, 'oh Willie thank you for thinking about me too. Let's see. which candy we want'. I pranced over to where Willie and Mr. Sal were standing in front of the candy counter in Mr. Brooks store, and the three of us made a big deal of choosing the candy. Five for me and five for Willie and five for you mama! We chose them one at a time, by our favorite colors and by their flavors. Oh mama! It was such fun seeing those boys wishing they were us!"

Willie slid his hand into his little jacket pocket and produced a small brown bag which he proudly presented to Eliza. "Here's your candy mama!"

Willie's mama was overwhelmed. She knew that her son was having the best day of his life. This was something she couldn't have given him because it came from having someone other than his mom show him that he was worthy of being honored and appreciated for just being himself. That Sal was some kind of man!

She extended her hands and took the bag of candy from Willie. "Thank you!" She said to both Sal and Willie.

Mary said, "Mama Mr. Sal let us each eat two candies on the way home. But he said we should save the rest for another time, so we don't spoil our appetite for dinner."

"That's a good idea. You two go and get washed up. The food will soon be ready." She turned to Sal as they left. "Sal I just don't know how to thank you. They are so happy. And I am so happy. You have been such a blessing to me and my children."

"Eliza, I meant what I said last night just before Marshall came. I want you to be my woman. That means I will stand by you and be your helpmate in all things big and small."

Eliza looked at him. She knew what she wanted to say. She also knew that once she said it, there would be no turning back. "You were right when you compared me to Yellow Feather. I have been falling in love with you and trying to convince myself that I must be crazy for even thinking about trusting another man. But you seem so different from anyone I have ever met Sal. You are very thoughtful, and selfless. I want to believe that being with you could have good results for me and you as well as for my children."

"They would be our children," he said. The look on his face was very stern and sincere. Sal wanted her to understand that he wanted all of her, and that included the children she had borne with other men.

"You know I am still married to Alex right?"

"Yes. I know he left you while you were still married."

"What do you want us to 'be'? I can't be your legal wife."

"Well for now, we can share our lives in any way that makes you feel comfortable. In time, if we choose we want something more, we can go to live with my people and get married in my tradition. We don't live by the white man's laws. All I know is that I have fallen in love with you and those two children in there. We belong together." Sal spoke sincerely.

Mary and Willie hurried back into the room and jumped into their seats at the table, oblivious to the conversation that was in progress.

The eye contact and silent assent between the two adults concluded that the question of how they would go forward had been adequately explored and resolved. Eliza and Sal were a couple, just like that. Details could be discussed later, but they both knew that they wanted to be together in whatever way they could.

Eliza put the plates of delicious hot food on the table. Sal blessed the food, and the family enjoyed a wonderful dinner together. Willie kept recounting his story from Brooks Store like it was the gospel. For all practical purposes, gospel being defined as good news, it was Willie's gospel. Yeah, Willie's gospel. "That's right mama. Them boys wished they was me!"

Chapter Eight

Life with Sal as a partner had a rhythm like none Eliza had experienced before. It was consistent. He was reliable and assuring. He was consistent. He kept his word when he made a promise and if he couldn't he would let her know ahead of time. She never had to fear that Sal would not be present when she needed him. If she said "Sal, winter is coming and the children's coats from last year don't fit anymore," he would come home with two new coats. No questions asked. That was Sal. She felt safe and confident in herself as a woman. It was so empowering to love someone who reciprocated her affections unconditionally. The colors of the sun's risings and suns settings merged and swirled to create a beautiful abstract landscape that became the backdrop for Eliza's life with Sal at her side. As the days became weeks, the weeks became months, before either of them realized it, they had been blending their lives together for over a year.

Sal's home was further from town than where Eliza lived. However, it was bigger with more space for the children than her small cabin. Sal had built the brick house himself. He preferred to have his woman and children live there than for them to stay in the house that Alex had provided for his new wife. He said that he was not jealous of Alex. He just knew he could do better. Eliza was agreeable. She was ready to be in a larger house, with a bigger kitchen and separate bedrooms for Willie and Mary. So, they moved, and life was good. So good.

Outside of the house there was a porch where Sal and Eliza often sat after dinner, with Mary and Willie gone to bed. Sal and Eliza worked hard during the day. She was doing laundry for some white folks in the area, and always still attending to her midwife duties when called. He was busy with carpentry jobs all over town. But, these sunset talks were a favorite part of the day for them both.

"So how is the work over at Mr. Beam's barn coming along?"

"It's almost finished. I will be glad when I can collect my money and move on to the next job. Mr. Beam like to watch me like he think I don't know what I am doing."

"Maybe he is watching you because he is tryin to learn something. Maybe he thinks he can watch you so he can do it himself next time," Eliza suggested

"You know, you are probably right. Because sometimes he would come really close and ask me a question like, 'So why do you use that nail?' Or 'How many inches thick is that piece of wood'?"

"He can forget it. He might as well go on bout his business, pay you when you finish and send for you again next time he needs something. Ain't nobody better than you. And cain't nobody learn what you do by standing there watching," she said smiling like 'ain't nobody better than you and you belong to me!'.

"You sho right Eliza," he said.

There were those kind of mundane but interesting talks, and then there were the other ones when Eliza really got to know what kind of man she was with. Sal was very spiritual and perceptive. It wasn't something he spoke about or wore like a shirt with a name on it. He just lived it and breathed it.

For Sal, everything was connected to what he said his people call "The Great Spirit" or God.

One evening while they sat on the porch sipping iced tea, Eliza had been telling Sal about something very funny that Willie had said that day.

"Eliza," Sal interrupted. "You ever wonder why God gave you a child like Willie? I mean what do you think Great Spirit was trying to tell you, or TEACH you?"

"You know. I have wondered about that. At first, when he was born, I thought God was tryna punish me. I must have done something. I spent many nights lying awake trying to go through my memory of everything I ever said or did that might have offended God. I couldn't really come up with anything that severe."

"My people don't see Great Spirit as some stern father, or overseer, who watches us to find our imperfections so that we can be duly punished and corrected."

"Well aren't we imperfect? And isn't God perfect?" Eliza was confused

"Yes. We call God Great Spirit. It's all the same to me. God is perfect and we are not. But God knows we are not. God created us imperfectly so that we could work hard to become more like him. That is our purpose for being here. Why would God, who is all knowing, punish his creation for doing what he or she was born to do...making mistakes and learning from them and for submitting to his will?"

"Gee. That makes sense. Sounds so simple when you put it that way."

"So, you said that at first you thought you were being punished. What do you think now?"

"Well," Eliza continued. "Willie has made me more patient and tolerant. He opened my heart. As he began to grow and show us who he is, there was no way I could not love him. There was no way I could wish he had not been born. That is a big turnaround from how I felt that day when my mother pulled him from my womb."

"I can see that when you are with him." Sal admitted.

"It took a long time. At first my heart was broken. I was also hurt that Marshall didn't want him. I had a really hard time Sal." Her eyes were welling up as she was revisiting that pain from her past like it had happened yesterday. Sal reached over and wrapped Eliza in his arms like he was a big blanket. The cascade of tears poured out from her heart to her eyes, to her chin, to her heaving chest, while Sal just held her and rocked her. What started with a whimper became a moan and then a wail arching to a mournful sob and back down to a whimper.

When she became completely quiet, Sal continued rocking her, while wiping her face with the inside of his big hands. She looked up at him and said in almost a whisper, "I am sorry. I didn't mean to put that on you."

Sal gently replied, "Woman. What is it you think I am here for? Do you have any idea how long you needed to do that? You needed to share your feelings about this major disappointment in your life, and have someone you trust, to rock you say that all is well, and you are just fine."

She couldn't say a word. They sat like that, Eliza in his arms, Sal rocking her, until it was pitch black outside and the choral harmony of crickets and frogs singing in the night, had become louder than their breathing. They went to their bed, made passionate love and fell asleep in one another's embrace. During the night, they awoke and made love again. By morning, Eliza felt like a new woman.

Love making with Sal hit so many of her sensitive 'spots'. Her body became liquid in his embrace. She wanted to melt into him and never let go. It reminded her of intimacy with Alex because he had satisfied her in a similar way. Her climax was always so powerful with her husband. She always felt euphoric afterwards. Like she couldn't even think clearly. The difference was that with Sal she felt free to open all the way up. There was no stress. No tension in their love making. With Alex, there was always the emotional undercurrent of, 'Is this good enough for him'? She trusted Sal's feelings for her and knew that they would be the same the next day, as they had been the day before. Not so with Alex.

Several weeks later, Sal got word that his dad was very ill. He needed to go home. The journey through the woods and over rough terrain to get to the town where his family lived, near Hyco River, was long and dangerous. There were poisonous snakes, wolves, bears, and not to mention two legged thieves that sometimes hid in the forest looking for lone travelers to rob.

"I need to go by myself," he said. "It would be too much for you and the children especially at this time of year. It's too cold."

"I really hate to think of you out there by yourself. It's a long journey. Cain't somebody go with you?" Eliza was worried

The Secrets of Hattie Brown

"Awww babeh. I'm a grown man and I've done this many times before. In fact, I can travel faster on my own. I know every tree by their first name. The squirrels and rabbits even come out to greet me. 'Hey Sal. Where you been? We ain't seen you in a long time.' I'll be just fine," he tried to assure her.

But Eliza wasn't laughing. She didn't feel good about this. One thing she had learned to do was to trust her gut.

"I promise. I will get there as fast as I can, see about my father, and then I'll be back in two shakes of a lamb's tail."

She knew he had to go. This didn't change her bad feeling about him going. But, she told herself that maybe she was just nervous because Alex had gone away and didn't come back. Maybe she was afraid of losing Sal. She convinced herself to relax, just a little, not all the way, and help him to get ready for his trip.

It took him a couple of days to assemble all of the gear he needed and to get the horse ready. Eliza baked him a tin full of biscuits. She also rolled up and tied a quilt that she had made for their bed. This was to keep him warm when he took a break from riding. The journey was long. Sal and the horse would both need to stop and rest.

The morning he left the weather was very cold. Eliza watched him ride his horse down the road until he was completely out of view. She felt a chill in the marrow of her bones. 'It's just winter,' she told herself.

She missed Sal so much. He had only been gone for a day, but it may as well have been a year. He was such an integral part of her life, whether he was physically present or not. Just knowing that he would be home in a few hours or a few minutes was a source of comfort every day.

"Mary. Come help me carry these clothes inside." Eliza was removing laundry from a clothesline out in the back of the house.

"Yes Mama," Mary replied as she ran to help her mom.

Both mother and daughter were startled when they looked up and saw Marshall watching them. "Marshall! You scared me!" Eliza was aghast

"If I was a bear, I'd be eating my dinner right now." He laughed at the terrified look still frozen on their faces.

"Okay. I'm sorry," he apologized, still smiling but sincere.

"Go ahead Mary. Put that basket in the kitchen and start folding those clothes. Mrs. Randal is expecting me to bring them around pretty soon." Mary followed her mom's instructions and dashed into the house carrying the basket full of clean clothes. "So how you Marshall? How is Ella and the children?"

"We are all well. Thank the Lord. I came by to see you because I have some news that I thought might interest you. Where's Sal?"

"Sal had to go see about his father, over by the Hyco River area."

"Wow. That's pretty far. He went by himself?" Marshall looked concerned

"He did. I'm not so happy about it but I understood he had to go. Sal said he could move faster by himself, and he would be fine. Said he knows the roads and the woods very well."

"Well when is he coming back?"

"I'm not sure. Marshall what news?" Eliza was growing a bit impatient. It was clear that Marshall's news was noteworthy.

"Well I was at The Colored Cafe the other night. In walked Sammy Jeffers. You remember Sammy?

"That's Ginni Jeffers' son, right?"

"Yeah. That's the one."

"Didn't he leave and go up north?"

"He did. He just came down to visit his folks. While here, of course he made sure to visit the ole watering hole, Colored Cafe, and see who he could see. Truth is, he just wanted to brag about how good life is up there."

"So that's the news? You saw Ginnie Jeffers boy and he doin good up north?"

"Well no. That's the first part of the news. The real news is what he told me."

"Marshall what is it you want to tell me that you really don't want me to know?" Eliza had known Marshall for a very long time, and she knew when he was stalling.

He figured he had better go on and spit it out. "Well Sammy said he saw Alex Cowen on the train he rode to come down. Said Alex was working as a porter. Alex told him that the pay wasn't that much, but a man could do good if he knew how to treat the white folks so that they would give him hefty tips. Alex was saying he had the game down tight. He knew how to make them feel like a million dollars. They want to feel like it is still slavery times, and he gave them exactly that. Shucking and a jivin. Grinnin' and a skinin'. Said he would be thinking about punching them in the nose, while smiling in their faces. That's what got him through it. That and the tips he put in his pocket at the end of a day's work. "Yes boss! No boss! Anything else I can get for you boss?"

Eliza's response was a combination of awe and disgust. "So that's what he left me to do? Go kiss up to white folks for a few extra coins?"

Marshall did not answer her question. He just stood there looking like he smelled a fart.

"So, where does he live?"

"Seems like he mostly working on the trains all the time. But when he is off for a day or two, he goes to Norfolk where his Auntie lives." Marshall decided not to tell Eliza who else lived in Norfolk that constituted the REAL reason Alex was going there when he was off from work. She would find that out in time, but not from him.

"Well at least I know that Mary's father didn't fall in a ditch somewhere. He is still alive. Thanks Marshall. This is something I should know. She feigned indifference. "I appreciate you making time to come and tell me." Marshall stayed for a while. He shared more of the details about Alex's work on the railroad.

After Marshall left, Eliza confronted herself in the mirror of her heart. Alex! She had carefully wrapped him up in a neat little package and given him his own corner in the recesses of her selfness. She had allowed Sal to enter and fill the spaces that had been left empty by Alex's abandonment. What about the love she had for Alex? She never questioned it. She never tried to exterminate it. Just tucked it away. Out of reach. Out of reach, but not dead, by a long shot.

Chapter Nine

Sal had been gone for a week. Eliza thought he would have returned by then. During his absence, she had realized that her menstrual was late and she was feeling nauseous in the mornings. She was pretty sure what this meant since it was her third time feeling this way. They were going to be parents together. She was looking forward to the look on his face when she told him. He had lost a baby before, and a wife. This one would live and be healthy so he could shower all of his love and affection on their child, like he had already been doing with Mary and Willie. Eliza thanked God every day that Sal had become her lover, protector, provider and friend.

After another week passed, and no Sal. Eliza knew that something, for sure, was very wrong. She asked Marshall to gather some brothers from the church and go see if they could find out what happened to her beloved Sal. Marshall understood her concern and promised that on the weekend they would go and see what they could find out.

That Sunday evening, Eliza was sitting on the porch after dinner. Children were in bed. She knew that Marshall should be back soon. They had left before dawn on Saturday. Sunset was well on its way to the dark of night. The orange sky was now being taken over by purple hues, spreading arms to embrace blackness. It was very quiet. Too quiet. Even the crickets seemed to be holding their voices at bay. Piercing the void of silence came the sound of horse's hooves. She heard them approaching before she could see them. There was a rhythm to the pounding of the hooves on the grass covered grounds in front of the house. Eliza's heart picked up that rhythm and pounded just as loudly as the hoove's percussion.

As soon as Marshall slowed his horse and stopped in front of her house, the other two brothers on their horses behind him, she knew he did not have good news. She knew it by the shallow look on his face. She knew it because the quilt that she had sewn for Sal, was tied to the back of the saddle on Marshall's horse!

Eliza felt her lower lip tighten. She clasped her hands in her lap and took a deep breath.

"Eliza, I don't have good news. I'm sorry," Marshall's tone was grim.

"I know. I know. Just tell me what happened." She wanted him to say that Sal was sick, and he would be coming soon, but she knew in her heart that Sal would not be coming.

"It seems that while Sal was on his way to see his father, he had finished the water in his canister and needed a drink. There was about two hours of riding left to his journey. He passed by a spring where he stopped to fill his canteen. It was getting dark, and Sal didn't see that there was a snake at the edge of the spring. The snake bit Sal on the leg before Sal even saw it. He immediately jumped on his horse and rode at top speed to try and get to his village where there were doctors who knew what to do. The people in the village told me that when Sal did reach there it was already too late. The snake had been a very poisonous one. These kinds of bites need to be treated within thirty minutes. Otherwise, the results are almost always fatal."

"Fatal," She said the word as a statement, not as a question. She understood what he was telling her. He was telling her that this man, who had loved her like no other, this giant who had picked her heart up from the depths of despair and showed her how to laugh again, this man...was no more.

"Is there anything at all that we can do Miss Eliza?" One of the other men asked

"No. Thank you both for going with Marshall. I appreciate your kindness."

"Eliza. You know that Ella and I are here for you. Anything you need, don't hesitate to ask," Marshall comforted. His sympathy was sincere.

"Thank you, Marshall. And thank Ella for me," Eliza replied, but she was numb. Outside calm, inside tsunami

Marshall carefully untied the quilt and handed it to her. Eliza accepted the folded memory into her arms and hugged it close as she began to rock and reminisce. This was the only emotion Marshall and his companions saw in Eliza on that day. He gently touched her shoulder, mounted his horse, and the three men rode off into the blackness of night, leaving Eliza rocking and hugging the quilt covering her belly. The crickets had resumed their symphony providing the soundtrack for her grief.

Nine months later, Eliza gave birth to Hattie Roberta. The love child conceived with Sal Tobin.

Chapter Ten

The memories of Sal were rich and robust. Those twilight conversations, just Eliza and her man, on the porch, had changed her in ways she had not understood until he was gone. She felt like when she met Sal, much of the landscape inside of her heart was uncultivated. Quite the barren, flat, dry soil. With his wisdom and insights Sal had plowed, planted, watered and shed light on the inner being of the girl born Eliza Betts. Understanding this now, she knew that this beautiful garden planted by Sal, that had grown her up to be a woman, was what would get her through the horrible experience of losing him.

The first weeks and months without him bordered on being unbearable. Taking care of Mary and Willie, nurturing Sal's baby growing within her womb, as well as her chores as a laundress and midwife, kept Eliza busy enough to get through her grief one day at a time, and stay sane.

Edna and Isaac came to stay with Eliza and the children when Sal died. They knew she needed more comfort than she was saying. When it was time for them to go home Isaac spoke earnestly to his daughter.

"Eliza, I think you should come home with us when we leave on Friday." Her dad was concerned

"I don't think you should be here alone with these children...you pregnant and all..." Edna wanted to keep an eye on her daughter. She knew that Eliza was not talking about what she was really feeling.

"Mama, Daddy, we will be fine. I have done this before. It's my third pregnancy!" Eliza didn't want to leave home. She felt closer to Sal there.

"Listen Eliza. Don't be a hard head. We know you can do this on your own. But why should you? Come home. When the baby is born and you feel ready, I will bring you back myself."

She felt cornered, and she knew that they were right. So much can go wrong with a pregnancy and with the delivery. She trusted her mom to guard her health and her baby's health more than any other midwife.

"Okay. I know y'all want what's best for us. I need a couple of days to get ready."

"We can wait." Isaac said

"Tell me how I can help." Her mom was relieved.

This is how it came to be that Hattie Roberta was born in Virginia, although she grew up and lived her entire life in North Carolina.

The birth was normal. Eliza cried when they first put Hattie into her arms. "Mama. She looks just like Sal!"
"Yes, she does. Isn't this a wonderful gift he has given to you? Praise the Lord!"

Edna called Isaac to come and meet his new granddaughter. It was clear that he was happy to see mother and baby both doing well.

"I will go and get Mary and Willie. They have been waiting to greet her."

After the two siblings hugged their new sister, the entire family stood in a circle around Eliza and Hattie, while Isaac prayed for mother and children.

They stayed there in Virginia for several weeks before returning to Woodsdale.

Chapter Eleven

The day was bright and sunny. The springtime breeze was light and airy, dancing around Eliza's long skirt tails as she hung laundry on a clothesline in back of the house. The children were playing on the front porch. She was singing a song she had known her whole life....

Trials hard on every hand and we cannot understand the ways that God will lead us to that blessed promise land
But He'll guide us with His eye and we'll follow til' we die
And we'll understand it better by and by

By and by when the morning comes
All the saints of God are gathered home
We'll tell the story of how we've overcome
And we'll understand it better by and by

The song had transported her to a place where everything either made sense or no longer needed to. She was so caught up in her singing, that she didn't hear Mary at first. "Mama! Mama!" Eliza turned with a start. Mary's voice sounded urgent.

"What's the matter Mary?"

"Mama there's a man out front asking for you. I don't know him, but he said he is your friend."

"Okay I'm coming."

Friend? The only male 'friend' she had was Marshall Mason and of course Mary knew him. Who was this? She walked around the side of the house so that she could get a peek at this visitor before he saw her. When she turned the corner on the side of the porch, she saw the backside of a very familiar silhouette. Tall, slim, and solid. He was talking to Willie. His horse was tied to the front porch railing.

Everything solid inside of Eliza suddenly turned to jelly. Holding on to the thin thread of reserve she had left, she exhaled a very cool, "Alex!"

He turned to face her. His face was as beautiful as ever. Somehow it had matured and with a tad more plumpness. And those eyes, looking though her. She felt transparent.

"Eliza. How are you?" All of this decorum for the children, who had no idea who he was. She would keep it up until they were out of earshot.

"I am well. Thank you. what brings you this way? I had heard you were workin on the railroad." This was hard. She didn't know if she wanted to curse him and shoot his horse (Sal's guns were locked away) or cry her heart out and tell him how badly he had hurt her.

In his eyes she saw 'I know I hurt you' but he said, "Well I was traveling through town, and had to stop and look you up. At first, I couldn't find you because you have moved. I went to Brooks store in town and inquired. They were able to direct me."

Since they were doing 'eye talk' because of the children, the look she gave him back was 'yes you did and I am hurt and really angry at you', but she said, "I see. How long are you in town for?"

Mary and Willie were sitting on the porch, closely watching their mother talk to this stranger. Hattie was content on her pallet next to Mary. Eliza knew she was going to have to have a private grown folks' conversation with Alex. She wanted to find out the real reason he had come. She didn't believe that he was just passing through and also knew that if that conversation was going to happen, she had to orchestrate it because they were on her turf.

"Well I'll be around for a day or two," Alex said. "Um can I get a glass of water?"

"Mary, get Mr. Alex a glass of water."

Suddenly the blatant reality hit her. She had just told Mary to bring HER FATHER a glass of water. Compassion for her little girl who had never known her dad, clamored to the surface of her considerations. That compassion had to push through a lot of anger, disappointment and resentment to get to it's position on top, and cause her to say, "Well Mr. Alex, I am just about to start dinner. Would you like to join us?"

She had forgotten that winning smile Alex had when he was pleased to the bone. "Well I don't mind if I do," showing all of his pearly whites as he accepted the glass of water from his daughter. "Thank you, little miss. What's your name?"

"Maaaary" she said, rocking from side to side with her belly protruded like 'Ain't I the cutest lil' thing you ever did see?' Indeed, she was.

The Secrets of Hattie Brown

Over dinner, Alex entertained mother and children with stories of life on the railroad trains of America. He spoke about black people traveling north to start a new life, black people traveling south to visit their families who still lived there. The funniest stories were about the rich white people who clearly wished there had never been a Civil War and that their families still owned plantations with brown people doing their every bidding.

As the children listened intently, Eliza was quiet, somewhat wrapped up inside of her thoughts and feelings.

The woman inside
The one who had been left like a dead animal in the forest.
Carcass to rot.
Alone, for all he knew
The woman inside who was left feeling like less than enough for him.
That woman whose guts nearly melted away from starvation because of deceit and feeling like a useless rag.
That woman???
Now, that woman was elated.

He had returned! This meant that maybe she had been wrong and maybe that woman wasn't so bad after all. Maybe he was sorry and knew that he had been cruel and neglectful. Even maybe he was going to say that he had been hit in the head, taken away, and forgot who he was until now…Silly girl. She was playing games in her head.

"Stop it," she told herself.

But this, she kept concealed inside. Instead she let her mental state, the stoic, warm but nonchalant one, show on the outer skin of her being.

Alex was laughing at them when he said, "Some of these white folks, ha, you can tell that they used to have a lot of money but now they jus' getting by. Their clothes are expensive, but old. If you look closely, their shoes are just as worn and dusty as a barn floor. Eliza knew that he had "looked closely" because Marshall had told her that Alex's work on the railroad was carrying the luggage, serving the food and drinks, and shining the shoes of rich white folks.

Willie seemed to be in awe of this stranger with such stories of a life he knew nothing about. "Mr. Alex, is it fun to ride the fast-moving trains? I mean, do your head get to spinning when you look out of the windows?"

Alex laughed. "No Willie. I don't get time to sit and look out of the window. I am working all the while the train is moving. Sometimes I am on my feet for twenty-four hours. Even when I lay down to sleep, I might hear someone call 'George!' That's what they call all of us, George. That means someone wants a drink, or a blanket, or maybe even a song and dance. We porters do it all. Anything to make the rich passengers feel like they done landed in a special heaven for white folks."

Mary's face was lit up like a star twinkling in the darkest night sky. She had never encountered a man like Alex. He was so handsome and animated. "Do little girls ride the trains?"

"Well there are some little girls once in a while. But it is mostly businessmen traveling for work, and grown folks wanting to move to someplace where they will be able to make more money to take care of their families. Once in a while there are little girls traveling with their mamas. But one thing is for sure."

"What's that?" Mary quizzed

"I ain't seen not one little girl as pretty as you!"

Well that was it. Mary was done. Eliza watched her melt like a stick of butter in a hot skillet. She looked at her mom, eyes like an owl, covered her mouth with her cupped hand, and muffled the sound of the silliest, most infectious giggle a girl had ever produced.

Eliza smiled at her, at him, and thought to herself, Alex, still the charmer.

Mary and Willie went to bed as the newest members of the We Love Mr. Alex Club. They had both asked if he would be there in the morning.

Hattie had been bathed, swaddled in her favorite quilt and was already drifting off into dreamland. Eliza laid her down by the hearth so she would be visible and warm while her mother spoke with Alex. Alex was staring into the fire of the hearth and seemed to be very deep in thought. His awareness of Eliza's return to the room brought him 'back' with a start. She sat in a chair opposite him.

"Eliza! Everything okay?"

"Yes. Everything is okay."

"What wonderful children. You have done well."

She didn't respond, just waited. The pregnant pause was accompanied by the crackling and popping of the logs in the fire, and the baited breathing of two people who knew that the words that were about to be said, would either open and infect old wounds, or act as a balm to heal and close those gashes forever.

Alex knew that he was the one who had to speak first. After all, he was the one who had run off like a thief in the night. He also respected Eliza for allowing him the privilege to try and explain. She could have just dismissed him the moment she saw him. She could have embarrassed him in front of the children, especially his daughter.

Instead, she had gracefully allowed him to establish and maintain a level of dignity in the eyes of her children. He was a lucky man. Maybe she still loved him?

"Eliza," he looked directly at her, "before I say anything, let me first say, I am sorry. God knows I never meant to hurt you. I took something from you that you ain't never gonna get back. It might not mean much now, but you deserve to hear me say those words. Then I want to thank you for letting me stay and have dinner with you and the children. It meant a lot for me to meet them and my daughter is so beautiful and so smart."

While Eliza was putting the children to bed, she had a moment away from him, to decide upon her strategy. She would not speak until she had heard everything he had to say. Then, she would let him have it and tell him to get out! There was nothing he could possibly say, that would change the reality. He had abandoned her without a word and been gone and out of touch for too many years to count... but it was six years, eight months and twenty-four days! Oh, she HAD been counting...

When she didn't respond to his compliment about her children, their daughter, he waited a moment, and then continued.

"At first, I left with the idea that I would go north and get a job making good money and then after a few weeks, I would come back and get you and Mary. I knew you would wait for me, cause that is who you are. I thought of telling you about my plans and then decided not to. You have your laundering work and more important your midwife work. I knew you want to stay near your family as well. Me, I don't really have much family to keep me grounded here. Honestly Eliza, I missed you and Mary more than I even wanted to, but once I had left you like that, I knew I had to make good before I had to face you again. Weeks turned into months and the work I was getting wouldn't hardly keep a roof over my head and food on the table. I was embarrassed that I had left my family and not made any progress worth shaking a stick at. Then I heard that they were hiring porters at the railroad station. I went down there, got a job, and finally saw that I could make some money that could enable me to get my family back. Eliza, I worked day and night. I rarely took a day off and I was saving every penny. My plan was to get an apartment big enough for you, me, and Mary, and then I knew you would agree to come back with me. That's when I got a friend to write you a letter for me. I told him what to say and he wrote it down. In the letter I said that I love you and I am sorry. I said that I was going to come and get my wife and daughter very soon and asked you to please forgive me. Weeks later, the letter was returned. The envelope said that there was no such person at that address."

"Around the time the letter came back, I saw a friend from back in Norfolk on the train while I was working. He told me that my mother's sister was very ill. I knew that I should go home and see about her. She was the last of my mother's family members still living. I arranged for a few days off and went down to Norfolk.

"When I got there, I found my auntie looking weak and thin. She was coughing a lot and didn't have much of an appetite. Some ladies from her church were tending to her, since she had no children and her husband had died many years before. When I spoke with one of the ladies, she told me that my aunt had tuberculosis, and the doctor says there is nothing that he can do except try to keep her comfortable. Considering that, she said my aunt was doing well. Some people die right away. I spent time there with my aunt, but they say that thing is catching, so the same lady suggested I come and sleep at her house. She could fix me up a pallet in her kitchen and I was welcomed. I went home with her and met her husband, her three sons and her daughter, Charlotte."

"My aunt lived for another three months. I went home as often as I could to see her and give her some money to help buy food and pay for doctor's visits. Each time I went home I would stay for a night or two at the home of Charlotte and her parents. Charlotte is the same age as me. Eliza, I am just gonna tell you how it was. I ain't proud, but this is how it was. Charlotte was friendly and I knew she liked me. Life on the railroad was lonely and tiring. Each time I went home to see my aunt, Charlotte was there willing to listen to my stories and be impressed by this boy living life in the city. I got to messing around with her. We would wait until her folks were asleep and then go out to the barn and be together until dawn, when we would sneak back into the house. I was enjoying myself Eliza. But in my heart, I knew I had a wife and daughter who I was working to get back with. I didn't know where you were. But I knew I was going to try and find you. I can't believe I was so stupid."

Eliza held her peace, although inside she was seething like a volcano about to erupt.

"I was planning to tell Charlotte about you and Mary when I went down for my aunt's funeral. But something happened that changed everything Eliza. I got in town, just in time for the funeral. After the burial, while we were having collations at the church, Charlotte's dad asked me if I would be coming to stay at their house afterwards. I said that I thought I would since the last train was leaving at that very moment. He told me I was welcomed and could ride back to the house with them in their wagon. I had seen Charlotte, but we had not spoken. She was busy helping the women in the kitchen."

"People started leaving, as it was getting late. I saw Charlotte's dad speaking with the pastor before he came over to me and asked if I was ready to go. The whole family loaded into the wagon and we headed to their house. When we arrived, Charlotte, her dad, and me went into the kitchen and the rest of them seemed to disappear to I don't know where."

"I had been so busy dealing with my aunt's passing, funeral and burial, that I had not noticed until this moment, that Charlotte was not the same girl I had been fooling with. She looked very sober and actually a little scared."

'Have a seat Alex.' I turned around to find myself looking down the barrel of a hunting rifle. I remember looking into that big long black hole and seeing my life pass before me. I knew I was going to die but had no idea why. Charlotte's dad must have read my thoughts because he began to fill in the blanks for me.

'You been sneaking out to the barn at night and laying with my daughter?!'

"He asked me, but he was telling me! Eliza I was terrified. All I could say was a very weak, 'Yes sir', my voice shaking like a leaf in a storm."

"Well now she pregnant. And you gon' marry her!"

"I looked at Charlotte. She looked even more frightened than I felt. Since she knew her daddy better than me, I figured I was right to believe that he would shoot me dead if I showed as much as a hint of resistance. So, I kept my mouth shut."

"The three of us were like statues in the kitchen. A man with a rifle pointed at a terrified young man seated at a table next to a very frightened girl. The sound of horse hooves clamored to a stop outside. There was a knock at the door. Charlotte's dad didn't move, he just hollered, 'Come in'."

"Who entered through the door but the pastor of the church!"

When Eliza heard this, she thought that if it wasn't her life, if he wasn't her husband father of her daughter, she would be on the floor laughing right now.

"Reverend thank you for coming. I know it's been a long day for us all. But I wasn't gonna let this here young man get on a train and ride out of my daughter's life without taking responsibility for what he has done!"

"I understand Deacon. Are we ready?" The minister seemed nonplussed. Like he came to pick up a basket of biscuits and he would be on his way very soon.

"Yes! WE are ready" said the father of the bride.

"The ceremony took all of ten minutes. I felt like this was happening to somebody else. Like Alex had left the room and Charlotte was marrying and pregnant with the baby of a man I didn't know."

"...then... I now pronounce you man and wife." And he was gone. Out the door, clippity clop as his horse carried him away and home to his well-deserved and needed rest. Just another day in the life of a pastor. Ha! My life was destroyed" Alex paused for a moment.

Somehow, Eliza knew that this story had an addendum. She stayed silent.

"Charlotte was crying, I was still trying to figure out what had hit me. I knew that if I told her now, that I was married already, she would tell her dad and he would surely kill me. He would kill me for deceiving his daughter in the first place, and then for saying 'I do' in his kitchen when I knew I had already said that with somebody else. I kept my secret. Now I was expecting a baby with another woman. This is a position I had never wanted to find myself in. I did what I do best. Get out of town. I told her dad that I was expected back at work and if I lost my job, I would not be able to take care of his daughter and grandchild. So, he put away his gun and gave me permission to leave in the morning. I had to promise that I would be coming home at least twice a month to check on my wife and child. We agreed that with my work schedule it would be best for Charlotte to stay with her parents."

"When I got on the train the next morning, I breathed a deep sigh of relief. I had no intention of ever showing up there again and was more determined than ever to find you and Mary so I could reclaim my life as it should be. The more I thought about this plan, the more I knew it wasn't right to abandon yet another child and its' mother. I decided that I had to accept the responsibility for my deeds at least until the baby was born and I could safely tell Charlotte about you and my daughter. I figured by that time she will at least allow me to escape before she told her family the truth about me."

"At that time, it sounded like a perfect plan. For the next few months, I would be obedient to my promise to her dad and show up every other weekend. I would be nice to Charlotte and she would be happy. Every time I went back, she was bigger and bigger, and nicer and nicer. She would cook my favorite foods, show me lots of affection," he looked at Eliza like he wanted to stop and apologize again, "and then always tell me about the baby and have me touching her belly to feel it kick."

"Finally, the time came when she was due any day, so I went back to Norfolk as often as I could without losing too much time on the job. Then I went and HE had been born. A little boy, who looked like I spit him out. My heart exploded with love and sank into deep sadness at the same time. Once I laid eyes on that little bundle, I knew I would not be able to dismiss his birth or his mother."

"This is how I ended up starting a family with another woman, Eliza. We had one more child a year later. I have been living this lie for too long, and I just can't live with it anymore. I came to find you and tell you first. Then I will go 'home' and tell Charlotte. Whatever punishment I have to go through, I will own. I created this mess. It's time for me to clean it up as much as I can. I won't be able to make up for lost time, but if you will allow me, I want to be a part of Mary's life. I never stopped loving you and my first baby girl."

He looked at her and waited for her reaction or response. Now that it was her turn, Eliza didn't know where to start.

The Secrets of Hattie Brown

Should she start with the anger? Did she owe him an explanation as to how and why his wife had two children by two different men? She was thinking, and Alex was waiting. Eliza decided on catharsis first. She deserved to vent, she wanted to vent, she needed to purge, and he had earned it. No matter the circumstances!

"First of all, let me say that your sorry is of no use to me. When I think of the nights I laid awake crying until my eyes looked like those of a diseased cow. When I think of all of the phony smiles and laughs, I had to conjure up so that Mary would not know her mother was dying on the inside. When I remember the days, I hoped that Marshall might come by and give me a few dollars, out of the goodness of his heart so that my daughter and I would have a little meat on the table. You left us destitute Alex! You left us alone. And you left me ashamed to face people at the church. They looked at me like there must be something wrong with me. Man left me and his daughter like we was trash he needed to dump. I suffered Alex! I suffered! You left me vulnerable. Marshall was my friend and he knew our story, so I allowed him to be the only man who I let close to me and Mary. He would have never been able to get as close as he did if I didn't feel so much in need of emotional and financial support. I was broken, Alex, thanks to you!" and then she spit it out, "Willie, is Marshall's son!"

Alex was listening intently but showed no surprise or curiosity.

"When you didn't come back or send word of any kind I waited. I just knew that you would come back for us, me and your daughter, and for the love that we shared. But there was no sign of you. I thought you might be dead. Caught some sickness and just passed away. Because I could not believe that anything other than death could keep you from us forever. Then Marshall came and told me that you were alive and working on the railroad. That someone had seen you and you were well! That sealed it for me. I knew that you were not the man I thought you were, and the love I had been holding on to was only meaningful to me. But at least I was glad to know that one day Mary might know her father, since you weren't dead. This is why I allowed you to stay for dinner. I knew that this might be her only chance to get to know you, before you run off again." That last comment was meant to rip at the core of his heart. If he even had one.

Alex just watched her. He looked remorseful and ashamed.

"Why Alex? I tried my best to be a good wife. I gave you everything I had. I put up with your moods and your sharp tongue! I put up with you coming home drunk and smelling like other women. I gave myself to you without holding anything back. But you, you broke my heart..." Eliza felt herself losing her grip on the quiet storm she had been raging. It was becoming a hurricane about to let go and unleash an ocean of emotion. But it was too late to try and hold back. The words came spilling out of her heart. A cup running over, a pot boiling over because the fire was too high, a balloon with too much air about to burst...

"I am the mother of your child. I opened my heart and took you into the most sacred part of me. And you crushed my heart like it was nothing! Just a fly buzzing around your ear."

By now she was becoming short of breath and her voice was shaking. She knew that she was on the edge but didn't want to stop. In a flash, in the middle of this scene with Alex, she heard Sal's voice encouraging her to let go, get it out. He always did that for her. She felt him in the room, cheering her on. She allowed the tears to come and roll down her cheeks like tunnels of pain intersecting at the tip of her chin and dropping like a waterfall to her chest.

Alex came to her. First, he stood in front of her looking deep into her eyes, then he took both of her hands into his. He kissed each of her palms and then each finger. Very slowly he crossed her arms over her chest and then pulled her body close to his. He encircled her with his arms and pressed her head to his shoulder. "I'm sorry. I'm sorry. I'm so sorry..." He just kept saying it almost like he was singing a chant. It was as if he believed that if he said it enough times, she would believe him and it would heal her heart. Take away the pain.

She didn't want him to hold her. She wanted to punch him and kick him. But she felt herself melting into his warm and seductive embrace. She heard herself whimpering into his shoulder and her legs began to feel weak under her. Almost on cue, Alex picked her up and carried her to the chair where he had been sitting. He sat down with Eliza on his lap, all in one smooth movement, and began to hold her and rock her and stroke her head. The warmth of the still crackling fire, and their shadows dancing on the walls of the otherwise dimly lit room, seemed surreal. Somewhere in the recesses of her being, she couldn't believe that this was happening. She was with Alex Cowen. Probably the only man she had ever really loved. She allowed herself to liquify into the moment, her head on his shoulder, his arms around her waist.

Eliza awoke with a start. It was dawn. Alex was wide awake and staring at her. "Oh. I fell asleep." Eliza felt a bit dazed.

"You did. I am glad you got some rest." Alex looked like he had not slept.

"You've been awake all this time?"

"I have. I just wanted to look at you. To watch you breath. It's been a long time."

She didn't know what to say, so she said nothing.

"Eliza, I meant what I said. I am going to tell Charlotte about you and Mary. I will have to still take care of her and my children. But, I want to do what I can, what you will allow me to do for you, Mary, Willie and Hattie."

"Alex. You go and do what you have to do, and then we can talk. Honestly, there's a lot of dust on the footprints behind us so I am not sure I can trust you. But time will tell. Your deeds will prove whether or not I can take your word seriously." She didn't know what to believe but at this point, she felt she had nothing to lose. If he came back, okay, but if he didn't, it would be life as usual.

This was about the time in her life, when Eliza accepted a certain fact about herself, her path, and her fate.

The Secrets of Hattie Brown

This is a portrait quilt made by the author. It depicts her grandmother Hattie Brown. Portrait quilting is an intricate and challenging art form. Barbara had to learn the skill set required because, although she is a quilter, as was her mother Sudie Brown, she had never made a portrait quilt. This quilt is based upon one of the only two photos of Hattie that the Brown Family has, because of the fire that destroyed everything a few months after she died. That original photo, which was the i inspiration for the quilt, is of Robert and Hattie together. Since she died in 1931, it is certain that the picture was taken before then.

Between the Books

A note from Hattie

You see why I am proud of my mama? You see how powerful she was? So many challenges, so many broken dreams, and she just kept right on moving forward. My soul looks back and wonder how she got over so many disappointments. Sometimes I would ask her questions about her life because I wanted to know more. She would always dismiss my queries with an "Aww that ain't nothin' for a little girl to be troubling herself about." And then, when I was a grown and married woman, I asked her and she was more explicit:

"Mama. Tell me more about who my daddy was?"

She was blunt. "His name was DICK."

She knew that would shut me up. Finally, I accepted that much of her past was so painful that she didn't want to resurrect it with reminiscence. I stopped asking.

However, I can speak about what I saw with my own two eyes. I spent my early years watching my mama and Alex Cowen reconstruct their broken relationship. Through the eyes of a small child, I saw affection in the way they looked at one another. It made me feel safe. My mother's face lit up with delight whenever he came home. Then there was a tinge of sadness whenever he left, which she tried to conceal but I saw it. I often wondered why Alex stayed with us for long stretches of time, and then he was gone for long stretches of time. But, answers to questions such as that were not children's business, back in those days. One thing was clear to me. Alex Cowen owned a piece of the real estate that was my mama's heart, and no thing or no body would ever inhabit that space, besides Alex and Eliza.

This part of my childhood kind of went by in a blur. The most I can tell you is that during that five or six years, at the end of the 1800s, my brother Andrew, and baby sister Emma were born, and Alex died.

In those days it seemed like just about every week somebody we knew was dying of pneumonia, the flu, or tuberculosis. I overheard mama and Marshall Mason talking about how Alex got sick with the flu, and in a matter of days he died. He had gone to visit his "other" family when this happened. So, mama never got to say goodbye to her beloved Alex. He just left one day and never returned. Mama would, for the rest of her life, refer to herself as a widow. Alex's widow. She lived and died as Eliza Cowen. All of her children, including me, carried the name Cowen. It speaks to the fact that in her heart, every man she had been with, was just a place holder for the love of her life.

Alex's death was sad because he was a fine man after all was said and done. He loved my mama and he took good care of all of us. More globally, it was sad because another colored man who had big dreams, and the intelligence to realize those dreams, had died with shattered aspirations lying at the foot of his grave. Each broken shard symbolized another aspect of his birth into a time period and a society that barred him from the achievement that he craved. He had left mama when Mary was a baby and shined white people's shoes while they called him George on the railroad. All in pursuit of his dream to be a whole loaf where only crumbs were being offered. My mama knew better than any other human being alive, how Alex saw himself and his potential for greatness, versus what America would allow him to become. This was an itch that could not be scratched by our people, who were at this time less than fifty years after the end of enslavement.

I think you're ready to hear my story. You have met my mother and know of my siblings. Now, you will understand some of the choices I made for my life, and the ways in which I chose to deal with the consequences of those decisions.

Book Two

Hattie Cowen Brown

Chapter Twelve

"A B C D E F G, H I J K L M N O P, Q R S, T U V, W X, Y and Z, Now I know my ABCs, next time won't you sing with me!" The children's voices resonated loudly when they sang 'Sing with meeeeeeeeeeeee!'

"Sing it again," said the teacher. And the recitation restarted...

Ten-year-old Hattie Roberta Cowen stood in the back of the classroom filled with white children seated on wooden benches. She sang along, but more to herself than as a part of the ensemble of students' voices. She was there to keep an eye on Joseph, the teacher's four-year-old son. He was small to be in school, but Mr. James Lucas wanted his son to get started early with his pursuit of reading and writing skills.

Hattie knew her place. She was allowed in the classroom because she was a servant to the Lucas family. She watched Joseph and helped Mrs. Lucas with the other two smaller children after school. She lived with the family and her food and board were her salary. Eliza lived in the house just up the road. She was the laundress for the Lucas family, and also the midwife who had delivered their children.

After Alex's death, Eliza's family struggled to make ends meet. Finally, she was obligated to downsize. She moved to a rooming house, found a "situation" where Hattie could live and work, and sent Andrew, Emma, Willie and Mary to stay with a family friend.

Hattie preferred to live with her mom and missed her mom. But Eliza had explained to her that this experience would give her the chance to learn how to read and write. This was something that nobody else in the family knew how to do.

Her mom had consoled her, "You will see me most times every day when I come to do the laundry. When you have a day off on Sundays, we can go to church. You will see Andrew, Mary, Willie and Emma, and you can come and have dinner with me. You know I'm only ten minutes up the road from the Lucases." Eliza wanted her children to achieve things that she had not. Hattie understood this, so she did not complain, and she tried her best to take advantage of the opportunity that was being afforded to her. She stood by and listened as her mom negotiated her future.

There was more to it than just wanting to live with her mom. Hattie had witnessed something firsthand when she would go with Eliza to deliver or pick up laundry.

Life in the white world was different. It was a world where people of color had to take on the persona of one who is subservient and sub…well sub everything. Subclassified, subdominant, submissive, substandard, subordinate, sub sub sub. To put it simply, submerged below the surface of their world. It was not subtle it was overt.

Eliza was pretty much in and out of their influences, but when Hattie went to their homes with her mom, she would observe. The servants moved around like ghosts to be seen but not heard in any form or fashion. She didn't want that for herself. To be a 'sub' personality. It seemed unnatural and uncomfortable. This is not how it was when she was at home or at church. There, she was free to be Hattie like all of her siblings, friends, and family members. They were people, not inanimate objects of servitude. But she was obedient and her mom seemed to indicate that this was a means to an end, so she would do it and do it well.

"Miss Lucy, you have had three children in less than four years. I can keep up with your laundering, but don't you need more help with the children?" Eliza was the midwife who had delivered the children. She asked this question a few weeks after the third child was born.

"Eliza, I do need some help. I stay tired and don't even feel like I am doing all that I should. Even with a housekeeper to cook and clean, I still need someone to help me with the babies. If one of them is sick, or not sleeping well, then the other two don't get the attention they need."

"I think I have an idea. My little Hattie was a great help to me when my baby Emma was born. She could be your helper for the children," Eliza suggested, having thought this out carefully.

"Well Eliza, that sounds good to me. I will have to ask my husband, just to make sure we can afford to hire another helper."

"Well how about we exchange room, board, and a place in the back of your husband's classroom, for Hattie's help with the children?" Eliza knew exactly what she was proposing, a better future for her girl, an education. That was worth more than a few coins.

Lucy was the granddaughter of a wealthy plantation owner who had owned dozens of enslaved Africans. She was born with a silver spoon in her mouth, which had become somewhat tarnished by her marriage to James Lucas. He was educated, but not from a family as wealthy as his wife's.

Down to the DNA threads pulsing in her body, Lucy was one who craved servants to do her bidding. Eliza's proposition sounded like a win-win to her.

"Eliza, I like this idea very much. And Hattie is such a good little girl. I will discuss it with my husband and let you know tomorrow when you come for the laundry." There was an edge of excitement in the sound of her voice. Eliza knew that this meant she was going to INFORM her husband. That's what it meant when a southern lady said she would "discuss" something that she wanted.

And so, it was that Hattie became a boarder at the home of James and Lucy Lucas in 1899, as well as a student standing in the back of the classroom where Mr. Lucas taught the children of the local white families. If any of the parents questioned why a "lil yalla nigga gal" was in the same classroom with their child, Mr. Lucas would explain that he had his hands full with all of the children in the room, so he had engaged Hattie to be responsible for his son, who was too small to be there without supervision. That explanation pretty much satisfied them as long as they were sure that she would not be a part of the social activities and therefore interacting with their progeny.

Hattie was a light skinned colored girl with highlights of brown and red gold in her complexion. Her hair mimicked the curl pattern of Sal', straight, curly long black thick ropes that hug on her shoulders if she did not tie them up. Her brow was like a canopy over the nose, which was straight and snubbed down at the tip. Hattie's body spread out below those honey colored piercing eyes, long for her ten years of age. The fabric of her ankle length dresses danced around her ankles when she walked or ran. Hattie wasn't just pretty, she was beautiful.

Hattie's charge, Joseph, was as dull as a broken pencil point. He had about as much interest in learning letters, as a catfish is interested in eating barbecue ribs. He would only feign attentiveness when he saw his father give him the "pay attention or I will beat your behind" look. Then he looked totally engrossed. But in truth, the words of his father, the teacher, were flying in the air above his head, like a swarm of bumble bees looking for blossoms to pollinate.

One day when they were walking home from school, Hattie asked him, "Joseph. Why you don't pay attention and learn your letters? You gon' be in trouble when your papa finds out that you can't even sing the song right."

"I wanna play with my toys in the yard. Why I gotta go sit in that ole room all day. Those kids don't even like me," Joseph whined.

"Well you better learn your letters. Otherwise he gonna make you study in the evening instead of playing with your toys. You can't win this one Joseph." Hattie also knew that if he wasn't learning, she might get blamed for his failure.

"Nooooo. In the evening! That's my free time! You think he would do that Hattie?" Now she had his attention.

"I know he would do it. Beside's he wantin', I mean he wants, you to learn. It's embarrassing to know that the teacher's own son is not learning nothin', I mean not learning anything in his classroom." Hattie was surprised that she was self-correcting her grammar. Guess mama was right. This school room experience WAS a means to an end. She was learning how to speak like somebody with book learnin.

"No Hattie. Please help me to catch up. I will try, if you help me."

This was how Hattie was able to justify HER study time in the evening. She was "helping" Joseph for a short while before his evening play time. At the same time, she was reinforcing her own knowledge of the fundamentals of reading and counting.

After school and before their evening study time, Hattie had to help the cook prepare dinner and then bathe the other two children to prepare them for bedtime. She was literally working from the time she got up in the morning, until she rested her head on the pillow at night. Her bed was a pallet on the floor next to where little Emma, the youngest of the three children, slept. Emma was still a toddler and had the tendency to awaken during the night for no known reason. She just wanted somebody to rock her. This was also Hattie's job. She had to get up, sit with Emma, and rock her until she went back to sleep. This was the life of Hattie Cowen at age ten.

By the time Hattie was thirteen, she knew everything there was to know about taking care of the Lucas' three children. They all loved Hattie and truthfully preferred her company to that of their mom or dad. Joseph was now eight, Huger was six, and Emma was five. Hattie played with them, sang to them and told them stories. Sometimes she would point to a rabbit running across the yard, or an ant crawling on the ground, and make up stories about them. The children would giggle with delight when she did this.

"Ooh! See that there rabbit running across the yard?" Hattie pointed at the little brown rabbit scampering in the distance. "Why do you think he is running?"

Joseph liked to show that he was the smartest, since he was the oldest. "He is chasing a butterfly!"

"Where Joseph? I don't see no butterfly," Emma asked

"He feels happy and he just want to run!" Huger suggested, while saying the word run as if he himself was running and happy to be doing so.

Now Joseph wanted to get back at them for not going with his story line. He said, "What he got to be happy about? He jus' a rabbit."

Hattie would let them sort it out and then she would resolve the conflict with her story. Truth was, whatever they suggested was gonna be the "wrong" answer. Because Hattie's objective was to get them interested and then she would make up her story using bits and pieces from their ideas. But, they never caught on to her little tactic.

"So that rabbit, his name is Sam. A few minutes ago, he saw a butterfly while he was sitting in the bushes over there. The butterfly said, 'You can't catch me!' In a tiny butterfly voice. Sam said, 'You stupid butterfly. I am faster than you! I am a rabbit' The butterfly repeated her challenge, 'You can't catch me!'. Sam jumped up to reach for the butterfly, and they took off. It wasn't long before Sam realized that the butterfly had made a fool out of him because although he was fast, he could not fly. Butterfly was right, he could not catch her. Instead of following the butterfly and making a fool of himself, Sam ran in a different direction, leaving the butterfly go on about her butterfly business. That's when we saw him right there. By that time Sam was just running because he was happy to be a rabbit with fast feet and fast legs, and he just wanted to ruuuuuuuun! She looked at Huger when she said this part of the story. Then he ran home to his mama and he told her what had happened. She told him that he should not be sad that he could not fly. Cause he had a lot of other things to be happy about. He was just a rabbit, but he was freeeee, (Hattie spread her arms wide like eagle's wings) and he had plenty of wonderful food to eat around the forest, and his mama loved him! This made Sam happy and he is somewhere right now, looking for some other rabbits to run with. The end."

All three children were happy. "Yay!" They clapped their hands and waved them in the air. "Tell us another one Hattie!" screamed Emma.

"So, tell me Joseph, what can we learn from Sam?"

Joseph knew what she wanted him to say, but he was rebellious. "I don't know. I can't learn nothin' from a rabbit." Joseph spat the words

Huger chimed in, "We learn that we should be happy with how we was born and don't let nobody fool us into wanting to be somethin' else!"

"Good Huger!" Hattie congratulated him. "Good idea! And Emma, what did you learn?"

"I like Sam. He is smart. I learned that we can always change our mind and do the right thing," she said this with such confidence. To make it more compelling, she looked at her big brother Joseph, and nodded her head a single nod in his direction as she said the word 'thing'.

Joseph said, "Shut up Emma. You don't know nothin'"

Hattie laughed at them and with them.

This was how they spent their evenings after dinner and studying were done. Life wasn't perfect, but it was tolerable. That is, until that night when Mr. Lucas came into the room while Hattie and Emma were asleep.

Chapter Thirteen

Hattie had learned how to read, write, and do simple arithmetic during her years of occupying her space in the back of Mr. Lucas' classroom. She felt privileged, as many of the girls she knew at church, including her sisters Mary and Emma, were illiterate. In fact, most of the adults at church relied on someone else to read and write for them. Folks who were literate understood that it was a privilege that called them into service for those who could not read and write. It was not a badge of honor to be lorded over one's family and friends. It was a divine gift to be shared generously. Only by the grace of God did someone find themselves in the position to get any level of education. She had dreams beyond servitude to the Lucas family, and wondered what life had in store for her. So far, she felt like an autumn leaf floating in the air. No longer attached to the tree but no idea where she was headed. She was just waiting for the wind to decide her fate. That cold, blustery wind woke her up one night, while she laid on her pallet next to Emma.

At fourteen, Hattie's body had changed inside and out, since she first came to work as Miss Lucy's helper. The body of a ten-year-old and that of a teenage girl are quite different. She didn't even feel like the same person. First, she had grown to be even taller. Her breasts were like those of a woman, as was her hourglass shape; waist thinner, hips wider, legs shaped like the letter 'v'. Then there was that day that she felt something warm and thick running down her legs. When she looked down, she saw that it was red! Blood! Oh Jesus! She thought she was dying for sure, ran to the kitchen and told the cook.

"I'm dying! I'm bleeding from here!" she screamed as she pointed below her waist.

Cook smiled. "No chile! You ain't hardly dying. Not unless every woman in the world is dying every month..."

Hattie was perplexed. "What do you mean? I'm bleeding! Blood means you have been cut right? It means something is wrong, right?"

Cook helped her to clean herself up, gave her a small bundle of clean white cloth to place over her vagina to "catch the blood," and bid her to sit down in the kitchen. "Just relax honey. You gon' be just fine. I promise you ain't dying right now. I'm gonna send for your mama. She will explain everything to you. Meanwhile here, drink this tea."

That had been a year ago. Hattie laughed at herself when she recalled her hysteria that day. Silly girl. It was her first period, her monthly bleeding. Now she was used to it as it was just a part of the life of being a woman. She was thankful for the cook though. She would have hated to go to Miss Lucy with something so personal.

Miss Lucy had been looking at her differently lately. Sometimes, Hattie would notice Miss Lucy staring at her from across the room. This was noteworthy because most of the time, the children's mother just ordered her around without much interest in who or how she was. Somehow, Hattie wondered if Miss Lucy's attentiveness was related to the fact that her husband had been spending more time outside in the evenings with Hattie and the children during study time. He too, was looking at Hattie differently. She tried to behave normally and not show her discomfort when he was around. But he made her feel like he was looking through her clothes. She felt like Mr. Lucas' eyes were resting on her body in places where they were not supposed to be looking. This made her feel uneasy. It was like a thousand ants were crawling over her body. She wanted to move from his gaze but dare not create a ruckus. It was like his eyes had hands that were touching her and invading private places that nobody but Hattie and her mama had seen. He had a wife. She thought, "Why doesn't he go look at his wife, like that?" She wondered why this was happening. One evening, she saw Miss Lucy watching them from a distance. Hattie, Mr. Lucas, and the three children were huddled over books and papers on a table. Miss Lucy didn't look happy. Her face was turned up like she smelled something bad in the air. Still, Hattie was a young girl; not worldly by any measure. So, she dismissed her discomfort and reminded herself that she was a great weaver of stories. Probably just making too much of nothing.

"Emma lay down!" Hattie was ready to sleep but Emma was still playful.

"Okay Hattie. Hattie tell me a story," she begged

"Okay here's a story. There was a little girl who would not go to sleep. So a monster came and ate her up!" Hattie made an ugly face and a monstrous sound. She knew Emma was afraid of just about everything.

"No Hattie. I mean a happy story. A bedtime story," she pouted, pleading in a sing songy voice.

"No more stories tonight. It's time to sleep!" Hattie was tired.

After a while, she noticed that Emma's breathing became rhythmical and that was the only sound other than Hattie's own breath. Her day was at an end. Now she had her time to enjoy her own thoughts and dream her dreams. This was her favorite time of each day, private moments. She was ready to drift off to sleep when, in the distance, she heard the slish slosh of slippered footsteps in the hallway, moving towards Emma's bedroom. The sound became louder and louder, closer and closer. Miss Lucy had gone to bed early with a headache. Joseph and Huger were already asleep. Cook had gone home. She had last seen Mr. Lucas in his study downstairs before she and Emma came up.

So, most likely it was Mr. Lucas on his way to his bedroom down the hall. She snuggled back under the covers and closed her eyes, ready to go to sleep. There it was again. Slish slosh, slish slosh. Only this time, the pace of the movement had slowed, then stopped. She heard the doorknob turn and the hinges on the door whine softly. Pretending to be asleep was the best thing to do. Maybe he was just having a last look at his little girl before turning in.

With her eyes closed she could not see what was going on. All sound had ceased. She knew that the door had not been closed, so she assumed that he was still standing there. All of Hattie's senses had been activated and she wasn't feeling good about this. Self-talk kicked in. Stop worrying. Mr. Lucas is a nice man. Don't he always slip you candy when nobody is looking? Didn't he tell you that you is very smart for a nigga gal? Hasn't he made you his little helper to teach Joseph when he was being hard-headed? He a nice man. All the children like him. Mr. Lucas don't mean you no harm. Relax'.

Her attempts to calm herself were not working. Hattie was terrified. She was right to be terrified. In her naivete Hattie had no way of knowing about the demon that lived inside of Mr. Lucas. The demon that had been passed to him from his father and grandfather and their fathers before them.

They liked to molest young black girls. They enjoyed abusing their power over these innocent victims. During the time when people of color were property, they didn't have to pretend to be a friend and admirer to get the young lady to trust them. Enslaved girls were raped, often impregnated, and had their babies sold away.

Now that era had ended, but Mr. Lucas was a "modern day" molester. He knew that in order to get near his prey, she had to trust him and even like him a bit so that she would not tell when he did his dirty business. His wife might make life difficult for him if her daddy learned that she was unhappy. Her daddy had financed the building of the schoolhouse and several other projects that James Lucas had needed money for. He needed for Hattie and himself to enter into a sort of private agreement. She would 'allow' him to have his way with her in exchange for special favors, like candy and compliments, maybe a new frock once a year if she was really good. Clearly Mr. Lucas thought Hattie was ripe for the picking, because this is why he had come to Emma's bedroom that night.

Hattie felt fingertips pressed into her shoulder, shaking her as if to wake her. At that moment, she wished she was dead, so he would leave her alone. He knew she wasn't dead, therefore Hattie had to pretend that she was being awakened. She looked up sleepily to see his finger placed over the middle of his lips, pursed into a silent "Shhhhhhh..." he motioned for her to get up and follow him. What choice did she have? This was a defining moment for black girls and women of this time in American history. What choices did they have? Very few, that would allow them and their husbands, brothers, and sons to stay alive and safe. White women had all of the choices in the world. They had only to tell someone that a black man had looked at them directly in the eyes, or said hello in a friendly way, and the next day, his family would see his dead body swinging from a tree. But black girls and women, the choice was tolerance. The choice was humiliation for the sake of staying alive. The choice was spiritual assassination.

So little Miss Hattie, got up and followed Mr. James Lucas. He led her down the carpeted steps and into his study. He closed the door behind her. She was trembling. "What's the matter Hattie? Why you shaking? You cold?"

"No sir Mr. Lucas. I am just wondering what did I do? Why you woke me up and brought me down here?"

"Oh no Hattie," he laughed and spoke just above a whisper. "You haven't done a thing wrong. In fact, I thought it was time me and you had a little talk. My wife took some sleeping pills and the children are out for the night. It's just me and you. Sit down."

Hattie stared at him, waiting for what was next, as she sat on the edge of a chair nearest to the door. He sat opposite her. "Hattie I have watched you grow up into a beautiful young woman, and I like what I see. I think you want more out of life than what you have here, day in and day out, right?"

She played it safe. He thought she was stupid. "Well I don't know Mr. Lucas. I don't know what I want. I guess I want whatever my mama tell me to want." Ha! Yeah! Remind him about Eliza Cowen. White folks respected mama and knew her to be somewhat fearless. Maybe that would jolt him.

"Well Hattie, you almost grown. You got to start thinking for yourself. Thinking about what makes you feel good. I can make you feel good Hattie. I can make you feel real good."

Something changed in his demeanor. There had been a shift as he started to talk about how he could make her feel. It was like there were images in his mind that Hattie could not see, but his behavior portrayed what they were, quite graphically. She saw that look she had seen before when he undressed her without touching her. he crossed the room to where she was sitting. Hattie was still dressed in her sleeping gown. It was thin but not sheer. The imprint of her heaving breasts was absolutely visible through the folds of the fabric. The imprint of her thighs was evident through the fabric as well.

Mr. Lucas crossed the room and stood directly in front of Hattie. He said, "I want you Hattie. You so beautiful. I will give you candy every day. When I go to town, I will tell my wife that I need to take you to help me shop and carry some of the items. You will get to go to town at least once a week. Hattie I want you. Hattie I love you!"

She couldn't believe what she was hearing. No white man or any man had ever spoken to her like that before. She didn't even know how to react except that she was feeling dirty and disgusted. This felt like an out of body experience, except before she realized what was happening, Mr. Lucas had pulled down his pants and grabbed her hand to place it on the hard pink, veinous meat dangling between his legs. He had his hand over hers and was using her hand to squeeze that thing!

"Ah yes," he moaned with his eyes closed, chin pivoted towards the ceiling. "You see Hattie. This is how it can be. Don't it feel good?" She was stunned, staring at him blankly.

Mr. Lucas had become somebody she did not now nor never had known. He didn't even seem to see her anymore.

He was calling her name but not looking at her. Then he reached out, eyes still closed, then caressed her breast with one hand, while the other handheld on to Hattie's, squeezing and pulsing his member. "Hattie! Hattie!"

"Hattie! Hattie!" A little girl's voice was calling from upstairs.

Oh God. Emma was awake. Mr. Lucas jumped to attention and pulled up his pants, all in one sweeping motion.

"Go see to her," he ordered as Emma was on her way down the stairs. Hattie ran from the room and met Emma at the bottom step.

"What's the matter Emma?" Hattie asked breathlessly.

"I woke up and you wasn't there. What you doing Hattie?" Emma asked, rubbing her sleepy eyes.

"Oh, don't worry. I just came down for some water to drink. Come on, let's go back upstairs." She took Emma by the hand and led her up the stairs to her bedroom. Mr. Lucas had forgotten that his little girl often awoke during the night looking for Hattie to sing her back to sleep. Next time he would be more careful. Maybe he should keep her at the schoolhouse after all of the children left for the day. Yeah. That's what he would do.

The next morning Hattie got up and prepared Emma for breakfast and school. When she went into the kitchen, she saw her mom there laughing with Cook. Eliza was enjoying a cup of coffee while cook prepared biscuits for the family's breakfast. When Hattie entered they were laughing and gossiping about something that had happened at church the previous Sunday.

Hattie had not slept at all. She kept seeing the scene with that man over and over again. Him touching her, putting her hand on that thing, making her squeeze it. She had washed up as soon as the little girl had fallen asleep, but still she felt dirty. No matter how much she washed her hands, they still felt like she had been squeezing dog shit between her fingers. Would she ever feel normal again? Although this was a secret Hattie would rather keep, she couldn't wait for daybreak so she could get up and tell her mom.

"...And sister, it was a shame how everybody was laughing behind her back. I felt sorry for her." Cook was tickled. "Morning little Miss Hattie."

"Morning mam. Morning mama." Hattie was so glad her mother had come early that day.

"Morning darlin'. How you feelin today?" Eliza looked at her daughter. Right away she knew that the smile was not sincere. Edna had taught her, long ago to see through folks. Certainly, she could read every one of her children, as well as she could see through a glass of water.

Hattie couldn't tell her mom the real truth in front of Cook, so she just said, "Not feeling too well today mama. I think I might be getting a cold. My head is hurting and my throat is kinda sore. You think maybe I could go home with you for the day? Joseph can walk the children to school."

Right away, Eliza knew something was up. Hattie never asked to come home with her during the week. They always had their little chats there at the house while Eliza sorted the laundry.

"Don't you worry," she told her daughter. "I will speak with Miss Lucy and have you excused for today. You probably need some of my special tea from those leaves in my garden."

Hattie was relieved. Her mom spoke with Miss Lucy, took the clean clothes off of the clothesline, folded them and put them away. Before long, mother and daughter headed down the road to the house where Eliza lived. They didn't speak until they were inside of the house and the door was closed. Hattie knew that what she had to tell her mom was not news that anyone else should hear.

She proceeded to tell her mom every detail from the previous night's events. She did not leave out a single detail. When she finished, Eliza's eyes were flooded with tears, and fury.

"Hattie. I am so sorry. I feel so sad that this has happened, and so angry. We have to be careful how we handle a situation like this. If we openly accuse Mr. Lucas, he will say that you came into his study and he told you to get out. He will say that you are lying on him. Folks will believe him, and you will be punished."

"What can we do mama?"

"Well first, I don't want you to spend another night in that house. I will have to make up a reason why you won't be coming back. Then, I will need to find someone else who needs a laundress so I can keep the money coming in without having to work for Miss Lucy anymore. That may take a little longer. Lemme take care of getting you out of there first." Eliza spoke authoritatively but gently, pointing her finger at Hattie as she spoke, as if these were steps she knew well and had taken before.

Hattie later learned that Eliza went to see Miss Lucy and told her that her father, Isaac Betts, was sick in Black Walnut (a little white lie to the little white lady), and her mother Edna was asking for Hattie to come and help with taking care of him. So, Eliza would be sending Hattie to Virginia right away. This suited Miss Lucy just fine, since she loved the idea of removing Hattie from her husband's field of vision anyway. Eliza thanked Miss Lucy for making good on the agreement that had been made five years ago which had enabled Hattie to learn to read and write. And the deed was done. Hattie was no longer in place to be Mr. Lucas' victim. In fact, Eliza did send Hattie to stay with her mom for a few weeks, just so she could recover from the horrible experience with that disgusting man.

Chapter Fourteen

Hattie was a curious girl, always asking questions and looking for hidden meanings, always turning over rocks, so to speak. The best option for her, after the Lucas nightmare, was to spend time with her Grandpa Isaac. He was such a different kind of man. Hattie enjoyed going to the farm with him and having great conversations about anything Hattie could imagine. She also loved being with her grandma Edna. Grandma Edna was sweet and kind and always seemed to know what Hattie wanted even before she asked.

One day when she was walking in the garden with Isaac, she asked, "Grandaddy why did you plant the corn on this side of the yard instead of over there?" she asked as she pointed to the other side of the field.

"Well we pick the place to plant a seed depending on how much sun it needs. Corn needs a full day of light. The sun rises in the east and sets in the West, so this place right here is where it will get the most sunlight on each day." It was his pleasure to share this knowledge with his granddaughter. Since Nelson had died, none of the others were very interested in farming. They would do whatever he told them to do, but their hearts weren't in it. They complained it wasn't fun and would rather play in the yard. Nelson had loved getting his hands dirty and watching things grow.

She would also ask her grandpa questions about the world outside of Woodsdale and Black Walnut. "Grandpa why are colored people treated bad by a lot of the white people? And will it always be this way?"

The Secrets of Hattie Brown

"Hattie, only God knows when that will change and how it will change. But I can tell you that education is important. I have worked hard my whole life, but I never learned to read and write. You do know how to read and write and that gives me hope that things can begin to change with you, your children and their children. Even now there are people working to bring about change. There's a man named George H. White who got himself elected to the United States Congress. That's a group of menfolks who talk about what's going on in the country and make decisions to change things, sometimes. Usually the things they discuss ain't got much to do with us colored folks. But George H. White went to school and became a lawyer. Now, as a member of Congress, he is telling those white men that lynching innocent black men and women should be against the law. So, people who do it should be punished by the law. This is how change begins. People must stand up and say something even if they think nobody will listen to their truth."

These kinds of talks with grandpa were very stimulating to Hattie. They made her aware that the world was a much bigger place than she had ever imagined. Sometimes she felt sad when she learned about how life had been for her people, and sometimes she felt proud to be born into a family that had survived such terrible hardships. She knew that she would teach her children to be strong and independent.

Edna had taught Hattie how to make biscuits using her special recipe and also how to fry hot water cornbread. The cornbread was Hattie's favorite. Edna also took Hattie with her when she went to "catch" babies, as the midwife's work was called, for families around Black Walnut. Hattie loved every single minute she spent with her grandparents. She learned a lot about them, and even more about herself.

Grandma Edna had talked to her about what happened with Mr. Lucas. She told Hattie that this is something that many colored girls and women have had to go through since even before she was born. She told Hattie that it did not mean that she was a bad girl, but that he was a bad man. She should not be angry at herself. And thank Jesus that the little girl came down the stairs when she did. It could have been worse. This comforted Hattie.

Eliza came to get her when it was time to go home. "I have a surprise for you," she told Hattie.

"What mama? What you got for me?" Hattie loved surprises.

"Before we go back to Woodsdale, I'm gonna take you with me to a special meeting."

"Meeting?" Hattie knew nothing about meetings except the ones they sometimes had at church, and they were never for children.

"That's all I am gonna tell you for now. When we get there, I will tell you more."

They took the train to Richmond. When they got off of the train, they walked to a church about fifteen minutes from the train station. It was a big church building standing in the middle of a church yard with an adjacent cemetery. Hattie was all eyes. So much to see. Why was mama taking her to this particular church? They attended Prospect Hill Baptist Church back home. Mama never mentioned being a member of another church.

When they entered the church through the front doorway, Hattie saw lots of activity. People swirling around doing all sorts of things. Everybody seemed busy and involved with very specific tasks.

"Stand here Hattie. I will be right back." Eliza left Hattie and walked across the vestibule of the church to speak to someone who was seated at a table near the entrance to the sanctuary. They spoke for a moment and then Eliza pointed to Hattie. The person she was speaking with nodded affirmatively and Eliza motioned to Hattie to come and join her. They went inside the sanctuary and were directed by an usher to take a seat in a certain section.

They sat quietly as the sanctuary filled up with people. Some sat near them, some sat on the other side in a separate section from them and some sat at the front. These people at the front looked very important and they were whispering amongst themselves. Everyone was wearing a badge that said, "The Independent Order of St Luke" and they had different titles on each badge. Titles like, "Worthy Chief," "Vice Chief," "Senior Conductor," "Sentinel," or "Member".

Here is what Hattie saw and heard once the doors closed and the meeting began:

The Worthy Chief on taking the Chair gives one rap with the something that looked like a wooden hammer and says: "Being about to open this Council, officers take your positions. Vice Chief, you will see that the entrance is closed and properly guarded."

What followed was a series of formalities, none of which Hattie understood. One person said something about the "entrance being closed and properly guarded." Then someone asked about a password that everybody was supposed to know. Hattie didn't know a password. Her mama had not said anything about a special word. Someone walked around and shook the left hand of all present, three times, while each of them whispered something in his ear. He didn't come over to Eliza and Hattie. She guessed he knew that they were not informed. She wondered then, why were they allowed to be there if you were supposed to know some special word in order to be present? Hattie hated not knowing what was going on.

Next, they prayed to God giving thanks for the preservation of our lives and for permitting them to assemble again. They asked to be kept from bitterness and prejudice and malice. The prayer seemed to go on for a very long time when finally he said, "We ask through Jesus Christ our Lord, Amen." Everybody said "Amen" and then stood up.

Hattie wasn't sure what to do. She stood up with her mom. Then Eliza put her hand on Hattie's shoulder and whispered into her ear, "Stay here, and just pay attention. You will now understand, why we are here." Hattie was kind of nervous, and excited, and of course her curiosity was at a mountainous peak. She watched her mother enter the aisle from the row where they sat and walk towards the front of the sanctuary.

"Worthy Vice Chief, this stranger seeks permission to be initiated into the mysteries and enjoy the privileges of our Order," the vice chief said.

"Stranger, what is your name?" The vice chief faced Eliza.

"Eliza Cowen," her voice was strong and confident.

"What is your age?" He asked

"I am forty-four years old," she responded.

"Do you enjoy good health?"

"Yes I do."

"Are you willing to take a solemn obligation to keep secret the forms, ceremonies, entrance words, and other private business of the Order and this Council, of which you now request to become a member?" He asked as he looked directly at her.

"I am willing." Eliza said facing him.

"Stranger, every individual before being admitted to membership in this Order must prove his or her qualification by submitting his character to the scrutiny of those which he wishes to associate with. All those whose characters cannot bear this scrutinizing test of our Order are at once rejected as being unworthy of enjoying its honors, rights and benefits. Stranger, the nearest approach to true happiness in this world is the wisdom, health and peace of mind which flows from a conscious rectitude of mind and conduct. The Great Creator has established certain laws upon which our happiness depends. The fundamental design of our Order is to promote vital piety. You have now been made acquainted with the nature of our obligations; are you willing to learn, practice and teach them, to the best of your ability, as far as you may beinstructed?"

"Yes, I am." Eliza stated.

"Worthy Senior Conductor, you will conduct this stranger to our Most Respected Worthy Chief, that she may receive further instruction." The vice chief turned to face the Worthy Chief and spoke in reference to Eliza.

Eliza was directed to kneel in front of the Worthy Chief and a blindfold was tied around her head. The members came forward and stood in a semi-circle behind Eliza. Hattie noticed that the room became a bit darker and a candle was lit and held by the Senior Conductor.

The Worthy Chief said to Eliza, "Stranger, what seek you here?"

The Senior Conductor told Eliza to say, "Light." When she said the word "Light" the Senior Conductor removed the blindfold and allowed Eliza to look at the candle. Then the lights were turned up bright like they had been before, and the members all sat down in perfect silence.

The Senior Conductor then introduced Eliza by speaking. "Most Respected Worthy Chief, in compliance with the instruction of the Worthy Vice Chief, I present this stranger to you, who seeks for further instruction into the mysteries of our Order."

The Worthy Chief said, "Worthy Senior Conductor, you will conduct this stranger to the alter and place him in the proper attitude to take the obligation of the Independent Order of St. Luke."

The Senior Conductor led Eliza to the altar, and at the same time the Past Worthy Chief comes forward and tells Eliza to repeat some words after him. Hattie could not hear everything they were saying. But it was something about "obligation". Next, her mom was led back to the Worthy Chief by the Senior Conductor, who "introduced" her.

The Senior Conductor said, "Most Respected Worthy Chief, I now present you Sister Eliza Cowen for the second time, who has been duly obligated as a member of this

The Secrets of Hattie Brown

Council, for further instruction." The Worthy Chief stood and shook Eliza's hand. He pinned something on to the white blouse that Eliza was wearing. From where Hattie was sitting it looked like the black satin ribbon that everyone else was wearing. Now everyone stood and The Council sang their song of benediction.

Good night, good night to everyone,
Be each heart free from care,
May every one now seek their homes,
And find contentment there.

May joy beam with to-morrow's sun,
And every prospect shine,
While dearest friends laugh merrily,
And keel in view the sign.

Lord bless the Council,
Keep them all together,
In this sacred temple,
In one mind together here.

In a social band let love and union be
Sounding through creation;
    Come and join with me—
And when we are all done
Meeting here together.

Let us meet together in that Grand Lodge above.
Almighty Jehovah,
Descend now and fill
This Council with thy glory,
Our hearts with goodwill.

Preside at our meetings,
Assist us to find,

Barbara Brown Gathers

True pleasure in teaching
Good will to mankind.

This was the end of the meeting. Afterwards, many people came over to shake Eliza's hand and to welcome her as their newest member.

Hattie wasn't sure what had just happened, but somehow she felt proud of her mama and honored that Eliza had chosen to include her in this special moment.

Mother and daughter were walking back to town to catch their train to Woodsdale, when Eliza informed Hattie, "We have one more stop to make". She turned the corner and walked them through a doorway entering a big stone building that had a sign which read "Saint Luke Bank and Trust Company." Eliza told Hattie to sit in a chair by the door and she went over to a desk where there was a man sitting and writing. There were piles of papers everywhere on the desk, but they seemed ordered, organized. She saw her mom reach inside of her bag and give the man some dollar bills. The man took the money and handed Eliza a piece of paper. She thanked him and turned back to rejoin Hattie as they headed out of the door.

"That place is called a bank. It is owned and operated by the Order which I just joined. A bank owned and operated by colored folks. I put my money in our bank to support the organization, and to grow my money. I have plans for the future which calls for me to spend some money and to save some."

Hattie just didn't even know what questions to ask. There was so much new information to take in.

The Secrets of Hattie Brown

On the train ride back to Woodsdale, Eliza told Hattie about the woman who was the leader of The Independent Order of St. Luke. Her name was Maggie Walker. She had been a poor country girl born in Richmond, Virginia. Maggie had worked hard and been educated all the way through college. She wanted to help people who were less fortunate than herself, which was why she became a member of and then the head of the Order. The Independent Order of St. Luke was a group that helped elderly and sick colored people as well as families that had experienced a death and needed some financial assistance. Now, they also had opened the bank, had a newspaper, and a department store. Maggie Walker was a teacher, so she also felt it was important to teach the children about the importance of education and financial management. Eliza told Hattie that one of Maggie Walker's favorite sayings was, "As the twig is bent, the tree is inclined."

"I wanted to be a part of a group that is doing so much important work for our people. Our church helps out where they can, but I wanted to do more. Plus, you know Saint Luke was a doctor. He was a healer. Since I am in the healing business, I believe I belong in this organization."

"No mama. I didn't know that Saint Luke was a doctor." Hattie had not read the Bible very much.

"Yes. Read the book of Luke in the New Testament. In fact, Miss Reading girl, when we get home, you can read it to me. Ha! I got my own reader girl living in my house!" This was Eliza's way of showing her pride in Hattie's educational achievements. In this way, Hattie began to read the Bible every day. Sometimes she would read out loud to Eliza, and other times she read to herself.

"Mama, thank you for taking me with you to experience these things. I didn't know that you were involved in such an important kind of work. I feel proud of you. I believe you have shown me that I must also be sure to be of service and help people in any way I can. Life is more than just looking at what's at the tip of your nose."

Hattie had learned a lot on this day. She was sure that when she had children, she would not forget Maggie Walker's powerful saying, "As the twig is bent, the tree is inclined."!

Chapter Fifteen

Hattie reviewed the time she had spent in Virginia like a long slow sip from a favorite and nutritious drink. She definitely had a much broader perception of who she was and who she could become; a young colored girl with a voice that could be used to make the world a better place.

Her work every day was now to assist her mom with the laundry she took in. With Hattie's help, Eliza could manage a bigger workload and therefore make a bit more money. They worked together like the gears of a machine. Hattie washed the clothes, Eliza rinsed and wrung them out, and Hattie hung them on the clothesline outside. When they were dry, together they would fold them in neat little bundles and deliver them to their owners. In this way, Eliza's business ran more efficiently than ever before and she was able to increase the number of customers she serviced. All she had to do was tell a customer that she was available to take on new people, and that lady would tell a friend at church. The white ladies were always looking for reliable and honest colored 'girls' to work for them. Eliza had a reputation for being just that. In this way, her savings, although small, began to grow. She was saving towards the goals that Hattie knew about since they had gone to that meeting of the Order of St. Luke. Also, she wanted to get all of her children living with her under the same roof and to save money to buy a small piece of land.

Every evening after dinner and cleaning up the kitchen, Hattie settled on her bed, a pallet on the floor, with an oil lamp and read the Bible. Reading this book was like an adventure for the young curious minded girl. She started with the gospels of Matthew, Mark, Luke and John. Jesus' story and message was very inspiring to Hattie and was helping her to make some decisions about what she wanted for her life.

Hattie enjoyed going to church. On Sundays, Hattie spent the whole day at church. First there was Sunday school. She would sit with the little children, aged six to ten, and read a Bible verse that was aligned with the topic that the adults were studying. Then she would use that verse to make up a story, sort of like she used to do with the Lucas children. This was how she explained the lesson for the day. Hattie always picked one of the children to tell the story to the adults at the end of the Sunday school gathering.

One Sunday after Sunday school, the superintendent said to her, "Great job Hattie. You're doing a great job with those little ones."

"Thank you sir," she responded.

During the church service, she would sit to the side of the sanctuary so that when it was time for the sermon, she would get up and read the scripture to the parishioners. Actually, the pastor could read the Bible. Hattie wondered why he needed her to read it. Then one Sunday after service, he shook her hand and said, "Little Miss Hattie, it's nice to have someone like you to show the other young people the benefits of book learning. I want them to see that if you can do it, so can they. I know how to read because my big brother can read, and he gave me a Bible. We had to work in the fields from sunup to sundown. We would stay up at night while everyone else was sleeping and study those letters and sounds until I had them memorized. After I learned, then I would stay awake by myself, reading the Bible over and over and over again. You gotta want it and be willing to sacrifice to get it. I want these young people to see that in you."

Hattie felt honored and proud. "Thank you, Pastor. It's my honor and I believe it's my duty."

One Sunday there was a special service in the afternoon. Afterwards everyone enjoyed a dinner prepared and served by the women of the congregation. Hattie and the other young girls of the church were the servers, while the older women were in the kitchen heating the food and preparing the plates. She was pouring lemonade (her mom's special recipe) into the glasses on a table filled with many of the younger men of the church.

"That's all I get? You ain't gone fill it all the way up?" Was he joking or serious? Hattie looked at him quizzically. He knew she was confused, so he sent another jab in her direction. "Well I mean, I see his glass is fuller than mine," he said pointing to the glass of the boy seated on his right side, who was grinning and enjoying the flirtation.

Hattie was pretty quick though. She came back with, "Well some folks deserve more than others." She gave him a very haughty look, turned and sashayed to the next table, without giving him more lemonade. She left him sitting there holding his glass.

She smiled to herself as she poured lemonade at the next table and wondered where she had found the nerve to be so sassy. Although the experience with Mr. Lucas had been horrible, a byproduct of it was that she looked at the opposite sex differently. She knew that there was something to be "had" with a man of her choosing. Not now, but some day.

Unbeknownst to Hattie, she had just engaged in the first of many tete a tetes with the man who would become her husband and the father of her nine children.

Barbara Brown Gathers

His name was Robert, Robert Brown. His father, William Brown was one of the ministers of their church. His uncle, Trustee Robin Brown, was a highly respected church board member. In fact, the Brown family was like church royalty. There were so many of them and they were all very smart, active in the church and hard working.

His oldest sister, Annie approached Hattie one day after choir rehearsal. "Your name is Hattie, right?" She was quite a bit older than Hattie, tall and very dark skinned.

"Yes ma'am. I am Hattie." Hattie wondered what this was about.

"My brother, Robert, he been talking about you a lot. Says he thinks you're pretty," she said looking at Hattie as if she was trying to get a sub-dermal view of the girl. This made Hattie somewhat nervous. She felt naked under such scrutiny, although she blushed and smiled at Annie. "So, I said to myself, let me go and meet this Hattie and find out what all the talk is about." Annie continued to study her like she was a ripe banana about to be eaten. "Your mama is Eliza the midwife, right?"

"Yes, that's my mama."

"I see. Well are you courtin' anybody? I think my brother wants to come a courtin' but he don't want to ask. He said you got a pretty sharp tongue. He likes that, but he scared you might say no."

"No mam I am not courtin' anyone. But he would have to ask my mama about that."

And that is how it all started. Annie told Hattie that Robert was interested in her, and then, told Robert what Hattie had said. On Sunday, Robert asked Eliza's permission to walk Hattie home from church and Eliza said yes.

"So how was your walk?" Eliza asked her daughter as she entered the house.

"It was pleasant. He seems like a nice fella," Hattie responded. "He asked me if he could walk me home again sometime."

"And you said...?"

"I said I would ask you and if it's alright with you then I would like that."

"I guess it's okay. I don't mind if you find a young man and get married. You are getting older and it is better for a girl to be married and having a family, than for her to be out there on her own. Might even mess around and get yourself in trouble with a baby. I want my daughters to have what I didn't, a man who would stay put and raise their children together. Robert is a preacher's son, so at least I know he came from a God-fearing home."

Late that evening, there was a knock at the door. Hattie and her mom were sewing a quilt. It was one of their neighbors who had been a friend of the family since before Hattie was born.

"Evening Joe," Eliza welcomed him in.

"Good evening Eliza, Hattie." Joe looked very serious. Normally these late-night knocks at the door came from someone who needed a midwife, but Joe and his wife had passed that age.

"I am sorry Eliza. I have bad news." Eliza braced herself and waited. "Marshall Mason is very sick. He been down with a fever for two days. They called the doctor, but his medicine is not working. He says that if the fever don't come down, Marshall is not going to make it. Ella asked me to come and get you."

"What else is happening besides the fever?" Eliza needed more information in order to decide what medicine she should to prepare.

"Well Ella says he woke up feeling very hot day before yesterday and he feels weak. Can't get up and do much of nothin'. He also has a rash on his arm, itching and feels very warm to the touch." Eliza knew what to do.

"Hattie get my bag of medicines and let's go." Before leaving with Joe, Eliza went to her pantry and got two red onions. When she saw Marshall, Hattie thought he looked very sick. She knew he was her brother Willie's dad, but otherwise she didn't know much about him. He and her mom seemed to be very good friends, though. It was not often that Hattie saw her mom look worried and saddened when she was working to heal someone's illness. But this time was an exception. Eliza looked like it was important to her life that she save Marshall's.

Eliza asked Ella for a knife and handed it to Hattie along with the two onions. "Cut each of these onions into three slices."

While Hattie cut the onions, Eliza, Ella, and other family members made a circle around Marshall's bed, bowed heads, joined hands, and prayed.

"Father God, we come to you as humbly as we know how, thanking you dear Father for your tender grace and loving mercy. Lord your child, Marshall Mason is in need of a healing right now. Right now, Lord. Lord touch his body and heal what ails him. Touch his body and break this fever dear God. Lord God Marshall needs you this evening. Ella needs you and his children need you dear God. We know that Marshall is your servant and he will continue to do your work after he is healed and back up on his feet. Lord have mercy on Marshall Mason. You are the master maker and healer of men. You promised dear Lord that you will deliver us from evil, like you delivered Daniel from the lion's den. Lord, we know that you are able to heal the sick, make the lame walk, and open blind eyes to see. Father God we pray you send a special healing touch from heaven down to Marshall this night Lord. We love you, we praise you, we thank you. These and all blessings, we ask is the name of your son Jesus Christ. Amen, amen, amen."

Eliza turned and motioned for Hattie to hand her the sliced onions. She pointed at her bag, "Look inside and hand me the white cloths inside." Hattie looked inside the bag which contained dried herbs, bottles of powders, and vials of dark liquids. Nestled in the corner of the bag were two white rolls of cotton. Hattie took them out and handed them to her mom.

Eliza was standing at the foot of the bed. She moved the patchwork quilt from Marshall's feet. Very carefully, Eliza covered the bottom of each foot with three slices of red onion which she then bound with the white cloth. Once the onion slices were secured, Eliza proceeded to wrap the entire foot. Each one was bundled in white cotton.

The family stood around the bed, watching her work. They didn't know that silently, as she wrapped Marshall's feet, she had continued praying for his healing. She had prayed over the onions and then prayed over the cloths when Hattie handed them to her.

Hattie was so deeply moved. She had seen her mama work many times before, "catching" babies, making herbal medicines for the sick and shut in. This time, she saw a different something. Eliza seemed to be there in the room, but somehow not there. She seemed to be working with her hands yet there was also another kind of work in progress simultaneously. Hattie could not verbally explain what she was witnessing, but in her spirit she saw it clearly. Her mother was a spiritual healer using physical means to carry out her work. Hattie felt so privileged to be able to watch this, understand what was going on, and to be the daughter of such a woman. At that time, of course, Hattie did not know that long after she was dead, two of her sons and two grandsons would become men of the cloth, who did rub oil on the foreheads of those in need of healing, witnessed by parishioners in the churches they pastored.

She didn't know that her children, grandchildren and great grandchildren would become ministers, missionaries, educators, doctors, lawyers and many other vocations where addressing the needs of others was their primary passion in life.

Needless to say, by daybreak the next morning, Marshall's fever had broken and he was calling for some grits and bacon. His wife Emma and their children were elated and singing the praises of one family beloved friend,

Eliza Cowen and her assistant who cut the onions, daughter Hattie.

Hattie asked her, "Mama, did you know for sure that Mr. Marshall would get better?"

"I have been doing this for most of my life, like my mother before me. It is a special gift. I know that if it is God's will for a person to live, then I can heal them because God tells me what to do. Marshall now has more time with his family and friends, by His grace."

Hattie thought that was so awesome. "Mama I want to help people and be of service. What is my special gift, passed down from you and Grandma Edna?"

Eliza looked at her daughter with a twinkle in her eyes, "Just keep a livin' honey. Just keep a livin'"

Chapter Sixteen

"Hattie! Can you go outside and get me a diaper off of the clothesline?"

Hattie's big sister Mary was visiting with her baby daughter Margaret. Mary had married a man named Sam Obey and they had already started a family. The Obeys lived in the house next to Eliza, and of course, they all attended the same church.

"Here you go Mary." Hattie looked at the mother and baby with thirsty eyes. She loved children, especially babies. "You need anything else Mary?"

"No. That's it. But you wanna hold her? She is full and dry now. All she wants is some rocking and playing." Mary knew that Hattie would love this.

"Sure!" Hattie carefully took little Margaret into her arms and gingerly perched on the edge of a nearby chair.

"Relax Hattie. She ain't gon' break," Mary laughed.

Hattie gazed lovingly at her niece. She was so little, so soft, so new. Hattie loved how Margaret smelled, like a tiny fresh and clean gardenia blossom. The little round face looked up at her and smiled. Hattie loved this tiny bundle of sweetness. But, even more transparent in her mind was that she wanted to have many babies of her own.

Speaking of that, Robert Brown had become a regular visitor at Hattie's house. He had asked Eliza for permission to "court" Hattie some months earlier. Since then, he walked her home from church on Sundays and after Wednesday prayer meetings and always stayed for Sunday dinner. As time went on, Robert would often come by their house some evenings after he finished his farm work. They would sit on the porch steps and talk about all sorts of things. He liked Hattie because she seemed to be so mature and smart. She liked Robert because he was manly and flirtatious. She felt like a woman when she was with him. Not just a female, but a woman; attractive and desirable. He looked at her like she was dessert after a good meal. When she spoke to him, he seemed to listen so intently. He would say things like, "That's why I like you so much Hattie. You a smart gal." She would blush.

One evening when Robert came Hattie was still in the kitchen with her mom finishing up the dinner preparations. He spent time outside talking with her brother Andrew. They liked one another.

"Man, how you doin'?" Robert asked. They sat on the porch. Hattie came out and handed them each a glass of her mama's iced tea. "Thank you, Hattie," He gave her one of his enigmatic smiles.

She flashed a quick smile at him and dashed back into the house.

"I'm good. What's new with you Robert?" Andrew asked.

"Nothin much. Hey, are you gonna play in the church baseball game this Saturday?"

"Yeah. I am thinkin' I wanna do that. In fact, looking forward to it. These guys ain't ready for me and my right arm!" He bragged.

"You probably right. Why don't we play on the same team? That would be so much fun. We can beat them down to a pulp." Robert was enjoying this.

"Perfect. In fact, did you hear about that colored fella from Ohio? That Catcher who is playing in the American Professional League?"

"Yeah," said Robert. "I think his name is Walker…Moses Fleetwood Walker. Is he the first one of us to play with them? "I still can't believe it. A colored man playing professional baseball!" Andrew threw up his hands in amazement. Just then they heard Eliza calling, "Y'all come on in here and eat."

"Okay mama. Right away." Andrew rose, taking his empty iced tea glass with him, and headed into the house followed by his sister's boyfriend.

The following week, Robert showed up after work. He looked tired but when he saw Hattie, his demeanor seemed to lift and brighten. "Evening Robert. How was today?"

"Girl they worked me to the bone today! I am beat. But still, I had to come and see my girl."

"Awww. It's good to see you. I am glad you came. Dinner is ready so come on in." She said.

After dinner, Robert said, "Miss Eliza, that sure was some good food. Your collard greens taste like my mama's greens. I didn't think nobody could make greens as good as Hannah Brown's. Thank you so much. I am about to head home now. It's been a long day."

The Secrets of Hattie Brown

Eliza said, "You're welcomed Robert. I'm glad you enjoyed it. Before you leave could you go out to the shed and help Hattie to bring two bundles of firewood for me? Just put them on the porch."

"I'd be happy to do that for you Miss Eliza". He said

It was dusk. As they prodded to the shed in back of the house, the only sound was the crunching of leaves under their feet. The air was crisp and smelled fresh like the pine trees that were all around them. When they entered the shed, it was hard to see because daylight was waning.

"Where's the wood pile?" Robert asked.

"It's over here. I wish Andrew had bundled it better. It's gonna be hard to…" Hattie had turned to head towards the silhouetted pile of wood in the corner, when she felt Robert's hand on her arm. She stopped, almost scared to turn around.

"Hattie." he said. There at a moment when the whole world stopped, there in the approaching darkness Hattie Roberta Cowen was frozen. That spell was broken when he called her name again. This time it was softer, more sensuous, like rabbit fur. "Hattie. Come here. Come here baby." Robert said sweetly.

Ooh, nobody had ever called her baby. Hattie knew what was about to happen, but she didn't know how to proceed. What was she supposed to do? She turned around to face him. She could see the outline of Robert's head and could feel both his hands now holding her arms. Her hands were clasped in front, feet planted squarely on the dirt floor.

"Hattie, I like you a whole lot. You know that right?" He said

"Yes. I do. I like you too Robert." She said as she felt his grasp on her arms tighten.

"I have been wanting to kiss you since that first day I saw you at church. I been waiting Hattie."

It felt like he wanted her to say something, but she couldn't. She had never kissed a boy and she had no idea what was appropriate for a girl like herself. Did 'nice' girls kiss boys? Robert reached down and separated Hattie's clasped hands. He lifted her hands and put them around his waist. She allowed it. But when he pulled her closer, it threw her off balance and she stumbled into him. So unceremonious! Ugh! Embarrassing and clumsy. But he quickly made it all right by chuckling aloud.

As she joined him by making it a moment of humor, he said, "Yeah, you fallin' for me baby. Hattie, can I kiss you Sweet Hattie?" His voice was becoming raspier and more urgent.

It was dark, she could not see him, but she could feel his breath on her face. She did not speak, but she tightened her grip around his waist, and that was her 'yes you can.'

She felt Robert put his arms around her back and he pressed his body so close, that she felt his heart beating. It was beating hard and fast. For a moment, they just stood there in that embrace, cicadas singing outside, stars twinkling, breeze breezin'.

When Hattie felt the softness of Roberts lips on her ear, she gasped. It felt so good and so gentle. The next kiss was on her cheek. He was working his way to her mouth in smooth gliding movements. Little kisses and pecks, tracing a path to her waiting, desirous, open mouth.

Just before he kissed her mouth, he squeezed her harder, closer to him, and he said, "Oh Hattie. My beautiful, sweet Hattie." When Robert's lips pressed against hers, Hattie thought that they might elevate from the ground and just float away. She wanted to breath him into herself, crystallize this moment in time. Make it endless. The kissed lasted until they were both out of breath and had to end it. Still they continued holding one another, letting go in slow motion.

"I guess we better get this wood back up to the house," he said, his voice still sounding like she felt. Hattie was dazed and felt and reluctant. She did not want to leave the shed and return to life before the kiss. As they were walking back to the house, he said, "That sho was a beautiful kiss Hattie. It felt so good to me."

"Me too. I am glad we did." Hattie smiled shyly

"They put the wood on the porch. Robert poked his head in the kitchen door and said, "Night Miss Eliza."

"Good night Robert," she said.

Hattie saw a look on her mother's face that said, 'Y'all took too long to be just getting some wood.'

After Robert left, Eliza said to her daughter, "Hattie, what is it you like so much about that boy?"

"Well mama Robert makes me laugh and he is a lot of fun to be around." She couldn't say, I like him cause he kissed me real good.

"I see. Well I hope he is serious when it comes to being responsible for a family. I hope he knows that hard work is not a choice, it's a way of life."

It was that night, the night of their first kiss when Hattie learned that her mama wasn't really that fond of Robert Brown as a good choice of husband for her. Eliza saw something in him that she didn't exactly say then, and they never spoke about it again.

After that night, whenever Robert came for dinner, Eliza didn't have to ask him to help Hattie to get the firewood from the shed. As soon as dinner was finished and Hattie had washed the dishes, they would make their way out to make out in the shed.

Autumn's breath chilled the air. It was time for harvesting and there was a lot of work to be done everywhere. Pulling up crops, cleaning the store houses, drying the tobacco and taking it to the processing plants were the main things to be done. The entire community was involved on some level. Everybody, even the mules, worked harder. Then when the harvest was done, it was time for celebration and a little relaxation before the time to start all over again.

Honestly, Robert was not fond of work. But he knew that it was required in order to have food to eat, and his father not badgering him about being lazy. He was the kind of guy who enjoyed talking to girls, eating good food, and fooling around with the fellas. Everything else was just what life demanded and he succumbed. Besides his big sister Annie, he had a younger brother, Hester, and six younger sisters. Robert's mom was his favorite girl.

He was her favorite because Robert had compassion for how much work she always had to do. She got up before everybody and when everybody went to bed, she was still working, cleaning, sewing and preparing the yeast dough for the breakfast bread.

In the evening, Robert was the only somebody who would say, "Mama, I am about to go to bed. You need help with anything?" Or he might just say, "Mama, you want some company while you do that?" She loved Robert because he was thoughtful and considerate.

He adored her and was her first born. He adored her because she always made time for him, even though she had the younger babies. When Robert was upset, either because of a fight with Hester or he was tired of his dad's work orders, he could always go to Hannah. "Aw don't worry sugar plum," she would say. "Don't let nobody steal your joy. You mama's special boy!" She would smile that warm loving smile and it was water to his fire. Only Hannah could calm him down like that. Annie was the daughter of his dad, William's, first and deceased wife. His mom called him her "Big Boy". Everybody at church knew that he was Miss Hannah's big boy, even then at twenty years old.

Needless to say, when the workday ended during harvest time, Robert would quickly run off to Hattie and Eliza's. He wanted to escape before his dad could give him some "extra" work to do. He loved sitting in the kitchen watching Hattie and Eliza prepare the evening meal.

"How you get that dough to be so soft?" he asked Hattie as she was kneading the dough to make bread. Little did she know that her bread making was one more reason why Robert liked Hattie.

"Well it's a combination of how much flour to how much water and then mixing it up just right by pulling and squeezing the dough. It takes patience." Hattie knew she was very good at making bread. She had been taught by her mom and by the cook at the Lucas house.

"I just love watching you. It's almost like your hands are dancing when you work that dough. You seem to be very focused on what you are doing. Almost like it's only you here in the kitchen by yourself."

Eliza had been listening and spoke up. "Well that's how you s'pose to be when you makin food. You gotta think about what you're doing and pray for the people who will eat it. Hattie knows that. I taught her."

Robert was a little scared of Miss Eliza. She seemed to see through him, and he wasn't sure what she was seeing. As long as she let him keep seeing her daughter, she could see whatever she want to see.

They heard booted footsteps outside on the porch. "Hey lil Emma. Give me a hug."

Without even looking up from her kneading, Hattie called out, "Andrew take off those boots before you bring that mud into the house!"

"I know, I know," Hattie's little brother Andrew said as he marched into the kitchen barefooted.

"Well you always forget and then leave a mess on the floor!"

He ignored Hattie. Typical teenage boy. "Hey Robert! How you?"

"I'm good Andrew. How are things going out there?" Andrew was coming in from work on a local farm.

"Man, it's hard out there. One day it's too cold and the next day it's too hot. The mules are too lazy and too slow."

"I know exactly what you mean." Robert liked Andrew. He was a smart kid and he was very self-confident. He loved Hattie but stood his ground if he felt she was testing his 'manhood'.

"Hey mama! How you Willie?" Mother and son smiled at Andrew and laughed at the fact that he was still ignoring Hattie. She laughed too. "You don't have to speak to me. But I know one thing, you better not be leaving behind your dirt for me to clean up."

Eliza had finally managed to put her household back together. Willie, Andrew, Hattie, and Emma were all together again, living under the same roof. Of course, Mary was married and lived with her husband, nearby. Soon he would get a job at a tobacco factory and they would move to Reidsville.

Robert felt very comfortable being around Hattie and her family. Hattie was his "main" girl. Of course, there were a couple of other girls at the church who he would flirt with. They figured if he was flirting, then he was still looking. Hattie knew he was a flirt, but as long as he kept looking at her like that when he watched her making bread, she knew he wasn't going nowhere! Those girls could forget it. Robert was hers.

Barbara Brown Gathers

Fall was a good time. A happy time, a prosperous time, a festive time.

Normally springtime brought warmth and sunshine, but this spring the chill would linger. The winter had been cold. Very cold. Cold was the weather, and cold was the climate in the hearts of William, Annie, Robert and Hester Brown. First the baby, Bertha, was stricken with tuberculosis and died in a few days. They buried her and then Hannah, Robert's mother, came down with the same. They worked hard to save her. The doctor came, Eliza went with her ointments and tinctures, but nothing worked. Hannah died. After that, one by one, each of Robert's younger sisters died of tuberculosis. Within a season, the coldest winter of his life, he lost them all. A family of ten had been reduced to only four in a matter of three months.

Robert was devastated. He felt empty, angry, and very sad. Why? How? It wasn't right. He wasn't sure that he could ever get over these losses. Certainly, his life was forever changed. He was no longer a big brother to five little girls, and no longer Hannah's Big Boy. He missed hearing his little sisters singing his name when he came home. They would all run over to him and hug his waist, knees, and thighs, depending upon their heights. His mom had been the buffer of the tension between him and his dad. Now she was gone. How would he navigate those waters? No more late-night talks with his mama, watching her preparing the dough for morning breakfast bread. Then who was he? Truly, Robert didn't know.

Springtime came, and found Robert Brown living in this state of emotional limbo. Most of the time he was just going through the motions of life's daily demands. The only time he felt alive was when he was with Hattie. She was now his passport to a new life. At least with Hattie he felt like he belonged somewhere. Since his mother and sisters had died, the home seemed like an empty shell. Robert's father William was often out doing church work as a minister, and his brother Hester had a girlfriend who he spent a lot of his time with. His sister Annie had married and moved away some time ago. Home was no longer home. It was merely a house.

Chapter Seventeen

Months later, on December 8, 1907 Robert Brown and Hattie Cowen said, "I do", becoming a husband and his wife. Hattie was happy and ready. Robert was happy and relieved. They both had a desired status in the society and therefore, a purpose for living. Love was a factor, but love was not the predominant reason for the bond. Couples married to secure the future for themselves individually and then collectively for their families. They paid a debt to the ancestors who toiled and had limited or no choices to marry and carve out the life they desired. This included the making AND keeping of their children. Ironically, the wedding ceremony took place in the home of Charles Lawson who would later become the father in law of their unborn son, Lander.

"Good morning Mrs. Brown," Robert said.

"Good morning Mr. Brown," Hattie replied with her cheeks still flushed. Deflowering felt like an intrusion. It was work, and it was painful. However, Robert had been gentle and took his time with kissing her and touching her in ways that made her feel willing to submit to the what simply felt like an intrusion. Afterwards they had slept, wrapped in each other's embrace.

"How you feeling?" he asked as the rising sun shone on her face.

"I feel good. I feel like I'm Mrs. Robert Brown," she sighed.

"No. I mean how you feeling down there." He gently rested his hand below her stomach.

"Not bad. I ain't in pain no more."

"Ready to go again?"

"I'm ready," she said blushing.

Robert was excited and anxious to make love to his wife. Their wedding night had been wonderful, but not really about love making. He could not allow himself to be fully expressive because Hattie's virginity was something that needed attention and care. He knew that if she was going to enjoy being his lover, the first time for her had to be right. She had to be introduced in a way that would invite her to like doing it. Some girls were all but raped on their first night with their new husband, and therefore came to see sex as their duty. Women like that were not so much fun in bed. They made the man feel like they were doing him a favor. Robert wanted to have a wife that gave herself to him as a gift every time. So, he had to be careful and caring with Hattie on the occasion of her first sexual experience. He was glad that he had been fooling around with some of the girls who let him have "his way" with them. Now when it was important, he knew how to proceed.

This morning was his turn to pleasure himself AND his bride. He kissed Hattie on the forehead, on her nose, and then on her lips. She looked into his eyes and saw his desire for her. This made Hattie feel like she was the only woman in the world and that Robert was the only man that there was.

This time, she felt no pain, only ecstasy. Robert had started out slowly, kissing her, touching her everywhere on her body, opening doors, unlocking secrets. He suckled her breasts and kissed in between them. When finally, he entered her private place with his swollen hardness, she was relieved and desirous. His movement was slow at first and as the momentum increased and became more urgent, she felt something so blissful, so delightful. Both Robert and Hattie were caught up in a euphoric state that was enchanting. Passion was mounting, sweat was beaded and rolling, breathing was heightened, bodies were moving in sync.

A knock on the door suddenly interrupted them. "Robert! Hattie!" came the voice of one of the mothers of the church.

Robert cursed, "Shit." He uttered. "Just a moment," he called out as he and Hattie scurried around trying to get their clothes on. It took a minute or so before he could open the door.

"Mornin' son. We cooked breakfast for you and your bride," one spoke up. There were three other women from the church, standing behind her holding baskets covered with plaid cotton dishcloths. Robert could smell the biscuits. "Normally it is something that your mother would do. Since she is has gone on to be with Jesus, we thought it is our duty to carry on."

"Oh, thank you Mother Jones. We appreciate it so much." Robert knew that these women certainly meant well. She was trying to look past him to see his wife inside the house. However, he also knew that his father was now an eligible widow in the congregation. This gesture of kindness would certainly earn some positive recognition from the good preacher, since Hattie and Robert were now sharing a room in the back of his father's house.

"Hattie!" Robert called to his wife. "Come on out and say hello. We have a wonderful surprise this morning."

The Secrets of Hattie Brown

Hattie came to the door standing slightly behind her man. "Well good morning Mother Jones, Sister Brooks, Sister Hill, and Sister Bland." The learned eyes of the older ladies appeared knowing that Hattie had the afterglow of good hot sex first night of marriage. They all nodded and smiled to respond to Hattie's greeting.

Robert was thinking, 'nosy ole biddies, that's all they came for', but he said "You ladies are so thoughtful. God bless you!"

Hattie concurred, "Yes thank you so much." She reached for the baskets with a slight courtesy as she accepted them from two of the ladies. Robert accepted the other one.

"Well," said Mother Jones, "we will be getting on now. Y'all have a beautiful day. God bless you. God bless your marriage." And with that, the four matrons turned and left.

Husband and wife closed the door and exploded with peals of laughter. They laughed at the fact that their lovemaking had been interrupted and how they had to appear to have decorum when they were actually totally flabbergasted. They laughed at the ladies who came in good spirit, yet also because they wanted to see how first morning after the wedding day was looking for the new couple. They laughed while guessing which of the three sisters with Mother Jones, was looking to be a candidate for the next wife of Minister William Brown. They laughed until their bellies ached, and then they resumed their love making. The lovers drank of each other like two thirsty travelers in the desert who had arrived at an oasis. Afterwards, they were thankful that they had biscuits, bacon, hard boiled eggs, and grits to fill their empty stomachs, and refuel their tired bodies.

This was Hattie Cowen Brown's Rite of Passage into being a sexually active woman. It had been gentle, loving and passionate, with a tad of hilarity. Just what her husband had wanted.

"So, Sister Bland, you are going to make the potato salad right? And Nelly, your collard greens are the best. We need to have plenty food to feed our visiting minister and his congregation from Wilmington next Sunday. Sister Lottie can you make some string beans?" Mother Jones was the president of the Women's Auxiliary. It was important to organize the preparation of collations. The church reputation was greatly influenced by the quality of the food they served to guests after a worship service. Folks either went away talking about how good the food was or whispered amongst themselves about how the collards had too much salt, or the fried chicken was not cooked to the bone, or maybe the iced tea was too sweet. Mother Jones wanted to make sure that the reputation of Prospect Hill Baptist Church would retain its standing as a church with the best cooks in the county!

"Hattie, your sister Mary usually makes the sweet potato pie, but she has moved to Reidsville. We sho' gonna miss her pie. How about you make the sweet potato pies? We need at least four. And, Louvinia, you can make your delicious pound cake? Okay, did I forget anything?"

'Whaaat? Hattie thought to herself. She didn't even ask me if I know how to make Mary's sweet potato pie'.

Robert's cousin Blanchie raised her hand, "Yes Mother Jones, what about biscuits?"

"Oh my. How could I forget that? Yes please. Blanchie, can you make the biscuits?"

"Of course," Blanchie said with a very smug smile. She believed her buttermilk biscuits to be the best of them all.

Mother Jones added, "I will make a ham, and Sister Bailey could not be here today, but she will fry the chicken. Who else can fry some chicken?" Two sisters raised their hands. "Great! I think that should do it. Next order of business, please let us hear from the committee of three who visited the sick and shut in, last Thursday..."

Hattie was a bit stunned. She knew how to make a lot of things, but not sweet potato pie. Perhaps mama could help her.

After the meeting, she went to visit Eliza. "Mama we are having a special guest Minister at the church next Sunday and Mother Jones has assigned me to make the sweet potato pies since Mary is no longer available to do it. She just assumed that I know how, but I don't. I can't go to Reidsville right now to see Mary. Do you know how she makes them?"

Eliza hollered. Her laugh was robust like a rooster crowing at the break of day. Hattie looked at her, confused. What could possibly be funny about her request for a sweet potato pie recipe?

Eliza was still laughing when she said, "Ha! Young people. Who do you think taught Mary how to make them pies? You think she taught herself?"

"Mama, you taught her? Oh, I didn't know. I guess I never really thought about how she learned. Just ate up every piece of her pie I could get my hands on. So, you can teach me?"

"Well little girl, making sweet potato pie is not hard. What makes it especially good is the thoughts you're thinking and the prayers you're saying while you are mixing it up. Don't forget. The prayers are the secret ingredient. You know we don't measure much of nothing, mostly pinches and handfuls, but I will try and give you some measurements at least for your first time making it. After that, you can adjust it according to your taste buds." Eliza was happy to pass down Mama Edna's Sweet Potato Pie recipe to her middle daughter. "Get a pencil and a piece of paper out of the drawer and write down what I tell you. You do know how to make pie crust right?"

Hattie had the pencil in her hand and was ready to write. "Yes mama. I made Robert an apple pie last week."

"Good. Use the same pie crust recipe for your sweet potato pie, and get you some medium sized sweet potatoes..."

Chapter Eighteen

Oh lord I want you to help me
Oh lord I want you to help me
Help me on my journey, help me on my way
Oh lord I want you to help me

The percussive rhythm of feet hitting the wooden church floor and hands clapping to the beat of the congregational song was moving beyond the four walls of the sanctuary. Hearts sang out, hands here and there waving in the air with heads bowed and eyes brimming with tears. With the start of each new verse, the volume rose and became more infused with emotional calls for God's presence in the moment, right then.

The guest minister in the pulpit was Reverend J. Allen Kirk, a pastor of Wilmington's Central Baptist Church. He had been introduced by Robert's father, Minister William Brown.

"Pastor Kirk is here with us to share a story of faith and redemption. A story that will surprise you if you haven't heard it before, and further enlighten you if you know about it already. Pastor Kirk has been going around North Carolina and many other places to share the details of an event that took place a few years ago, but still trembles our hearts when we hear of it today. For those of you who don't know him, I introduce, and for those of you who do know him, I present, Reverend Allen J. Kirk."

Reverend Kirk stood up to the warm and spontaneous applause of the congregation of Prospect Hill Baptist

Church. He stood at the podium. "Thank you, beloved. Isn't it wonderful to be in the house of the Lord?"

"Yes! Yes!" came replies from the congregants.

"I said isn't it wonderful to be in the house of the Lord?" he said louder this time.

"Yes! Yes!" they said as many 'hallelujahs were shouted around the room.

"I said...isn't it WONNNNNDERFUL to be in the house of the Lord one more time?"

Applause, amens, affirmations of yes, praise the Lord, thank you Jesus, resonated from wall to wall.

"Giving honor to God, Pastor Jones, Minister Brown, members, saints and friends. Truly it is a great privilege for me to be here with you today. I have crossed the thunderous waters of the River Jordan and made it safely to the other side by the grace of our Lord and Savior Jesus Christ. Amen?"

"Amen"

"I want to share the story with you of how we got over. Of how the Lord has once again brought us from a mighty long way. He has never failed us, never left his people destitute and helpless when the enemy has threatened us. I won't be long today, but I will be thorough so that you will understand what took place and why it is important. Our plight is not a new story. The people in the Book of Romans had experienced a time very much like ours. Our text is from the book of Romans, chapter twelve, verses 17-21. And it says: Recompense to no man evil for evil. Provide things honest in the sight of all men. If it be possible, as much as lieth in you, live peaceably with all men. Dearly beloved, avenge not yourselves, but rather give place unto wrath: for it is written, Vengeance is mine; I will repay, saith the Lord. Therefore, if thine enemy hunger, feed him; if he thirst, give him drink: for in so doing thou shalt heap coals of fire on his head. Be not overcome of evil but overcome evil with good. May the Lord add a blessing to the reading of his word."

"Rome was the largest city in the Roman Empire. They had a great influence in the world of that time. But," there was a problem that created a rip in the society. Jews and Gentiles did not get along. The book of Romans was written by Paul, as a letter to the people of both these groups. Paul wanted the people of Rome to remember that God's will is the way and they should behave accordingly."

"This reading from Romans, speaks to how we, the colored people of Wilmington have made it through a terrible thing that happened to us. We know God, and we waited on him to lead us in the direction that he wanted us to go. We didn't follow the lead of our enemies, nah, because we knew that they were wrong, and that is not how God says we are supposed to treat one another. If we acted like them, then we would have been just a wrong as they were. Let me tell you what happened.

Maybe you heard of it as a "race riot" started by colored men. That was not the truth. So often God's people we are lied on and mistreated. But Jesus was rebuked and scorned and taught us how to receive such treatment with dignity and grace. Amen?"

"Amen reverend" is what came from the crowd. They were listening intently. Most were fascinated by the story which they had heard drips and drabs about. They wanted to hear more. Of course, there were those who were thinking, 'here come another one of these colored men talking against the good white folk. He is a man of God and should not be preaching hate.' But they stayed silent and just said 'amen' by the movement of their mouths, not their hearts.

Hattie for one was sitting straight up in her seat and poised for what she knew would give her a lot to think about, pray about, and process. She was also thinking about a surprise secret she had to share with Robert later, after they went home.

"For those of you who do not know much about the Wilmington of ten years ago, let me just tell you that it was a mighty great place for colored people to live. In 1897, over a thousand colored people owned some sort of property. We had our own schools, our own newspaper, our own churches. In fact, there were twenty-two barber shops in Wilmington, and twenty of them were owned by colored folks. We were also very involved with the politics of Wilmington. Many men of color were in high leadership positions. Yes. It was a mighty great place for colored people, Wilmington was.

Now don't fool yourself into thinking that the white people of our city were happy about this state of affairs. They were not. They were angry and wishing slavery had not ended just a little over thirty years before. Many white men of Wilmington had been soldiers, even officers in the Confederate army. They were still angry about losing. The Republican Party had been trying to help us since slavery ended; to get on our feet and become independent. It had been nine years since they had controlled the government and kept the Democrats weakened. Now it was time for the election. The Democrats had fought against every good thing the Republicans tried to do for us. Now they were determined to win in the election that was soon coming.

There were many tactics used to discourage us and to even scare us into not voting on Election Day. It came and went with the white people being unhappy with the results. They wanted the colored people and the Republicans who supported us to get out of Wilmington. They did what they could to stop us, and that was a terrible day brothers and sisters, a terrible day. November 10, 1898, there were many white men who participated in this event. Some of them went to our wealthier colored families and put guns to their heads and forced them to leave town on the train. One of those white men was Josephus Daniels. He stirred up the problems, whipped the flames of the fire by talking to local whites who owned property and held offices.

Josephus Daniels owned the white newspaper. In his paper he wrote articles about how the white people need to knock the colored people down to size. That if they don't do something quick, they will be running white lives. He had cartoons in his paper that showed us as serpents and devils. Then there was a woman, named Rebeca Felton, the first woman ever elected to the senate, who was an important part of this movement as well. She gave a speech and said that white men should "lynch a thousand times a week if necessary to protect white women against the black rapists." This made the white men very angry and even more willing to go out and do something.

That day mobs of over two thousand white men stormed the town. I was in my study at the church, working on my sermon for the next service. One of the deacons rushed into the room: 'Pastor, we need to get out of here. There are white men everywhere in the street. They are carrying sticks and guns and waving their fists like mad men. I gotta go find my wife and children! It's not safe.'

"Immediately I ran out of the back door of the church and made it to my house which was just behind the church. My wife and children were terrified and hiding in a room in the back of the house. We left everything we had and ran for our lives. We hid from the violent mob in a graveyard. The shrieks and screams of children, of mothers, of wives were heard, such as caused the blood of the most inhuman person to creep. Thousands of women, children and men rushed to the swamps and there lay upon the earth in the cold to freeze and starve. The woods were filled with colored people. The streets were dotted with their dead bodies. Every colored man who passed through the streets had either to be guarded by one of the crowd or have a paper (pass) giving him the right to pass by."

"That day, those mobs of white men destroyed the offices of the colored people's newspaper and were trying to kill the owner Alex Manly. They were very angry at him. Manly had responded to Rebecca Felton's comment by writing that white men should take care of their women and that many white women willingly sleep with colored men. That day they didn't catch Manly, but they burned his building to the ground and destroyed his printing presses.

They went on to kill many people of color that day. There is no way to know how many died, although some say as many as three hundred were never seen by their families again. Some who left home that morning, just never came back. They were shooting us down in the streets like dogs, then loading the bodies on the back of a wagon and throwing them in the Cape Fear River. They were screaming that they would 'choke the Cape Fear River with black carcasses!"

Screams of "Jesus, Lord have mercy. Oh lawd!" were scattered throughout the audience as the reverend continued his story. Some just shook their heads in pity.

"After that they had a meeting," he waved a piece of paper in the air, showing it to the congregants. "I know you can't see the writing, but I am going to read it to you. It was posted all around town, 'Attention White Men. There will be a meeting of the White Men of Wilmington this morning at eleven o'clock at the Court House. A full attendance is desired as business in the furtherance of white supremacy will be transacted.' They did assemble that day and out of that meeting they drafted a document called 'The White Man's Declaration of Independence'."

"Many colored men did take up arms and try to fight them, but they were far more armed than we were. Some of us hid in the forest for weeks afterwards. Many fled and moved to Brunswick County. Those who stayed faced racism and large reductions in pay. It was nothing to see a sign posted that said, 'Wanted one hundred workmen whites only'."

"This terrible time in our beautiful town, changed our lives forever. In fact, the next governor who was elected was Charles Aycock. Name sound familiar? Of course, our most recent governor of the state of North Carolina. Aycock was one of the leaders of the white supremacists!"

"I have prayed and asked the Lord, what is my mission. Why did he save me and my family from dying on that horrible day? The Lord has given me the task of going around and sharing this story with those of you who do not know it. The Lord told me to encourage you and to tell you that 'weeping may endure the for a night, but joy cometh in the morning'. Yes, the Lord has sustained us and protected us and covered us with his mighty long arms. From slavery to today, he has kept us as a people and continued to bless us. I am here today to tell you that there is a God, his son is

Jeeeeeesus who died for us, and the Lord will never forget about us.

Our bible text from Romans says, 'Vengeance is mine; I will repay, saith the Lord. Therefore, if thine enemy hunger, feed him; Be not overcome of evil, but overcome evil with good.'

"So, you might ask me, reverend what good can we do to overcome this evil? Well brothers and sisters that is a mighty good question. You might be surprised at my answer. I didn't come here today to tell you to hate the white man...'

"Nah! Hate is not the way," somebody yelled out.

"I didn't come here today to advise you to get a gun and go out to shoot the first white person you see or do something to poison their cows or chickens!"

"What can we do rev?" The crowd was emotional.

"I came here to talk to you about what you are teaching your children. We were on the right track in Wilmington. What has happened is a temporary setback. It is temporary only if you do your job good! Teach your children to be independent. Make sure they learn how to read and write. You should have a classroom right here in the church. Teach them everything you know and then get people who know more than you to come and teach them. Your children should know that their world can be as big as they are willing to make it. There is no limit to what they can create if they are willing to work hard and be disciplined. We can't give up beloved. That is what the enemy would want us to do. The Lord sent me here today, to tell you, yes, that you can repay the evil with good. Yes! Raise your children to be proud of who you are, of who they are, of how far we have come in spite of the perils we have faced as a people and determined to become an example of the greatness of what the Lord can produce. We are an intelligent people. We are a talented people and we are truly a blessed race of people. Amen?

"Ayyyyyyymen! Yes Lawd!" People were rocking, and waving their hands in the air, and looking around at one another nodding in approval. Even the nay sayers were now participating in the revelry. They could go along with what he was saying. It was about the children, not about hating white folks.

Reverend Kirk was a bit winded, sweating and moving back and forth across the pulpit. It was clear that he was very much invested in his God given mission to infuse the parents of colored children with the spirit needed to raise their children as good Christians and progressive people of color. "In conclusion, my brothers and sisters, I would like to leave you with the word of God as a road map to get where we need to go. Deuteronomy, chapter six, verses 21-25 tells us; Then thou shalt say unto thy son, We were Pharaoh's bondmen in Egypt; and the LORD brought us out of Egypt with a mighty hand: And the LORD shewed signs and wonders, great and sore, upon Egypt, upon Pharaoh, and upon all his household, before our eyes: And he brought us out from thence, that he might bring us in, to give us the land which he swore unto our fathers. And the LORD commanded us to do all these statutes, to fear the LORD our God, for our good always, that he might preserve us alive, as it is at this day. And it shall be our righteousness, if we observe to do all these commandments before the LORD our God, as he hath commanded us.

"Raise your children thoughtfully, brothers and sisters. They can't raise themselves. Raise your children to be independent, to be wise, to be children of Almighty God. If you have children, this is your divine appointment. Do this well and when you close your eyes and you are a citizen of this earth no more, the Lord will embrace you and welcome you and say, well done my child, well done."

As Reverend Kirk returned to his seat behind the roster, Minister William Brown came forward while the congregation gave Reverend Kirk a standing ovation for his wonderful sermon. "Let the church say amen."

"Amen!"

"Let the church say amen again!"

"Ayyyyyyyymen," voices sang out.

"Did you enjoy the message that was brought to us by this man of God today?"

"Hallelujah, yes Lord!" There was more applause

"Well now is the time for us to show our appreciation and help him to continue his work. Please give what you can. Deacons, please come forward and prepare us for our offering."

After church service, the collations were delightful. The atmosphere in the church dining room was festive and neighborly. Clearly Reverend Kirk and his church members totally enjoyed the cooking of the sisters of Prospect Hill Church. Hattie's Sweet Potato Pies were a huge success, and there was not a crumb of crust left when the meal was finished.

Chapter Nineteen

"So what did you think about Reverend Kirk's sermon?" Hattie had been anxious to ask her husband this question since they left the church. She waited until they were home in bed because she wanted his full attention.

"Well he is a good preacher. Seems like a smart man. He been through a lot." Hattie had hoped for more of a reaction, but that was Robert. He was more on action and less on words.

She went with what he gave her. "I felt sad. Every time I hear these stories about how our people are mistreated, I just feel angry. I don't know what to do with that feeling. Reverend Kirk helped me to see that the solution is not quick, but if each of us does what we can, there is hope for us through our children."

"You're right. We each have something that we can do to make things better."

"What do you think about what he said about raising children?"

"Oh, definitely. You gotta teach your children the right ways of the world and also raise them up in the church."

Hattie deep inside was a bit "underwhelmed" by his responses. She had hoped for a stronger commitment, verbally, to something she felt so passionately about.

But she was on a roll, and things WERE moving along, so might as well keep moving towards her ultimate goal, which was to tell him...

"So, who you gon' teach? You got any children?" She was playing with him and he knew it.

"Well none that I knows of. But there could be somebody out there somewhere," he laughed at her and with her. He was sure that Hattie knew he didn't have any children. She was teasing.

She laughed and hit him with her pillow. He grabbed her, taking the pillow from her and kissing her sweetly on the lips. He was about to start up something, but Hattie was not ready for that yet.

"Robert, I went to see mama yesterday."

"Really? How she doin?" Robert wanted to make love, why was she bringing up her mother right now?

"Well she's fine. But I went to see her about me. I wasn't feeling well."

"Wasn't feeling well? You didn't tell me."

"I know. I thought I knew what it was but wanted to check with mama before I told you."

"Yeah, and what she say?" He was wondering if he should be worried.

"She said..." Hattie measured her words and let them out in a slow drip, one at a time, "I...am...definitely..." now she started smiling "most surely"...smiling more and just kind of staring at Robert, studying his face, watching to see how it would change from worried to happy once her next word was out.

"Hattie! Stop fooling now! What is it?" He actually looked worried. Was something terrible wrong with his wife? So many young people died of Consumption and other things those days. Maybe she was smiling to keep a strong face for him to be less upset with the news. "Hattie just spit it out."

"Well mama examined me, and she said that I am definitely three months pregnant!" Whew! She felt relieved to get that secret out! Now she could tell everybody! She, Hattie Roberta Cowen Brown, was having a baby!

Robert's whole countenance morphed from frustration and impatience to delight. His face lit up like the full moon in a summer sky and he grabbed his wife hugging her so tight she squealed.

"I guess that means you're happy," she said with assurance.

"Happy?! I can't think of any one thing I have wanted more than for us to begin our family. I am so happy Hattie!" He kissed her again. This time there was no interruption to his advances. They made love passionately in celebration of their new status, as parents.

Bessie Brown was born six months later, easily sliding out of her mother's womb into the hands of her grandmother, Eliza. A beautiful little curly headed baby girl. For the next nineteen years, Hattie would become pregnant, on an average of every two years, for a total of nine births. She bore five sons and four daughters.

Everything changed. Every single moment of Hattie's day was scheduled with responsibilities either towards her home, her baby or her husband. She knew what it was to work hard. Hard work was a way of life known to Hattie for as long as she could remember. The difference was that this was her "real" life, not working for someone else's advantage. These tasks were significant in the very cells of her being, because she loved everything and everybody she was working for.

Little Bessie was Hattie's mirror image. People would see mother and daughter and go to oohing and ahhing about how "chile you spit her out." Bessie had the same straight curly hair texture, same light complexion, same straight teeth and bright smile. She had long slim hands and fingers like Hattie and really loved helping her mama clean up around the house. Although she was just a bit more than a toddler, it appeared as if she was going to be a tall girl, just like her mother. Hattie was so proud of her little sweetness. She took Bessie everywhere with her. There was no Hattie without Bessie.

Robert was happy that he had a family. The loss of his mother and sisters had left him feeling quite destitute and alone, as far as family relations were concerned. He had been closer to his mother than to his dad. Although William was still around, his place in Robert's life had always been more custodial than warm and fuzzy. Little Miss Bessie was a welcome addition to her father's heart space. She looked at him, smiled, and he was defenseless. He would pick her up and wriggle her over his head. Sometimes she would drop spit right on his face, and he loved it.

"Be careful Robert. She just ate. You gon' make her throw up!" Hattie cautioned.

But Bessie, she had no problem with being the center of his attention and affection. She would scream and laugh out loud, showing every square inch of the smooth pink gums inside her mouth.

"Oh, go on Hattie, she ain't gon' break!" Robert was enjoying himself as much as Bessie.

"Just be careful. She is still a baby. Anyway, mama sent me a message earlier. She wants to see me. Is it okay if I run over to her place and come right back? Bessie is fed and diaper changed. Dinner is done and I will be back in time to serve it."

"Sure. Go ahead. Tell her I said hey."

Hattie reached her mom's house in less than fifteen minutes. Normally the walk took almost half an hour, but she was moving nearly twice as fast as usual. Eliza was not one to summon her, especially since she had a young baby and a husband at home. It must be something important.

"Hey mama. Hey Willie." Hattie found Eliza sitting at the table in her kitchen holding a cup of steaming hot tea. Willie was laying down on a cot in the corner of the room. "How you doin'?"

"Not good daughter. Not good," Eliza replied. Her face was ashen and sallow.

"What's the matter?" Hattie looked around the room. There was a mist of sadness in the air. Mama looked remorseful, and the normally lighthearted Willie, looked broken somehow.

"We got the news today that Marshall is dead," Eliza's eyes were brimming with pools of moisture.

"Oh no mama! Willie! I can't believe this. What happened?"

"He went home to Black Walnut to see his dad. Ella said he had a pretty bad cough when he left home. She tried to tell him that he should stay home until he felt better, because the cough was terrible. She even suggested that they send for me to make him a cough syrup. He told her that he would be fine. It was just a cold. So off he went." Eliza was struggling to relay this story. Her speech was slower than usual. "Marshall was Willie's father, but first, he was my friend. We grew up together."

"Did he make it to Black Walnut?" Hattie asked

"Yes, he made it there, became sicker and took to the bed. They told Ella that he started having chest pains when he coughed and had no appetite. He also had trouble breathing. Finally, when the doctor came, he said it was pneumonia. Marshall died that same night."

"Mama, I just don't know what to say. God bless his soul. Willie I am sorry you lost your daddy." She looked at Willie. He was curled up in a fetal ball on the bed, looking more despondent than she had ever seen him look. "What can I do?" She wasn't sure how she could ease her mother's pain, but whatever she could do, she would.

"Well, Willie and I need to go home for the funeral. They are gonna bury Marshall there in Black Walnut. Can you take Emma and Andrew home with you until I get back?"

"Sure mama. Is there anything else?"

"No. Everything else is between me and The Lord. Marshall stood by me so many times in this life. He was a good man Hattie. He was kind, honest, thoughtful and generous. There was only one Marshall Mason. Only God knows all what he did for me. Marshall knew me like nobody else." She was rocking back and forth and wringing her hands as she spoke. It was so hard to see her like that.

"Willie, where is Emma?" Hattie asked.

"She in the back with Andrew."

Later, Robert looked up from his chair in the front room, to see his wife returning home with her brother Andrew and baby sister Emma. "Hey. How y'all doin'?"

Hattie explained what had happened while she added two more plates to the table setting. Emma and Andrew were happy to be with their sister and the new baby girl. They stayed there for several days, while Eliza went to Black Walnut to attend the Going Home services for the man who had been her friend and the father of her first son.

Chapter Twenty

It was both the easiest and the hardest time in the young life of Hattie Cowen Brown. Loving husband, baby, and home took little or no effort. She felt like it was why she had vacated Eliza's womb at birth. The hard part was that it was starting to feel like the lines between who she was as a person, and who she was as a wife and mother, had blurred to the extent that she was becoming a stranger in her own skin. Exactly who was she now? Roberts sex partner and housekeeper? Bessie's milk supplier, playmate, and constant companion? No problem with any of that, except...as a girl, she had dreamed of some achievements that would affect more than just herself. More than just the circle of people around her. Now, of course, it was her dream to be a wife and mother. What was important to Hattie was to have one and only one husband, father of ALL of her children.

Although she knew that her mom had been through some painful experiences with the fathers of Hattie's siblings, and she knew that her mom was a good hearted and God-fearing woman, Eliza's reputation in their society was smudged because she did not have a husband. Eliza identified herself a widow, but that didn't seem to help very much. Hattie wanted to be admired by people and known for being holy and chaste. Another secret aspiration that young Hattie had dreamt of was to open a small school to teach the colored children of her community how to read and write. She wanted her school to be sort of like the one Mr. Lucas had. As she was growing up and watched her mama feed and clothe them with money earned from her own businesses (laundering and midwifery), Hattie knew that she would one day also start a business of her own. Further, she would teach her children to work hard and to be entrepreneurial in spirit and in deed, so as not have to rely on others to keep a the roof over their heads and food in their bellies.

What about those dreams? Were they the pipe dreams of a child? Or had the meanderings of the young mind been showing her pathways she might travel if she chose? Well, now she had chosen. That was that and she might as well forget those other things because wife and mother is who she was. Unless the good Lord were to add a few more hours to those twenty-four, then she didn't have time for anything else. Hattie would keep this as her seventh secret within herself. There were so many. Maybe, she thought, one day she would at least share them all with her daughters. They would want to know. Women were expected to put family and home first, and not have much of any other interests, except of course, church activities.

Anyway, there was nobody to tell. Of course, mama might understand. She had not forgotten that day she went to the meeting of the Order of Saint Luke. Clearly Eliza also wanted to impact a bigger segment of her world. But outside of mama, most of those other girls she knew were just happy if they got a man to marry them and fill up their bellies with plenty babies. They would think her dreams were a waste of time and downright stupid. Who ever heard of a colored farm girl thinking about things like that? So yes, she would keep this as a sacred promise to herself. But one thing she knew for sure. Her children would be the blossoms of her budded dreams.

Speaking of her children, she was pregnant. Baby number two was due any day. Eliza had come to stay with them to help out with Bessie and other chores while she waited to deliver her next grandchild. Mary already had seven children. With Bessie and this one coming soon, Eliza would have nine grandchildren!

Bessie was three years old now and running everywhere at once. She was talking about everything and challenging everyone's authority, just a little bit. Everyone except of course her daddy, who she both adored and feared. She knew that he loved her. Still, there was a bit of an unpredictable edge in Robert's countenance. Even a little girl like herself was smart enough not to risk incurring his wrath. Bessie had observed that most nobody fooled with Robert Brown. But Robert wasn't around at this time of day. He was out doing farm work, while Bessie played outside in view of her mother and grandmother.

What little Bessie could not know was that Robert had become progressively more and more reticent, and sometimes melancholic since his mother and sisters had died so abruptly. Hattie had noticed that his behavior had become unpredictable, bordering on unstable. Most often, he was the same lighthearted jovial Robert she had met that day at church. But there were those fleeting moments when he would become a stranger. She would look up at him and say to herself, "Ha! Where did Robert go and who is this standing in front of me?"

Andrew had come to stay for a few days with them to help Robert with some chores around the farm. He and Robert were talking over dinner. Their banter was animated and chirpy. Like two birds chattering about how a day in the skies had been. Robert said, "You didn't think I saw you fall down off a that mule out in the fields this afternoon." His voice had a chuckle in it, like he thought it had been a humorous site to see.

The Secrets of Hattie Brown

Andrew laughed, "Oh! You saw me. That old mule. I was trying to move him along and he bucked on me!" Andrew too, was seeing the humor in the moment, now that it was past.

Suddenly, Robert bolted up from the table, and yelled at Andrew. "That was stupid. I don't know what you were thinking. What's wrong with you?! If that mule had kicked your ass you would be of no use to me or yourself for the next week! That was just stupid!" That said, he left the table, went to their bedroom and got in the bed.

The rest of the meal at the table was eaten in silence by the family. Nobody could believe what had just happened.

It was a hot and humid August day in Person County, North Carolina.

"Mama why did you decide to be a midwife and laundress instead of living a simpler life as a farmer's wife?" Eliza and Hattie were outside doing laundry. One could hear the sound of the clothes being rubbed up and down the rippled washboard. It was constant and rhythmical, zoom zah, zoom zah, zoom zah. Eliza scrubbed and rinsed, then handed the garment to Hattie, who wrung it out and hung it on the clothesline. In this heat, the clothes would dry quickly. The smell of Hattie's homemade brown soap was pungent.

"Since I was a girl in Black Walnut, I knew that scratchin and diggin in the dirt was not for me. I even hated feeding the chickens first thing in the morning. My brother Nelson used to help me out so I wouldn't get into trouble with Mama Edna. But I loved helping with the delivering of the babies. I used to pray that my mom would take me along every time she went. The families were always so relieved when she showed up. I knew it's what I wanted to do with my life; help people to feel okay when they were worried and not feeling well. Living life is like growing a tree that bears fruit. Those fruits are the product of the choices we make along the way. If it's bitter, if its sweet, if it makes your belly hurt, it's all about what choices you made while that tree is maturing and growing up. We never stop growing and we never stop making choices. The fruits just keep on a comin'. You know Willie can't get much of a job. He might never have a lot of money. But I always want him to have a place to live, even when I am no longer here on this earth. That's why I saved my money and bought that piece of land, which I have signed over to him.

"I know mama. I am so proud of what you have done. Do you think I am growing good fruits with my life?"

"Well time will tell honey. You been married now for five years? You chose a man to marry and have children with. How's the fruit tastin' so far?"

"Well Mama I love Robert, that's for sure. Most times he is mighty kind and loving. I get the feeling that he don't really like farming but he is doing it because it's the only thing he knows. And mama, truth is, Robert don't know how to manage money at all. We don't have much, and he sometimes goes down to the juke joint and spend money on I don't know what. If I don't take in the laundry to bring money into the house, there are days when we might not have much to eat. I don't complain though. I figure he will wake up and see that he can't do that. We about to have another mouth to feed. What kind of fruit would you say that is?" Hattie actually had no idea how to answer her mother's question, so she just told her what she did know.

"I would say that's a fruit that is a bit sour and hard. Men who spend money on who knows what, when they have a family to feed, don't usually 'wake up'. Ain't nothin' to wake up to. They like it. Just up to the women in their lives to take it or..." Eliza was blunt liked a burnt-out cigar stump. She threw her laundry soaped wet hands up, in exasperation, and raised her shoulders.

Hattie sure did appreciate having her mama to confide in. There were things, however, that she had not shared with Eliza. Things that made the fruit even more sour.

Just then, she felt a wet, warm fluid running down her legs and onto the ground beneath her feet. She looked down as did Eliza. "Okay," Eliza said excitedly, it's baby time." She escorted her daughter into the house and onto her bed. While Hattie began her breathing and resting between contractions, Eliza made a fire and put the pots of water on the stove to boil.

Bessie sat quietly in the corner of the room. She had seen her mother's midsection expand over the past nine months. There was something important and very serious going on, and she did not intend to miss a beat. She watched her grandmother coaching her mom through a certain way of breathing, and through what looked like painful episodes that would come and go. Sometimes Eliza would say, "Bessie hand me that!" Or "Get me that!" Pointing at various items that Bessie had no names for. Finally after several hours, Grandma Eliza started telling Hattie to, "Push! Push! Push!" She was screaming quietly and was very calm. Bessie later wondered if this was how it had been when she was born.

He came bursting out of his mother's womb surrounded by a flood of colorless fluids, still connected by a long round moistened cord. Bessie was astounded!

Grandma Eliza lifted her open palms upward and uttered, "Thank you Jesus! Thank you, Lord."

Robert came home from work some hours later to find Hattie and his new son asleep. She opened sleepy eyes on cue, as if his very presence in the house was enough to arouse her from slumber and looked at her husband with pride and love. As he approached the bedside, she lifted their newborn baby, from her arms to his.

"Your son, Mr. Brown!"

Big calloused brick like hands, engulfed tiny fragile life, "My son. We gon' name him after my cousin and my father, Ernest William," he said kissing the little brown bundle on the forehead.

"I like that. You and Ernest been together like brothers your whole life. And Papa William will be so happy!" Hattie exclaimed.

Chapter Twenty-One

There was a smoky texture to the air. Visibility was clouded by a blue haze through which she could hardly see. In the distance, there was the silhouette of a man. He was big and tall, and he was... Robert! He was not alone but was holding the hand of a woman who wasn't Hattie. They were walking together, then stopped and faced one another. Robert put his hands on the woman's breast, fondled them, then he kissed her. As they caressed one another, he put his hands on both of her buttocks and pulled her into the embrace to close the distance between their bodies. And then there was one silhouette in the mist. The blackened form of two bodies molded together.

She sat straight up in the bed. Abruptly awakening, she had the burning certainty that her dream was more reality than fantasy. This feeling was very discomforting for someone who was already suspicious. She got up and went outside to pray on the porch. The sun was just barely piercing the horizon.

"Morning Lawd. I come to you this morning as humbly as I know how. Lawd, I know you showed me that dream for a reason. Except, dear God I don't know what to do about it. He is my husband. We have two children. Am I supposed to tell him about this dream? Should I show anger? God, how do I live with this? I feel betrayed. People been looking at me funny at church, like they know something I don't. Even his cousin told me that he be flirting with some of those same girls around the church who we grew up with. And now there's some younger ones too. She said I need to watch Robert. Dear God, I don't want to believe it, but it is becoming harder and harder to fool myself. When I married

Robert, I thought it would be me and him against the world. Now I just don't know Lord. I just don't know."

Hattie began to weep. Her heart was hurting. She was seeing the illusions of herself, a young girl in love, being shattered and swept away by a reality that was unceremonious with sharp edges. She paused for a few moments, just staring at the sunrise. Listening for that quiet divine inner voice, that would comfort and encourage her. Then she continued.

"Dear Father God, I pray for you to guide me and help me to walk this rocky road with grace and balance. Lawd I know you will be there always, as you promised. You ain't never left me yet. I will wait on you, for wisdom and for direction. These and all other blessings, I ask in the name of your son, Jesus Christ. Amen."

Whenever Hattie prayed, she was comforted immediately. The solution might not be long term, but it would get her through that day. It felt like the Lord was telling her to bide her time. Just be watchful and silent for the moment. Her heart was relieved and found a modicum of peace in the fact that she had her God as a guide and master.

"You okay?" His voice startled her. She nearly jumped out of her skin when Robert touched her shoulder from behind.

"Oh! Good morning. Yes. I am okay." She was okay, for now. Thanks to the power of morning prayer.

"You got up extra early and didn't come back to bed." He sounded concerned.

"I woke up and decided to come outside for a little morning worship before the children wake up."

"Well long as you are all right." He hugged her and kissed her cheek. "I am gonna go get ready for work."

"Okay. Breakfast will be ready."

And so it was. Hattie continued to be vigilant in her duties as wife and mother. Meanwhile, she allowed the certainty of her husband's unfaithful dalliances to marinate inside of the remote crevices of her mind, and within the confines of her heart's private places. These were locations within, that even Hattie herself rarely visited. Those remote crevices where her secrets were stored. Secrets of dark moments, secrets of light moments, secrets. Life was awfully busy. But she didn't forget, and her ears were always open for a solution to her problem.

Chapter Twenty-Two

Florida James Brown was born on May 14, 1914. Now Robert and Hattie had three little mouths to feed. Bessie was five, Ernest was two. Living expenses had increased while income was stagnant.

"Robert, what are we going to do to make some more money?"

"What are you asking me? Can I work any harder? Are there are more hours being added to God's twenty-four?" His arms crossed his body, hugging his resistance to whatever she was about to say.

"No, love. I know how hard you're working, and the number of hours a day you are out there in the fields. It's just that we need to increase our income."

"I know that. Do you think I haven't thought about it?" he asked, eyes peering into hers

"Of course I know you think about it, but you don't speak about it. I thought if we could discuss it, then we could make a plan. You're not in this alone. If we work together, I know things can improve."

Robert's eyes softened, just a tad, as a shallow inhale and exhale escaped his nostrils. "Okay Hattie. What is it you have in mind? Cause I know you already have a plan."

Under her skin, Hattie was jubilating, but was careful not to show that she felt triumphant.

"Well, I was thinking that I could take in more laundry. There's a white family that just moved in up the road. I know they are gonna need a washer woman. I can go up there and introduce myself. Let them know that I am their girl. Then, Sister Mary showed me how to make molasses. I can start making blackstrap molasses to sell. That would also bring in a couple of dollars. If I get a few regular customers, they can return the jars when they need more so I only need to buy jars one time."

Robert leaned forward, listening intently. "So, where do I come in?"

"Well I will need for you to grow and harvest the sorghum."

He was quiet, looking up at the ceiling. This was the part of her plan that scared her. Adding more work to his already heavy load. But caring for three small children, housekeeping, and doing laundry was as much as she could handle with her twenty-four hours. She waited and prayed during the soundless moments it took for Robert to digest her idea.

"Okay Hattie. But I can't plant a whole field. I just don't have the time, the land, nor the help. Cause you know that tobacco is the money crop. We will start with a small patch. I gotta scrape up some money to buy the seeds. Grow your business and then see what happens after that."

She wrapped her arms around his big neck and hugged him tightly. "Thank you, husband. It's gonna work. I know its gonna work."

Robert nodded agreement and embraced his wife. They slept like two spoons nestled together, that night. Hattie was sure that they were headed in a good direction.

Sunday, Hattie was so happy to see her big sister Mary at church.

"Heeeeyyyy! Mary!" They hugged outside on the grass in front of the church.

"How are you? I could hardly wait until first Sunday to see you," Hattie said

Mary had been married to Sam Obey for several years. His family had been neighbors with Eliza. The newlyweds moved to Reidsville, North Carolina because there were jobs to work in the tobacco factory. Mary had given birth to seven children and was pregnant again. Reidsville was pretty far, so Mary only came to their church on the first Sunday of each month.

"Sister! It's so good to see you. How are Bessie, Ernest and baby Florida?"

"Everybody is good. Thank the Lord. It's time to go inside, but after church I got something to tell you."

"Okay. Let me round up my brood and we will be right in."

Hattie took her place at the front of the sanctuary so that she could easily stand and read the scripture when the pastor was ready. After that, the service went by in a whir. She was looking forward to talking and sharing with her sister. It had been three weeks since they had seen one another. It was hard not seeing Mary on a regular basis. Hattie loved her big sis and valued the advice she always offered. Mary was strong willed like Eliza, and more aggressive than Hattie. She didn't take much mess from anyone.

After church, there was always socializing. The men sat around discussing matters of work and who knows what else. The women would serve the men and children before settling into their own style of gossip and sharing. Hattie was mainly interested in getting her husband and children served so she could grab Mary and find a private corner somewhere.

"I love this skirt Mary. Where did you get that fabric?" Hattie asked, beginning their girl talk.

"Miss Sally, the lady who I clean house for, she gave it to me. Said she didn't want it. She bought it some time ago, but now doesn't like it. "

"Well you made good use of it. It goes perfect with that shirt waist blouse and cute little hat. Mary, what's new? How is the pregnancy coming along? You should be a pro at it by now."

"I am. Each baby lays different inside though, but it all boils down to the same thing. Even before they born, they don't care about what you want or need. It's all about their comfort and feeding. I'm fine. Margaret is a big girl, so she is very helpful with her younger brothers and sisters. In fact, she got a job, working at the tobacco factory!"

"Fourteen years old, and workin already! Everybody has to work if we gonna eat and keep roofs over our heads. In fact, I am so glad you taught me how to make molasses awhile ago. I decided to start making it to sell. We need to increase our income. I am doing laundry, but I need more customers. So, I asked Robert to grow the sorghum for me.

And then in October when it is harvested, I will make the molasses and sell it. I am so excited Mary. Robert said he gotta find the money to buy some sorghum seeds, but otherwise he will plant me a patch of it. I know it will go well. Then next season, I believe he will plant me a whole field of sorghum!"

"You sure Robert is gonna do all of that extra work? Hattie, you know he is not crazy about farm work. Now he has to ~~do~~ carry his load growing tobacco, and add some more? I hope he don't disappoint you."

"No Mary. He promised me. He said he will do it, and I believe him. He knows we need more money. We got three children now."

Mary hugged her sister. "Okay love. Let me know when you are ready to make the molasses. I will come and help you, so you get it right your first time making a big batch."

Hattie nodded in agreement, but privately shared her sister's apprehensions.

"How is life in Reidsville? It seems like you so far away. I really miss you Mary."

"Life in Reidsville is haaaarrrd. From the time I open my eyes until I near about pass out in the night, I am working and taking care of folks. Sometimes, I feel so tired, Hattie. I wonder is this all that life will ever be?"

"I know. I feel the same way sometimes. Sun up to sun down. Thank the Lord we have Sundays for a little break, and a chance to see one another. How is married life with Sam?"

The Secrets of Hattie Brown

"Hattie, Sam is mean. You know I am not so good at keeping my mouth shut if I don't like something. If I talk back at him, he slaps me. He don't care Hattie. He will beat me in a minute if I say or do something he don't like."

Hattie stared at her sister in disbelief. Her eyes began to well up. "No Mary. No. So what you gonna do?" Not Mary! Hattie thought. How could her husband treat her like that. She had bore his children, cooked his food, taken care of him and their home. What kind of man was he? That question frightened Hattie. What kind of man was this? If he would do that, how harsh will he become? How badly will he hurt her sister in the future? Cause Mary is not likely to change.

"Well for now, I am just trying to learn to keep my mouth shut. I'm pregnant and I have seven children. You tell me, what else can I do?"

Robert came over to where the two sisters were sitting. He handed Florida to Hattie. "He hungry. When you finish feeding him, I will be ready to go."

Mary could read and write a little but not as well as Hattie. "I am gonna write you a letter every week to see how you doing. Get somebody to read it to you and write me back. I will just say 'how you doin' and when you respond say all is well or everything is the same. This way, I will know how you doing without telling your business to whoever is writing the letter for you."

"Okay. I will look forward to that. Thank you, Hattie."

The two women hugged with tears rolling down both their cheeks. After nursing Florida, Hattie joined Robert who was waiting for her in the wagon with Bessie and Ernest.

"I told Brother Allen about your plan to make molasses. I was asking about some sorghum seeds. He said he had some left over from last year, and he would give me enough to plant a patch!"

"Oh Robert! How wonderful! I told you its gonna work out. I told you!"

Later that week, Hattie. Went to the General Store in town, to buy some supplies.

"Hello Mr. Brooks. How is the family?"

"Hey Hattie. We are all well, thanks be to God. How y'all?"

"We are all just fine, Mr. Brooks."

"What can I get for you today?"

"I need a sack of flour, a sack of cornmeal, and a bag of sugar. How much are your potatoes today?"

"Potatoes are fifteen cents a pound."

Hattie recounted the change she was holding tightly in her fist. She felt embarrassed to have to say, "No. That's okay. Maybe next time."

"Now Hattie, you know you can take the potatoes and pay me when you get it." He had known Eliza since before Hattie was born. When she was growing up, Hattie always came into the store with her mom, and then with Mr. Lucas' cook. He knew them to be honest and hardworking people.

"Thank you, Mr. Brooks. I don't want to run up a bill. But pretty soon, I will be able to get a few more things when I come in."

"How so?"

"Well I am planning to start a molasses business. My husband is out there planting the sorghum this very day."

"That's a good idea Hattie. Everybody loves some good molasses for their biscuits. In fact. You make it, I will sell it here in my store."

"You will? Oh Mr. Brooks that would be so helpful. Everybody comes to town to shop here."

"Yes, they do. And I will start telling folks in September to look out for the molasses that's is coming in October! So they won't buy it nowhere else. In fact, I know what, how bout I give you the jars to put it in, and we deduct the price of the jars when I sell it. But we can work that out later. The sorghum seeds haven't even sprouted yet."

"Thank you, Mr. Brooks. I like that idea. I was wondering how I would be able to buy the jars before selling any molasses."

Hattie went home feeling content, accomplished, and proud of herself on that day. This is what she had wanted since the days at the Lucas' house. She wanted to be validated as someone who could take her ideas and make them blossom. That is what having a business was all about. This was the kerosene on that little spark of an idea she'd had while growing up watching Eliza use her talent and intelligence to make a living.

This was a rare occasion when she had a positive memory from the time in Mr. Lucas' classroom. One day he had quoted some man who he said had been from a place called Greece. She didn't recall the man's name, but what he said was, "A thought is an idea in transit." Hattie knew that this thought had been traveling with her for her whole life, and now finally, the idea was going to find a landing place in her life. She would have success, make extra money for her family, and show folks that she knew how to grow a dream.

Robert was impressed to know that she had managed to arrange for her molasses to be sold at R.P. Brooks General Store.

"Everybody shops there, white folks as well as colored. They gonna be talking about my wife the businesswoman! I am proud of you Hattie."

That night, she hardly slept. Her mind was reeling with ideas, plans, and more plans.

Summer was warm and humid with a regular showering of rain from the heavens. This was the perfect gift for the little sorghum seedlings. They grew and grew so tall. Hattie loved to stand and watch their willowy stems wave in the breeze, back and forth. Back and forth. Like a choreography created in heaven.

She knew she would need help, at least the first time. The leaves and heads from each plant had to be removed and then put in a big pot to boil for several hours. After prayer meeting one Wednesday night, she began putting her plan into motion. A group of the ladies were sitting around chit chatting.

"Sister Lawson, in a few weeks I will be making up a batch of molasses. I was wondering if you would come over, bring some of your fried apple pies, and spend the day helping me." Fisher Lawson was sweet spirited and kind. Her fried apple pies were the best. Period.

"Of course, Hattie. Sounds like fun. We can put out a long table and spend the day eating, talking, and enjoying each other's company while we make molasses. In fact, why don't I ask Charlie to come along and bring our mule so he can run the grinding mill?"

"What a perfect idea Fisher! I didn't even think about that. I would appreciate Charlie's help, and his mule!" They both laughed. "Also, I will give everyone a jar of molasses to take home as a thank you gift."

Hattie asked several other sisters for their assistance, and they all agreed to come and bring corn bread, fried chicken, boiled ham, creamed corn, lemon aid, ginger snaps, and cakes. The plan was in place. Hattie knew that Mary would be joining them as well. Soon it would be harvest time.

Chapter Twenty-Three

Tobacco harvest starts in early August. The work of removing and curing the leaves could go all the way into October or November. There were other steps between the curing and delivering the tobacco to the owner of the land they were share cropping on. There was a deadline. The tobacco auction house closed in November.

"How's the harvesting going, Robert?" Hattie asking as she was feeding Florida, while Bessie and Ernest sat at the table eating their breakfast of bacon, eggs, and biscuits.

"So far, so good. I could always use more hands. But I don't have money to pay anyone to help me, so I just have to put in the hours…me and the mule."

She slid him a guarded look, feeling anxious about what she was going to ask.

"The sorghum will also be ready to pick soon. I know you will get to it when you can. The weather has been chilly. If it freezes, the sorghum is not good for molasses. Not good at all."

Robert peered at her over his coffee cup, with not very well concealed agitation, "Don't worry Hattie. I will get to it in time."

She knew her husband. The subject was closed.

Days and weeks went by. Robert was mostly home to eat and sleep. Otherwise, he was totally immersed in the process of picking, curing, tying (Hattie and Bessie helped with this part), drying out and airing the tobacco before delivering it to the packhouse to be pressed flat. This took considerable time, after which the year's harvest was delivered to the tobacco warehouse. This is when the harvest was weighed, and Robert got a full accounting of his wages for the year. Before there was any profit, the house rent, cost of the seeds, and the use of the mule and wagon, all had to be deducted. With one bad crop, a farmer could find himself in debt for several years going forward.

When Hattie saw Mary at church, the first Sunday in September, she shared her concerns. "You know Mary, that sorghum is sitting out there ready to be harvested and Robert has no time to do it. I could go out there and pull up some of it, but there's no way I can do it all. That's why I asked Robert to do it in the first place. I am doing everything else, but the growing and the harvesting... that's all I asked him to do."

"You know that if the temperature drops below freezing, you won't be making no molasses, right?"

"I know. Mr. Brooks has agreed to support us by giving me the jars on credit and selling the molasses in his shop. The sisters here at the church have already promised to come and help with the first batch. I am so nervous Mary. Some nights, sleep won't come. I don't dare bring it up to Robert again."

Mary was sympathetic. "I am sorry Hattie. This doesn't sound good." She put her hand on her protruded midsection.

"Oh sister, I am sorry. Here I am complaining about my stuff and didn't even ask about you. How you feeling?"

"I am all right. Sam is busy at the tobacco factory most days and late into the night. No time to be foolin' with me. When he gets in, Margaret will let me rest while she heats up his dinner. I just stay quiet and keep my distance. That's how I am managing these days. But after this baby is born…well I have some thinking to do."

Hattie hugged her sister. "I love you Mary. How about we go and see Mama, Willie and Emma after church?"

In the days ahead, summer waved goodbye as the trees changed their attire. Her hopes became translucent and her outlook was clouded with doubt. Hattie felt as if the trees were laughing at her, dressed in colorful clothing of gold and scarlet. She didn't want those colors, stay green! Each falling leaf shouted a refrain, mocking her dreams. Dancing to the beat of her misery.

Robert entered the house looking angry and distraught.

"What the matter?" she asked

"That damn mule. I don't know what is wrong with him. He sat down in the middle of the field and would not move. I spent the last two hours trying to make him get up. Finally, the only thing that worked was dragging, pushing, and beating him back to the barn!"

"Oh Robert. That is terrible. Now what?"

"I don't know. But right now, I gotta get some help so I can move the yield along. Brother Charlie Lawson has two mules. I am gonna go over to their place and ask to borrow his mule for two days. I know he is further along to being finished than I am because he has his sons to help him. So maybe he will say yes. Otherwise, there is no way I can get this done."

"I see. So how you gonna get there? It's cold out, and it's getting late."

"Hattie, I don't have a choice. I will walk. If it gets too late, I will stay the night with Charlie and Fisher. Come home in the morning."

"Okay. Let me get your coat and hat. The last thing we need is for you to get sick."

Truly, Hattie was concerned about this dilemma with the mule. But honestly, on the top of her list of concerns, was the fact that the temperature was dipping, and dipping fast. That morning, she had been outside hanging laundry on the line, with just a sweater on. Now, merely twelve hours later, it was too cold to go out without a coat.

Robert left. Hattie cleaned the kitchen, folded laundry and put the children to bed before retiring herself. She tossed and turned through the night. Around 3AM she got up and put a second quilt on the sleeping children. The house was getting chilly. If Robert had been there, he would've got up and made a fire in the hearth.

Outside was pitch black as she stood peering out of the window, trying to guess what the temperature might be. If only it would not drop below freezing. There was no way to tell until sunlight. So, Hattie Brown sat at that window until the sun showed its mournful face over treetops that were glistening with circles of ice fathered by overnight precipitation.

She ran outside, coatless, crying, arms flailing, "No! No! No! Please Lord no!" She saw the bowed heads of the sorghum flowers, lowered as if they were in prayer at a funeral. Hattie dropped to her knees, right there, in the cold damp field, with dead sorghum surrounding her, sobbing, broken, and disgusted.

When her husband returned later that morning, the climate inside the house was more frigid than the weather. At first, she pretended not to hear him come in, too busy with the quilt she was working on. Then he spoke.

"Hattie, I am sorry. I know this meant everything to you. I swear before God I will make it up to you. I am really sorry. Please understand that I was stuck tween a rock and a hard place."

Finally she looked up, eyes puffy from crying, "How did things go at the Lawsons?"

"Well the best he could do was lend me the mule for today. After that, he needs it back. I just stopped by the house to greet you and the children for the morning, and now I am going to get to work and make the most of this day."

"You want something to eat?"

"No. I had breakfast with the Lawsons."

And just like that, life went back to "normal" for Robert and Hattie Brown. But what is normal, when your dreams have been shattered? What is normal, when the only thing you have ever tried to do, that was as much for your benefit as for the benefit of others, is dead before it springs from the womb of your desires? What the hell is normal, when you feel like all that you seem to be good at, is cooking, cleaning, and having babies? This was the meaning of normal for most of the other girls in Hattie's circle of friends. After this disappointment, normal took on a different meaning, an evolved hue, in her heart; although on the surface of her being, it was still wearing the same old house dress. To look at her one would think that she was a mother, wife, good standing church member, and quite satisfied with that lot. Hattie knew that she was all of those things and glad to be so, but there was more to what she wanted to share with the world.

Chapter Twenty-Four

"Well mama, I haven't seen my blood in more than a month. Then this morning, I woke up feeling sick to my stomach. I am more tired than I should be at the end of the day."

"Hattie, you already have three children. You know what pregnancy looks like on you. I don't understand what you want me to tell you. Do you want me to say, 'Oh daughter, don't worry, it's just a bad cold.'?"

Head turned upwards, shoulders slumped, "No mama. You're right. I know what it means."

"Then what is the problem?"

"The problem is that I don't know how we can feed another mouth. When that mule went down, and Robert had to borrow the Lawson's mule, he could only keep that mule for one day. He needed it for more than that if he was going to finish all of the harvesting work. So, when he delivered the tobacco and it was weighed, we came out just even, once the rent and other expenses were paid. He had an income of zero dollars for a full season's work. I've been taking in laundry and doing some house cleaning work to make up enough money to feed us, while Robert gets ready for the next season of planting."

"Hattie, this is the life for colored people like us. Work, work, and more work. Sometimes there is no pay and whatever it is, there's never enough for our reward. That ain't never stopped us from having babies. We have them, and by the grace of God, we feed them. When they get big enough, they become workers too, and help support the family. That's just how it is honey."

"I wanted more, for me and mine. You was born a slave. I was born free. Don't that mean I am supposed to do more?"

"Yes. You don't think you are doing more? You can read and write. During slavery, if it was known that you were able to read and write, you would be beaten severely, and sometimes even sold away from your family. The person who taught you could go to jail. Even if they was white! So that right there is 'more'. You can teach your children. Then they can teach theirs. You stand at the end of the line of illiterate people in our family. That's a gift I could not hand to you myself. Best I could do was arrange for somebody else could give it to you."

"Really mama? Beaten or worse? Jail for a white person? Why?"

"Cause they believed that a slave who could read and write, could think and reason their way out of bondage. You know, in those days, if you were off of the plantation, you had to have a pass written out that said you have your master's permission to be on the road by yourself. If you didn't have that pass, the paddy rollers would take you somewhere and sell you and keep the money in their pockets. Many of those paddy rollers were poor whites who could not read or write themselves. They wouldn't even know what the pass said, but they knew you better have one. On some plantations, those colored people who could read and write, would make passes for the ones who wanted to try and escape. This is another reason why they were a danger to the masters. They would sell away their favorite servant, if he or she turned out to be a threat to the security of their property. Sometimes, when folks got caught, they would beat them until they bled to death, if they didn't tell who wrote them the pass. You know, I was a little girl when the Civil War came and went, then slavery ended. Once I became a mother Mama Edna told me all about these things, so we could continue to be grateful for how far The Lord has brought us since then. It ain't everything we might want, but it's a whole heap better. And with that, we keep on moving forward and keep on having more babies who can grow up and make us proud."

What Hattie had not told her mom, was that she was still having those dreams about Robert with other women. And there were times when she caught certain 'sisters' at church looking at her and talking in hushed clutches. When she turned her head in their direction, they would stop talking and conjure up phony smiles, laughing in her face.

"Well Mama, I see what you mean. And you're right, I have already started teaching Bessie and Ernest their letters. They are both very smart. And soon as Florida learns how to talk good, he gone start learning too."

"Hattie as long as I have a crust of bread, me and mine will never starve. We are family. We will take care of one another. Try not to worry. It's bad for you, the baby, and for the other children. As for Robert, well, he gon' just have to do better. Simple as that."

Hattie loved visiting with her mom. She always felt better when she left. Eliza seemed to have the answers to so many of her daughter's questions.

"Come on walk with me. I have to take this laundry over to the Howards."

Her sister Emma came into the house. She had been outside playing games with Bessie, Ernest and little Florida. "Emma, would you keep an eye on the children while I go for a walk with mama?"

Nineteen-year-old Emma, who was soon to be married to Major Hill, was always happy to spend time with her niece and nephews. "Sure Hattie, you know I will."

The Howards were a white family who Eliza had worked for since Hattie was a little girl. During the one mile walk to the Howards property, mother and daughter laughed, reminisced, and pointed out various medicinal plants growing along the roadside. When they reached Mrs. Howard's porch, Eliza knocked on the door.

"Hello Miz Sallie."

"Good afternoon Eliza. I see you have company today. How are you Hattie? You a big grown woman with children huh?"

"Good afternoon Mizz Sallie. Yes, ma'am. How is Mr. Howard? And how is Jessie? I understand he got married last year."

"He did. He and the wife are doing well. You know he moved to Wake County. Got a job there as the bookkeeper for a tobacco company. They gon' have a baby soon too."

"Really, a bookkeeper?" Said Eliza. "Gone on now!"

"Yes. In fact, he went there to work on the cutting machine. But recently he got a promotion because their bookkeeper died. So now they are moving to a new house and will have a little more space for the new baby. When he visited last weekend, he said that they are now looking for someone to fill the job he left. He also does the hiring for the company. Said they pay better money than here, and the salary is guaranteed. Not like having to weigh tobacco and pray that he will make enough money to have a profit."

Hattie asked, "What kind of workers is he looking to hire?"

"Well most he told me was that he was looking for men who are strong and can work hard."

"Ms. Howard, when is Jessie coming home again?"

"He said he'd be back next Sunday."

"You think we might could have a chat with him when he comes?" Her eyes were sparkling with the glint of an idea being born.

"Sure Hattie. You know Jessie looks at you and Eliza like family. Come on by after y'all finish church on Sunday."

During the walk back to Eliza's house, Hattie shared her idea with her mom.

"Well good luck with that. You know your husband better than I do. For your sake, I hope he goes for it."

Chapter Twenty-Five

"Well hey now Jessie Howard!" Robert and Jessie, both around the same age, shook hands.

"Robert Brown! Hattie, it's good to see you. Look at us. All grown up. Robert I ain't seen you in years! Come on in and sit down."

Hattie and Robert entered the farmhouse of the Howards and sat in the parlor with their son Jessie.

"So how is life. How y'all doing?" He cocked his head

"Well the good Lord had blessed us," Robert began. "We have three wonderful lil babies and a fourth one on the way." He turned towards Hattie and smiled. The smile was not joyous at the root, however. It was a serious smile.

Hattie understood the message of that smile. She still couldn't believe they were sitting there with Jessie Howard. It had been a real challenge to convince Robert to at least come and hear what the man had to say.

First he had said, "No Hattie. Not a chance. I ain't pickin up and movin to someplace I know nothing about. Suppose we go and I lose the job. Then what?"

"Well Robert there is nothing saying we can't come back if it don't work out."

Then he said, "How am I gonna go begging Jessie Howard for a job. Like I can't even take care of my family, so 'please Mr. White man can you help me'?"

"No, Robert it wasn't like that. His mama mentioned that he is looking for strong men who can work hard, on account of his new job as bookkeeper. He is also charged with hiring for the company. I thought about you because you are a strong man, and you work hard. I know you are a good man and Jessie Howard would be lucky to have you working for him. No, Robert. You ain't beggin'. If anything, you're doing him a favor. Having you as one of the men he hires will make him look good to his bosses. That will put money in his pocket and in yours." Hattie hoped this would convince him.

So here they were. He had agreed to come, but she knew he was not one hundred percent convinced that he would move so far away from the only town either of them had known since birth.

"Three children and one on the way! Well congratulations! Me and Blake have a baby on the way too. I am hoping we can get your mama, Hattie, to come stay with us when it gets near her time. She don't know nothing about birthing no baby, and we don't know anybody in Wake County who we trust like Eliza," Jesse Howard said.

Hattie smiled. Always proud of her mama's reputation.

"My mama told me y'all would be coming by today. What can I do for you?" Jesse asked.

Hattie saw that Robert's right foot was rapidly bouncing up and down in place, and his hands were laced together in his lap. He did that when he was nervous. The pit of her stomach fell. This was the moment of reckoning. She was surprised when Robert straightened his posture which elevated his shoulders by a couple of inches, puffed out his chest, and smiled showing his beautiful shiny white teeth.

"Well yes, Mr. Jessie, Hattie told me that you are looking for men who are good workers to hire for work in your company over in Wake County. I been working tobacco since I was a little boy helping my dad. So, I thought maybe I could help you out."

Ha! Only Robert with his cunning way of twisting words could have turned his shame and guilt into an offer to provide a prospective employer with an offer to "help him out".

Obviously, Jessie went for it.

"Now you know Robert, that's about the best idea I heard today. You are a good man and I know you to be honest and trustworthy. Your mother in law is jus' like a mammy to me. I would love to do this for you and for Hattie. But also, it would help me out a lot." Jesse agreed

His bouncing foot became still. Her baby fluttered as if it was pumping a tiny fist in the womb. Hattie's face was stoic, as was that of her husband.

"What is the pay like? And what would my job be?" Robert wanted to get down to the nuts and bolts.

"Pay day is every Friday. The wages are $7.00 per week. You work about fifty-eight hours a week, and sometimes more during the high season. I would hire you as a leaf picker. Your job would be to sort the leaf tobacco into the various grades required for the different brands of goods to be manufactured…cigarettes, cheroots and so forth. But once you are there and get the settled, I would really like to train you to be a machine watcher. In the tobacco industry there are some new machines that make the work faster and require less workers. The machine watcher monitors the machine to make sure it's running right. That salary is $9.00 a week."

"How much do people pay for rent in Wake County."

"Well the rent is affordable on the salary I just quoted. But for the first year, I will let you and your family live in the house we bout to move out of. I had paid the rent for the whole year, not knowing that we would be moving so soon. In exchange, Hattie could help out my wife with laundry, cleaning and cooking."

"Well Mr. Jessie, this sounds like a very good opportunity for me and my family. How long will you be in town?" Robert asked.

"In fact, I am leaving in a few hours. Gotta get back for work tomorrow," Jesse replied.

"How bout me and Hattie come to Wake County next week so we can see how it is?" Robert suggested.

"That's a good idea Robert. You a smart man. I wouldn't move my family to some place I have not seen first." Jesse admired Robert.

"Thank you, sir. Well we will be going now. What's the name of the town where your house is?" Robert inquired

"That's Holly Springs. When you get in town, just go into the General Store and ask them to direct you to my place. When exactly are you planning to come?" Jesse inquired

They discussed the details of the visit to Holly Springs Township and said their goodbyes. Robert and Hattie headed back to Eliza's house where they had left the children after church.

Their visit, some days later, was a pretty quick, go and come back turn around. They visited Jessie and Blake Howard, saw the house, which was much larger than where they currently resided. Robert later told her about his visit to the tobacco factory where Jessie had shown him the machines that were the newest technology in the business. Robert was impressed on all accounts.

Hattie spent time with Blake Howard and spoke with her about pregnancy, childbearing, caring for a baby, and living in Wake County. She felt like this was someone she would not mind working for. Although she had not known Blake back in Holloways, like she knew Jessie, Hattie found her to be pleasant and different from many of the white girls her age who she had encountered over the years. Blake treated Hattie like a new friend who was visiting from home, not like a niggah gal who will be washing her clothes. Of course, Hattie was assured that a part of that respectable regard, was that Blake knew her mother. Eliza's stellar reputation as a midwife and herbalist, gave her children a bit of a higher status with folks around town, both colored and white.

Hattie's reservations were that she would be so far away from her mama, siblings, and other family members. Also, she had been a member of Prospect Hill Baptist Church since she was a girl. They would have to find a new church home. But she was ready for change. This could be the event that would change her life for the better. They could have a fresh start, where nobody knew them. Maybe the bad dreams would stop. Yes. She could raise her children here. This could be the resolution, for many of their problems, the answers to many of her questions.

Two hours later, Hattie and Blake stood at the window inside the house, and watched their husbands shake hands. Robert was smiling. Both women could infer that he had accepted the job. Their eyes met, both twinkling with delight, as they embraced. This was a significant moment for both women. Hattie had a new job and a new life and Blake had help, companionship, and the pregnant daughter of Eliza Cowen to guide her through this pregnancy. During the ride on the train back to Holloways, Mr. and Mrs. Robert Brown discussed the plans for their new life in a new town.

Chapter Twenty-Six

Two weeks before Robert's birthday, Hattie had a baby boy, Robert Junior. He was the first of their children to be born in Wake County. They had moved and settled in quickly and with ease. Hattie worked for the Howards, took care of her children and home, while Robert got accustomed to the life of working at the tobacco plant.

For Hattie, Junior's birth represented the beginning of a new era for their family. A time of prosperity, of rededication to what was important, God, marriage and family. A time of greater security, financially. Robert had a regular salary, and after that first year of rent that had been prepaid by Jessie Howard, his salary was adequate enough to pay the rent. And then, as per their agreement after the first year, Hattie began earning a regular salary from the Howards for her work at their house.

It was a challenge to adjust to a new community, find a new church and new friends/neighbors. But for a young working wife and mother, change is a way of life. With children, one is constantly making adjustments based upon their needs and evolving temperaments. For Hattie, it was almost business as usual. Life was about her love for her husband and family. Everything thing she did was fueled by that reality.

Robert, well for Robert not as much. He was happy that they were more secure financially and his children were well fed. He felt accomplished in this regard. Still, he missed the old watering hole where he used to go after work on pay day and drink with his buddies. He was too far away now, and the men in this place seemed different, more churchy. Like old men. He was a good church going man himself, but still he liked a little raucousness to pepper up his life every once in awhile…just a little.

It wasn't long before the Browns were expecting the next addition to their family.

Lander Elevin Brown came sliding into the world, screaming his head off! Eliza was smiling brightly as she pulled the head, then body, of her newest grandson into the world.

"Okay little man, you are here, we are here, just relax." She laid him in his mother's arms as Hattie fed him her breast milk for the first time.

"Lord have mercy! This boy greedy!" Hattie was exuberant, though tired after the overnight labor to delivery.

Lander was a healthy, beautiful, and vibrant baby boy, with a head full of curly black hair. They had named him after the son of John and Sophronia Williams, their friends at Prospect Hill Baptist Church.

The children were growing like string beans. Bessie was nine, and the best helper a mother could want. Ernest was seven and thought of himself as Papa Robert's shadow. Whenever Robert was not at work, Earnest was right there by his side, following him around and mimicking his every movement.

One Sunday after the once a month service at their new church, First Baptist Missionary Church, one of the sisters pointed at Earnest following his father around the church dining hall, and said to Hattie, "Look at that boy. He even walks like his daddy!"

The Secrets of Hattie Brown

"Florida, bring me that pot over there," Hattie ordered. This little five-year-old enjoyed being at home with his mother and the babies. He didn't mind helping his father and Ernest do manual chores around the outside of the house, but he preferred staying around the kitchen, watching his mama and Bessie prepare the meals, and playing with his two year old brother Robert Jr. who was toddling around. They had also acquired a family dog.

"Go outside and run around a little bit with Butch." Sometimes Hattie felt he needed to get out more. That he would do. Florida enjoyed playing with the dog. "But be careful. Don't go too far down the road." Mom had already noted that Florida was a risk taker. He was very adventurous. Once, Earnest had run into the house dragging Florida by the scruff of his neck. "Mama, this fool was out there using a stick to push around a snake. Lucky it wasn't one of them poisonous ones, but still. What's wrong with him?"

Everybody, except baby Lander, had reading and writing lessons with Hattie every day. It was quite a sight to see the Brown children all lined up at the family table with paper and pencils in front of them. Bessie and Earnest could already read and write simple sentences. However, Florida loved studying his letters more than any of the others. Always the first one at the table, he was sharp and quick to catch on. In the fall, Bessie, Earnest and Florida would be attending the local school for colored children. Robert and Hattie Brown, with five children, had now been married for twelve years.

There would be four more children before the end.

Chapter Twenty-Seven

One morning as Hattie wrapped Roberts chicken sandwich in a red and white checkerboard towel, she opened his lunch pail and noted something different nesting inside. It was a little brown bottle, which when opened had the very distinctive odor of bootleg whiskey. Just then, Robert entered the kitchen, smiling brightly.

He kissed Hattie on the cheek without noticing what was in her hand. "Robert, you drinkin' bootleg whiskey on the job?" She showed him the bottle she was holding.

Without missing a beat he responded, "Me and some the boys had a couple drinks after we knocked off. Yeah. What are you doing questioning me about my business?"

"I am questioning what you might be doing that could cause problems for our family, is what I am doing."

"Look Hattie. I am a man, not a boy. I know what I am doing. A little drink after work ain't gon' hurt nobody, and it sho' aint gonna hurt me or OUR family!"

"Listen Robert, I am not trying to suggest that you are not a man. It's just that you and drinking don't mix well. When you start drinking, some measure of trouble ain't far behind."

The conversation was escalating, and Hattie did not want to wake the sleeping children. Robert was clearly putting up that stone wall that would lead to him walking out without resolving the conflict anyway. So, she best close it out while she could.

"I just want the best for you. We have been doing so well here in Holly Springs. I hope everything is good at work."

"Some days, I need to take a break before I come home to you and the children. The work is very hard, and it ain't easy being called nigga or boy all day by those no count white trash who I have to work with. Jessie Howard is not around. He works in the office. Some days, me and the other fellas like me, well we get together and talk about how we hate the way things are for us colored men. We all want more, you know Hattie."

Her heart softened. "I do understand love. Just be careful okay. Don't let Mr. Jessie see you drinking around the plant, and don't get yourself so drunk you get into a fight or some other trouble to get yourself arrested. Please Robert."

"Don't you worry, my dear. Everything is fine and gon' be fine." He kissed her, took his grey lunch pail from the table and he was off to work.

Hattie went ahead and got her day started. Went outside to feed the few chickens they kept for eggs. "Hey Fannie!"

"Mornin' Hattie." Her neighbor said as she was passing by. Thomas and Fannie Brown were no blood relations to Robert and Hattie, but as nextdoor neighbors, had become good friends since they had moved to Holly Springs.

When they first moved in, Thomas had come over to welcome them and offer to help with anything they might need.

"That is so nice of you Thomas. Thank you. I will definitely take you up on that offer should anything come up. For now, I think we are good." Robert was appreciative.

"That's just fine. Well I am just up the road so don't hesitate to ask. Really."

"We won't," Robert replied, shaking hands with Thomas.

As Thomas began walking away, he turned, with a second thought, "By the way, y'all looking for a church home?"

"Yes. We are!"

"Well the colored church here is First Baptist. We meet once a month. Tween times we have Bible study at folks' homes. This Sunday is our service. How bout you and your family come along?"

"Well that would be perfect Brother Thomas. Thank you so much."

Robert and Thomas got along well. Thomas and Fannie lived on rented property which was house and farm. Thomas worked on his own account, growing tobacco, like Robert had done back in Woodsdale. Sometimes, on weekends, Robert would go over and give him a hand.

Hattie liked Fannie, except sometimes she tended to be too much of a gossip for her tastes. Hattie was all about righteous living, her husband, and her children. Other people's business? Not so much. Whenever she saw Fannie coming, she knew there would be some juicy news in the mix before their conversation ended. Fannie seemed to know what was under every rock in every church member's front yard. She even knew some of the white people's secrets.

How in the world did she have time for all of that? Hattie just didn't know.

In the coming weeks. Robert started coming home just a little later, and sometimes later than a little. She knew he was drinking, and she hoped he was with 'dem fellas', as he had said that day when she brought it up to him. She did know that the dreams had started up again. Robert walking away from her, in the mist there were shadows all around. Smoky shadows of females she could not identify.

To add pepper to an already hot soup, Fannie had told her some local news that was new to Hattie. "Hattie have you heard tell that there is a colored ho' house in town?"

Hattie felt a stirring in her heart. "A ho' house!?"

"Yes," she continued in her high-pitched whiny voice. "I heard that there's a ho' house in town, and some of our men be going over there in the evenings. I told Thomas I better not hear that he has even been walking past that place!"

Hattie faked a giggle. "Fannie, you know Thomas is not going into no place like that."

"Hmph! He better not."

Hattie stored this information in her mind, hoping that it was just storage, never needing to be applied actively.

Chapter Twenty-Eight

Two days before Lander's second birthday, Hattie gave birth to a pretty little girl with big brown eyes. They named her Virginia, after the state where both Hattie and Eliza were born. This was the last of Hattie's children that Eliza would deliver.

Eliza came to stay with them a week before the delivery and remained to help her daughter with the children for two weeks after Virginia was born. Since moving to Wake County, Hattie had not had the chance to visit Woodsdale as often as she might have liked to.

"Mama, I sure do miss you, Willie, Emma and Andrew. I don't get to see Mary neither. I haven't seen Andrew since he and Ann had their baby boy." Jesus! It must be almost a year!"

"Yes. We miss you too. Willie is always asking 'where is Sister?'"

Listening to the sound of her mother's voice, observing her posture, Hattie could see that Eliza was aging. Her voice had developed a bit of a crackle in it. The words flowed smooth even and with wisdom from her mouth, but they were delivered more slowly. It was like she had to think about each word before she poured it from the vessel of her mind. Hattie noted that her jaws were sagging and looking hollow under eyes that told of deep pain, tremendous disappointment, and yet still curated a fire that was burning brightly. Eliza was still the bold and beautiful mom she had always known, but she looked like life had drained. "How you feeling mama? You look tired," she asked deeping concerned.

"I am tired honey, more tired than you know. This life has been full of knocks and bumps. I've seen my way through them all, and now I am just worn out."

"I'm sorry mama. I pray that the load will lighten as you are getting older. I pray for you every day."

"I know baby. The Lord knows what is best."

"Mama, I am going to try my best to come to Woodsdale more often so I can see how you doing. Bessie is bigger now; she can watch the children while I am away. I think you should consider going to live with Emma and Major. This way you will have someone to see after you if you don't feel well."

"Yes, we have been talking about that. As soon as I get back, we are gonna all move into the house on that property I bought, Me, Willie, Emma and Major."

"Mama! That is good news. I won't worry as much if I know you are with Emma. And the land Mama!!! I am so proud!. You have been talking about that ever since I can remember! Eliza Cowen, you are some kind of woman."

Within two months after Virginia's birth, Robert quit the job at the tobacco factory, rented a house with farmland in Fuquay Springs (still Wake County) and they moved.

Another change in their way of living. There was once again the financial uncertainty of being a tobacco farmer, although the business was much better than it had been years before. Hattie was now two hours walk away from her job at the Howards' instead of ten minutes. With a baby, a toddler and little ones who were attending school, her life became even more complicated.

One day, Robert had come home from work, looking exasperated and convicted. "I'm done Hattie. I am just done."

"Done?"

"Yes done. I can't take it anymore. All day every day. 'Niggah this, boy that'. None of them is my boss but they all treat me like I am dirt under their feet. Some of the other guys just 'yassuh boss' and keep on working. Robert Brown is not made like that. I've done it until I can't do it anymore. I feel like it is making me into somebody I don't want to be. I don't believe God made me to be nobody's door mat, Hattie. I quit. If I had not quit, I know I would have killed me a white man today."

"You quit! You quit? What did Jessie Howard say? Couldn't he do anything to stop them from treating you like that? I mean it's not like that job is on a plantation during slavery times and they are overseers!"

"Jessie Howard is one white man. He treats us different privately, but he gotta look out for his job and feeding his family. He is not going but so far out on a limb. He wasn't happy to see me go, but he understood."

Hattie was thoughtful, quiet. She felt for her husband. She totally understood what he was feeling. But she was worried. How would they make it?

"I know what you are thinking Hattie. But don't fear. I was talking with Brother Thomas the other day. He was telling me that growing tobacco is pretty good business nowadays. A man can make enough of a living to even hire help at harvest time. I have already went to look at a house to rent with some land over in Fuquay Springs. The house is a good size for us and the children, and it's a nice piece of land for a farm. I have saved up enough money to get us started with the rent, and to buy a wagon and a mule. Thomas will even give me some tobacco starts and some seeds so I can plant in time for next season. Hattie we will have plenty and it will work out. I rather be my own man, standing tall in front of my wife and children, then to have to stoop low to the ground, bowing in front of somebody I can't stand. Our children should grow up feeling proud and believing that they deserve the best. I thank God that we can do it. Some of us don't have the means to make changes."

"You want me to quit the job working for the Howards?"

"Well no. We are gonna need that money to help us get started. But after awhile, I don't think you will need to work for them anymore."

"Okay Robert. When will you take me to see the house and the land?"

Chapter Twenty-Nine:

The Letters

Hattie kept her promise to be more vigilant about visiting her mom. In fact, Eliza had not been feeling well.

On one of her visits, Emma (who did not read or write very well), showed Hattie a letter that they had received from Margaret, Mary's oldest daughter.

My dear Aunt,

I will drop you a few lines to let you hear from me. I am well except my eyes. They are giving me a lot of trouble. Son had been sick, but he is getting along all right. Now Emma, how is grandmama getting on? She wrote Mama she was sick and didn't get any better. I am mighty sorry she didn't get better. Mama said she was coming to stay with her and now she has been gone for over a week and we have't heard from her nor from you all. Write me at once and tell me how she is getting on and have you seen or heard tell of mama. Bye. Write soon.

From Margaret (Reidsville, NC)

"Emma. She is saying that Mary came to visit you a week ago. Where is she?" Asked Hattie

"We haven't seen nor heard from Mary," Emma replied.

"Lord Jesus. I hope she is all right," Hattie said concerned. She recalled the conversation that she and Mary had shared at Prospect Hill not very long ago.

The Secrets of Hattie Brown

Hattie returned to Fuquay Springs with a heavy heart. She worried about her mother's health and wondering what had happened to her sister Mary.

A few days later, Hattie writes a letter to her Uncle Henry's wife Ella, because Ella was literate.

My dear Aunt,

I wrote you yesterday that I would be home on Saturday. But I see it is so I can hardly come and give justice to my chores here. Mama is better, I hope. If she isn't please let me know at once and you be sure to meet me Wednesday night at Woodsdale train station. I will have to wash a little on Monday, but please meet me Wednesday night. If anything happens, please send a telegraph to Varina c/o Mr. Jessie Howard. If I live I will be home Wednesday night but if mama don't get any better please let me know.

Yours truly, Hattie Brown

Hattie did visit that Wednesday. She spent time with her mother, sister and family members, did what she could to help, and then had to return home to her husband and six children.

The next time she wrote, was two days before Christmas.

My dear mother,

Today I will write a letter to let you hear from me. I am not feeling so well this morning. My nerves are kind of upset, but I guess it comes from studying about you. I hope you are getting along ok mama. It is very cold mama. Please ask Aunt Ella to write to me and tell me exactly how you are doing. Tell Aunt Ella I will send some molasses as soon as I find a stone jug to put it in. Please write soon.

Your daughter,
Hattie Brown

New Years Day, 1922

Mama,

I am happy to say we have sausages and collards and tomatoes. Boiled hams, chicken, two kinds of cake, corn bread, biscuits and butter milk are on the table and we are all of good mind this first day of the new year. I am happy, and not for myself. I am a child of God. Mama stay at the cross, in due time it could heal all aches and pains.

Robert said to tell Andrew that if he wants to come and stay this year. He will be glad and give him a good salary. We have got good land and plenty of it. Robert needs his help to till the land, help plant it and to burn the land. Also, he needs help to cut fire wood. if Andrew doesn't have a job, tell him to come on. But for Jesus sake, Robert doesn't want him to bring Ann.

Aunt Ella, I will send the molasses to you next week, I hope. Half for you and half for Mama and Emma.

Hattie Brown

The same day, twelve-year-old Bessie also wrote to her grandmother:

Dear Grandmother,

The Secrets of Hattie Brown

Tonight I am well and glad to know that you are better. I was aiming to come down there if grandfather and them had come here. But they did not come and that knocked me out. I will come when I can, and you come when you are able. Give my love to all. Papa said tell Uncle Andrew that he should write and let him know if he is coming so someone can meet him at the train station.

Answer soon,
Your loving granddaughter
Bessie Brown

Finally, Hattie had heard from Mary. She was asking for some money to help her with the very difficult time she was having. It seems that Emma had also heard from her a few days after new year's.

This letter is from Mary to Emma:

My dear sister,

I will write to let you hear from me. I am well and I truly hope when you get these few lines they may find you all getting along all right. Emma, I know you all are mad with me, but this is all right. I saved my life by leaving home.

Emma please write and tell me something about how my mama is. I ought to have written but was afraid you all would write to Sam and tell where I am. Emma tell mama I will be home as soon as I can. The times are dull here and work is hard to get. Even when you get work the pay is so small you can't do very much with it. Emma, could you send me two or three dollars at once? I am in bad luck, and when I come home I will bring you three dollars. And Emma, if you see Mary Lewis ask her if she sent that two dollars she owes me to Reidsville. If she ain't sent it, you get it and send it to me at once. Emma, don't you tell where I am. I don't want Sam to know. He beat me and I took James and Gladys and left. I could not leave my babies; Margaret will take care of the other children. She is grown now, but I am in a hard place. Please send money at once. Please. You won't lose it. Write me at once. I will be home in a little bit soon as I can get straight and get some clothes for James. I have been very sick since I been here. The ladies in the rooms where I am staying sure is nice to me. They are real nice people. If I had three or four dollars I would soon get straight. Emma, let me hear from you at once. I wrote to Hattie the same week I got here and haven't heard from her. Write soon and tell me all the news there.

Your sister,
Mary Obey - Lynchburg, Virginia

Of course, Mary had no way of knowing that the Mary Lewis, who owed her money, had died of Consumption (tuberculosis), a few days after Emma received her letter. She was buried at Prospect Hill Baptist church during a snowstorm. So, no money would be coming from Mary Lewis.

From Hattie to Eliza, two weeks after New Year's Day 1922:

My dear mother,

I will write again to see if I can hear from you. I haven't had but one telegram from you since I came home. I don't know what is the matter with you and the reason you don't write. Are you any worse, or not? I feel like you are getting along all right though because the prayers of the righteous prevails much.

All are well here and enjoying good health. Mama, I am fat as a pig and eat like a dog. I have given Bessie all my skirts. I ain't got but one skirt now that I can wear well. I will be so glad when you are able to come for a visit.

Well Mama, I had a letter from Sister Mary this week. She asked me to please send her some money and when she gets well she will work and then pay me back. It makes me feel sorry for sister. She said we was mad at her because she wouldn't let Sam kill her, and we wouldn't write to her. She says she did not get any letters from us. I am going to send her the money tomorrow, though I ain't got it to spare. But I don't know her condition. Only the Lord knows mama. Everybody will reap what they sow.

Have you heard from Andrew? Robert is expecting him to come and been waiting get word from him. So, if you see him, please let him know that Robert said to let him know what he is going to do.

Tell Aunt Ella, that I am going to start her molasses tomorrow which is Saturday, and I will send a gallon; half for her and half for Emma.

Bessie and Florida send their love to you. I will close now, Good night

Your daughter, Hattie Brown

Barbara Brown Gathers

From Mary to Eliza Cowan - January 29, 1922

My dear mother,

I will write you a few lines to let you hear from me. I am very well and hope you are getting along all right. Mama, why don't you all ever write to me? I wrote to Emma and she didn't think enough of it to answer. I guess she is hot because I am not at home taking a dog's fare. Mama, I been here almost three months and I have been trying ever since I been here to get some money to send to you. It takes all I can not to pay my room rent and get something to eat. I wrote Emma to send me two dollars and I guess that is why she didn't answer my letter. But that is all right. I guess the works will open up after awhile. I can't get much work to do now. Say Mama, I will be coming to see you as soon as I can.

When have you seen Mary Lewis? How is she getting along? Give my love to all and if nothing happens, I hope to be there in May. Mama, get you a box of pine tar, put it in a bottle with water and drink that water. It will help you a lot. I have been very sick since I been here, and I got me some of that. My cold is just about all gone.

Write to me and give me all the news. Excuse me for not writing to you before. I thought I would write to Emma and it would be just the same, but I see she won't write. Mama please don't think I have thrown you away or don't love you. I love you as I always did. I am trying to make something to be of help to you. So, write soon.

Your loving Mary

The Secrets of Hattie Brown

Hattie was so worried about her mother and her sister. She could not be physically present with either of them as much as she would have liked to because she had her own obligations at home. But she prayed without ceasing.

Hattie's hands and forearms were covered with flour as she kneaded the biscuit dough.

"Bessie, come here and sit down. I want to write a letter to Emma so your Papa can take it to the post office when he goes to town in the morning. Get a paper and pen and write what I tell you."

From Hattie to Emma - February 5, 1922

My dear sister,

Today I am well, and all the family are well. When these few lines reach your loving hands, I pray they will find you all the same. Emma, what is the matter? Why you all don't answer my letters. I have written to Aunt Ella twice and have not got an answer at all. I have sent Mama a box and have sent Aunt Ella molasses, and have not received an answer from that. Please write to me as soon as possible please and tell me how mama is getting along. Is she dead? Is she bad off sick? Or is she well? What is the reason why you all don't write Emma?

It is raining today, but I went to church and had a very nice time.

Emma, if you see Andrew tell him I said to write Robert word whether he is coming or not. Emma, don't you sit down til you answer this letter, and also let us know what Andrew is going to do. Tell him that Robert is sick and wants him to come on the next train that is running. He should come this week, not next week. This is not a joke. If he doesn't have the money for the train, tell him to borrow it and Robert will send it back when he comes. Don't forget, Emma.

Answer soon, soon, soon
(answer by return mail)

Your Sister

From Hattie to Emma - March 9, 1922

My dear sister,

Tonight, I will answer your letter which I received today. It found us all well and this leaves us the same. The baby, Virginia, is little ill but I don't think it amounts to very much. Well Emma I sure was glad to hear from my Mama. I stay in trouble all the time. I can't sleep and sometimes can't hardly eat. I'm telling you Emma you don't know how it is with me. I am so far from home and always dreaming dreams that are troubling. I had a dream the first of January and it was so straight. I would tell you if you could read this yourself Emma.

Please ask Aunt Ella to write to me for you and mama, as often as you can. I am upset that you all won't tell me nothing about how mama is getting along. Is she able to sit up? Does she have a good appetite? I do wish to the good Lord that Mama was with me. I feel like you all get tired of waiting on her. I would be glad if I had her here to look after her and do all I could for her. Tell mama if I don't get home next week, I will try to send her a little money. Write and let me know what she is eating, and I will fix her a box and send it too. My mama is my all day study and all night dream. If mama would die, I believe I would die too. The good Lord knows best, don't he? Well Emma, you pray for me and I will pray for you.

Please write me word whether you have seen Andrew or not. If you see him, tell him Robert is looking for him and please come. I am sending you some postal cards and ask Aunt Ella or some to write for you every other day and let me hear from my mama. Please answer soon.

Love, your sister,
Hattie Brown

Hattie's prophetic dream forecasted the imminent demise of Eliza Cowen. Between March and May 1922, she continued to write to Emma and Eliza and to visit whenever she was able to get away. She was now a wife and mother of six children. There was always something to be done at home. In late May, she received a postcard from Emma, written by her Aunt Ella. Two words were inscribed on the back side of the card: COME SOON.

"Robert, I gotta go home. I think Mama is very sick. Emma sent word for me to come." Hattie was sick with worry.

The train seemed to be crawling in mud, rather than rolling fast on tracks. Hattie's heart was fluttering. Her stomach was in a knot. She didn't want to stand but it was hard to sit. The churning sound of the train's clackitty clack was sharpening the edge on her last nerve. The only thing she cared about at this moment was seeing her mama's sweet face, alive and breathing.

Suddenly, there was a loud clash and the train jolted to a stop. Hattie was thrown out of her seat on to the floor. For a moment, she was not sure what had happened. A nearby passenger came and helped her to get up.

"You okay Miss?"

"Yes. Yes. I'm fine. What happened?"

"Looks like the train's had a break down."

Just then a conductor entered the car. "There is a problem with the locomotive. We are trying to get it fixed as quickly as possible."

NO! They don't understand! There can't be a problem! There can't be any delays! She must get to her mama! Hattie was hysterical. Sitting in her seat, waiting for the movement of the train to resume, having a quiet and very private break down.

When she arrived in Woodsdale three hours later than anticipated, she made her way to Emma's house breathless.

Walking into the house, she could smell death and see the ashen mask that was her sister's face. As their eyes met, Hattie knew without Emma having to utter the words.

"When?" She asked.

"About three hours ago. She tried to wait for you Sister. But her heart...it just gave out." Hattie was stunned. She stared at Emma as if she had spoken in a foreign language that Hattie could not comprehend. As the impact of Emma's words finally hit home, Hattie collapsed on a nearby chair and began to wail. "Mama no. Mama no Mama no! I tried to get here Mama. I tried."

They funeralized Eliza and buried her in the cemetery at Prospect Hill Baptist church.

Robert and the children joined Hattie and the rest of the family in Woodsdale to say their last goodbyes. When they returned home, there was a letter that had come while they were away. It was for Hattie, from Eliza.

May 24, 1922

My dearest daughter,

The Lord has put it on my heart that my time is not long. I know you don't want me to say this, but the truth is the light. I hope I will see you while I am on this side of God's earth, but in case I don't there are some things I wanted to say to you. So, I asked Ella to write these words for me.

Love of self is the most important relationship to have after love of God. Don't ever let any man, woman or child convince you that there is any other truth than that. For a time, I did love Alex more than I loved myself. That caused me a lot of pain till I learned better. I've suffered enough heartache for two lifetimes. But what kind of life would it be if we had the good without the bad? We would never grow closer to God. We would never really get to know ourselves.

When people disappoint or even hurt you, find it in your heart to forgive them. Jesus taught us, "Forgive them for they know not what they do". You will feel better in forgiveness than in holding anger and hatred. I been hurt many times. More than you will ever know. Sometimes by men folk and sometimes it's just how life decides to teach us things. Pain is growthful and growth is painful.

I don't have a lot of regrets. Even though life is hard for colored people, I learned how to get around the walls blocking us. What single colored woman with children do you know who was able to buy land? I am leaving that piece of land to Willie, so I know he will always have someplace to live.

These days I am so tired and have shortness of breath most of the time. Feels like the life is draining out of me. I submit. The fight has been long and hard. I believe I left more here than I brought with me when my mama pushed me out of her womb. I'm good. My children are my greatest gift to the world. You, Hattie are at the center of my heart. The Lord has blessed you, and yours, for generations to come. I know this, without a doubt.

Emma and Willie are looking after me, and I don't want for nothing, except to see my second born baby girl. Come soon Hattie.

Your loving mama
Eliza Cowen

Hattie collapsed holding the letter over her heart. Her mama was gone. What was she gonna to do without her mama? She felt an emptiness, an inner, bottomless pit. Eliza had always been there. This woman's face was the very first she had seen when she slid out of the womb and was placed upon her breast to nurse. Of course, Hattie didn't consciously remember that moment, but she knew that Eliza had been her companion for life.

She hugged her stomach with arms crossed over it, and rocked back and forth, wailing, moaning, recalling the many memories of her mother. Tears cascaded down her face, to her cheeks and her chin, dropping on her collar bone like a waterfall. Memories of the day she snatched her out of the reach of Mr. Lucas and his sexually abusive influence. Then the fact that this woman, a colored woman born enslaved in 1860, had died leaving a piece of land to her disabled son, which she saved for as part of an organization started by another powerful and progressive colored women. She had been hit with the loss of lovers so many times, yet still got up and pushed forward. Many women would have crumbled and become either whores, alcoholics, or died depressed if they had been rejected and abandoned as many times as Eliza had. Hattie thought about the life of this woman who had nurtured her, and loved her, and brought her from a mighty long ways. She would miss her mother. And she would always remember that Eliza believed in being loving, trusting God, and not waiting for a handout. She believed in getting your own.

She wished that she had made it in time. Her mama was gone, and this was the most final pronouncement she had ever known in her life. There was nothing she could do to bring Eliza back. What was there she still wanted to say to her mama?

Chapter Thirty

Thanksgiving, The Following Year

There was a lot of activity in and around the Brown homestead on this blustery fall holiday in 1923. The wind carried the clean, fresh, aroma of pines trees in autumn. Birds chirped in sync and harmony with the brush of Hattie's broom sweeping the overnight dust from her porch. Inside the house, Bessie was playing with baby Virginia, who was squealing with delight.

"My turn! My turn!" Screamed little Lander as Robert Junior dominated the pushing of their play wagon, an old wooden box, around the yard.

"Now give him a chance Robert. You're five, he is three. Be fair!" Hattie was used to being referee between her boys.

Running from across the yard, "Mama. Have you seen Florida?" Ernest's nostrils were flaring and sweat beaded on his forehead.

"No. I haven't seen him since breakfast. Didn't he go to the fields with you and Papa?"

"He did. But he is no use out there, mama. Florida jus wanna play and wander around. Papa told me to watch him. I turned my back for a second and he was gone. Now I can't find him nowhere. Papa gon' take me to the judgment hall for sure."

"Come on Ernest. Papa won't beat you for something like that. He knows how Florida is. I am sure he is somewhere around here. Just keep looking."

Ernest was at the beginning stages of having the swagger of a teen boy. He was only eleven, but his walk, talk and attitude were at the border of adolescent snark.

"I'm sick of him. Always wondering off! Why I gotta watch him all the time?"

"Because he is your brother, and each of you has a 'take care'. Florida is yours. Think about how you were at eight years old."

She could see that he shut himself down because he dared not talk back. But he was not buying her explanation.

"Yes mama." He ran towards the back of the house. "Florida! Floreeeeedaaaa!

Bessie came to the doorway with little Virginia hoisted on her right hip. "Mama, should I start washing the collard greens?"

"Yeah baby. Go ahead bring them out to the porch and put them in that bucket of water. Also, bring my knife. I will chop as you wash. Check and see how the ham on the stove is doing."

Just then she turned around to see Florida barreling toward her holding his face, with Ernest not far behind on his heels.

"Mama, Ernest hit me!" Here stood her little half baby half big boy, wanting his mama to defend him.

"Ernest, where did you find him?" Ernest stood still looking like the cat that ate the mouse. Arms crossed over his chest, his jaw was clenching as one foot was forward tapping to the beat of his conquest.

"He was behind the barn playing with that ole stupid dog!"

By now Florida was hugging his mom around her waist, almost hidden behind the folds of her floor length skirt. She could feel his heart beating fast like a dragonfly's wings.

"Ernest, next time you watch Florida more carefully! And Florida, you can't be running off without letting your brother know where you are. Y'all are brothers. Stuck together for life. You better learn how to get along. Now we have a lot to do. Our guests are on the way from Holloway right now. They will be here in a few hours. Florida, take that pail over there, and go get mommy some water from the well and bring it to the kitchen. Ernest, tell Bessie to give you the largest basket in the pantry, and you get me some sweet potatoes from the barn. We harvested some nice ones last week from my garden."

She thought about her conversation with Robert the previous night. She wished she could get Robert to soften his heart towards his dad. She thought of how much she wished she had even one more chance to tell Eliza that she loved her.

"Robert, he is your father! You know he loves you, and our children adore him. They will only be here for two days. And, truth is, I will be glad to have some time with my friend Virtee. It's been so long since we have been together, and I miss my friends from Prospect Hill Church. She is bringing her baby boy, James, who is the same age as Lander. Then, I thought you would be glad to see Thomas Lawson. His family and yours have been together since the slavery days! You all were good friends when you were boys. You need to let go of those old raggedy memories you have about your dad. It's a new day. Your life is different now."

"He ain't never had a good word to say to me about nothing I do! Always looking for my mistakes and trying to make me feel like less than a man. I will make the best of the visit, but glad when he is gone. You watch. He's gonna have something to say. Some criticism about something."

Well, that was about the best she could expect and hope for. Robert was not a man to change his mind easily, once it was fixed upon something. That is unless he decided it was to his advantage to do so. That decision normally came from him and not from anybody's convincing conversation. Truthfully it was one of the things she loved about Robert. If he made a promise, he kept his word. The day was here. His father would soon arrive, and Robert was not around. He had kept himself busy with tasks away from the house, since after breakfast.

The collard greens had been washed, chopped and put on the stove with a piece of smoked pork swaddled amongst them.

"Bessie, the last time Grandfather came, he loved your cornbread. I am going to let you make it again. I will make the layer cakes."

"Yay!" she cheered clapping her hands. "I love it when Grandfather comes. He is so smart. I am proud when our neighbors come over for one of his sermons. I be thinking, 'That's my grandpapa up there.' And he makes some beautiful cabinets too. You think he gone bring you another one this time mama?"

"Not sure. But he hinted that he was going to make something special for his newest grandchild, and since the baby is due next month, well…" She looked at Bessie and blinked one eye while nodding her head. Bessie grinned, and kissed her mother's bulging middle.

"Maybe another girl, mama?"

"Well we will see what the Lord has given us this time."

The collage of delectable aromas airborne from Hattie's kitchen, throughout the house and into the front yard, was enticing, inviting, and appetite conjuring, by the time William Brown, Thomas and Virtee Lawson, and little James arrived. The wagon was loaded with offerings of food and other gifts for Robert, Hattie and the children. Hattie would never speak the words aloud to anyone, least ways her husband, but she knew the true source of Robert's resentment towards his dad. That resentment was fueled by things that Hattie didn't know or quite understand. Things that had happened before she met Robert. But it was clear that Robert still harbored a feeling of something that was not loving towards his dad.

William Brown was a tall handsome dark-skinned, strong bodied, man. His skin was the color of an eggplant. Smooth like one too. Hair was tightly curled, now mixed gray. His lips had a purple line around their perimeter. Not bad looking for a more than sixty-year-old man. His reputation as a jack leg minister, coupled by his striking appearance, had fluttered the eyelashes of many ladies, young and old around Holloway Township.

The Secrets of Hattie Brown

When Robert's mother and sisters had died many years ago, he noted how the women in the church were vying for his father's attention. Bringing him cakes and pies and inviting him over for dinner Sunday after church. Hattie's husband had commented to her once when they were speaking about his mother, that he didn't believe his father really missed his mom.

"Why you say that honey?"

"Cause I didn't see him turning down any of the favors being offered by those women. He was enjoying the attention. Then he up and married Bettie Bland. Her husband hadn't been dead that long either. And she had all those little children for him to raise. My mama was such a wonderful woman. Nobody could replace her. And don't forget, my mother was his second wife. The first wife, mother of my two oldest sisters, died a few years before I was born."

It was then that Hattie realized her husband was still mourning the passing of his mom. She had been only thirty-six years of age when she died.

"I understand love. You feel like he should have stayed to himself more after she died."

"Exactly that. Not running up and down the road courtin' women."

This was something they would have to live with until he could tell his dad how he felt. And that was not going to happen. Their relationship was not one of show and tell. It was cordial and respectful, but warm and fuzzy? No. Alpha males, both father and son.

Everybody heard the clip clop ahump clip clop ahump clop clop ahump calamity when William Brown's wagon rounded the bend to Robert and Hattie's front yard. The Brown's emerged from all of the places where they had been working to prepare for visitors. Robert, Ernest and Florida came from the barn, Hattie and Bessie came from inside the house, joining Lander and Robert Jr. who were already on the porch. They all merged to create a welcoming circle for their visitors.

As hosts and visitors converged upon one another, it was a challenge to tell where one body ended and another begin. Outside of that colorful circle of adoration, one could only see arms outstretched, feet on tippy toes, and cheeks pressed to cheeks.

"Virtee! Girl I ain't seen you in a month of Sundays! Come on in the house!"

The men and children unloaded the wagon while the women went on into the kitchen.

"Where is Mama Betty? I thought for sure she would be coming with Papa William?"

"At the last minute, she said she wasn't feeling well. I kinda felt it was something else, but I just told her that we miss her. She said to give everybody her love."

"Well you know Mama Betty has ten children and lots of grandchildren. Maybe she just wanted to be with them for the holiday."

"Could be."

The Secrets of Hattie Brown

Hattie could see that Virtee knew more than she was saying. This was something she actually liked about this woman; she was not a gossip. If she knew something to be a fact, she would tell you. Otherwise, she kept her mouth shut about what she was supposin'.

"So Hattie, how is life here? We sure miss you in the women's circle at Prospect Hill. We get your letters, and prayed together when your mom was sick, God bless her soul. But it's just not the same as having your sweet face amongst us. And personally, I miss our talks."

"Virtee, life is good, just busy as ever. The farming is going well. I have been able to quit my job working for the Howards. That freed up a little time so I could tend to a small vegetable garden for our food, and also grow sorghum to make molasses. Robert helped me to get it started and I am able to maintain it myself. Of course, I have the children's help with weeding and watering. Then I am able to make molasses and sell to people around here. I enjoy that, plus it brings me a little spending money to buy a new skirt or blouse here and there. You know Bessie is getting to be pickier about her appearance these days. She's a teenager. I think there's a lil boy at church she has her eye on."

"You're kidding. My oh my how the times do speed by! I remember when she was born. Held her in my arms. Now she ready to court! And you bout ripe as a juicy peach! When are you due?"

"Baby should be here very soon. Feels like it could be tonight," she giggled

"I can usually make a good guess. But this one, it's hard to tell if it's a boy or girl. Sometimes it feels like one and then other times it kicks like the other."

"I know what you mean. My James was like that," she responded laughing. "Even now, sometimes I still don't know. One minute he up under me in the kitchen, watching everything I do, and the next he is rolling around in the mud with his brothers."

There was a burst of laugher from the men outside on the porch, which reminded these two women that their intimate, alone time was limited. Virtee leaned in towards Hattie, with a conspiratorial whisper. She asked, "What about that "problem" we had discussed when you were back in Holloway?" She nodded her head towards the porch to indicate the subject of the "problem."

Hattie felt a little embarrassed, even though this was her friend, who she trusted and had confided in. "Well Virtee when we first moved here, I thought we left the problem behind us. But it seems to have followed us here. Not as often though. He is very busy with the tobacco business, and he is older now you know. But every once and awhile, I see something, or smell something that makes me sure he done been with somebody else. And then of course, there's my dreams. But still he is my husband. He is a loving father and he works hard to take care of us."

"Still having those dreams. So how are you handling that? Do you say anything to him?"

"No. I just keep on doing what I am doing. Taking care of my home and my children. Making molasses and loving him. I believe, one day, he will stop."

"I know what you mean. Ain't much more a girl can do. He comes home every night, right?"

"Oh yes. He always comes home. Most days in time for family dinner."

"Well honey. Count your blessings. I heard tell about Harriet's husband. You remember Harriet…"

"Harriet Cordings?"

"Yes. That's the one. Well her husband stays out when he feels like it. When he comes home, if she asks any questions he gets rough with her. She came to prayer meeting with a bruise on her arm last week. Now that's somebody who needs prayer!"

"How terrible. My sister Mary was in a situation like that. But you know what, she took her two babies, left the bigger children with him, and disappeared. She had a very hard time at first but is doing much better now."

Just then, Robert, and Thomas Lawson came into the kitchen. Each man sat a covered dish on the table, which was already laden with clay bowls and oversized pots.

Robert asked, "What y'all looking all secretive about?"

Thomas laughed. "Yeah, you two look like that rabbit I caught eating my cabbages." Both men looked at one another, neutralizing the women's continued silence by haunching their shoulders with both extended hands turned up and eyebrows elevated.

"How long before we eat?" Robert asked.

Hattie said, "Oh in about 30 minutes. Bessie just put the cornbread in the oven."

"Okay. Cause I am starving." Robert said

"Be ready soon love," Hattie said.

The family stood in a circle around the table as William Brown said the blessing over the food. He took his seat at one end of the table, and Robert sat at the other end. The two seats that indicate their paternal dominance in the family. As the vessels of steaming hot food were passing around in a circle, from person to person, the room was quiet except for the clinking of forks and spoons. Hattie remained standing, helping with the passing of bowls until all plates had been filled with food and everyone had been served. Then she fixed her plate and joined the family, seated on Robert's right side.

William broke the silence. "Hattie, this is a wonderful feast. I don't know where to stick my fork first."

"Thank you Papa William. Bessie helped me with all of the cooking."

William smiled at his granddaughter. She blushed, chewing with bulging cheeks. The children had all dove into their plates on a mission to clean them and get seconds.

"And Papa William thank you for the beautiful cabinet." She gestured towards the new beautifully crafted wooden chest that had been placed near the pantry when they were unpacking the wagon.

"Oh I was happy to do it. One more life added to our family. I wish my daddy Hanibal and Mama Lizzy were here to see all of these grands and great grands that have come from them."

"So, you been keeping busy back in Holloway?"

"Yes, I have. My bother Robin and I are still the only carpenters in town. So we stay busy. Between that and church work, we are always on the go. But I am getting older now, and sometimes wish I had somebody to help me. Somebody I could train like the old white man trained me and Robin so many years ago."

Thomas asked, "Robert why didn't you ever learn how to do carpentry?" Hattie held her breath. This was a sore spot, unbeknownst to Thomas. She hoped Robert would not be baited.

Robert seemed pensive for a moment, "Oh, I guess I was just busy doing farm work. Everybody had to work to bring in money. You know, we had a lot of mouths to feed, when my mother and sisters were here."

Hattie exhaled. The moment had passed.

Thomas accepted the response without further discussion. Everybody knows that fathers normally teach sons their craft. Hattie was thankful that his intuition had shut his mouth on that subject.

"Bessie, who made this cornbread?" William was teasing her

"I did Grandfather. Mama said you would like it."

"Well your mama was right. It's the best I have tasted. Did you churn the butter too?"

"I did grandfather." Bessie was proud

"Well now, you've done well. Pass me that molasses." All adults at the table showed appreciation for Bessie's culinary prowess. Hattie was proud of her girl.

In general, the conversations at the table were fluid, discussing numerous topics, from church business, to farming challenges, to how the world was changing.

"Papa, how is Uncle Robin doing?" Robert asked.

"Well he is coming along. Doctor said he has the Dropsy. So, his feet be swollen sometimes to the point of making it hard for him to walk."

That night, the home of Robert and Hattie Brown was filled with cozy pallets on the floors of all rooms. The adults slept on the children's beds and the children slept on the pallets.

The next day, church members came over and sat in the front room of the house, where Papa William delivered a sermon entitled, "Didn't My Lord Deliver Daniel?". It was well received by all. Robert seemed to be a bit more relaxed as folks congratulated him on his dad's excellent skills as a preacher. They even took up an offering for William. When everyone left, he privately gave the offering to Robert "for the children"

The next morning at dawn, William, Thomas, Virtee and little James left to journey back to Holloway. It was a bittersweet parting. Everyone had enjoyed their time together. Even Robert was sorry to see his father leave. Hattie could see it in the way they looked at one another as William climbed up onto his wagon seat, and Thomas signaled the horse to get going.

Hattie and Virtee promised to continue writing to one another. Their goodbye was also doleful. Hattie was glad that Robert and his dad had been together. William was sixty-eight years old. She knew that if anything were to happen to him, it would hurt her husband. She also knew how much she still missed her own mother. Good memories, or bad memories, your parent is still your parent.

Chapter Thirty-One

It was 1924, a very tumultuous year for the Browns. Uncle Robin finally succumbed to the Dropsey in April, Robert's daddy William's heart failed in October, and Bessie married Jeff Ray in November. Although each of these events were separate and significant entities within themselves, they all wrapped around one another like intertwining ivy vines on a wall.

Simply put, Robin's death set off a season of depression and ill health challenges for William. They had been very close since William's birth two years after Robin's. Their families always lived in the same neighborhood after they married and had children. Prospect Hill Church was home for both of these men. Robin as a trustee, William as a minister. Robin's death shook William to the very fibers of his existence during the months after his brother's demise.

Bessie had been courting a young man she met at church. Jeff Ray was ten years older than Bessie, but they fell in love, nonetheless.

"I know she is young," he said to Robert and Hattie, "but I love her and I promise to take good care of her."

After privately discussing Jeff's request, Robert and Hattie gave consent. They knew the Ray family to be good people. It was a very big family; Jeff had lots of siblings, and they were well respected in the church community. A wedding date was set for October, three months away.

"Robert, I have been thinking about the wedding proceedings. Wouldn't it be wonderful if your father came and performed the ceremony? There's a special bond between he and Bessie, and it would surely bring him some happiness. He has not been well since Uncle Robin's passing." Hattie was thoughtful

"You know Hattie, that is a great idea. I will send him a telegraph tomorrow." She knew he would agree. Father and son had been getting along much better since that Thanksgiving visit.

William happily said yes to come and administer nuptials for his first grand baby. Now, the plans were in full swing.

"Mama. I been thinking about my dress. I want something really pretty to wear. But how can we afford food for guests and a new dress for me?" Bessie asked.

"My sweet darling, I have been pinching off money and putting away for a long time. Looking forward to this moment. In fact, I made an appointment for us to go see Miss Sally about making you a dress. I could sew it, but she is a really good seamstress. And I want my big girl to have the best! There is some fabric I have been saving for a special occasion. Let me show it to you." Hattie spoke as if conspiring.

She went into the bottom of a storage chest next to her bed and pulled out a beautiful piece of white lacey fabric. Bessie ran her hand over the surface of the cloth, like it was whipped cream. In her eyes, Hattie saw surprise, appreciation, and excitement.

"Oh mama! This is beautiful! I love it. Thaaaank you! When do we go to Miss Sally?"

The ladies of the church volunteered to bring a variety of foods, side dishes, for the special day. Hattie would fry up some chickens, and Robert would roast a pig in a pit outside, overnight. The wedding and reception would be at their home.

Days before the wedding, Robert came into the kitchen. He looked sallow and withdrawn. In his fist, he was holding a piece of paper like it was oxygen...like if he let it go, he would stop breathing.

"Robert! What is the matter?" Hattie asked.

He showed her the telegraph.

It read, "Your papa has died. Come soon."

Signed, Betty Brown (his father's wife).

So, all wedding plans and preparations subsided and the family had to pack up and go to Woodsdale. Hattie had not seen Robert so broken since his mother died. He was quiet, and remote.

Hattie went into action. "Bessie, come here. I have something to tell you."

Bessie had been in the back of the house washing clothes. "Yes mama?"

"Sit down honey." Hattie knew how much Bessie loved her grandfather.

"Papa William has died." She stopped to give her daughter a moment to absorb the words she had just spoken.

"Oh no, mama. not Papa William! What happened?" she exclaimed while sobbing. Hattie showed her the crumpled telegram. Bessie was so much like her mother. Grief stricken or not, she knew that this meant things had to be done and she needed to get on task. "What do you need for me to do mama?"

Bessie rounded up the children while Hattie began packing their things for a trip to Woodsdale. Robert just sat, staring at the hearth, dazed, silent, eyes glazed over as if they were not seeing the now, but focused upon another time and another place. "Robert honey, you wanna talk about it?" Hattie wanted to comfort him but wasn't sure what he needed. At the funeral, Ernest and Florida hovered around their dad. They had never seen him cry.

The Going Home service was well attended and William was buried, like Robin and Eliza, in the church yard at Prospect Hill Church. The funeral was actually on the day that had been scheduled as Bessie's wedding day, which was now pushed forward a month.

Betty did come to Holly Springs for the wedding. She was of great help to mother and daughter with wedding details and chores. It was a comfort for them all to be together so soon after William's passing.

The nuptials were performed by their pastor, and the wedding was quite lovely after all.

Jeff worked and lived on the farm property of Dr. J.M. Judd., in a very small nearby town called Varina. This was where he and Bessie made their home. The following year, on a beautiful summer morning in August 1925, Dr. Judd delivered their first baby, Robert and Hattie's first grandchild: Christine Hattie Ray.

Barbara Brown Gathers

Chapter Thirty-Two

"You're pregnant!" Hattie exclaimed.

"I am!" Bessie was grinning.

"And here you are helping me and the midwife to deliver your brother!" Hattie was aghast.

"Yes, mama. Looks like my new brother is going to have a built-in playmate, for life." Bessie said excitedly.

That was in February of 1926. Hattie gave birth to a curly headed little boy with the deepest dimples, Azel RD. In October, Bessie bore Jeff Jr. So, Robert and Hattie became both the parents of a new son, and grandparents for the second time within a span of eight months. 'RD' and Little Jeff didn't have very long to play together though. Jeff Senior and Bessie Ray decided to join the throngs of people of color who were leaving the south and trying their luck in the northern cities.

Just months after Baby Jeff was born, Bessie came to give her parents some news.

"Jeff says that now there are two children, we need a better style of living for our family. Colored people can't really make much money here in the south, and he is tired of farm work. Jeff has been talking to a friend who moved north and is down here for a visit. He says that racism is a bit easier to get around in the north, and there are jobs to be had in factories. Jeff and his brother James want us all, me and the children and James wife and children, to move up there together."

"Well where are you going? New York? Detroit? Chicago?" Hattie could tell by the harsh tone of his voice, that Robert was asking because he didn't want Bessie to go anywhere. Period.

"The friend told Jeff about a job at a chemical manufacturing plant in Camden, New Jersey. He and James are going up there this weekend to see about the job and to see what the housing situation is like."

Within two weeks of this declaration, the Rays had packed up and left Holly Springs to move to Camden. The brothers had rented a house big enough for them all to live together. Hattie felt incomplete without her right hand. Even though she had married and moved away, she still lived nearby and they still saw each other often. But with this move to New Jersey, she didn't know when she would see her first born, again. Hattie had eight children, and now one of them was outside of her reach. The only thing Robert had said one night as they lay in bed was, "If he mistreat her, I will kill him." Hattie knew that Robert didn't t think any man was good enough for his girl. What was the big deal about going north anyway?

Virtee was three when RD was born, and she was more than glad to vacate her mama's lap and head outside to run with the boys. She was a girl who loved rolling around the yard with her brothers. Sometimes Hattie would yell at Robert Jr. and Lander. "Careful! She's a little girl you know! You can't knock her down like that!" But Virtee would jump right back in the game, as if to say 'Come on with it. I can take it!'

Meanwhile, Virginia, at five, was now Mama's helper. She watched baby RD while mama worked around the house and played with him. Two years later, when Hattie was pregnant again, RD was Mama's lil sugar pie and coveting his position as 'the baby'. He was more inclined to hang around in the house with Hattie and Virginia, than to go outside to rough it with his brothers and Virtee. RD was a quieter and more introspective little boy who enjoyed playing by himself.

The new baby girl was named Rivers Ardenia. Born on January 19, 1928, she was cute as a little doll. Rivers had big pear-shaped eyes and bright as the midday sun. She was light skinned like her mom, Bessie, Virginia, and RD. Although Rivers' hair had that straight curly, curly straight texture, it was more curly than straight and thick like a bush. She was a perfect baby. Ten fingers, ten toes, and strong little plump legs and arms waving in the air. She giggled anytime a family member came nearby to play with her. This was the ninth and last child that Hattie would bear.

The rhythm of their marriage was well established. Sex, work, church, and the children. Pregnancy, work, church and the children. Sex, work, church and the children. Every moment of their day was emulsified with fulfilling the tasks that maintained this pattern of living. Until that day, when everything changed.

In general, Hattie's life was good, except for missing Bessie very much and craving for a heart to heart talk with her mother.

Bessie was her first born. Bessie's birth represented the first time she knew what it felt like to have a tiny version of yourself to cradle in your arms. Theirs was a very special bond. She missed Bessie's sweet spirit and funny stories. Bessie had inherited the story telling gift from Hattie. That girl could make up a story about a ball of biscuit dough.

Hattie missed her mom most, early in the morning when she got up to pray and meditate while the house was still quiet. Sometimes she even imagined that she was talking with Eliza. She would say things like, "I miss you mama." Or "I'm okay mama. The children are growing so fast. You know Bessie is now a mother too."

Otherwise, Hattie was happier than she had ever been. Her family was blossoming. Earnest, Robert and Lander were big enough to be of tremendous help to Robert with all of the aspects of planting, growing, harvesting, and selling the tobacco. They were not wealthy, but money was quite adequate.

Hattie knew that education was a number one priority for any children she might bring into the world. She had not changed her mind about that. Everybody except Florida, Rd, and Rivers attended classes at the local school for colored children. When Hattie visited the school, the teacher always had high praises for the Brown children. They were smart, well behaved, and ready to learn.

Now Florida, well he was another type of bird all around. Although he had attended the local school at first, both Hattie and his dad wanted something more demanding for him. He was smart and quick to learn, but he was easily distracted if his intellect was not being stimulated. In the local school, with mixed ages in one classroom, older children had to be more tolerant and patient while waiting for the younger ones to catch up. Sometimes they even assisted the teacher with tutoring the little ones. This was not the environment where Florida would best be served educationally.

Each of the Brown children had a godfather and a godmother. Florida's godfather was Mr. Ira Burton, a very close family friend who they had met at church when first moving to Holly Springs. The Burtons owned the farm they lived on. Mr Burton's son, Leroy and Florida had become best friends over the years. They were the same age.

One Sunday, after church, Mr. Burton made a great offer to Robert and Hattie.

"There is a colored man named Berry O'Kelly, who has opened a school for colored children in Raleigh. The school, said to be one of the best, has a campus, with eight buildings, including a dining hall and dormitories. They teach reading writing and arithmetic, and they teach trades. I want to send LeRoy to this school, and we want Florida to go with him. I think it would be good for both boys. Florida is sharp as a razor. This will set him on the right path. If you consent, I will pay his school fees for as long as he earns good grades. You would only have to provide him with some pants, a couple of white shirts, a tie and a suit jacket, because they do wear uniforms to school every day."

Robert was astounded. "Mr. Burton, thank you so much. Yes I heard about this man, Mr. O'Kelly. He is very a very rich businessman in Raleigh."

Hattie said, "You know Mr. Burton, I worry about that boy. He needs more than we can give him around here. He is so smart and so talented. We appreciate your kindness, and generosity."

And just like that, a few weeks later, Florida was off to school with his best friend, Leroy Burton. Hattie had everything to be thankful for, and everything to be happy about.

"Robert, have I ever said thank you for my beautiful children, and for this life we have built together?"

"Well I don't know if I ever heard you say those words, but over the years I've learned a few simple things being with you. Love is in the biscuit dough. Your thank you is in the way you smile when you see me coming in from the fields, tired and hungry. Hattie, love and appreciation is in everything you do around here. I need to give gratitude. You gave me a loving family after my mother and sisters died. I was alone the world. Where would I be without you? I am not sure that I have always treated you like how you deserve to be treated."

Hattie was deeply moved by his sentiment. She had seen this side of Robert opening up in recent months. With the death of his father, the marriage of his first born, and then the birth of grandchildren, he seemed to show a more sentimental side of his nature. This Robert reminded her of the snappy boy who had teased her at church that day when they first met. Also, Hattie wondered about how Robert was feeling. He didn't seem to have the same pep as he used to. Well, he was getting older, she thought.

They were laying in bed, talking. The room was aglow with the light from the oil lamp.

She wrapped her arms around his neck and pressed her body against his, feeling the warmth of their shared affections. The embrace evolved into deeper intimacy as they began to undress one another with hands and eyes. Hattie felt like she was seeing her husband's naked body for the first time. Like their love was new, and fresh. Then she saw it.

"Robert. What is that?" She pointed to a round red sore, with a punched out looking middle and a raised border near the tip of his penis. It appeared to be wet.

"I don't know. It doesn't hurt. I just figured it's a bump that will go away soon after it drains."

"Well how long has it been there? I haven't seen it before."

"It's been awhile. You know, most times we undress in the dark."

"I think you need to see Dr. Cheek. I don't like how this looks."

"Aw Hattie, it ain't nothing. I can't be running to the doctor for every little cut or scratch."

"Robert that looks serious to me. You need to see the doctor. We will go to his office tomorrow once the children are in school."

The next day, with babies RD and Rivers in tow, Mr. and Mrs. Brown went to see the local physician, Dr. Cheek. After examining Robert, Dr Cheek's face was grim.

"I have known and cared for your family for many years. I am going to give this to you both straight. Robert it looks like you have bad blood. It's called syphilis. I have taken a swab of your blood to test it. While we wait for the test results, you need to know that this disease is contagious. If you two have intercourse, I want you to use these."

He handed Robert three small packages.

"These are rubbers?"

"Yes. They will protect Hattie. That's if she is not already infected."

Hattie gasped. "You mean I could already have it too?"

Dr. Cheek said, "Yes. Hattie. Syphilis is very contagious. It can be in the blood for some time before the symptoms show up. Now, with this sore on the penis, and you two don't know how long it's been there......"

The ride back to their house was deathly silent. Robert was in shock. His face had turned ashen gray. He had not been able to make eye contact with Hattie since Dr. Cheek had uttered those words, 'It's called syphilis.' Hattie was crushed. When they arrived home, Hattie took the children and went for a walk down the dusty road. She saw a beautiful bird in a tall tree and felt envious. So free, no worries, no burdens. She thought of Psalm fifty-five, "Ah but if I had the wings of a dove, I would fly away and be at rest."

She had walked further and longer than she'd realized. Rivers, being carried on her hip, was beginning to feel like a bag of bricks, and RD was complaining.

"I am tired Mama. When are we going home?"

Just at that moment she heard their wagon behind. Robert pulled up alongside them.

"Come on Hattie. Come on home. The children will come from school soon, and I know you all must be tired of walking."

She did not utter a word. Just handed him Rivers, so that she could help RD to climb on and then take her seat next to her husband.

RD said, "Thank you Papa."

As the wagon turned around to head for the house, she saw that bird, perched on the same branch, about to take flight. And she, back in the cage.

She made it through dinner, homework, stories of their day at school, being referee between the boys, and bedtime, all of the usual stuff. The children were always so animated, nobody seemed to notice that their mom and dad were quieter than usual. At bedtime, when the house was settled she sat in front of the hearth, staring into the flames. Robert came into the kitchen.

"Hattie. You coming to bed? It's been a long day." His voice was soft, like cotton.

"Coming to bed? Coming to bed? Coming to bed!" There was a loud clap of thunder outside that shook the frames around the windows.

"Mama!" Virginia screamed

Hattie went to the girls' room, "What's the matter baby?"

"The thunder. It scared me," she spoke, terrified

"It's okay Sugah. Don't worry. Mama is here." She engulfed her child in her arms and rocked her until she fell back into a restful sleep.

When she returned to the kitchen, he was still there, waiting. Looking like he knew what he deserved and was patiently waiting for it.

"Hattie, I am sorry."

"Stop Robert. Just stop. I don't want to hear it," She interrupted in a venomous whisper, not wanting to awaken the children. A streak of lightening cast a flash of light in through the windows. Just for a split second she saw Robert's face in the bright light. She saw fear in his widened eyes and his right foot was rapidly bouncing up and down in place, hands laced together in his lap. Like a little boy about to get a whupping.

"You sorry for what? What did you think was going to happen? Out there fooling around with every Mary, Sally, or Jane who would open their legs to a married man! Exactly what did you expect Robert?"

He was silent. This put kerosene on her fire. The volume of her voice was turning up, but then so was the sound of the rain tapping on the roof. In the dimly fire lit room, she stood up and pinned him with her eyes. Her shadow loomed large on the wall. His was dwarfed, sitting in the chair. Then she stood very still, shut her eyes, and replayed the thoughts, visions, and painful memories from the past twenty years. Just for a moment. Robert was completely silent. Fighting back the tears, she opened her eyes and looked at the man sitting in front of her.

"So you think it's the first time you have been caught doing your dirt? Huh? So you think you have been getting away with this deceit all of these years? Really? Is that what you think husband? Well I've got news for you. I have always known what you were doing, and so did half of the people in Woodsdale. Why do you think I was so willing to move away from my mama, my sisters, our church, and the only town I have known since I was born? I was hoping that your behavior was because of where we were and not because of who you are! But then we moved here, and after awhile the same thing started up again. Women giving me subtle hints, like telling me about the local whore house that opened up. Or pointing out someone at church and saying, 'You know she be chasing everybody's husband'. Robert, I have been through it all, the hurt, the embarrassment, being laughed at behind my back. Now I am just disgusted. Because it was all for nothing. You ain't never gonna change. It's who you are Robert. You are a womanizer. What do you need me for? To cook your food? To take care of your babies? To wash your clothes? Or to make you look like a man of good standing in the church community? What, Robert, do you need me for? Cause I don't know. What kind of man goes out and brings bad blood home to his wife? Men fool around, of course. Everybody knows that. But they are careful, and they protect their wives. You done went out there and picked up a contagious disease and brought it home to me like an alley cat bringing a dead rat to the kitchen table!"

Now she was finding it difficult to hold back the tears. As the rain had become torrential, banging on the roof top, her tear ducts had been filling to flood levels. Robert looked heavenward, as if he was in prayer. Tears shimmered in her glossy eyes, she scrunched up her face.

"Oh now you are praying. And what exactly can you say to God? The only thing you can say is, I am sorry. God will forgive you," Hattie's voice began to tremble. "but I tell you...."

And then it came, the flood, the cascade of tears. She crumbled to the bench near the table, and the wail began. It was the wail of a mourner who has lost a beloved loved one through sudden death. Truly, Hattie had lost her dreams of the perfect marriage, of an adoring husband who was committed only to her. She had lost the fantasy that had been implanted in her heart, so long ago. It was dead. Killed by the truth. Murdered by her own refusal to accept what she had known since she met Robert Brown. Now this was the price she had to pay.

She was aware of him staring at her but felt like she was all alone. She wanted to crawl up into a fetal knot, becoming smaller and smaller until she disappeared into nothingness.

Robert walked over to where his wife had now put her head down on the table. She did not look at him, but could feel the heat of his body, very close by. When he put his hand on her shoulder, she flinched.

"Go away Robert. Just leave me alone. I can't even stand to look at you."

She heard his footsteps shuffling their way back into the bedroom, and the creak of their mattress being compressed by the weight of his tired body. After awhile, the only sound in the house, was that of the constant rainfall splattering on the roof, and the low almost inaudible dirge of Hattie sobbing. Her heart was shattered.

She was running, fast. The road ahead was endless and paved with dead birds. Somehow though, she did not step on them but just kept seeing them ahead. And then she heard her name being called.

"Hattie! Hattie Cowen!" She didn't want to acknowledge the call. She didn't want to turn around to see who was coming up behind her. She knew the voice but didn't want him to catch up. She kept running and running and wondering why the birds had died.

"Hattie! Stop. Stop running!"

He caught up, running alongside her, out of breath. It was Robert. But he looked different. His face was that of her husband, but his body was small, like that of a boy. She towered over him.

"I'm tired Hattie. I can't run no more. Stop please." He was breathless.

She outran him by speeding up and was looking for someplace to escape. Was there an old tree, or a big rock she could hide behind?

"Haaaaaaaaatie!" The sound of his voice became remote, as if he was no longer chasing her and she was moving away from him. Then, there was silence. The crisp air was whistling in the blustery wind. When she stopped running and turned around, the little boy/man, Robert, was lying face down, on the road. He was stretched out on top of dead bird carcasses. The last thing she remembered was smelling the stench of the dead animals, and running towards Robert, terrified that he too, was dead.

"Mama. Mama? Why are you sleeping out here with your head on the table?"

Hattie opened her eyes to see the entire kitchen lit up with the brightness of daybreak. Ernest was standing over her, looking confused and concerned.

"Oh," she said sleepily "I was so tired son. I just rested my head for a moment, I thought. Thank you for waking me. Lemme get up and get myself ready to start breakfast. Is everybody up?"

"Yes mama. Everybody is up and getting ready. Are you okay mama?"

"I am okay son. Yesterday was a long day. That's all. Just help me out with the others. Go and put some fire under them. Don't wanna be late for school."

Ernest was obedient, but as he walked away, she wasn't sure that he believed her excuse about 'tired' and 'long day'. Well for now that was the best she could do.

Chapter Thirty-Three

Their Last Christmas

On October 30, 1930, Bessie and her husband Jeff became the parents of their fourth child, Gladys Melvina. Hattie and Robert were so happy about being grandparents again. Hattie had birthed enough babies to know how fast they grow. She wanted to see her grand babies at every stage of their development. She wanted to hug them everyday. She wanted them to know her. To come running and tripping over their feet when they would see her coming. Of course, it was hard not being able to see the babies on a regular basis. She was afraid that they would not even know her because they didn't see her enough.

Soon it would be Christmas and Hattie wanted it to be their best ever. Her marriage was in a good place, and her children and grands were growing up beautifully. She started planning for the festivities right after Thanksgiving.

November 30, 1930

My dearest Bessie,

I am so happy when I think about sweet Gladys being here and healthy, with five fingers and ten toes. I can't wait to kiss them all. How are little Jeff, Christine Hattie and Wilma doing? You feeling okay? I worry about you all the time and hope you are getting along all right up there. The weather is cold. Do you all have enough heat? Do you have a warm coat to put on when you go out?

We are all well, thank the Lord. Your brothers and sisters are growing up so fast. I hope you will recognize them when you see them. Your Papa is also doing fine.

Bessie, do you think you all might able to come down for Christmas? I just feel like this is to be our best holiday ever! But I know it can't be the best, if you and my grandchildren are not at the table. I know that the Ray family would be so happy to see their sons and grandchildren too. You all could make us so happy. See what Jeff has to say about it and let me know. I have saved up a few dollars, I could send, to help you all pay for transportation. I know it is hard with Jeff the only one working, and you just had a baby. Kiss the children for me.

Your Loving Mother

Next, she started thinking about the menu. There would be the usual, boiled ham, fried chicken, collard greens, baked sweet potatoes, potato salad, biscuits, molasses and a cake with icing...but it was Christmas! What could she add to make it super special?

"Robert we are going to need a few extras for the Christmas dinner when you go to the store in town next week. The vegetables in the garden are ready. I will have Virginia and Virtee help me with the harvesting. I've got plenty molasses made. But I will need some brown sugar and a couple of other things. I know that you will have to double the amount of lard we usually buy, since there will be a lot of chicken frying going on," She said this with a wide mouthed grin.

"You seem so excited about this holiday. It's been a long time since I have seen you looking like a thirsty plant that has been watered."

"Family holidays are so important to me. They feed me us memories that never fade. When we gather together, the love in the air is so thick, you can slice it with that big cutlass you use to chop the tobacco. I am hoping that Bessie, Jeff, and the children will be here with us."

"Now that would be a treat. I want to put all four of those grand babies on my lap at the same time! I will be going to town on Monday. Figure out exactly what you need and let me know. I will pick up everything."

On Sunday, after church, Hattie spoke with Sister Burton. "Sister Burton. When are the boys coming home from school for the holidays?"

"I think they are coming next week. Ask my husband. He knows their schedule. I am sure he will bring Florida to you, as soon as they hit town."

"Good. I miss him and can't wait to see my child. By the way, I remember, last Christmas Eve when we had our service here at the church, you made some delicious candy for everybody. What was it called again?"

"Oh. The Brown Sugar Candy. Everybody loves my Brown Sugar Candy!"

"It was so good. I had to stop myself from eating it and leave some for other folks." She laughed. "I want to make some for my family this Christmas. Can you tell me how?"

"Oh sure. I would be glad to share the recipe. I learned it from my grandmama."

"I would appreciate it. Robert is going to the store tomorrow, so I need to tell him what to buy for me."

"You will need some butter."

"We can do that. Bessie used to churn it, and now I have taught Virginia how to do it."

"Okay, so you are going to need some cream to make your butter. Tell Robert to come by our farm. I will send you some cream from our cows."

Hattie's eyes were sparkling. This was going to be some Christmas!

"Then you need brown sugar, a tin of that evaporated milk, some vanilla extract, salt, and you can use either walnuts or pecans."

"Our pecan trees are loaded with nuts."

"Good. That will work just fine. Now listen carefully. It's not hard to make Brown Sugar Candy, but you gotta get everything in there at the right time."

Hattie had a pencil with a point that and been cut using a kitchen knife, and a piece of paper. She wrote down every word.

"Sister Burton. I am so excited. Thank you very very much. My family is going to love this! I will tell Robert to come by your house on his way back from the store tomorrow."

"Anytime sugar. It is my pleasure."

On the way from home from church, Robert said, "Tomorrow after school, I am gonna take Ernest, Junior, and Lander with me to the woods, so we can find and cut down our Christmas tree. In fact, I think I will take RD with us too. He is big enough. Lander can look after him while Ernest and Junior help me to pick up and carry the tree."

Hattie replied, "I was wondering when you were going to get it."

After dinner, Hattie, Virginia and Virtee started making decorations to hang on the tree. Virtee went outside and collected pinecones to which they tied strings for hanging. Virginia mixed flour, salt, oil, and water to make a clay that could be shaped into ornaments for the tree. They used juice from crushed Sumac berries, which grew wild down the road, to give the clay a red color.

"The clay is ready mama." Virginia was excited

"Okay, call Virtee. Let's sit down and make these ornaments."

Mother and daughters created a variety of balls and other shapes, punching holes in the top so that a string could be inserted. They baked them until they were hard. Hattie removed the hardened clay ornaments from the oven and put them on the table.

"Don't touch. As soon as they are cooled down, we will put the strings in them so that they can be hung."

Later, when she looked out of the window, she saw her husband and sons coming with the biggest, greenest, most beautiful pine tree she had ever seen, a smile danced on her lips. It was a challenge for them to get that huge tree into the house and standing straight up. Mommy and daughters squealed and clapped as they watched father and sons perform with machismo. Even little RD tried to be a part of the manly tasking. Afterwards, everybody helped to decorate the branches of the tree with the ornaments and pinecones Hattie and the girls had created.

Robert said, "It's beautiful. But I think it is missing something."

"What? That's all we have," Hattie asked curiously.

"I will be right back." Robert went to their bedroom and came back with a little box in his hand. When he opened it, everyone exclaimed!

Virginia swooned, "Icicles!"

The little box was filled with strips of silver foil tinsel. Robert had bought them and hidden them as a surprise for this very moment.

They each took a few strands from the box and added them to the tree until they were all used up. The family now stood, in awe, staring, surrounding their tree.

The silence was broken by the voice of Robert. "Dear God, we thank you for this life you have given us. We thank you for our family, our home, and the harvests that you have so bountifully provided for us. Thank you Lord, for Jesus. Please continue to bless us and to feed those who are less fortunate. These and all blessings, we ask in the name of your son, Jesus Christ. Amen.

Hattie knew that her family, individually and collectively, had been deeply touched by this sacred moment.

Chapter Thirty-Four

Christmas Day

"Mama, is Sister coming home for Christmas?" Virginia asked.

"I don't know honey. I wrote and asked her to come. But I haven't heard back from her."

"I hope so. I want to see my nephew and nieces." She grinned.

"Well I am thinking that if they were coming, she would have said something by now."

Hattie didn't tell her daughter that although she was certainly happy about the holiday and its festivities, there was a little chunk of her heart that was sad. She didn't know why, but she felt compelled to see everybody she loved, this Christmas. Now it was December 25th, and it didn't look like that was going to happen.

Robert came into the house with both arms full of logs. He laid them down in front of the hearth.

"That should be enough to take us through the day and into tonight. Gin, go to my room and get my hat. It's chilly out there!"

Virginia left the room and he turned to Hattie. "Now what's wrong? I have been watching you for the past few days. There is something eating at you."

The Secrets of Hattie Brown

Hattie let her guard down. "I am worried about Bessie. She didn't write back and that is not like her. I hope they are not having serious money problems and she is ashamed to tell me."

"Well it ain't over till it's over It's still Christmas Day baby! We have the whole day! Meanwhile, the rest of us are here, and we love you! I bet Bessie is just fine."

"I guess." She tried to lighten her mood.

"Where's that pretty Christmas dress I bought for you?"

"It's hanging up. I will put it on after I finish cooking. Don't want to cover it up with this apron." She smiled at that notion.

"I am looking forward to seeing you in it!"

Her man. He had worked his charming magic on her once again. She was still sorry to think that she might not see her daughter and those babies, but she was willing to wait and see what the day might bring.

Hattie had just finished mixing chopped pineapple with icing and slathering it on top of the bottom layer of the cake, when she heard a noise outside. She peeked out of the window, while wiping her hands on her apron.

"Oh my God! Lawd Jesus! Oh my God! Thank you Jesus!"

She saw her beloved Bessie, stepping out of the passenger side door of a Model T Ford automobile, carrying a baby in her arms. Quickly taking off her apron and patting her hair to make sure it was laying flat in place, she ran outside.

Robert had already been outside. He, and the boys were all circling around the car and excitedly listening to Jeff, Bessie's husband, talk about the vehicle.

"My landlord was getting a new car so he sold me this one. And since he knows me and I pay my rent on time, he let me have it on credit. It cost $300, and I have six months to finish the payments."

Hattie grabbed her daughter and hugged her while taking the baby from her arms. Then little Jeff, Wilma and Christine appeared from the back seat. Hattie didn't know which one to grab first.

"Bessie! You didn't answer my letter. I thought you weren't coming."

"I know mama. I'm sorry. I wanted to surprise you. Also, we were waiting to see if we would get the car in time for Christmas."

"Well I am happy happy happy! Come on inside." By this time Virginia and Virtee had come out of the house and joined the hugfest.

As mother, daughters, and granddaughters made their way towards the porch, the men were still discussing the car.

"Well how fast does it go?" Robert asked

"It can go up to forty-five miles per hour! But with my family in the car, I don't drive that fast. They say it has the power of twenty horses!"

"Wow! Man that is something else. Show me how you turn it on. Can I take it for a little spin around?"

"Sure! Lemme show you."

In the kitchen, Hattie and Virginia helped Bessie and the children get their coats and shoes off. Jeff Jr. was still outside with the guys. He had attached himself to Robert as soon as he got out of the car.

Inside, the two women were looking one another over.

"Well I see you won't be wearing those wasters that I gave you. Honey, your waist looks like you just had a baby!"

"Well I did mama. Please don't remind me! I am hoping it will shrink back down. I am trying to eat less."

"You still my pretty baby girl! Nothin' is gonna change that," Hattie said pinching Bessie cheeks.

"And you Mama. I have to say, you look happy. Both you and Papa seem very content."

"I am. I think your papa and I have turned a corner in our marriage. We have both matured and that makes life better. You will see. Every married couple has their own style of growing up together."

"Mama, can I go outside with Gin to play?" Christine asked.

"Sure go ahead. Just put your coat on," Bessie said.

"The children look wonderful Bessie. You are doing a good job."

"Thank you mama. I'm trying my best. Kids are a lot of work and living up north is very different. For one thing, people are not as neighborly. If my sister and brother in law didn't live in the house with us, it would be even more challenging. We help one another with childcare, with cleaning, even cooking. Still it's a full day, from sun up to when Jeff comes home from work, dinner is served, and kids put to bed."

"So now you understand my life a little better huh?" Hattie smiled.

"I sure do and think of you often. You made it look so easy. Like you didn't even have to think about it. Now I understand how much vision and planning it took for things to run as smoothly as you always made it. So how are my brothers and sisters doing?" Asked Bessie.

"They are all good. With Florida gone off to school, it puts a little more work on Ernest, Robert Jr. and Lander around the farm. In fact, let me tell you a funny story."

Bessie eyes sparkled with anticipation.

"Last spring, when the weather was just getting warm, it was time to start planting our kitchen garden. Your father gave the seeds to Robert Jr. and Lander to go and till the ground, make rows and plant. They turned the ground and made the rows one day before going to school. Next day would be for planting. The following morning, I woke them up extra early to do their work before going to school."

Lander said, "Aw mama. I'm so sleepy. Can we do it when we come home?"

Robert Jr. sleepily chimed in, "Yes mama. It won't take that long."

"I said okay."

As soon as they returned home in the afternoon, they took the seeds and a hoe from the barn and went off to our garden. They came back about two hours later, laughing and joking with one another.

"All done?" I asked.

In unison, they said, "All done," grinning wide.

"Well, after a little over a week, during which I had been watering these rows every day, nothing was growing. Nothing was sprouting. Not even a little green tip of leaf pushing its way through the dirt."

"Really? Those seeds should have sprouted after a few days," Bessie said

"Yes. There was corn, collard greens, sweet potatoes, tomatoes, and some okra."

"Oh yeah, Something is wrong here." Bessie said.

"Exactly. But I just kept watching them every day and wondering what happened. Then one day, I took RD and Rivers for a walk in the far field. You know the one way behind the barn?"

"Yes. We used to play over there," Bessie said

"I am walking my babies, and talking to them, and way over yonder, I see a corn stalk sticking out from behind that big tree. So I hurry over there, and my God, Bessie, behind that tree, all together in a huge clump, was little baby tomato plants, collards sprouts, the okra were getting tall already and the corn was shooting up!"

Bessie started laughing. "How in the world did that happen?"

"Well when you father came home, I told him. He called both boys in here and asked them what happened when they planted the vegetables?"

"At first Robert Jr. started saying, "Well we planted everything just like you showed us to do Papa."

"I looked at Lander and could tell that he had already figured out that this was a set up. So he came clean right away."

He was crying even before he started speaking, because he knew what this was going to mean. "Well Papa. We wanted to go play catch, in the fields with some of the other boys from school. So instead of planting like you told us, we dumped the seeds behind the tree. Robert Jr. said that when the garden doesn't grow, we could just play dumb and swear we did everything right. I was scared Papa. But I did want to play too. And I knew I couldn't do it by myself. So that what's happened. I'm sorry Papa. I'm sorry Mama!" His voice was shaking.

"He looked at me, as if to say 'Save me', as he was now bordering on hysterical."

"So what happened?" Bessie asked

"You know your father is not a man of a lot of words. He simply pointed his finger and said very quietly, 'To the judgement hall'!

Bessie put her hand over her mouth and stifled a giggle, "Not the judgment hall!"

"Yep. They both got a beating. Robert got more because he is the oldest. The next day, they had to get up at dawn and go do the planting. Your father told them that if they were late for school, they would find themselves in the judgment hall again. And, he told them that those seeds had better start sprouting immediately or else.

Mother and daughter said in unison, "Judgement hall." Nodding their heads and laughing simultaneously.

"The next night over dinner, Ernest was making fun of them. He asked, "How in the world could you two be so stupid? And tell me what did you think we would be eating come harvest time? At least, tell me, did you learn anything?"

"Both Lander and Robert looked at one another, as if they had discussed this question already, then they looked at Robert."

Robert Jr. said, "Well Papa said, if you plant a seed, something is gonna grow somewhere, and everybody, especially you, will get the benefit or punishment for what you planted. He said it never fails. And Papa said we should remember this as we go through life. You will reap what you sow."

"Well good you learn that now, rather than later. I hope you got the lesson sealed in your dumb heads," Ernest told them.

"Wow! What a lesson for them and for everybody. I learned so much about parenting from you and Papa. I hope I will do as good as you two." Bessie was impressed.

"Aww, that's already in motion my love," Hattie noted.

While they were talking, Hattie had been heating up the food and Bessie had been setting the table. It was like they had rung the dinner bell. All at once, the whole clan came through the door.

"Food ready?" Robert said. "We are hooongry!"

Hattie laughed, "Well I am glad you are hooongry cause I haven't been doing all of this cooking for it to be left in the serving bowls. Yes! Food is ready. Everybody sit."

Adults sat around the dinner table, with Robert at the head. There was a smaller table nearby, for the children. When all were seated, Hattie said, "Let us pray." Robert prayed a long and beautiful Christmas Day prayer, and the passing of steaming bowls and hot platters commenced.

A few days later, when the Ray family left to return to New Jersey, there were tears all around. Hattie's throat was thickened with sobs. Even Papa Robert's eyes were flooded with tears as they waved goodbye to the Model T Ford and its beloved passengers. Their departure was bitter sweet. It was simply wonderful having Bessie at home. However Hattie realized that once your child leaves and starts a family of their own, they never really 'come home' again. When they come, they are still a visitor with their own 'home' to return to. She could see that theirs was a happy home. Jeff was attentive towards Bessie and clearly loved his children. This made Hattie happy. After they left, even Robert had to say something nice. "She looks good. Looks happy."

Chapter Thirty-Five

Days later when Hattie thought about their Christmas dinner, she realized that she had not even tasted the Brown Sugar Candy. From the time she put it on the table, it began to disappear from the platter. Before she knew it, the platter was empty. Oh well, she would just have to make it again. Sister Burton was right. She must remember to thank her again.

"Robert, did you get any of the Brown Sugar Candy? I didn't even taste a crumb. I guess it must have been good."

Robert was sitting on the side of the bed, elbows on his thighs, resting his forehead on the palm of his hand. She was waiting for him to respond to her question. When he didn't seem to hear her, she said, "Robert. What's the matter?"

He looked up at her with clouded eyes. "I am not sure Hattie. I didn't want to say anything before because I didn't want to ruin the Christmas spirit in the house. But I have not been feeling right."

"What do you mean?" she asked

"Well for one thing, I am gaining weight. My feet are swollen from time to time. I pee a lot and sometimes I see red in my pee."

"Red as in blood?" The pitch of her voice was raising.

"I don't know what it is. Look like it could be blood." He seemed confused "And then sometimes after I eat, I feel nauseous like I wanna throw up."

"Robert, I appreciate you wanting to make our Christmas as joyous as it was, but this sounds very serious."

"I know. I am going to see Dr. Cheek tomorrow. Come with me."

The next day, they went to see the doctor. After examining Robert and listening to the list of symptoms he was experiencing, the doctor said,

"The medicine you are taking for the syphilis, is called 606. It does have some side effects. Not everyone experiences them. However, it sounds like your kidneys are having a bad reaction to this medicine. What you described, we call it nephritis, which means your kidneys are inflamed. The only other medicine we have is Mercury, and they don't really use that anymore. They say 606 is better."

"What can I do Dr. Cheek?"

"I can give you something for the kidneys, and meanwhile keep giving you the 606 so we can get the syphilis healed up. You will still have some symptoms, but once the syphilis is gone, then we can work on the kidneys."

Hattie could see that her husband was uncomfortable with this option, but he knew that this choice was six in one hand, half a dozen in the other.

"Okay. Dr. Cheek. I will continue with the 606. How long will it take for the syphilis to get better?"

"Well we can't know for sure, but my guess is anywhere from two weeks to two months. It really depends upon how long you had this disease, which we don't know. As soon as it is cleaned out of your system, we will begin treatment for your kidneys. Meanwhile, you will continue to experience some of these symptoms from time to time. I want to see you every week, without fail Robert. Don't miss an appointment. This is your life we're talking about!"

"Okay, Dr. Cheek. I will be here every week. Thank you."

Hattie said, "I will make sure of that."

Dr. Cheek smiled at them both, "What would you do without this woman?"

"I don't know Doc. And I definitely don't want to find out." Robert was smiling, but Hattie noticed his knee rapidly bouncing up and down.

On the way home, she assured him. "Don't worry love. I am here with you. I will take care of you. We will see this through together."

"Thank God for you Hattie. You are my world."

Chapter Thirty-Six

A few weeks after Christmas, Robert came back from the Post Office with a telegram from Bessie. He handed it to Hattie. She looked at him, waiting for a clue. His face was blank. When Hattie read the telegram, she felt her legs give out from under her. Robert caught her in his arms and eased her down on to the nearby chair.

"How could this happen? Oh my God! My poor baby!"

The telegram read:

My husband Jeff died yesterday morning. STOP
His brother died last night. STOP
They both had pneumonia. STOP
My sister in law and I are making arrangements to bring their bodies home. STOP
Will write soon. STOP
Bessie

Bessie was nineteen years old, with four children, one of whom was less than three months old, and her husband was dead. No job, no money, no husband.

Hattie was devastated, and so worried about her first born. What was she going to do now? Maybe she should come home, until she can get on her feet.

Hattie didn't really get the chance to be a part of Bessie's recovery from this devastating loss.

Chapter Thirty-Seven

The End

During the months following that visit to Dr. Cheek, Hattie and Robert did not miss an appointment. His blood test was showing signs that the syphilis was being cured, but his kidneys were not good. He was still seeing blood in his urine from time to time and was always tired. He had also developed some strange behaviors and would sometimes say things that were incoherent.

"Gin, come over here. Get up on this table. I am gonna cut you up like a little pig."

"Virginia, daddy is just fooling. Go ahead outside and play."

Hattie neutralized the moment, but she was concerned. What was wrong with him? Hattie felt like a grief sandwich, mashed between her husband falling apart mentally and her daughter's life being devastated. She couldn't cry. Tears would not flow. She couldn't eat. Food would not fill her emptiness. She couldn't sleep. It just would not come. What do you say or do when life is broken beyond repair?

It was early March 1931. Springtime with its rain showers was in full effect. On the way back from seeing Dr. Cheek, in their open wagon, suddenly, a torrential downpour caused both Hattie and Robert to get wet through and through. Hair, garments, shoes, socks, all soaked. The rain stopped before they reached home. This meant that they had to ride with the cool breeze that comes after rain, chilling both Hattie and Robert to the bone.

When they finally made it into the house, and got out of the wet clothes, Hattie made some hot tea. They sat in front of the hearth to warm themselves. Both thought that this would be sufficient for their recuperation from getting wet and chilled. It was enough, for Robert.

By dinner time, Hattie was feeling feverish and had a head slicing headache.

"Hattie go and lay down. I will have Gin make you some soup."

"No. I don't want anything. I just want to lay down." She laid down, and she never got up. By the next morning she was having chills and sweats. Robert went to get Dr. Cheek.

After examining her, he said, "She has the flu. This is very dangerous. It could turn into pneumonia. Keep her warm and give her these pills every four hours. I will come back tomorrow."

The next day, Hattie was worse. She was coughing, had a sore throat and her muscles were aching. Virginia stayed nearby always anxious to do whatever her dad suggested she could do to help mommy feel better. Make her tea, boil some chicken to make a broth, put cool cloths on her forehead. The boys went out to the fields to try and keep things going while their papa was unable to work. It was hard for them to see him so incapacitated and worried. Virtee, like Virginia just watched her mama and kept asking Virginia, "What's wrong with mama?"

"It's just a waiting game Robert. It definitely looks like pneumonia now. I'm sorry. Keep giving her the pills and pray. I will see you tomorrow afternoon."

By the following day, Hattie had become nonresponsive. She could see everyone around her. Worried faces, Sad faces. She wanted to reach out to them. Tell them not to worry. But she was locked inside of herself. Her voice no longer worked.

Her inner voice however was in full effect and quite capable of expressing her desires to her maker:

"Holy father, I come to you as humble as I know how. I believe my life is at an end. I know, dear God, that you have your reasons, even though I don't understand. I live by thy will being done. So be it. I pray that you will look after my children Lord. Please see to it that they will be cared for and protected like I would do if I was here. I want my children to grow up and be good people. I want them to have a family life. May my sons find loving wives, and may my daughters find men who will care for them and respect them. Lord I only ask that you protect them, keep them safe, and Father, when they knock, let the doors be opened. Please put food on their tables, and roofs over their heads. I have raised them to worship you dear God and I have taught them your laws. I pray that they will continue to walk a righteous path and to spread the Gospel far and wide. Lord I know that you will guard, guide and protect my children. Thank you Father. These and all blessings I ask in the name of your son Jesus Christ. Amen. Amen. Amen". She prayed this prayer, unceasingly, until she had no breath.

The Secrets of Hattie Brown

Robert was by her side, day and night. He prayed, he held her hand, he told her stories from his childhood. She stared blankly at him. In her heart she was feeling his love and concern and fear, but there was nothing she could do for him now. Her life had arrived at its final moment.

Four days after getting wet in the rain, Hattie Roberta Cowen Brown, at thirty-nine years of age, felt as if she was being lifted up from the earth. And then she saw Robert sitting below her, holding the hand of who she had been, his loving, adoring, wife.

Barbara Brown Gathers

Final Word

"The soul takes flight to the world that is invisible. At there arriving, she is assured of bliss, and forever dwells in paradise." - Dr. Feckenham, the movie, "Lady Jane"

After Hattie died, Bessie had come back home to care for her father and siblings. As Robert's condition worsened there was another tragedy that effected the plight of the Brown family.

One day, Virginia (age 8) and Christine Hattie (Bessie's first born - aged five), were playing inside the house. One of the girls put the broom in the fireplace. Just as it caught fire, they heard someone coming and knew that they would be in trouble if caught playing with fire. The broom was quickly stashed in a closet, and this ignited a fire which destroyed the whole house! Everything the family owned was gone up in smoke.

Bessie's son Jeffrey and her brothers Robert Jr. and Lander had seen the smoke from the fields where they were working. Jeff said to Lander, "Look! Somebody's house is on fire!" They ran in the direction of the smoke, only to discover that it was their house. Everybody got out safely, but the house burned down to ashes.

Bessie was able to make arrangements with church members and friends to take over caring for Rivers, RD, Virginia, Virtee, Robert Jr. and Lander. Each of them went to a separate dwelling. Earnest was old enough to go out on his own and get a job. The younger ones were terrified at being alone in the world without their parents and without one another.

In March of 1931 Hattie passed away. The fire was in August of 1931, and Robert Brown, at age forty-seven, died in June 1932. His kidneys gave out. His heart was broken. And the truth is, he always felt somewhat responsible for the untimely death of his wife.

Bessie had cared for him until the end of his life. She had lost her husband and both parents in the span of eighteen months. She was strong. She was smart. But Bessie was in need of some time to try and put her life back together. She asked some of her husband's relatives and her mother's sister Emma to care for her children, while she went back up north try to get employment and to establish a home for her family.

When they were informed of their father's death, and came together to attend the funeral, the children only knew that he had died. The truth about him having syphilis was not revealed.

Barbara Brown Gathers

Author's Note

I remember when The Color Purple movie premiered in 1985. Although it was a great movie, on many accounts, there were mixed reviews. "There is absolutely no balance in the movie," said Kwazi Geiggar, in the L.A. Times, "It portrays blacks in an extremely negative light. It degrades the black man, it degrades black children, it degrades the black family."

As I completed the final read-through of "The Secrets of Hattie Brown", before sending it to the publisher, I asked myself if this novel will be seen in a similar light as the one expressed about the Color Purple. Ironically, the Color Purple takes place from 1910-1940, The Secrets of Hattie Brown takes place from circa 1870-1932. As a student of history, I asked myself if the time had anything to do with the social practices and choices of the characters in these works, including both males and females.

There have been volumes and volumes of scholarly studies done on the after-effects of slavery in the United States upon the Africans as well as their slave masters. One such scholar Is, Dr. Joy DeGruy (Post Traumatic Slave Syndrome). Another is Dr. Naim Akbar (Chains and Images of Psychological Slavery). These are merely two, in a literal army of researchers and educators who have expounded upon this topic. There are certain identifying social aspects of folks just coming out of the trauma that was enslavement.

My point here, is to clarify that the men and women in this novel, many of whom are based upon actual people whose blood I share, are products of a society that was merely a few decades out of the slavery experience. They were doing the best that they could to carve out and define the meaning of life without a slave master.

As the mother of a son, I did not feel comfortable to share this story with the world, without being sure that the reader understands that people's behaviors and beliefs are always a reflection of the world that they live in.

I have noticed how the role and contributions of men in our families has morphed even in my lifetime. I never saw my dad or my uncles change a diaper or do laundry. But my son, and many of the young men in his generation, do what is needed without such lines being drawn.

So don't judge Hattie, Eliza, Robert, Alex, Marshall, and the others by a 2020 lens to evaluate their choices. If you feel the need to understand their behaviors and motivations, on a deeper level, I would invite you to do some research into the social and economic climate of the world that they lived in.

This is historical fiction. Although I have been researching our family history for more than thirty years, there are certain facts that are impossible to confirm. For example, my great grandmother Eliza was born in 1860. Slavery didn't end until 1865. What was her life like, really? People of color weren't even listed by name in the census until 1870. I have had to take the facts (dates, names and places that I know from documentations like her death certificate and censuses from 1870, 1880, 1900, 1910, 1920) and use those facts as the bones of this story. The meat, the flesh, the nuances, came from my imagination and my knowledge of African American history and culture, which is extensive.

Robert and Hattie had nine offspring. Their progeny produced at least twenty-four grandchildren, numerous great grands, great great grands, and still counting. The children grew up to be church leaders and entrepreneurs. Many of their grands grew up to become doctors, educators, lawyers, entrepreneurs and church officials. The next generation, great grands, produced ministers, doctors, entertainers, and other accomplished professionals. Almost ninety years after her death, Hattie's nine children have all gone to eternity. Yet still, her grandchildren and extended family gather on Christmas Eve every year to celebrate family and the importance of hugging one another. On these occasions we, me and my family members, share the story of Robert and Hattie Brown with young and old. Truly, this is the reader's happy ending. Hattie's prayers have been answered. We may never indeed know all of Hattie's secrets, but by observing the positive accomplishments of her children and their offspring, we see the answers to the prayers a mother might have prayed every day, especially if she realized that she was dying.

The Secrets of Hattie Brown

I am the granddaughter of Hattie and Robert Brown. Azel RD was my father. He is the little boy sitting on his mother's lap in this family photo, taken circa 1929 in North Carolina.

Barbara Brown Gathers

In case you are wondering:

- Bessie eventually remarried, Johnny, moved to California, and died in 1969. She visited New York often, to reconnect with her siblings, children, and grandchildren.
- Ernest married, had six children with his wife Lucy and died, Bishop Ernest Brown, pastor of Macedonia Church of Christ in Brooklyn, New York in 1983
- James (Florida) married Muriel and they had one daughter. He was a hardworking businessman opening and operating, James F. Brown Pest Control. He died in 2000 in Brooklyn, NY.
- Robert Junior married Annie Mae and then went into the military. After that, they moved to California. He died in 1958
- Lander married Lillian and together they had six children. He died, Bishop Lander Brown, Pastor of Antioch Church of Christ in Brooklyn, NY He died in 1992.
- Virginia married Thomas and they had three children, plus raised a number of foster children in their home. She was a deaconess and an internationally known missionary. She died in 2002.
- Virtee worked as a nurse's aid at Kings County Hospital in Brooklyn, NY. She was known in the family as someone who would always be there if somebody was sick or in need of care. Nursing wasn't just a job to her, it was a way of life. She died in 1983.
- Azel RD married Sudie and together they had two children. Azel died in 1995. He founded, A. Brown Pest Control, the first Pest Control Business owned and operated by an African American in New York City, and

was successful for over twenty-five years before moving to Florida where he died in 1995.

- Rivers married Percy and they had a son. Later, she married Scot (the brother of Virginia's husband, Thomas) and they had two children together. Rivers was a dietician for the school system and died in 1987 in Brooklyn, New York.

Recipes

Barbara Brown Gathers

Addendum

Here are two recipes mentioned in the text as dictated by the character who was giving it to Hattie:

Brown Sugar Candy

In a mixing bowl, you pour a tin of evaporated milk, add about three handfuls of brown sugar, that's using both hands to scoop, and a little less than a cup full of butter.

Stir that mixture over a low fire and cook for five minutes. Now you gotta stir it continuously and only for five minutes. Remove it from the fire and pour it into your bowl. When Robert goes to the store, tell him to have the man to weigh exactly one pound of powdered sugar. Take that powdered sugar and add it to your hot mixture along with a spoon of vanilla extract, a pinch of salt, and about a handful of them pecans off your tree. Now, Hattie, you gotta beat that mixture like it did you something wrong and you mad at it. It will become very thick. When it is so thick that you almost can't turn the spoon, it's ready. Pour that mixture into your buttered dish, use the spoon to smooth over the top to make it flat and level. Let it cool until it hardens. Then you can cut it into squares. Now if you are having a lot of guests, cut them squares pretty small, or else it is gonna run out before everybody gets some."

Sweet Potato Pie

The Secrets of Hattie Brown

1 1/2 cup of mashed sweet potatoes
(you gotta boil them first)

1 stick of butter

1 1/2 cup of sugar

1 teaspoon cinnamon

1/2 teaspoon of nutmeg

1/8 teaspoon of allspice

1/2 teaspoon of salt

1 teaspoon of vanilla

2 eggs, well beaten

1 tin of evaporated milk

Now when you go to Brooks Store, and buy your sweet potatoes, don't get them too big. They won't boil quite right. Get some medium sized ones. Boil the potatoes in a big pot. While they're boiling, get your oven started. Set it to about 350 degrees. Also get your mixing bowl ready. When the potatoes are soft but not overcooked or mushy, run them under cold water for a spell so you can peel them without getting burnt. But don't let them get cold, because you want potatoes to be warm enough to melt the butter. Put the potatoes in a bowl and mash them up real good. Put the butter into the potatoes and mix in until it melts. Take the sugar and spice ingredients and blend them together in a small bowl. Then add the vanilla and the spice mixture to the potatoes. Beat the eggs really well and add them. Finally, take the canned milk and start adding it a little at a time. Add some and stir, add some and stir. Keep an eye on it because you don't want it to get too juicy. If you feel you need to add a bit more, go ahead. But be careful, you don't want it too juicy. It should be like oatmeal. Pour the pie mixture into your crust that you already made and laid in a pie pan. Put the pie in the oven, while saying your prayers for the taste of the pie and the blessings upon those who will eat it. Bake about 35 minutes or until you see the pie set, looking solid. Take the pie out of the oven and let it cool. You gonna get so many compliments. A lot of people can make sweet potato pie, but not like this one.

About the Author

Barbara Brown Gathers was born in Brooklyn, New York to parents who had migrated from North Carolina. She was educated from elementary school through graduate school in New York City. Barbara has always had a strong curiosity about her family history and over thirty years ago, she officially became her family's historian. She has collected numerous interviews, videos, photos, and documents telling the family story.

Barbara always knew that when she retired from teaching middle school, she would use the historical data about her family to recreate a fictional version of what the family

Barbara Brown Gathers

history might have looked like in 3D. She is a multimedia artist, freelance educational consultant, a writer and quilter. Barbara's most treasured life accomplishments are being the mother of one son and grandmother to her three girls. She resides in Central Florida.

Made in the USA
Middletown, DE
17 May 2020